MURDERLAND

Fevered vision penned by
GARRETT COOK

Cover art and design by
Matthew Revert

Published by

PHX – 2013

Everything Bleeds.

www.morbidbooks.wordpress.com

MURDERLAND is published in the US and A by MorbidbookS and the Grace of God.

ISBN-10: 0615855075
ISBN-13: 978-0615855073
(MorbidbookS)

FOREWARD

If there was one thing that Hunter Thompson demonstrated through his writing and his antics, and we writers can take especial note, is that we are forever haunted by four ghosts, four 'patron haints' if I may be allowed to coin a phrase: the Buddha[1], David Hume[2], Heraclitus[3], and Werner Heisenberg. I bring this up because I am looking at a painting by Garrett Cook on my wall, and the hellish, lagomorphic landscape reminds me just how small, scary, and wonderful a world it is. With some thoughts on interdependence bubbling up after that, I realized I wanted to make things go ahead correctly.

One thing I've noticed is that a lot people review their friends' work with a less than critical eye. While it's nice to buoy your friends up a bit with praise, I think it does them a bit of disservice. I've seen reviews that are little more than a regurgitation of the jacket copy, and forewords that are no more than a rarefied verbal handjob. Why bother putting that kind of shit out there? I've determined that I'm not going to do that. So disclosure time: I am fucking terrified of Garrett Cook.

I met Garrett for the first time at the inaugural BizarroCon, and I picked up on his intensity immediately. Later that weekend he won the very first Ultimate Bizarro Showdown with some weird spontaneous meditation on bestiality that he screamed at full volume in front of a speechless audience. He beat me soundly. He beat all of us soundly, and hell- I had actual antlers hanging off my dick, scarfed handfuls of pills, and read apocalyptic John Entwistle fanfic. Garrett *yelled*. Ever since then, though we've become great friends, I remain afraid of him- afraid that the plane of literary excellence he dwells on will forever be denied me, barring some fortunate accident involving a radioactive typewriter bite.

Murderland, in brief, is the story of Jeremy Jenkins, a mild-mannered pharmacist whose cover story of being a moralizing nebbish hides that he is in fact a vigilante killing the popularly-sanctioned serial killers of his day, but is also one himself, targeting scores of young blondes who he believes to be the hosts of an invisible techno-chthonic menace that only he can see. It is here in Jeremy's insanity that he joins the ranks of other wonderful unreliable narrators such as Severian or Patrick Bateman: is Jeremy really a golden Adonis as he sees himself? Is there truly a Nanite invasion, or just a sick justification? A split personality also crops up as the assassin part of Jeremy's mind, and this personality is so effortlessly charming that it made me wish, as I did about William

---

[1] "The Kalama Sutta," *Anguttara Nikaya* 3:65
[2] *Treatise On Human Nature*
[3] "Panta rhei," Plato's *Cratylus*

Hurt's apparition in *Mr. Brooks*, that it would get a lot more face time with the reader.

"You kill like a girl. Pills, Jeremy? God, pills? I'm starting to feel that my faith in you is quite misplaced. I need a Cuchulain and I get a Borgia."

My one complaint about this bit, and quite a backhanded one at that, is that Cook's voice in this novel is so strong (especially for what was his debut novel) that the transitions between the main character and his 'secret sharer' were a little too well-done. That same narrative voice makes this a wonderfully strong read, and very brisk- I read it over lunches and breaks at work and barely noticed when suddenly the book was over, and had to do a bit of a double-take. I've read some comments about the futuristic or experimental language of the book, but did not see much of evidence of that. The running patter in Jeremy's head allows a graceful buildup to a nice piece of classic thriller-type climax: conveyed by *Murderland*'s top murder aficionado, both reader and Jeremy realize the true magnitude of his violence and its impact on the world of 'Reap.' Great stuff. Again the narrative voice is so strong that it tends to overwhelm the supporting characters, such as Jeremy's girlfriend Cass. Her emergence at the end of part 1 as a 'real person' seemed a bit pat, but I feel that is part and parcel with transition into the action of the next part, as well as her association to the world of 'Reap,' as you'll see in a minute.

If there is any part of the book you are about to read that falls even the tiniest bit flat, it is this alternate world of 'Reap', and I don't think it is Cook's fault at all. The dystopian shocker, as a genre, has a pedigree going back almost 300 years[4], but as a vital, living form of art seems to lack enough critical work being thrown at it. In *Murderland* serial killers are extended a sort of disability/affirmative action, that instead of causing them to be mocked as our Asperger's sufferers are, instead are lionized by letting the basest instincts of the public run wild. This is a marvelous concept, like something Aldous Huxley would have come up with had *Answer Me!* been around when he was alive. We are at first presented with what could be considered the 'world-gone-wrong' beef and potatoes: murder-themed restaurants, gangs of people dressed like Jack the Ripper, and TV shows tracking killing instead of sports. One character immediately stands out and gives us a hint of *Murderland*'s depth: serpent-jawed Godless Jack, who shows the potential of combining the self-righteous killer with the bodily transgressive for maximum creepy effect.

So what part of this book gives us trouble? And just barely, because this is a great book, and perhaps only a fellow writer with a head full of philosophy and nose for the Frankfurt school would

---

[4] *Gulliver's Travels* was published in 1726. Close enough for government work.

really go this far. There's a pitfall in this fiction that needs to be explored, and I suppose instead of being bummed that I am rambling away from traditional foreword territory, Garrett Cook may be pleased that I am inspired by his work to tackle a new term for the genre: 'The Reverse Uncanny Valley.'

The regular-ass Uncanny Valley is a theory, not considered scientific necessarily, that as simulacra (such as robots or CGI characters) become more realistic, human reactions to them become more favorable up to a certain point, at which point they drop off sharply. Plotted on a graph, this dip in reactions is the Valley. The commonly accepted explanation is that as more things become 'normal,' the details that are *not* are more noticeable, and the brain rejects the whole. I disagree. To me, I think that something about an almost-perfect robot causes us to consciously or unconsciously question exactly what it is that makes us human, and we can't put our finger on it. Thus, revulsion towards the object of our existential confusion. Obviously, if you want to sell a robot or market a cartoon character, no dice. As stated in the *Shrek* DVD extras, they had to make Princess Fiona less beautiful, because she was creeping the animators out. In a critical view, the idea of the Uncanny Valley is not a scientific one, supportable with data, but a philosophic and methodological one: we want it to be there as part of our aesthetics; we have decided that there will be an Uncanny Valley to avoid in the creation of simulacra.

However, a sort of mirror image exists, not a precise opposite, but a complementary technique, and for a lack of better term, I'm calling it the Reverse Uncanny Valley. Perhaps something like "Cook's Canyon" would be more appropriate- but I must confess I am hoping that Stigler's Law of Eponymy doesn't take hold and "Gulbranson's Canyon" will be what future scholars call it.

So taking it as a given that there is an Uncanny Valley showcasing how little we know about what makes us human, I think there's very strong evidence that the Reverse Valley tells us all about how our society is fucked up and staring us in the face every day. Only, no matter how weird and roundabout a way it may choose to tell us, the issues it confronts are very immediate and direct. The dystopia- the fractured place- in the future, well, it's *not* in the future, and it's revolting because we're standing at ground zero, realizing it on the same level as staring into the soulless eyes of a robot with a sweet, fuckable body and perfect face. Take *A Clockwork Orange*- perhaps the most recognizable and effective piece of dystopian fiction (book and film) ever. Bowler hats and penis furniture aside, it's really about kids talking funny, morals being challenged, the government not giving a shit about you, and violence lying in the heart of everyone. Timeless stuff, and apply it to the environment of your story, and you have dystopian lit first class. It's going to resonate.

Don't doubt me. I laughed when I read about the futuristic Stalin ad campaign in *Terraplane*, but I wasn't laughing when I bought that bottle of black bean sauce with a dancing Stalin on it at the Russian market a month later.

Of course there's a wide spectrum- ranging from the literary and heartbreaking *Random Acts of Senseless Violence* by Jack Womack to Bizarro like *Grape City* by Kevin L. Donihe. Womack's is the diary of a 12-year-old girl during an economic collapse, and her eventual transformation into a killer. No miracles or alternate history required. Donihe gives us a vision of a humanity so distorted that demons and devils have been brought to their knees by our perversity and brutality, and the story veers into surreal and absurd at every turn, but still shows us our true face right now.

That's the power of dystopian fiction. Despite the trappings of a usually escapist science fiction setting, its immediacy lets us know we are somewhere between ankle-and upper lip-deep in the flood. The heavy hitters of this literature are credited with social change and literary influence unlike any other genre. Apart from the stylistic swishes I mentioned earlier (consequences of an industry-wide ignorance, and the equivalent of spiked shoulderpads in post-apocalyptic movies), *Murderland* shows that Garrett Cook is well on his way to being one of those heavy hitters. Protagonist Jeremy reminds us that we're just a couple of newspaper articles away from going native wherever we are, and that is in the classic spirit of running straight down to the bottom of the Valley. Perhaps now that Cook knows why he should ... maybe he'll homestead for a while.

There aren't many writers I'd rather have down there.

-Jess Gulbranson

MURDERLAND

GARRETT

COOK

Morbidbooks

Everything Bleeds.

FRANCISCO de GOYA

MURDERLAND | Garrett Cook

Book 1: H8

"There's a brand new dance, but I don't know its name
That people from bad homes do again and again
It's big and it's bland full of tension and fear
They do it over there, but they don't do it here."

-David Bowie- *"Fashion"*

What a Wonderful World

I.

Sometimes he has the courtesy to wear shades. There is something oh-so-thrilling about making the asshole behind the desk feel like losing his lunch, but this time he doesn't. This time, he is wearing the shades, but it isn't quite courtesy, no, he doesn't really know the meaning of the word. He does this so the man will be able to look at him, and he'll be able to look down over them and cause drama, cause the man's blood to turn to ice. He waits for the question that bothers him most to do it.

"So, Jack, what made you want to do what you do now?"

He waits for it. He's been working on his timing for awhile. 3, 2, 1…0. He always includes the zero when he counts down, and that's when he goes. Down come the shades, and the surgically enlarged mandibles expand into a smile that other mouths are incapable of.

"Well, Richard, all the cowboy and astronaut slots were filled up."

He smiles, although he stares through time, looking through the crack in the closet door to see a room full of old boxes, neglected tools and dusty books. The place where they put the forgotten things. He hears the squeal of joy in the distance, knowing his mother is lifting it into the air or tickling it. He hears the front door open and the heavy footsteps of his stepfather. Only a few hours until everybody goes to bed and his mother brings up a little tray of food. Why live when you don't exist? He watches himself close his eyes and pretend that nothing is there, but he knows when he opens them the closet and the family and the baby will be there. If he closed his eyes on the set, the talk show would still be there, the audience would still be there, the Sun, big burning zero betrays its nature. We can only do what we can. There is less and less every day, someday, some wonderful day...

II.

The pimp likes the prophet, but the prophet is never sure about the pimp. The prophet opens the box, and the pimp smiles. He genuinely wants to hug the old man, although the stench is nigh unbearable. The pimp claps his hands, and the girl brings a stack of papers. The prophet looks them over, reads words that nobody else knows are there and nods his approval.

"Will this help?" asks the pimp, who genuinely wonders, although the old man's box is worth several hundred dollars.

"We can only do what we can," says the prophet. He knows hundreds of others think the same thing.

III.

Stupid fucking clowns. King shit Kyle springs his swordcane and Joey can't help but sigh. Joey draws his knife and tries to let them know he means business with his eyes. The Gacys aren't armed. Who would have expected them to be. They're big, but they're not armed. Their leader looks his boys over and looks Kyle's boys over and knows sure as mama's monthlies they're dusties if they even bother. Joey knows that Kyle just wants to make a mess though, if he wants to pomp he should go ahead and pomp, find some sweet bait make meatloaf. The top hat falls over Kyle's eyes as he advances.

Joey can't help but laugh. *Mr. Badass Ripkid leader made-up as the scourge of Whitechapel thinks he can stack the dusties but he can't even wear his fuckin' hat right. It seems for a second like a stupid way of life, but how else are you gonna feel free? So fuck 'im. Go along with it. Swallow your pride. Kyle's pathetic, but we can only do what we can.*

A Walk in the Park

The grey-haired man I've been following looks down at his watch yet again and yet again starts to fidget a little. He knows that the woman starts jogging at 8 pm every night. 5'2, blonde, 24, it could be said nubile as all fuck. The mundanes are over there chatting away about what Ashley said to Chris and then how Chris was out with Julie at the Johnny Rockets at the mall when he told Ashley he had to stay home and watch his little cousin. What scandal. I hope they set that bastard straight. Chatting away with a mechanical whir. Fucking robots. Cut them open and see all the wires for myself. See the electric guts and polymer skin. See the silicon brains. But I get back to ignoring them because I don't like the noises they make. Every night without fail when she goes jogging, the grey-haired man is there. I have not checked every night, but on my way home from work, I have checked frequently enough to know that every night without fail he is there. He's neither fat nor jolly, but the media has dubbed him Kris Kringle. This is because he is known to leave brightly wrapped packages full of their organs on the doorsteps of their families like a proud kitty cat. Or like Santa Claus, as they think of it.

Kris is the grownup equivalent of the precocious child who takes apart daddy's watch to see how it works. He deconstructs things. Returns them to where they came from when he's done. A savage who thinks he's a scientist. I don't know his story, but I know his work. I have, as I mentioned, been watching him. I've sat in the park at 8 o'clock too watching the young blond filthy yellow cunt filthy filthy filthy yellow cunt little mommy fills it up dumps it out, full then dropped off, full then empty, squeezes me out and doesn't think my little eyes might have looked and seen and remembered the bright gold sheen like all the other blondes not about that. Not about grudges. Fast, anonymous, above such things. Calm down and do it. Get home and document it, write it down, write it down, keep it near your head always keep it near your head. This is not for anyone to see. This is for me. This is not exhibit B or the documentary, this is for me. I am fast, I am anonymous; it is a matter of principle.

But I wonder what this guy's doing tonight. What card from the less than full deck he's working with does he want to play? What the fuck is his angle? Bag of groceries. Fuck you, Kringle. It's not that I doubt it will work, I know it's about 95% likely to, but it's sad and banal. It shows no respect for her intelligence. Simple trap. Animalistic. Primitive like him. Bag of groceries, my ass. I would like to think that she'd be smarter, but no. And I'd like to think that I could leave her to him. She'd be dead anyway, no real chance of bearing the child, but no, I can't let it happen. I have to do this. If he does it, she's just another thing to be taken apart, if I do it, then she dies for a reason, which is I think the least a woman dead at 24 could ask for. I'll just walk up, turn on my winning smile, lure her somewhere and open up the briefcase. She deserves better than this loser. I will smile, flash my big brown eyes, give her what she does deserve and GET THE FUCK HOME.

I hate this part of it, I honestly do. I just want to kill the little yellow sluts before the Dark Ones start to fill them up with their seeds and then they make more like me. Like what I should have been. They thought they had created the perfect little general for their legions. Charming, handsome, nice eyes, toned body, IQ 236. Gacy and Berkowitz combined. And most likely an average human being ahead of Mr. Kringle. And unlike the previously mentioned two, I am not gay, I am not stupid and I DON'T want to get caught. I am a righteous avenger of the wrongs done by my creators. I am retribution turned against monsters who make me do this. Who build the robots and the robots just walk around with their slow computer brains and wire guts and every once in awhile it seems there is a glitch in the program and the robots start to tear and dismantle each other. Mostly, there are robots mostly. But I look at the jogger, and I know that that little yellow cunt is made of skin and organs and juices and is ready, more than ready, ready and willing to be filled up with corruption by the Dark Ones in order to make another devil, another one of me, to come and to undo all my good works and all of my crusading and everything that makes me me and carry my head on a prideful pike and I can't FUCKING STAND IT. They will not duplicate me. I will destroy the devil factories the clone machines DEEP BREATH don't fuck up I won't fuck up I won't I won't I won't. Stand up, be casual. Look like a robot, look like a person. Don't look like anything special. Subtle, discreet, nondescript, Mr. Casual, Mr. Suave.

And then there's Kringle, suspicious, scary, more than a little off. Nothing avuncular, pleasant or especially trustworthy about him. He stands up, limping a little, plays up his age more than enough. That should have been enough for her to realize something's up. I have to wonder if she watches the news, if she sees the T-shirts and the DVDs and the television shows and the baseball caps, videogames, and the newspaper. He asks if she can help him with his groceries, help load them in his car, says he's got a bad back and hunches over to emphasize it. Then how did he carry them three blocks from the grocery store to his car, parked suspiciously in an alley near a public park? Why did he not park outside of the grocery store to begin with instead of a dark alley near a public park? It might be a public park in the Safe Zone, but still too many questions. I shudder when I once more realize that he'll still get away with it.

Too many questions. But, she doesn't ask any of them. Walks with him to the alley. Quick strike with a blunt object, dragged into the back seat. I do have to hand it to him, he's pretty strong and pretty good at parking discreetly. I take note of the license plate and the next day; call my friend Shauna at the DMV. As Godless Jack Cavanagh wrote in "The Complete Reaper," a photographic memory is one of a psychopomp's handiest tools. I find the car is registered to a Joe Strickland. Strickland. Eww. He'll never be too famous with a name like that. Nothing sinister. Nothing especially melodic or intense about it.

Joe Strickland, alias Kris Kringle. Alias Karl Edward Pratt. I see the name on the paper on his front lawn. Karl Edward Pratt. There we go. Much better reaper name than Strickland. Definitely. Kill count 14. Nowadays 14 makes it a hobby. Not a star, never. A murder enthusiast. I come to his house with my silenced .22 in my pocket. I hate guns, but I want this to end fast. This will be the first man I have ever killed and I would rather it be the last. I want this C list poseur barbarian out of my way and out of my mind once and for all.

I ring his doorbell. He comes to the door in a bathrobe. Part of me hates the idea of shooting a guy in a bathrobe. It seems like such an embarrassing way for someone to die. But then again, to be killed by this loser, whose handle has been mentioned on the news a mere three times. He's 55, 56 maybe. Way too old. He's in a young man's game, too. His face is sunken and tired, his teeth tobacco stained. His gnarled, craggy hands light a cigarette out of a three dollar pack.

"Something I can do you for you, young man?"

"Kris Kringle? Kill count 14?"

A smile crosses his face. It's always flattering to these guys when some armchair detective tracks them down for an autograph or a picture together or to answer some questions for his website. He probably hasn't had any yet. Godless Jack's address is on his website. There have been 28 published interviews with the I-80 Roadflare Stalker I've been told, 17 with the Ice Cream Truck Strangler. But not much Kris Kringle material, no. Derisive, stupid, primitive. Gimmicky, they think. I feel a little sick being mistaken for a fan of a pathetic son of a bitch like Karl Edward Pratt. A fan. I shudder to think how desperate, depraved and stupid his fans must be.

"No," I answer, my face grim and stony, "a fellow psychopomp."

He goes through newspaper clippings in his head. Thinks about Oscar coverage. Thinks about BLD news. Then moves on to the local Bundys. It's clear he is doing this because he examines my profile, the contours of my face, tries to get to the bottom of it. He doesn't recognize me. Of course he doesn't. I'm not a celebrity. I'm not a role model. I have no merchandise and my killings can't be rented at the local Blockbuster, so of course, he doesn't know my face. I relish it.

"Jeremy Jenkins."

Once more, he searches for the name and struggles idly for my face.

"What's your handle?"

I huff. "I don't have one."

Why does nobody see that I'm up to something more important? No end of annoyance. No fucking end of annoyance. My dissatisfaction registers heavily and he thinks I'm offended for an entirely different reason. Then again, who wouldn't?

"Don't worry, kid. You keep it up and maybe someday..."

"I haven't been caught."

He still doesn't get it. Very slow on the uptake.

"You should do something about that. Try letters. You really oughta read Godless Jack's books. They've done wonders for me."

I huff once again. "I don't need advice. The blonde in the park was mine."

The skinny grey old bag puts out his cigarette. "Look kid, I'm just doin' my best to get by. I'm trying to get some attention, some coverage. I can't go round worryin' who belongs to whom. It ain't my problem if some 'pomp can't stack the dusties. My meat's my meat; your meat's yours, man. You do your shit and you're still choked to death, ain't my problem. When the bait's sweet, it's sweet."

"You're nothing."

These are the last words he ever hears. I shoot him. He's nobody.

__Television Man is Crazy__

"In Ohio and Indiana, authorities report that Bundy award nominee, the I-80 Roadflare Stalker struck again. At 46 kills, it's possible he might just bring home the Bundy. What do you think Valerie?"

"Well, Chet, The Roadflare is definitely a contender this year and since Jack Cavanagh voluntarily removed himself from the Bundy runnings, it seems that Mr. Right, the I-80 Roadflare and Hacksaw Sally…"

"Nice to see a lady in the runnings, isn't it, Valerie?"

"Oh, definitely, Chet, if you ask me it's high time…"

The remote clicks. The talking heads bantering sport talk fade into cathode hell, burning and writhing alongside frames too numerous to mention. Cass yawns her way up from the quilt, and stretches up as if grabbing for something on the ceiling. The falling quilt reveals round breasts the color of bread dough and sharp russet nipples. Jeremy feels like rolling over and touching them, pinching them, kissing them, biting them, suckling on them just a bit, but Jeremy is trying to decide whether he believes she is a robot or not. He's seen inside her, tasted her and it feels warm enough in there. Oh, God, it feels warmer than anywhere to Jeremy. But, it might just be some kind of plastics from the dimension the Dark Ones come from. After all, she, like all the others watches all the murders on the TV going down, places bets on her favorites, screams in the chatrooms now and again, jeers the boring ones and maintains the brand loyalty that only a true junkie can have. She is entertained. In the middle of all of the shit and the violence and the noise and the death, she is entertained. Sometimes she might be entertained by the irony, sometimes by the repugnant nature of what this country has become. Sometimes by the chittering stupidity of the inane newscasters and the cacophonous blaring of the loud and pointless commercials. She is occasionally disgusted by how far this has gone. By how reap culture has been perverted from its purer forms and reduced to a pop culture cult. It used to be just people who really understood why people kill and the defiance and the intensity involved. It didn't used to be stupid teenagers who didn't even know the names Jack the Ripper or Albert de Salvo, although there are still plenty who idolize those two.

But still, so often she can't tear herself away from it. It makes Jeremy debate whether she is in fact one of the few intelligent people he has ever met, or if she is falling for the game too, just falling into the pit they dig for people who are looking too close. He stops and thinks about the razors he keeps in the briefcase and about how there might just be wires in her, God don't let there be wires, he thinks, god don't let there be wires. Don't let there be the fiberoptic cables that link up to the receivers for satellite images. Don't let there be neural uplinks to the Dark Ones. His breathing gets heavy and there begins to be a burning feeling in his eyes. His head begins to throb violently with a humming like a fork against a violin string. He cannot stop thinking about wires and cables and the mechanical whirring of the machines around him. Cass leans over and kisses him and relief washes over Jeremy's feverish brain. Human. Of course. Should have known. She is, after all a brunette. The Dark Ones will never touch her.

"I love you," she says. Her face gets bright and she looks at him as if he was the most interesting thing she had ever seen. She looks at him like a sunset.

"I love you," he replies.

And it is all that he feels. All he wants to say and know and think about. He returns her kiss voraciously. It expands and moves around her mouth. The kiss, once small has become a colossus. They roll over on top of each other. They writhe and shake, they coil around one another and they begin to explode with power and intensity. Jeremy's eyes are full of astronomy. The movements of planets and the blazing of bright new stars shine in them. His perpetual motion superpowered Swiss watch brain lets itself shut off, lets itself return to its roots as meat and juices. Cass sort of sees somebody she was a few thousand years back in Egypt or Mesopotamia or somewhere of the sort. She remembers being as she is at the moment: naked and exalting in the triumph of being and the movements of everything. There is Jeremy and there is Cass and they are creation. Crashing like waves and falling like torrents of rain.

And then Jeremy's elbow hits the remote and the channel changes. The room fills with venom oozing from the television and Jeremy can feel it. Jeremy smells the cloud of noxious hate and feels the flames of persecution lick at his feet. He feels more than a little sick.

"Karl Edward Pratt, Kris Kringle, was found dead in his home today at the age of 57. Kringle was killed by a shot to the head from a .22 revolver. Kringle was known for the particularly inventive and grisly qualities of his murders, involving dismembering his victims and delivering body parts to their families. His killings numbered 14 to date. And while compared to others, that might seem to be few, he will still be remembered for the viciously ingenious nature of those he committed. Pratt's identity was discovered only when police found a kitchen full of human parts and wrapping paper. The media and the American people alike remained ignorant of the identity of the visionary that so ably captured their attention. Karl Edward Pratt you will be missed. This is a true American tragedy."

The newsanchor, no longer a portrait of stony, ersatz integrity looks genuinely dismayed. He purses his lip in dissatisfaction in one of those rare moments during which he finds something truly sad. Jeremy is not altogether certain that those moments exist and is skeptical that somebody like Pratt would have earned one. But, this is the typical death knell of a minor celebrity. Thorough appreciation, a tragedy painted so eloquently, a career exaggerated. An explosion of relevance onto the life and the TV screen alike. Then, suddenly, the tragedy fades from the news anchor's face. The relevance oozes down a drain behind his desk. He straightens up, perks up and turns to the woman at the desk beside him, the bleach blond with the low-cut blouse and the wrong shade of lipstick. Jeremy wonders if she's related to the identical news anchor on channel 8.

"Back to you, Eileen."
Cass finally shuts off the TV and a frown spreads across her face.

"That's too bad," she says, "I kinda liked his work. And it's occasionally nice to see them cover something besides Godless Jack or Hacksaw Sally. And sometimes, he was just amazing. He really had his moments. Like when he sent the Haskell girl's parents her stomach and it was full of his cum, I mean, Jesus," her tone changes. It's more upbeat, more excited.

"And the statement her folks gave the press was completely priceless, totally vintage," Cass launches into a bad Texas drawl, "we appeal to you, our fellow Americans, to help get Safe Zone regulations repealed and get monsters like the so-called Kris Kringle who did this to our daughter off the streets. Gina was the most precious gift that God ever gave us and while we cannot have her back, new laws will allow many many people to have their little girls come back home."

Cass falls into utter paroxysms of laughter and Jeremy heaves a very long sigh. He looks angry.

"Cass, they're human beings and they lost their daughter. It's not funny. Imagine how your parents would feel. What would they be saying on their news if they lost you to some maniac? What would I be saying?"

Disgust creeps into Cass. She'll never get used to his moments of moralizing. They come so briefly and they seem so goddamn random.

"Maniac? Maniac? You're so backward sometimes, Jeremy, you know that? I can't believe you're using that word. Catholic school really must have gotten to you. Maniac. God, these people have problems, Jeremy. Real honest to God psychological problems. But they overcome adversity and rise up to provide us with hours of quality entertainment every week. Talk like that makes you no better than guys like Tommy Simmons and the Christian Victim's front. You should go out and...and..."

Jeremy has heard this from Cass as much as Cass has heard Jeremy's tirades. Just as much as she didn't want him to open his mouth about it, he does not want to hear it from her. So, Jeremy does the one thing that any right-thinking red-blooded American male does in such a circumstance: he acquiesces.

"I'm sorry, Cass, you're right. I was just saying that it was in kind of poor taste, because, well, you know, they have a right to be angry. After all, they did lose someone they love to this person. They might not have a right to scorn or be bigoted or persecute, since society has progressed beyond punishing people for being who they are, you're right. But, by the same token, you can't really blame the victims; they're people too, aren't they?"

Much of the time Jeremy does not quite believe this. In fact, much of the time, Jeremy does not believe this at all, as in this day and age, real human beings seem to Jeremy to be few and far between. And it is hard to fully process a concern for the rights of victims when one is in fact killing them. Jeremy is taking note of this, but still tires of such behavior in others.

"Sometimes, Jeremy, you're just too nice. It's a mean world."

She kisses him once more and it is a little less so.

He grumbles angrily in his mind at how they could possibly devote a whole news report to sheer trash like Pratt. No real reputation, no ideas that could benefit a community, no real redeeming social graces and even as a source of entertainment, he could often be pretty mediocre. TV is really puzzling to Jeremy, sometimes. As Jeremy often does, he wonders exactly what it is that makes him not a monster. This is more of a logical exercise than a line of deep moral questioning. In fact, he very quickly comes up with a variety of highly satisfying replies to this question. He remembers, first of all, that he is above guilt. It is something to be banished from his mind. He is above guilt and beyond evil actions. Jeremy Jenkins, it turns out, is far too relevant to deal in murky moral absolutes. Jeremy does the right thing. He stops and savors the quiet produced by all the squealing, mewling, nasty little Dark Ones that he has kept from emerging and kept from spreading the seeds of ignorance and wrath. Only this and Cass bring him the requisite peace and time to clear this head and allow him to enjoy the knowledge that thanks to Jeremy Jenkins, Paladin and Patriot the world is safe. He smiles down on Cass and means it. So seldom does he mean it. So often is the smile a tool and a sidearm. Cass has fallen asleep which is a shame because he considers letting her know that were he to divulge his actions he would be a media sensation, and that whether he does or not, he is a rebel genius and the greatest killer since the Black Death. He is not often proud of it, but she might very well be. He thinks about just how adoring and fawning she would be if she knew about his work, but realizes that he needs to remain anonymous. That TV and such things don't really become him much. He considers slicing her open and checking for wires, but instead he delicately and subtly lets his fingers slip into her, feels the chills and excitement of her not seeing or knowing about all kinds of manipulations and maneuvers.

No, no TV for him.

"I'm not a superstar," he tells himself, "I'm a superman."

Nurse, Veterinarian

As usual, I get up in the morning. No big surprise there. Then comes breakfast. I'm usually not crazy about breakfast. There should be a rule in relationships that you cannot converse with your significant other between the hours of six and ten am. Both of us sit there over oatmeal, staring down at the bowl for awhile like it's a magic eight ball that will tell us what to do with the rest of our day. It never does. Then she finishes up her oatmeal, usually a little after I do because she stops and plays with it a bit. She has to keep stirring and make little shapes in it, remind herself of the texture, remind herself that it's food. Sometimes she has a donut instead of oatmeal, but I don't really like sweets. I don't like the feeling that my body could be less efficient on account of what I'm eating. Today she drinks a Slash energy blend with her oatmeal, which means there's more time I spend with an empty bowl watching her eat before work. Even before her makeup, her face is beautiful. I always find myself looking at her mouth. I always find myself wanting to kiss her, but it feels like it's not appropriate at the moment. I feel shy.

"So much paperwork today," she says, "you'd think lawyers would be a little more organized…"

Her words disappear. I start thinking about her lips again. Then I think about how I want to go back to bed and get warm and I want her to go back to bed and get warm with me. It would be nice to grab something to eat later and then go to a movie. But the movie theater is dark and crowded and full of all these people. I can hear the clicks and the sounds of wiring and a hum of emptiness like a fluorescent light. I'd still sort of like to go to a movie. It would be nice to sit comfortably in the dark and enjoy something. Something that doesn't involve people getting dismembered. Last time we went we saw Marshall Kozack, the Nailgun Killer walk into a kindergarten class. The guy had a camera crew with him and everything. Because this place was in the Safe Zone none of the cameramen were an accessory to murder. Cass gawked at it, full of thrills and shock and amazement. That wasn't a movie, it was a massacre. It was a real massacre. I hope we could see a real movie and she could rest her head on my lap and I could feel close and feel our minds in the same room, at the same task.

"You know, Jeremy," she says, and she says it too often, "sometimes it seems like you're not in the same room with me all the time. I don't like it."

This comes up a lot at breakfast. She can see that I was wandering off. I wasn't wandering too far, I don't think. I was at the movies, that's all. Sometimes, I go places we could go instead of places we are. I'm not fond of breakfast, and I'm not all that fond of knowing I have to set off for work in a few minutes. I want to kiss her and I want to make plans. She wants to remind me what a day we both have ahead of us.

"I'm here," I tell her, "I think you should wear the blue skirt. They might take you a little more seriously. It looks more professional."

"It's kinda tight."

"I know, but it's not quite as short as the other one."

""You really think the blue one will make a difference?"

"It's less of a distraction."

"Thanks."

I regret that I don't hear a word she says until she kisses me goodbye. I wish my brain wasn't all over the place, but it just doesn't want to sit back and find some peace. I can't make it stop roaming around, not with what lies ahead. Some days I'm not sure we're like a paralegal and a pharmacist. Neither of us is boring enough. Well, I'm pretty boring on the surface, but not quite boring enough for my job. Cass worries sometimes that I'm too nice and too dependable. I think one of the things that thrills her about the relationship is when she gets me to come out of my shell and have some fun. She likes making me have fun. I like that. There's not much fun in my day. I wish I could participate more and communicate. I'd like to go out and communicate, be heard and talk to people. But that's not the way it goes.

The walk to work is always too short. I wish there were a few more blocks between me and the pharmacy, but the city only gets bigger when you don't want it to. The Starbucks you're hoping won't pop up rears its ugly head, the little Italian restaurant you used to like becomes a Pizza Hut. But my apartment won't get further from work, no matter how much I wish it will. Some days I think that I should probably be the one getting further away from the pharmacy. Not going to happen though. I take pride in my position as a "healer," no matter how little actual healing I do. Maybe I feel guilty for doing what needs to be done. Maybe I just don't want to deal with most people for more than a minute or two. Maybe med school would have been a better idea. Maybe I think too much. No. You can never think too much. Stop observing, stop keeping the notations handy for later, everybody and everything you're up against gets an edge. I do not think too much.

Well, I think too much for this job. I always remember how all the old people I actually like end up in the Obituaries. They're friendly, but not too friendly, never pry, don't talk about their condition, but I feel something of a connection. Then I never see them again. So, I feel like shutting off at work. So, I shut off today. Even the couple of people I like aren't feeling too pleasant. Some of them ask me if I saw the latest Cabana Boy victims. They have to stop and describe in detail how strange it is that you see dead prostitutes on the news. No comment. Too much to say. The day passes surprisingly quick like this. I don't feel like going home to Cass and the TV. I sort of feel like seeing people. Maybe.

So I head downtown and the girls begin to smile at me and the dogs begin to smile at me too and the cops wave hello and smile, too, and lookie here the old people smile at me and so do the teenage boys skateboarding. So, I'm beginning to really get tired of everybody. Everybody is so friendly and the world is so harsh. How can they be so friendly when the Cabana Boy is running around and Kris Kringle is dead and children were dying in Vietnam during the late 60s and early seventies? How can they? The sheer audacity of their decision to remain friendly makes me more than a little uncomfortable, to be honest. And really, they aren't actually being friendly anyway. It would be some feat for somebody to actually be friends with all of these people: an absolute miracle. And for all of these people to actually like me too would be quite a feat as well. I don't expect them to and I don't believe that they do. And if they were actually friendly, those big smiles and the waving and the joy at my passing would probably not be there. They would ask questions instead of assuming that they were happy to see me. Such an assumption is, in my book, very unwelcome. Were they actually friendly, they would instead say: "Jeremy, you look like something's wrong? Care to enlighten us about exactly what it is that has you looking so disturbed?"

And I, being their true friend, would oblige them. I would say:

"Our culture is being eaten by creatures from another harsh and unloving dimension and they are trying to impregnate our females with their vile hatemongering destructive seeds. I would tell you what it is that they look like and intend to do with us, but I think you just ate. Also, human monsters have quite frequently been appearing on the covers of such publications as People and Us Weekly. They endorse shoes and videogames and DVDs of their butchery are on the shelves at video stores and all major retail establishments. It turns out as well that our president just filled the atmosphere in

China with the equivalent of six thousand drums of Sarin gas yet again and again such stories end up on page H8 of the newspaper between weddings and honor roll announcements. Maybe it's just that the other news is much more entertaining, or maybe and this might just be it, maybe I am the only one who can see it. If this is so, I worry very deeply for my mental health. Do they see it? A massive spacecraft was recently unearthed by scientists working in Antarctica. It was covered with strange symbols indecipherable by all the world's best linguists and cryptographers alike. It seems very likely to me that this spacecraft is possibly connected to the same extradimensional beings who have been caused me no end of trouble and who utilized my own mother as one of their numerous breeding vessels. And because of all of these breeding vessels, I need very desperately to take action against them. And for this reason, every other Saturday, or whenever else I get the chance, I have to go out, find and shut down one of these vessels before they end up impregnated with something inhuman and completely vile. For five years, I have found yet another empty little blond whore, another womb for them to take over. I find them and I take out their uterus after cutting them open with a razor. And even after they're dead, I have to be really really careful that the Dark One embryo can't escape and find another host. I've seen it happen. You wouldn't believe the environments these creatures survive in. As I said, their home dimension must be an unspeakably awful place. And when I am not doing it on Saturdays, my schedule switches to Mondays and Wednesdays. And nobody has ever noticed, because number one, psychopomps are everywhere, and number two, I'm too damn clever. Because, you see I switch to Tuesdays and Thursdays on alternate months. Did you see it? Do you have any clue what I'm doing for you?"

And THAT is why those that are supposedly friendly are in fact not friendly at all. They're not friendly because no matter how happy they look to see you, how much light shines in their faces or comprehension in their eyes, the fact is that they don't comprehend any more than your average dog can. It's sad, but, no matter who Mr. Casual Greeting or Miss Nervous Smile actually are, they don't have the slightest clue who you are, so at best you are merely exchanging fake phone numbers on business cards you both printed out yourselves. I'm trying very hard to appreciate how nice people can be, honestly, I really am. But when faced with a kindness that only exists because it is tempered with utter ignorance, how can I help but be completely frustrated and lose faith in whatever the fuck it is that they're trying? The smiling, waving, satisfied hordes shuffle by and for a second they just become ducks in a shooting gallery, mechanically quacking to seduce me into blowing them to kingdom come. And then I count to 100, as I have taught myself to do when stress gets to be too much and I am tempted toward random violence. I think of how later on I will have Cass, and I will have bed and I don't hate them as much anymore. I think that I begin to pity them and the fact that they don't know that they're robots and couldn't do anything about it if they tried. Forgive them, Jeremy, they know not what they do.

I then make an important decision. One that I did not think I would ever see myself bothering with. I decide that I will stop and talk to one of those girls and maybe see, for once, if they are actually something at all. I admit I choose the girl to get to know based on looks, as I don't see them reading any books, I like carrying around any films I like or wearing shirts declaring allegiance to any bands I like. The girl I choose is very tall (almost 6 feet I think), very thin, with lovely red hair. I think the red might very well be dyed and it's more than likely that I'm right, but I wonder what color her hair really is since the red goes very nicely with the green of her eyes. And to initiate our interactions, she has said "hi" as all of the others have.

I then say "hi" in return.

I follow this up with the ever popular, "I think I've seen you around."

And I have in fact seen her around. Post office, Dairy Queen, the market. I've seen her around and still I would like to talk to her. Good sign.

"Yeah," she replies, "I live on Maple."

I consider momentarily that I should tell her that in moments of intense boredom I have done a lot of research on the city and know a very fair amount about its history. I am thinking that maybe I should tell her that the houses on Maple Street were built in the roaring 20s. They were built mostly by wealthy and irresponsible socialites who, in the end, drank, coked, partied, jeweleried and whored away every cent they had before dying lonely, broke and filled from head to toe with shame when the depression set in. But I recall that bringing this up might be considered gauche or just plain weird. Thus, I don't.

"Nice houses there," I say, since it's the best thing I can come up with at the moment, "I hear they're also pretty affordable for what you get."

"Oh yeah," she says, "You wouldn't believe what a steal the place was. My family only paid around seventy grand for the house. Six bedrooms. Six bedrooms and three baths. The plumbing and the electricity were total shit, but a couple thousand bucks, an electrician and some work and then the place ended up right as rain."

"You wanna get some coffee or some food?" I ask, interrupting her.

I decide that today this girl is definitely a person I need. I want to sit down and get to know this girl so that I will have met a nice person on the street that doesn't make me nauseous and fill me with revulsion. I cringe knowing how much I have to do this. Because these kindhearted and ignorant strangers need something akin to a fair shake I feel, since after all, I go out and do so much to try and stop this country and the world alike from going completely to shit. Why not interact with the residents of the world I'm looking out for? It makes a lot of sense. In my opinion, they deserve a chance every once in a while regardless of how much they annoy me. And my opinion is that of an intelligent, distinguishing, kind, decent and sane person. Usually at least. And I stop and I think about how awful it would really be if she said no. It would be more embarrassing than it was in high school to begin with, but more than that, if she refuses to go out then it will have ruined my day completely. I might just have to kill her for it, and I can't do that because she's innocent and there's no real threat of the Dark Ones getting to her from what I see. And if I kill somebody innocent and unlikely to be corrupted by the Dark Ones, then I will be just like the others on TV. I will be a petty, stupid little shark with legs like them. The THEM that Cass and the Reap kids are entranced by. And I'm better than *them*. I'm not a shark with legs, but God help me if somebody makes me snap and turn into one. I refuse to snap. I am not a great big mouth that demands to be fed big, meaty chunks of violence, malice and lost innocence.

"Sure," she says, "I'm starved."

So, we walk to a café I don't go to and I feel relieved. I have been given in the form of this redheaded angel of mercy the chance to redeem a shitty pointless sharkmaking day. Then, it suddenly strikes me why I do not go to this other café at all. I have to bite my tongue to avoid filling the streets with the loud echoes of my profanity. The other café is called "Murderland."

Murderland is a bastion of "Reap Chic."The names Murderland and Reap Chic never cease to annoy me. Neither do the people nor décor that populate Murderland and the popular Reap imagination. We go in and the clientele is a blur of Deerstalkers, dark shades, hooded sweatshirts, bondage masks, black cloaks and clown suits. The outfits are a gibbering, self-deprecating Halloween party that laughs at centuries of bloodshed and makes light of what are now, thousands of victims. All the Deerstalkers, all the cloaks, all the bloodstained clownsuits and flannel shirts and people walking black labs inside. The fictional blurs with the real as it tends to, when hockey masks and rubber chainsaws and machetes are held merrily in the air, waved about in a mock threatening fashions at the waitresses. I see one kid is even wearing yellow contacts to emulate the famous "Cobra Gaze" of Godless Jack. Mack the Knife plays loudly on the jukebox and I hear screeching voices singing along.

"Oh the shark has pretty teeth, dear…"

God, the shit these kids wear! The music they listen to, the way they conduct themselves. This place makes me long for the glory days of safe rebellion. I long for all the hippies and the goths and the punks and the metalheads, and all those other freaks that fade into the woodwork, 'cause, God, these reap kids don't just disappear and I get the feeling the way they walk and the way they listen and dress and hang on TV screens at bars, that Reap Chic might just be here to stay. This place reminds me that there's damn good chances that reap chic might just be here to stay.

"This place is so Reap," the redhead says. Her tone is more observational than disgusted or amazed. I had wished she would be disgusted or uncomfortable but it stands to reason that she'd been to reapjoints before and maybe to this particular reapjoint, it being within walking distance and all. And now I'm stuck here. Well shit.

"Yeah," I agree. So Reap.

A waitress dressed in a perhaps too tight lace up corset and a longish grey skirt with a petticoat, bloomers and long black boots seats us. It appears that she's going for Whitechapel whore. She pulls it off pretty well, although her breasts look huge and awkward in the tightness of the corset. Not only this, but it sounds like she's probably chewing gum. Not particularly Victorian, I think.

"'Ow do ya do, gov?" she asks me in the fakest of Cockney accents.

"Fine," I lie and try to fix my gaze on the menu, but the photos on the walls are too distracting. They depict the superstars of the trade. Ted Bundy is looking as oily and charismatic as ever. Gacy looks fat, stupid and content like a cow in a pasture. Berkowitz looks like he has no clue where the hell he is. Ramirez looks as if everything's really funny. Manson looks like he wants to look. He looks like he's ready to rip your throat out with his teeth and swallow it. I honestly don't know why the hell it is that reapers are so into Charles Manson. I don't see what it is that appeals to them about a schizophrenic wannabe rockstar who convinced a bunch of hippies that it would be fun and productive to ruin a perfectly good director's life. The guy is, after all, not even a real psychopomp. The computer printouts of fake Ripper letters and autographed photos of Mr. Right, Howard Shaw and the Girl Scout Slasher make me even more uneasy. It leaves me torn between thinking either this place takes itself too seriously or whether it's the circus it looks like. Or maybe the circus is taking itself too seriously. It occurs to me that this third possibility is more likely than the others. This third possibility is almost definitely the one. After making this conclusion, I finally get a good glance at the menu.

Milkfed veal. The Sharon Tate. I hate meat and I hate violence. I am a vegetarian, and confusing as it may sound, I maintain that I am a pacifist. Sloppy Joes. The Mary Kelly. Things I certainly don't feel like thinking about when I'm eating.

Some of the reapkids are throwing them at each other. They laugh from across the restaurant, give each other the finger. It appears that the swastika tattooed Manson kids look down at the Victorian foppery of the Ripper kids. One Ripper kid wipes the $2.00 sloppy joe off his cape and feeds it to the Son of Sam's dog next to him. The black lab wolfs down the sloppy joe eagerly and the Ripper kid exchanges obscenities with the Manson. All through this the waitresses go about their jobs. This is really just the order of things at reapjoints. My distraction becomes even more evident although the redhead has a laserlike focus on the menu. It astonishes me, really. She notices my discontent.

"What's wrong?" says the girl.

I duck a flying bloodsausage.

"It's just the veal," I say, "so inhumane."

I don't say enough to make myself look square, but I do say what I mean. I feel satisfied with my comment. The Whitechapel whore moves over to another table and I wait for the new waitress to come. She's dressed conservatively, somewhat tight conservative sweater vest, pleated skirt, heels. Traditional coed clothes. She's one of those "Bundy girls." Pretty, blonde co-ed. Look at that little-yellow-cunt-little-mommy-little-empty-womb-little-devil-hole-waiting-to-be-filled-put-it-in-and-drop-it-off, and then let it go. The Bundy girl pushes the bangs off her forehead so she can see better. She makes some semblance of meaningful eye contact.

"What'll you have?"

"Coffee," I say, "just a cup of coffee."

I fumble, a little distracted by some smaller, wispier Dark Ones around her.

"Black." I feel relieved when I discover that they're only scouts and not breeders. She's been discovered but it isn't too late. It's too late for her to live much longer, certainly, but it isn't too late to stop the Dark Ones from getting to her. This is a Tuesday and Thursday week, so tomorrow I'll deal with this. Right now I will sit and I will reaffirm my fucking faith in the kindness and decency of strangers.

"And you, miss?"

The redhead looks up from the menu, face full of certainty, "I'll have the Sharon Tate."

My eyes widen and I get scared. She seems to almost be dissolving into the scenery. Another robot playing belligerently in a crossfire of flying meat. How could I have possibly picked so badly?

"Oh the shark has pretty teeth, dear and it keeps them pearly white..." croons Bobby Darin. I don't want to be a shark. I am not an automaton made to eat other creatures. And yet, I can feel my teeth start to grow and go sharp. It almost hurts my mouth. This girl has just about turned me into a goddamn shark, and there is nothing in the world worse than another human shark. There are a lot of creatures out there who deserve to be eaten, but I do not want it to be my business to eat them. I callously wonder why these kids don't clean up their own messes. Why the rippers don't just pull out their trusty putty knives and scalpels and tear the Mansons to shreds. I wonder why the Sons of Sam don't just blow them both skyhigh. Only paintball guns. Only toys. The real things aren't in here. Except for me. This shitty day has gotten shittier. I can't believe this woman.

"I'm kidding," says the redhead, and I'm just relieved enough, "I'll have the Albert Fish filet."

Like Cass' smile, this girl's smile reminds me that she may very well be a person. It makes me examine the reapers and think what it is they might have going on. Most of them are robots, some don't really feel so passionate about violence, I think. Some are poseurs. Funny how sometimes a person might be a little more human or a little smarter or a little more compassionate just because they actually are a poseur. The waitress is most definitely human as I can see from the Dark

Ones examining her. Strange how they don't even know sometimes who's a robot and who isn't. It's funny that even they need to check. These are just larvae, these are just scouts, but the breeders are coming. How lucky this is a Tuesday, Thursday week. It makes me kind of sad though that one of maybe six human beings in the whole restaurant has to die tomorrow night.

"Can't see how anyone would do something like that to some cute, defenseless little calf. Do you? It just doesn't seem humane at all. I think it's really fucked up. But then again, ain't that the way, nowadays?" She doesn't look like she's all that affected by it.

It is. It really is, but I wish she or anyone like her could really grasp it. But it is "so fucked up" it doesn't make all that much sense to me. The comment, inane and generic as it is, makes me think of a John Lennon song.

"UFOs over New York and I ain't too surprised."

I'm not quite thinking when I say it and I'm surprised that I actually do. I usually keep those things in my head. I should have, I realize, because she looks at me like I'm from outer-mother-fucking-space. In a restaurant full of serial killer photos and teenagers tossing meals at one another, all of a sudden I look like a total freak. Amazing.

"It's a song."

It still doesn't quite register with her. The frustration, the shock, John Lennon's political and social outrage. My political and social outrage. My alienation. I want to explain how stupid and sick and alien I think all of this is, but I don't think anyone who says they feel it really does. I don't think anybody feels like I feel. I don't think anybody can actually see the town they're walking around in the country they're walking around in the time they're walking around in. It makes me choke it makes me feel more than a little awkward here. I am not a regular person. The hardware store clerk is a regular person. The redhaired girl is a regular person, and these freaks are regular people. She just sits there. I can count the seconds and my count reaches twenty-five before she opens her mouth again.

"Oh," she says, and I wish Cass were here. Because Cass jumps to those connections, she gets impressed and eager and clever. She comprehends. But I feel like I've been talking to a dog. I can't blame her, she's not the most well educated person you could meet. A little slow in fact. She's just about 19 now that I look at her. She's going to community college. She has to be an aspiring nurse or veterinarian. I wonder which one because I think it might make a difference. She looks sort of like the nurse type. She might not have gotten what I said but she's attentive at least. Outgoing. Something somewhat similar to caring as well. Yeah, sort of like the nurse type, but she might surprise me and in fact be a veterinarian. She might further surprise me and pull kindergarten teacher or beautician. Lots of beauticians around. Hair and nail salons everywhere. Blows my mind how many hair and nail salons there are everywhere, but a lot of the women around here need it. But it's either nurse, kindergarten teacher, veterinarian or beautician.

"What do you study?" I ask.

But after asking, I don't stop guessing. It's a habit of mine. Obviously, I do something that requires being able to read people really well. Need to know a little something about everyone you look at. Another one of those things brought up in Godless Jack's book. Always watch people. Get to know whoever you can and make sure you have everybody sized up. Wouldn't want to get a black belt in Judo or somebody with a can of mace for example. So, I think harder and narrow it down to nurse or kindergarten teacher. She doesn't seem quite mousy enough for a veterinary assistant and there are certain traits that make me think that beautician might be out of the question as well. Big, sensitive eyes. Little attention to hair and nails beyond the dyeing. Her clothes are also, I think, about seven months out of style. It seems to me that a lot of beauticians and veterinary assistants are robots. Even robots love puppies and kittens. I think a higher percentage of them than nurses. Nursing takes a fair amount of education and while the nanites reach about 97% of adults now. Still, that much time devoted to education, that much empathy, well, those things are pretty human traits. They might all be people. Maybe some are and some aren't. Kindergarten teacher or nurse definitely."

"Actually, I'm studying to be a teacher. I love kids. I just don't think I could deal with older ones. All the issues and too much math to remember. So, I'm gonna teach kindergarten, because kids are so simple and so nice to be around. Do you like kids?"

I think I like children. I like the human ones at least. I'm very fond of the hope, the fact that maybe this generation might not end up as more robots. And I like knowing that they don't belong to the enemy, or not yet at least. I feel so certain and happy sitting there with people who I know are usually people. I like knowing that they're not teenagers dressed up as their favorite killer yet. Maybe it's just fashion and maybe the problem's with me. But all the kids seem to be doing it.

"Yeah. I read to kids at the library on Tuesdays and Thursdays."

She smiles, real warmth.

"That's so sweet," she says, "You're such a nice guy."

"Yeah," I answer and then I look at the Bundy girl waitress and I look at the man she's talking to. The manager. I notice a family resemblance in their features. I read her lips. She says her rent's due in a week and asks him if she can work tomorrow night too to pick up some more hours. He agrees. You're the best, Uncle Stan. How immensely convenient. My Tuesday evening starts to fall into place, although I wish it hadn't. No need for stalking or research or asking around now. I'll know right where to find her. Thank you, Uncle Stan. Uncle Sam hearts Uncle Stan.

I sit, silently finishing up my coffee. The redhead talks for awhile about things that I don't really process and I respond with nods and looks of blatantly feigned interest. She doesn't quite notice. Thinks that she has, in fact, made a real and profound connection of some kind.

"Can I call you?" she asks.

"No," I reply. Then, I go home and have a real conversation. In retrospect, I think the redhead was a robot.

I Must Be Permissive, Understanding of the Younger Generation

On Tuesdays, Jeremy works at the pharmacy in the morning so that he can go to the library and read to the children in the afternoon. The reading room is lined with bright pictures of the Cat in the Hat, mythic creatures from the Narnia books, dragons, faeries, the Tin Man, Dorothy, the Cowardly Lion, the Scarecrow and any number of other images from fairy tales and children's books of all kinds. In the middle of the room is a rocking chair painted green with little gold letters engraved on it. The little gold letters read "Story Chair" and Jeremy always beams with pride and comfort when he sits down in it and picks a book. The large circle of children stares up eagerly as they observe him making his choice. They know what he'll choose, but they always like to see him pick it out. Children love rituals and routines and consider them bastions of safety and Jeremy's picking a book is one of the rituals they observe the closest and feel safest about.

He silently opens *Goodnight Moon* and then says hello to all the children before telling them to gather around. He tells the little ones to scoot closer in order to hear and better see the simple, bright but subtle little pictures. *Goodnight Moon* is completely without flash or pretention. Goodnight Moon is an institution in children's literature. Not only that, but it is an American institution, period. This is one of the reasons Jeremy likes it so much. And one of the reasons for which Jeremy selects it every time he sits down to read to all of the children.

If I have children, Jeremy thinks, I'll read them *Goodnight Moon* all the time. I think maybe every night. I'll read them *Goodnight Moon* and then I'll tuck them into bed and tell them I love them. Although a child should be exposed to a wide variety of things to expand their fragile little minds in order to avoid potential nanite infections. He hopes and prays (as close as Jeremy comes to praying) that his influence and that of the great patriot Margaret Wise Brown might just be enough to spare their little brains and their little souls. He does not for a minute believe it sufficient. Why? Because I don't for a minute believe it will be sufficient. Jeremy is wasting his time. Poor Jeremy.

A little girl, six, round-faced, cute and blonde lays her head gently on his lap and Jeremy fights to avoid crying. So, I take the sad like I often do. I put it where all the other sad goes and it's gone, like magic. Now Jeremy is all right and I am sad. I am sad that Jeremy knows the Dark Ones will come for her and fill her up with their evil and their venomous ideas. But Jeremy is not sad, no. I am. I tend to keep quiet. Quiet, but sometimes I have things to say. When I have things to say, they are always of the utmost importance.

Jeremy pats her head and smiles. Some of the littler ones are starting to fidget. Then, he points the book at them, a little like a gun and bang! The bright magic of the sweet little pictures brings them to their knees and they are crawling back to the story. A murder of crows devouring a corpse. Bandits gathering round to loot the treasure trove of stimulation.

Someday, he thinks again, someday if I have children, I will read them *Goodnight Moon*. But Cass isn't into children, Santa, or the Easter Bunny…

She's also not conscious of the Dark Ones. Cass may not be the one to send his innocent progeny screaming and clueless into an embattled world. For right now, he'll just do what he can with these poor ignorant things. Hope is all we have, he says to both of us and even I am uncertain if this is an unusual statement for him. It fits firmly inside and outside of his ethos. He's just glad for now, that these children are enjoying serene, wholesome children's literature and not comic books or movies or BLD News. Jeremy hates violence. I however am absolutely crazy about it. Sometimes, I just have to sneak up behind him and shake him hard and remind him. I have so much to do and so little time. Jeremy is at last finishing the book. Good. I myself hate it. Goodnight this, goodnight that. I don't see the point. I'd like to think he's smarter than all this shit.

"More," says a little brown-haired boy with glasses.

Jeremy looks around the children's room. *Grimm's Fairy Tales*. Killing. *The Chronicles of Narnia*. Right-wing Christian propaganda. *Alice in Wonderland.* Too complex.

Maybe too close to home. And there are various other bright loud plastic books about talking insects, bears and bunnies that are lonely and looking for friends, baseball capped dinosaurs munching hamburgers and having a good old time in the twentieth and twenty-first centuries. The books all beg for attention, howling and caterwauling like a zoo. Jeremy is unsure. A maze of saccharine, juvenile, amoral titles tries to drag him in. He is reminded of the mall and movie theaters and infomercials. He sees the nanites crawling on some of them. Sure, they're microscopic, but Jeremy sees them. He is painfully aware of their game. He's too good for them, Jeremy Jenkins ascendant devil will not be tricked into making more robots out of gullible innocents. I stop him from sweating since I am so tired of all of his fucking panic. It's no good. Another one of those feelings that I occasionally slice out and toss on the big intricate compost heap I've built. He finds something at last. Loving, fun, kindhearted.

"The sun did not shine; it was too wet to play…"

Crisis averted. I take a short nap, with my eyes open as always. Call me paranoid.

Jeremy finishes the book and returns home to Cass. Though no domestic prodigy, no more a potential housewife than a potential mother, Cass has made a pound of linguini and keeps a bowl of meatballs separate from the thick and crunchy marinara sauce she has made for Jeremy. He is quiet and reflective. Cass hugs him hard and she shakes him like she usually does when it looks like he's spacing out. She should know by now that Jeremy is never spacing out. Too smart, too productive, too powerful.

He looks at her now. He actually looks at her. So often he's remembering other times with her or trying to see wires under her skin, but now he is really looking at her. The roundness under the sweater, the sweetly predatory amber brown eyes, the maybe-too-pale skin, the tiny smile that sometimes gets enormous and threatens to devour her face, the longshort legs that her black skirt shows so well, the silent laughter and the muted depression and the inaudible footfalls. Jeremy is almost too shy to talk. It feels like back in school when the plaid skirts and forbidden cleavage would reach in and wrench the words from his throat. But, it's different now, too. He wants to say all the things that he sees and feels, but they might seem fake or not quite sane or like they're just lines to get what he wants from her. So, he says something that expresses nothing at all. Something that seems genuine, but is empty and weightless to her ears. The real words and the real thoughts are too heavy. I might just have to drag them away.

"You look nice," he says, and almost instantly regrets it.

"I look nice? Don't you have anything unique or real to say? I think I know that you think I look nice. You fuck me, don't you? You wouldn't fuck me if I was hideous or something. Don't even bother with that you look nice shit, Jeremy." Cass looks annoyed. She doesn't look small and sweet anymore, she looks huge and dour, a glowering renaissance statue of her, a desperate and perfect Venus who might as well be a Juno. She's still too beautiful for him to talk about coherently. He backs off. He gets tense and nervous, that feeling he gets at the ATM when he doesn't know if his paycheck has cleared yet and the rent is due. Is this it? Is she gone? If she goes, then Jeremy and I are alone. I sort of want her to go; actually, she's a distraction. I have a hard time getting through to him when she's around.

"I was just saying that you look so beautiful. I always think you look nice, and I love you so I felt like telling you. I love you, Cass."

"Okay," says a mournful, bitter Cass who still manages to plant a kiss on his cheek. I love it when she's like this. She gets very quiet.

"I'm sorry," says Jeremy. I can feel him creeping away, creeping toward me and the things that I pile up in my corridors. He resists walking down that path, somehow. Instead, he thinks what he was about to say before, but doesn't even consider saying it now. Silent laughter. Glowing melancholy. Light and darkness playing so ably on her sweet face. Chiaroscuro. He dips a piece of garlic bread into the linguini, methodically scooping bits of tomato and pepper onto the bread. He crunches into it hard. It's a little burnt. Everything's just a little bit wrong. Everything's slightly off. Something good must have been on TV. Something repugnant, actually.

"Poker night?" Cass asks.

"Mhmm," Jeremy says with his mouth full. This is his excuse every week and every time it works and manages to arouse no suspicion whatsoever. Nobody ever calls to remind him, and Jeremy hasn't seen his male friends for ages, but he knows that Cass would never check it out or think of asking to go with him. Jeremy's male friends are desk job kinds of guys with very little sense of humor and nothing great to talk about. Just the kind of people you pick up without even noticing. The kind of people someone as unassertive as Jeremy finds clinging to him. Completely foolproof. And when those other alternating days arise, Jeremy volunteers at a soup kitchen or goes to book discussion groups. Why not? The work he does is to preserve humanity and to preserve the intellectual integrity of the species as well. Cass is not stupid, but Jeremy knows that she trusts him completely. She might not understand if he explains the situation. I'm not the man they think I am at home, he thinks. Elton John sings in his brain, "No, no, no, I'm the Rocket Man!"

"You wanna come with? Jeff's actually bringing his new girlfriend this time. He thinks you two might hit it off."

Cass shakes her head as he knows she will every time.

"No, thanks. Poker is so boring. You just stare and wait and hope nobody knows what you're hiding. If I wanted that, I'd have dinner with my mother. Besides, Jeff's really condescending toward me and his last few girlfriends were too boring for most quilting bees. You have fun."

"Jeff's not such a bad guy if you get to know him, and Sheila's not stupid. Actually, she's an orthodontist."

"Yeah, I'm sure she's a laugh a minute. I think I'll just stay home and watch TV, if it's the same to you."

Jeremy shrugs. "I'll tell Jeff you said 'hi.'"

"I just don't feel welcome most of the time. It sounds like a guy thing. I can't believe you of all people are involved in such a crazy macho ritual. You're such a timid, sensitive guy most of the time, although there has to be a dark side somewhere in a guy who fucks like you do."

She flips her hair and gives him a seductive glance. I examine the context and I deem an erection completely unnecessary. Got to get going, places to be, people to be rid of. Not the time for dalliance or distractions, Jeremy.

MURDERLAND | Garrett Cook

"I've got a very dark secret life, you know. I'm really a spy for some malignant Eastern European country." He returns the seductive glance. It's cute, it really is, but I myself am getting exasperated.

"If you were a spy, you'd have a car, sweetheart." Cass smiles. Not quite coy. She kisses him once more, this time nibbling on his lip a little bit. She lets her tongue tickle and taunt his before the kiss separates itself. She hugs him tightly, the bitterness disappearing someplace else in her.

"Don't forget your case of stuff," she reminds him, thoroughly unaware that the case is full of razors and other serial killing paraphernalia and even more thoroughly unaware of what all of this serial killing paraphernalia is for. He tells her goodbye and rushes upstairs to grab all of his very important poker stuff.

Jeremy's important poker stuff is kept in a highly professional red leather briefcase. This is the second briefcase to bear Jeremy's important poker stuff. This one was a birthday gift after the other was dropped and badly dented. It is fortunate that the briefcase did not open up as it was dropped, for its contents are of a fairly uncanny nature. Jeremy says it is full of change rolls, poker chips, a couple books and an extra deck of cards, since he occasionally likes to use his own. The contents of Jeremy's briefcase however are as follows:

7 straight razors
1 meat cleaver
1 pair of two inch shoelifts
3 pairs of colored contact lenses: blue, hazel and green
1 fake beard
1 sanitary mask
4 pairs sanitized rubber gloves
1 syringe of liquid valium
1 bottle vicodin
1 bottle rohypnol
1 bottle morphine

Sometimes, Jeremy is actually glad that he is a pharmacist. On this occasion, Jeremy is also glad that Murderland does not close for another hour and a half. He is also glad that he noticed the waitress' conversation with her Uncle Stan. He sometimes wonders whether it is a lightning quick brain and excellent judgment that give him such an edge, or whether it has something to do with the fact that what he is doing is the order of things. Just too many coincidences too much falling into place and it's all so easy. So easy it almost hurts. But no matter what, tonight Jeremy's kill is going to fall into place and nothing will get in his way. Nothing can get in the way of the triumph of goodness over the Dark Ones. It all feels gnawingly perfect to Jeremy as he slips in his blue contacts, puts on the lifts and walks into the restaurant with a slightly different swagger.

The Jeremy who walks in is a hulking figure with a beard and sharp blue eyes. Tall, powerful, capable of throwing a woman around the way she likes it. Any woman who works as a waitress at a reapjoint likes to be thrown around. He has on a Yankees hat and a flannel shirt, which in this case are both very Reap. A consummate solitary predator type who lures innocent young things back to his house and slices them open. How ironic that that's just what this girl and so many others they're intrigued by. He gets stares from Ripchicks, Kelleys, Bundy girls and all manner of Reapers, even several male Rippers and Gacys.

"Come sit with me, love…"

"Come over here and play with Uncle Pogo…"

"I'm going to a concert tonight and umm…"

"You look amazing; it's just so perfect…"

"'Ave a little fun, boss?"

He walks through the gauntlet of flirting unscathed, not replying once and sending further shivers down the spines of all the Reapkids around him. All of the mystiques, the danger, and the quiet desperation are too much. Fingernails drum his shoulders from the booth behind him and he has to ignore them. He brushes off a tongue on his neck. This should really be enough for Reapers to know that this is a man here to kill a waitress. Idiots. They might very well lack the requisite presence of mind to kill like Cass always says. What poseurs, sitting there begging for the real thing to work his magic on them. Sitting ducks. Their parents should be even more worried.

He orders a salad and a coffee and he gives the waitress a big smile. She returns it. I whisper such exciting things to him.

Such exciting things. I am not a panderer or a seducer, no. I'm just here to make sure Jeremy gets his job done and gets it done right. I tell him that we need to be rid of her. I remind him of his mother abandoning him. I remind him of just what would have happened as a result of the breeders getting to her. Were it not for me. It really scares me, to be honest. I am glad Jeremy is on mankind's side and not against them, since he is an unstoppable juggernaut of destruction. They are terrifying beyond words, and they will get this woman. They will get her and they will fill her with their seeds. So, he waits and when he finishes his salad, he tips her a 20. He knows he'll see it again. That's when the Reap kids stop harassing him. They know damn well that he's chosen his date for the evening.

"What time do you get off?" he asks her with another smile.

She looks down at her watch. "About now, cutie."

And then Jeremy gives his winning smile again. It's reflexive by now. He wants to stop but he knows too much. He knows that he couldn't even think of letting her get away. He had, at first, wanted immensely to spare her, for some reason that I cannot begin to fathom. That would be completely illogical, though, completely illogical, and a threat to humanity itself. But this stupid had been in his head. Glad to see it exiled. Now he can't even think of letting a squawking, vicious baby Dark One squeeze out. Warn her? Let her run? Warn her, let her run? No. I have taken the fear and I have put in the usual place where fear belongs. No better place for it. The winning smile pastes itself on. The winning smile has something to win.

"You wanna go get a drink?"

Of course she agrees. Tall, nice smile, good tipper, pleasant with sickly sweet predatory pheromones. He can tell how lonely she is from all the times she checks up on her tables. Some of the kids have six refills by the end of the meal. Obvious, so obvious. So, they get in her car, and they head to a bar that Jeremy knows and has taken many women to in various permutations of his disguise. So many permutations that the witnesses couldn't come up with a description if they wanted to. He's been here a good seventy times and the bartender doesn't know him as a regular. She asks about the briefcase and he explains that he just got off work. Computer programmer, sorta boring. You don't wanna hear about that…

It's amazing how quickly he can bore her away from his story with technobabble. So, she accepts it. Never would have thought a real live psychopomp would be making his rounds at the little reapjoint where she works. It would be like a real leprechaun buying Lucky Charms. She's still in uniform and we laugh together at the irony. On the inside of course. Jeremy would never let a slipup like that happen. They talk. Nothing special, nothing at all worth bringing up. They get drunker and she gets more brazen. He keeps her from noticing that he has been nursing a single rum and coke.

She kisses him, puts her hand on his thigh and begins to rub it. Her hand moves beyond the thigh and it squeezes quite shamelessly. She licks her lips, and he, in turn traces his tongue across them. He puts his hand on hers. Whispers in her ear just as seductively as I whispered in his.

"Maybe we should go back to your place."

They get in her car and she gives him directions. They park outside of her building and he looks up at where she lives. Second floor, overlooking the fire escape. A real dream. It couldn't possibly be any more convenient than this. Jeremy hates elevators. Godless Jack Cavanaugh in "The Art of Reap" points out that obviously elevators and security cameras are the psychopomp's worst enemies. One of those awful books that Cass shoved down his throat. He kept on insisting that he wasn't into them, but he loves her, so he read them. Picked up a hint or two from the master, the superstar, the man who made murder higher rated than baseball, football and pro wrestling combined. He winces, remembering where he was taking his strategy from. He uses that book too often for his liking.

She brings him up to the apartment. Whites and pinks. Lots of lace. Too much lace. The sofa has a ridiculous floral pattern. It looks like she resides in a *Bed, Bath & Beyond*. Jeremy gags.

"Nice place," he says.

She smiles, and, stumbling, places her hand on his shoulder as much for balance as contact.

"I'm going to go change into something slinky and cute. Can you amuse yourself for a minute?"

"Of course, beautiful."

As she disappears into her bedroom, he opens up the briefcase and takes out the syringe and a pair of latex gloves. He stands barefoot quietly outside the bedroom door. She walks out , and the syringe greets her. We grab her by the throat and choke her. In a matter of moments she is getting very weak and sluggish. My eyes grow wide and I choke her for a bit. Just me, because sometimes I need to do it. This isn't pleasure, no. We synchronize ourselves and soon are acting seamlessly together. We have made ourselves a cohesive, fully functioning unit. She finally falls.

The valium in the syringe could kill a grizzly, but until it sets in, the strangling is necessary. She is most likely already dead, but Jeremy needs to make sure that the little Dark One isn't already in there, able to crawl out on its own. This is a legitimate and very sensible fear since Dark Ones are like cockroaches, able to survive most anything. He makes the cut and we reach in, great surgical team that we are. Filthy yellow cunt. Filthy filthy filthy. Little mommy we think. No children now. No noisy angry poisonous Dark Ones. He feels many cries go silent. Real child? Real infant? Real mother? The children at the library were different, hers would be, well...

Jeremy calms himself and removes the uterus, ovaries and fallopian tubes, along with her hands, the only part he made contact with. He hates using the meat cleaver. Everything then goes into the trash compactor. He carves a letter H on her head. It stands for nothing, but he does this to every tenth victim to help maintain the illusion that he is multiple reapers. The place stinks so he reaches into the suitcase for the air freshener and the screaming and the stench and most of the guilt are gone. Goodnight, moon, goodnight room...

Jeremy's Journal, April 11th, 1994

School psychologist tells me to keep a journal, so I'm keeping one now. He says I'm repressed and too unaware of my own feelings and pain. He says I need a creative outlet and to express myself more. Ted and Elise have a piano, a big, intimidating mahogany thing that everybody has too much respect for to touch. If they play it, bad music will surely come out, and since it's an expensive piano, they want to think it can only make good music, and the only way it can really do that is if it makes no music. I thought about taking lessons, but I'm sorta sure that piano's more expensive than I am, so I don't ask.

Ted dropped me off at the mall because he has things to do today. He left me a hundred dollar bill, which I am supposed to be impressed by and grateful for. So, I act impressed. I don't tell him that I can't wait to drive next year so that I can run over his legs and put him in a wheelchair for the rest of his life. I guess the school psychologist is right about me not expressing myself. I look at the bill in fained (is that how that's spelled?) amazement and I thank him in my usual "I'm so glad you saved me from life as an orphan" level of gratitude.

"You're very important to us, Jeremy," he says. I don't think he realizes that he talks to me like I'm one of his middle management cronies. He's talked to me about a business degree someday so that I can be. I always tell him that I'll think about it. It always of course means no. There I am repressing everything again. But then again, what kind of role models do I have? Where do they get off calling me repressed when I live with a guy who talks to his foster son like that? Sometimes I swear he must be from space or a cyborg or something. I swear he ticks like a clock and his legs are pneumatic.

"Enjoy yourself," he tells me, "try not to spend it all in one place."

And I so wanted a new pair of Air Jordans. I find it odd that I'm someone to be bought off. I'm fifteen years old and yet have become a sort of o authority figure. I am in charge of their guilt; I am proof of their Christian Charity. I am God's grounds for letting them into Heaven, in spite of their deep mediocrity. Other kids would feel like taking advantage of this, but other kids don't get that it wouldn't mean anything if I did. If there were something I wanted from them, it would be different. The only thing I want from anybody is something that I could only get from somebody who I'll never see. I want my mother and my father (if I have one). I wonder what kind of father he'd be. At the very least, he'd be one to understand that I have nothing to do at the mall. There's a bookstore there, but there's a library down the street. There's pizza there, but there's pizza everywhere if I want it. There's pizza at the supermarket which eventually becomes pizza in the freezer and then pizza at the table. There's nothing for me at the mall. Nothing.

The buzzing, honking and squeaking can be heard from the food court and you can see the glow of the machines from the B. Dalton. I've never seen an arcade so loud, so bright and so disruptive. I'm not fond of arcades, but this one has something really awful about it. You can't quite see it at first. When you walk in, on one side is the skill crane, something I don't consider aptly named. It's too random. I've tried it, the claw more or less stops wherever it wants to stop.

On the other side of the entrance is the change machine. The other kids line up there, letting it devour their fives and tens and taking the shiny quarters it vomits out. With those two machines spread so far apart, it feels like it's actually spacious. A whole wide world of amusements looks to present itself. But the machines are so close together that you can feel the frustration and drench yourself in the sweat that the kid at the machine next to you is working up. Tight, wet, smells awful…

It's what I imagine girls are like. The girls I've met at least. But they don't glow and make weird noises.

The only machines that are spread apart from the others are the cars. Go in, sit down, play with the steering wheel and all of a sudden they feel themselves rushing down a big, monotonous stretch of racetrack, and inside the little dome, they don't have to look at, smell or interact with any of the other children at all.

I find myself at the arcade so often, because I want to know who runs this place. I guess it's just trying to deal with an irrational, childish fear I have. I always find myself thinking that the arcade just runs itself. It's stupid, but if you watch it long enough, you can see it. The kids put the money in the change machine, the change machine spits out the quarters, and the quarters work the arcade machine. The machines all feed each other in a scary little ecosystem. It's crazy, but I feel like they don't need anybody. Nothing scares me more than the thought that the machines are doing their own work and I have to find that they aren't. But what proof is there?

It's so dark and anonymous that you can't find it. I never see people loading the change machine. I never see anybody watching all the kids or repairing the arcade games. They might even be fixing themselves. They might extend little wires into the back of the others, share electricity, share their power, and keep this whole bright, shiny city of machines running. I look around for clues. I hope there's an Out of Order sign on something every time so that I'll know somebody put it there, but nothing at this arcade is out of order. Nothing ever gets fixed, so it's almost like nobody's there to set them up or fix them. There are never signs advertising the new games, the new games just arrive and the kids know that the new game is in and they walk up to it and they play it. Where are the people in all of this?

Everybody's acting like a machine, absolutely everybody. The kids don't talk to each other at all, they grab the quarters, they put them in the arcade games and then they play the arcade game until the quarters are gone and then they either put more in, shuffle off disappointed, or one of their parents show up to pick them up. When they're not playing against each other, they're trying to outwit the computer, a lot of the time failing. So other than depositing quarters, they're not doing anything that the machines can't. And in the end, who comes out on top? The machines beat the kids and the kids put in more money to try and beat the machines. The machine is only serving its function and it gets paid for doing that function. The kid plays the machine, the machine plays the kid.

This time, it's really disappointing to me that nobody's there running the arcade. In this little world, there isn't a God and everything just runs itself. It's scary thinking that. It's scary thinking that maybe when I leave the arcade, everything outside is the same. Are they really that different from the robots they are at the arcade when they're in class, raising their hand when a question's asked and answering it? Deposit coin, serve function. Is my stepfather that different when he works all day to bring home money which he uses to buy a bigger TV or a new stereo? He still pumps coins into a little car and acts like it's the Indie 500 when he's driving it. Deposit coin, serve function. Outside the arcade, it's just an arcade. People feed machines which feed people, turn them into machines to feed the machines. People play the game, game plays the people.

It's so cramped and claustrophobic and smelly at the arcade that I'm direly in need of air. I go outside into the parking lot and there's an oldish man there in a long, smelly trenchcoat. He ducks between cars and underneath them, like he's running and hiding from somebody, but when he emerges, he puts a page of newspaper on the windshields of each car. The way he puts out the newspaper, ducks away and then puts out more newspaper, you'd swear that he was some sort of demented newspaper sprite. He doesn't quite act like a human being. It freaks me out at first, having seen so much mechanical behavior, but the more I watch him, the more it somehow relieves me to see how apelike his movements are. With all the jumping around, hiding and checking his surroundings, I think he'd be right at home in the jungle. The jungle would be a great relief to me. It would feel fresh and alive and like everybody's not full of wires. I think someday I'll go to the jungle.

I approach one of the cars, take the piece of newspaper off it and read it. I made sure to keep it and paste it here. I wasn't sure if it was some special newspaper or a page from the Weekly World News or something, but it seems authentic. I can't believe all the things in that clipping. They don't seem insane to me. They seem almost right. Nanites in things. People turning into robots. Extradimensional beings, evil things, looking to corrupt everybody. It has to be pure gibberish, but it is right there in the newspaper on page H8, where nobody looks. I think it's the page after wedding announcements, and they print it really small, don't even have headings on the columns. I hate it when you see something that has to be fake and has to be real at the same time.

It's a lot to take in, things I should think are just paranoid delusions, but maybe they're not. I look around for the old man amidst the cars in the parking lot.

"Where did you get this?" I ask him.

"Where do you think I get it?" he asks, not emerging from beneath the car he's hiding under, "it's a newspaper page. I get it from the newspaper. Where the hell else do you get a newspaper page?"

I don't know why I feel like apologizing to an insane homeless man for bothering him, but I do.

"I'm sorry," I tell him, "I was just curious."

"Killed the cat, curiosity. Haven't you heard that?"

I don't feel like backing away from him, because everything inside the mall feels scarier, especially since I haven't sorted out if the newspaper page is true or false. So I stand my ground and I nod. I don't make any move closer, because he feels that much like a wild animal. If threatened, he might bite or scratch or just go generally insane on me. I'm not sure I trust him, but I don't want to act like I'm afraid.

He gets out from under the car. His face is covered in what looks like it might be several beards, because one beard doesn't grow as thick as his. He looks like a picture of Moses, if Moses didn't bathe or go to a barber or slept under a bridge. Is he a monkey or is he a prophet? I have to wonder as he stands there, looking me over like I'm the strange one, like I'm the one that's likely to bite. I feel more than a little self conscious and nervous.

"Put that one back," he tells me, pointing at the page of newspaper, "people gotta see that."

"I wanna keep this one," I tell him, and he seems to notice that nobody but me has been reading the things. He seems to notice that people come out to the parking lot, see the things on their cars and they crumple them up. He shrugs then grabs another one from a bag he keeps concealed in his coat and puts it on the same windshield. He's got a lot of newspaper pages on him, and it looks like he wishes he could get every car.

I feel like a total idiot, but I just have to ask him. "Can I help?"

"Sure," he says, handing me a bunch of the pages.

People are coming outside to their cars, so I have to be extremely quick and extremely quiet. They all take a look at their cars, swear to themselves when they see the newspaper pages, and like the machines they are, don't think before tearing them up, don't think about the fact that something might be going down. I'm disappointed that nobody's going to read them, but I feel like it's important to try, because if these are true, people should know. People shouldn't be giving birth to monsters or turning into robots without knowing it's happening, especially when it's right there in the paper. I'm doing something right, which is more than any of them can say, more than my foster parents can say, that's for damn sure. Their idea of charity is taking in a kid, feeding him and sending him to some Catholic prep school. My idea of charity, this man's idea of charity, makes more sense to me.

It amazes me that he never gets caught, that he hides at just the right moments. He seems to feel people coming; he seems to have senses sharpened to fine points, like an animal or like some kind of psychic. It looks like he just tunes into how people feel, tunes into things psychically, and he can feel them showing up. Some people make him cringe. Sometimes, he almost gets caught because he sees something scary or hears some agonizing, awful sound, but he never does because he sees everyone coming. I'm not as good as he is, I almost get seen a couple times, but I'm starting to tune in.

I can start to see what's scaring him, but I'm not quite sure it's there. If it is, there are some problems, some big problems. There are little lights in the air, awful little lights and they start to flit around people. And that's if you look close enough, if you tune in, if you saw it in the paper maybe. Maybe if you see it in the paper, then you know it's true and then you can see it. Maybe modern people are wired to that extent. I know everybody else thinks what they see in the paper is always true, and if it's always true, then it must be there and you must be able to see it. It's so childish, so uncomplicated.

I crawl under the car with him and I offer him my hand.

"I'm Jeremy."

"I don't shake hands," he tells me, "germs."

MURDERLAND | Garrett Cook

That's a laugh. This dirty homeless man doesn't want to get my germs. I can almost feel them crawling on me, until I get a grip. For some reason, everything he says feels truer than everything that other people say. He has an odd magnetism about him in spite of the disdainful and scary qualities.

"What's your name?" I ask him, as if I had to remind him that I sought to know. The more cynical side of me thinks that he probably doesn't even know, that he's probably too far gone to hold up a really normal conversation, or else that he'll say that he's Jesus. The less cynical side of me wonders if I'd believe him if he said that he was Jesus.

"I'm General Lud. It's not my real name, but it's what I use. I've been waitin' for somebody to read these. Some people have and they help me sometimes and bring me food and buy me more newspapers. They can see that it's the truth. They sorta knew it already. I sorta knew it before I read. I knew that it sorta had to be true anyway. It's not that big of a stretch."

"So it is all true?" I ask, not needing to know whether or not I'm insane but just wanting to hear him say again that it's true, just wanting to hear him say it once more. Then it would definitely be true.

"Of course it's all true," he tells me, "it is, after all, in the newspaper."

I feel cold and alone in the world all of a sudden. This man doesn't help it, this man's ability to see the truth or to speak things that feel correct don't help it at all. When I go home, I read the little newspaper clipping over and over again for hours, and each time it says the same thing and each time General Lud is right. I don't know what to do about it right now, but I know that it will have to be something drastic.

A Debate With Hippocrates

Thorazine. Depakote. Welbutrin. Paxil. Vicodin. I quite
simply don't believe my eyes. I look up from the slips to make
sure Elvis has not risen from the grave to make my shift at the
pharmacy just a little more entertaining. Alas, no such luck.
My life has no room for whimsy. The man is as fat, but has
none of the King's flamboyance. The prescriptions are from a
doctor in Hartford. Three states over. This man is wearing a
University of Indiana T-shirt. His driver's license is from
Michigan. His accent however is definitely deep southern.
Florida or Georgia most likely. So, the daily grind of being a
pharmacist is broken up by a question: where the hell is he
actually from? Out of all the states I'm confronted with, I can't
come up with an answer. So I'm also left wondering why he's
here. Thomas Gennaro. The name rings a bell. I'm left even
more suspicious because I've never seen anyone who puts
matchbooks in the pockets of his wallet. He seems to have
plenty. The pocket is overflowing.
　"You collect matchbooks?"
　"Yeah."
　Some connection is starting to develop, but I can't place
it yet. I need to know more.
　"Can I see?"
The man looks extremely confused. He trembles slightly. I
think I know something. I think I know something amazing.
　"What for?"
　"It's an interesting hobby. I've never seen anybody do it
before."
　"Okay. I never thought it was that unique, myself. I
mean, people collect all kinds of things. All kinds."
　He takes them out, puts them down on the counter and
spreads them wide. Fifty five motels. Sloppy sloppy sloppy.
Shouldn't be seen outside the Safe Zone, should we? Victim's
families, vengeful cops. This is the work of somebody with no
semblance of self control and serious compulsions. Somebody
who takes a vast cornucopia of pills. It strikes me that his

fingers are lily white, his whole hands, but only up to his wrists. Chlorine. His face is very nicely tanned and I have a feeling that the rest of his arm is too. I've seen the newscasts, and with my photographic memory, blessing and burden, I can see every single motel mentioned by the shows Cass glues herself to. The Cabana Boy himself is here picking up what I would have to assume are some extremely ineffective prescriptions. Amazing. This one has killed a few cops in the chase, so he doesn't like showing his face. It also impedes his work for the hookers to know who's buying them for the night. A lot of people would be absolutely starstruck. This one is up for a Bundy and is considered a very weighty competitor. Fat pathetic little man. I can't keep the bile in check and I can't stop the blood from starting to rise up to my hands. My mind wanders back to the hardware store. A man who went through Vietnam was so impressed by this man's particular brand of brutality. The hierarchy of violence is funny. The hierarchy of fame is nauseating.

When you get right down to it, this man is nothing but another crazy drifter who kills prostitutes. Another truck stop avenger looking to right a violation that the media that glorifies and obsesses over him couldn't care less about. But he's famous, has a book deal, and sells T-shirts. He's famous, and yet he's nothing. He couldn't contribute less to society if he tried. As a historical footnote even, he'll be completely lacking in import. Contemptible no-account pop culture cliché. Contemptible no account pop culture cliché here and vulnerable in the pharmacy where I work picking up his prescription. Providence, providence again.

Examining the matchbooks, I connect all the places to the photos from the news. Every motel has a victim and every victim has a gruesome photo on the news to keep the hungry little animals fed on blood. If the news didn't slake their bloodlust, those Reap kids on the street would really be something. My mind ends up as a swirling blur of interviews with sheriffs and coroners and hotel managers. Even the occasional pimp with his face blocked out. The matchbooks themselves begin to feel a lot like crimes to me. I want to slit his goddamn throat just for having so many matches in his possession. I wonder if he ever did ME any favors, prevented any vessels from becoming possessed and taken by the Dark Ones. The disposal's different, though. A lot more complicated than chopping their breasts off after holding their heads underwater in a hotel pool. The Dark Ones can still incubate in a corpse if the plumbing's present.

Then, something funny happens. I completely forget about the very existence of the Dark Ones and obsess instead over how this bastard spreads from town to town, kills and then goes elsewhere. I get on a bus now and then to spread out, get off the radar and do some good a town or two over, but this guy, he's gone to every single state now. He only needs the pills because he himself is a disease. He needs to try to put himself into remission.

He has gotten a lot friendlier and he goes on and on and on about the matchbooks. I hear very little. I finally gather myself, tell him it's been nice talking to him but I have lots of work to do, so many prescriptions to fill and all. He takes his matchbooks and walks out, leaving me alone with so many pills. As a professional healer (yes, professional healer, a part time pharmacist is still a healer, I need things like this to get through my day), I am morally obligated to give this man his medicine, no matter how reprehensible and disgusting he actually is. He is a distinguished entertainer who needs to be in tip-top shape to work.

It's amazing how little time I have to argue with myself to accept that this is complete and utter bullshit. I'm so glad there's another guy named Thomas Gennaro in town. I replace his antidepressants with sedatives and his mood stabilizers with MAOIs. I have to put these in bigger capsules, but that's okay. I can't help but think of this other Thomas Gennaro as more than a coincidence. I'm on the right track. I'm doing the lord's work after all. Not quite the shit that was handed to me in Catholic school, but the lord's work can be done. A few days ago, I shot my first man. There was no pang of guilt or concern for the most part, no moral qualms to get in my way. He was a problem, so I shot him. After I shot him, that particular issue was resolved. Almost cathartic. Stands to reason that getting rid of Gennaro would be just as cathartic, even more so because he's more of a celebrity and more of an annoyance and really more of an everything than a small timer like Kringle. Nice to know that this media darling would no longer haunt me with his antics. So many others, though. Ultimately futile, I'd suppose, but I have to do what I feel is right and what might make me feel good later. I think it is quite likely that poisoning Thomas Gennaro will make me feel extremely good. Not even Thomas Gennaro, the name is irrelevant, like some comicbook supervillain, he's the Cabana Boy, he's his handle now. I'm not even killing Thomas Gennaro. That's a relief, because killing Thomas Gennaro might have made me feel bad. But, erase the legend, erase the handle, erase the Cabana Boy. Fifty five dead hookers will thank me. I'm not quite sure Gennaro works with the Dark Ones, though I'm sure the DVDs and the books about him are crawling with nanites, but just the same, it's good to be rid of a second worthless nobody who liked to take things apart. Human beings are not Swiss watches or Lego castles. Many of them are all wires, but the deconstructive urge is still too much. I think it was Yeats who said "things fall apart, the center cannot hold", in fact I know it was Yeats. The man was right. This is all starting to crumble. Why take it apart and see why it crumbles. Even the robots deserve better, though I have this irritating tendency to tell myself otherwise. I also have this irritating tendency to be uncertain whether it is in fact me telling myself otherwise. So, Kringle deserved it and the Cabana Boy deserves it.

I look down at my watch every five minutes or so. One old man, old woman, depressed housewife after another. Shuffle in shuffle out shuffle off the mortal coil. Shuffle shuffle shuffle vanish. Like a card trick without the amusement. Makes me feel like a machine. I always hate feeling like a machine. So many of the others are machines, after all, so I have to take pride in being a real flesh and blood man. No matter how proud I am of my guts and my grey matter and how tightly I hold onto them. Twelve glances at the watch per hour. Four hours of work following the Cabana Boy's departure. That makes forty eight glances per hour. It scares me how precise the timing of my glances is. In fact, the watch is pretty much just a prop. I am my own watch. Spinning gears momentary ticks in my head. Around glance twenty five, the Cabana Boy comes and picks up his medicine. I try my hardest not to seem nervous, but I'm so excited. Afraid he might be on to me, but the excitement and anxiety are the most apparent things. It's lucky he's way too far gone to even notice how much I fidget. Can't even see the sheen of sweat on my face or hear the heaviness of my breathing.

And after that, twenty three glances follow and I am ready to go home. I am ready to go home about four glances after he goes, but twenty three more is when I get to go home. Home where I can live and breathe and bleed. No detours this time. No conversation, no scooping out victims, no hunting for nefarious extradimensional beings seeking to corrupt and annihilate us gradually. My going home rituals are abandoned in favor of seeing the woman I love and being away from streets full of Dark Ones, Reap Kids and killers. I get to be away from all of that poison that's seeped in so deep everywhere else. I greet Cass with a kiss that almost makes me forget. The kiss asserts my skin and proves that in my veins there is red and not motor oil black. Every real person needs to prove these things sometimes. Cass looks confused and doe-eyed. She is legitimately taken by surprise this time.

"Jeremy?"

I say nothing. I see that there aren't words. Every time I see there aren't words. It feels like people can't communicate because there aren't good enough words. Words that really do taste and touch and smell. So, I don't use any and I let my kiss and my embrace say everything. There's nothing wrong with the silence. I see myself whisper the things I can't say right down her throat and making them into poems that I could never be articulate enough to put on paper. It plagues me that I think that the only things that I can do sincerely are kill and fuck. But, this isn't killing and it isn't fucking. The kiss is a language, a language that real people with real minds and real hearts and real souls speak to each other in a time when those things aren't comprehended.

Cass half cries. "I love you, Jeremy."

Then there's a miracle. I put an end to all of the almost crying I've done so much recently. I devolve into a truly honest mood swing. Nothing in me is prepared for this, although everything has been waiting for it. No, not devolve. I ascend into a truly honest mood swing. The tears are apotheosis, grailblood dripping down and washing away the poison and the motor oil, and the-the-the blood.

"Cass, I don't want to be a pharmacist anymore. I want to be alive."

She holds me and all of a sudden I'm saying things. This reminds me why humanity is worth defending and once more why I have to-

But this feels like the crusade. Wars are fought everywhere I suppose. No escaping them. But this is a better part of the war. This defines, validates, and explains the crusade. This is more active than the action.

"They're not all people, Cass. People look like people, but I think that they're not and what I want is I want to be a person, so I don't want to be a pharmacist. I thought maybe that I could could could…"

My crying begins to drown my syllables, yet, at the same time it crystallizes the things that they try to say. It kind of chokes my ability to stay coherent. I sound like a child, but Cass doesn't care. The blondes and the Cabana Boy's hookers and the the the-god, all the women that had to die. So many men could have cried and been honest before it came to this. So many. Maybe the hookers and waitresses and joggers weren't Cass, but I'm vulnerable and she's vulnerable and the streets are grey with wolves. Vicious animals that could come and take her away, as easily as- she holds me and I'm honest.

"You wanted to help people. All you want is to help people, Jeremy. But you're really just filling them up with pills. How are the pills really helping? What good will pills do?"

Some morbid and smirky part of me cracks a little smile at the question. I see the Cabana Boy writhe and twitch. Somebody is safe. The Dark Ones must be losing a little bit somehow. In my three years as a pharmacist, I think this is the most healing I have ever done. Cass is right. I just want to help everybody.

"I love you…" I stammer.

"Shh…I know, Jeremy, I know."

I relax in Cass' arms and feel my contribution. I don't need to kill tonight.

Obsolescence

Jeremy and I are not talking too much lately. It's a pity. Jeremy and Cass have both called in sick and I feel neglected. I should be above such things, but I'm not. I really wish that I had something very important to say because God, I hate just sitting around and waiting for my time to come. When Jeremy is bored, he can read a book, he can watch people and he can play any number of stimulating little games people play to keep themselves amused a little longer. But me, I just need to wait. I don't even have thumbs to twiddle. I just have to sit here and prepare to do my fucking job, my fucking all important job that doesn't get done without me. Pull the levers, manipulate the switches that need manipulating, reassign the mechanisms, whisper the things I need to whisper. But, Jeremy is at peace. I really want him to be happy, at least on some level, but I am utterly beastly bored.

Cass wraps her right leg around his, and runs her fingers up and down his arm. He rolls his eyes back and just enjoys himself. Jeremy is experiencing simple unrefined joy. I myself tend to believe that such feelings are not to be had. I believe that such feelings should be confined to dogs and apes and other such ridiculous primitives. The little animals. He likes and admires the little animals enough that he doesn't even eat them anymore. So much for evolutionary perfection. I wish that he would just come to terms with the fact that he's too useful for things like that. Would you like to sleep on a star, carry moonbeams home in a jar and be better off than you are? Or would you rather be a pig? Old Bing Crosby song seems so pertinent. So many take the easy way out existentially. Powerful, Adonaic, brilliant Jeremy has chosen the life of a farm animal. I almost think I'm at fault for turning his brain off when things get dull; I've coddled him to the point at which his banality tolerance is far too great. I'm occasionally the one that lets him play the little games that keep him amused, and now I have nothing to amuse myself with. Oddly appropriate. I think about Cabana Boy yesterday. Like a bored high school jock lacking the wit to come up with a good insult, I resort to a low blow.

"You kill like a girl. Pills, Jeremy? God, pills? I'm starting to feel that my faith in you is quite misplaced. You worry me. I need a Cuchulain and I get a Borgia. Not only that, but you're further mixing business with pleasure. And what about the Dark Ones? And what about the unrelenting plague of evil about to be loosed? So, Mr. Pharmacist, how do we cure all of this? Paging Dr. Jenkins…the world needs you, Jeremy. No healer, no warrior, no guardian. Neither the flame that purges nor the water that quenches. Excuse my pretention, but I must lay it on thick…" Like Cass says, "Same shit, different day." I have often contemplated whether or not I have feelings of my own, but now I see that they mirror his. Redundancy, worthlessness, hesitation…I exist to build a better mousetrap, yet shriek at the sight of vermin. Pathetic. The division between us stands at killer and killjoy. It actually hits me and I choke knowing that for him to do what I need him to do, he has to be joyless. And I end up as the agency that deprives him of that joy. Maybe there's a whole culture of stupidity and a heartbreakingly menial job to help with that, but my role is still quite prominent. If I were an entity that could stand on its own, I wouldn't be so frustrated by these idyllic interludes. If I were at all self-contained, I would not be wishing he would go and do something worthwhile or trying to whisper in his ear that she's a robot. Though I resent the Dark Ones, I suppose that can be called nothing but corruption. Jeremy's a hypocrite and so am I. I think she's a robot, I think it's all adding up for me, but it's not. If I thought otherwise, I would have too much else to understand.

Like why he is quite content to lie in bed and enjoy the kisses, caresses and the very touch of his girlfriend. His robot girlfriend. Nanites. That's the angle. There is always an angle. I wouldn't dare to think there isn't one. Be vigilant. Deny everything. Take no shit. Clean up emotional messes. These are my orders, my prerogatives. If I encounter something that I do not understand, I should eradicate it because if I don't understand it, it is in the way of the mission. So, I've decided on the angle. She is in league with the Dark Ones and trying to spread Nanites via physical and psychic contact. Simple but devious. It would be just like them to do something like that to him. Give him someone to love only to be poisoned and transformed by her. Reprehensible. And it has to be the case, because otherwise, Jeremy who has an innumerable amount of very useful things to do would not even think of being in bed with Cass. Is it true or would I like it to be? Perhaps I'm in a position where it doesn't matter. And that might just be why I'm on the inside and Jeremy is on the surface. Perhaps it's also because he has things to enjoy.

They kiss and it's once more electric. Once more an earthquake, tidal wave, hurricane kiss between desperate fleshy elementals. They are once intertwining and being once more a single body with one skin and four hands like a statue of some Hindu God. The hands float around each other and I can't keep track of which belongs to whom. They simply enjoy each other, take each other in like sips of wine or a chocolate milkshake. I can only feel the aftershocks really and the quickening of his heart. I can see him feeling what he feels and understand what it does to him, but I don't get any of it. Neither get nor comprehend. Neither kind of "get." But work must be done, Jeremy, work must be done.

Then, without fail, Cass does it. There are those who call addicts inconstant and unreliable, and that might be true about the addict, but the addiction is like clockwork. Every time she gets content and relaxed and stops thinking, she does it. And it always gets us talking. Even when I'm on the outs with Jeremy, he starts to listen to me. Cass turns on the TV. I always see a sinister smile on its huge blank face as another anchorman is spawned from the pits of god-knows-where. The magic lamp is rubbed and the slick-haired genie emerges to share the latest juicy gossip. Funny thing that now the anchorman and I have become unlikely allies. He works for the Dark Ones and I for the light, but we move toward a synchronicity not unlike the one I just witnessed. Only that one was just dawdling and denial, and this one is part of the crusade.

"Today, the Reap world was rocked by news of the death of one of its luminaries. Thomas Gennaro, 34, also known as the Cabana Boy, was found in his hotel room having overdosed on a variety of pills. Among these pills were antipsychotics, antidepressants, sedatives and MAOIs; a fatal cocktail of nineteen different medications. The authorities and Gennaro's friends and relatives have declined to comment on what might have caused him to take his own life.

Gennaro's exploits and merchandise have been a Reap sensation recently, paralleling such big names as Mr. Right and Hacksaw Sally. During the course of his career as a Psychopomp, Gennaro killed prostitutes in all fifty states and managed to kill a record seventeen police officers during a chase into the Safe Zone with only his wits and a Molotov cocktail.

Members of the Bundy Awards panel say to keep this in mind when you remember Thomas Gennaro, since this accomplishment and the ambitious spread of his killings more than overshadow his meager fifty-five victims. Seldom does a Psychopomp get a Bundy nomination and so much respect from the awards committee in spite of so few kills. This is what separates him from other Psychopomps with similar figures such as the late Karl Edward Pratt, alias Kris Kringle. In Ian Sterling's popular reapchic.com newsletter Gennaro was called "classic," "sublime," and "an American original." Thomas Gennaro, the Cabana Boy, you will be missed. Here are a few highlights from Gennaro's five year career…"

Jeremy is getting riled up and Cass is starting to cry. It couldn't be more perfect. Opportunities to wrest control like this one come along far too infrequently.

"God, I can't believe it…"

Jeremy wraps his arm around Cass and her tears are flowing as his had been earlier.

"I just can't believe it, the Cabana Boy…"

Jeremy is somehow sympathetic. I watch him have so many feelings but I don't understand half of them. Nonsensical. Insincere. Inefficient. Compromising. A pillar of strength, but not always one of integrity. I don't respect this at all.

MURDERLAND | Garrett Cook

"I know," he tells her, "You have the t-shirt, the crime scene DVD, the interviews taped and you preordered his book on Amazon. You loved him, and you loved his work so much. I know."

She looks up at him, face like the confused child she is, "And now he's…"

"I know."

Suddenly she's angry. Juvenile. Stupid and juvenile. Not even angry at him. Inefficient. Silly. Angry at God, for taking away the precious little dancing bear that filled her days with carnage and joy. I don't get it, but he does. Maturity and saintly patience are what he has to offer to this absurd mess. He doesn't listen when I whisper "robot," but maybe because that's me being immature. Not as grounded as it could be since robots aren't so sensitive and erratic. I don't know what she is. Fuck her. Fuck the little cunt. She's blonde on the inside, somewhere in there. Robot mess, organic mess, just a mess I say. She glares, and the glare hisses like a cat.

"No, Jeremy, you don't know."

And now it looks like he's going to start to implore her to be reasonable. Does that to me a bit too often. Meek little shit. Cat's hissing glare falls on timid little mousy and Mr. Mousy says "oh, miss Kitty, please don't eat me!" And all the important things, all the momentous events on page h8 are paling in comparison to this tantrum. Priorities, goddamn you, no priorities. I'm getting rather hot under the collar, even though I know in the end he's going to start listening to me again and remember what he's for. Good for him. Good for mankind. Good for me. Can't I be selfish sometimes?

"Cass," he says, "I know what it's like to…"

His words are buffeted out of existence by an angry Cass' violent interruption.

"No, it's like when John Lennon and Jim Henson and Vincent Price and…"

And now Jeremy is trying desperately not to explode. I hate how much I am enjoying this. He now wants to have an outburst. He now wants to tell her that he was the one who killed that monster and that the Cabana Boy was a lunatic, not an entertainer. But he has to push the words back. He has to give them over to me for safekeeping. He needs me to hold him back now. Knew he'd end up on his knees. So, the question returns. Do I feel bad that I'm exploiting the situation? The tender intimate moments where suffering drips off Cass into Jeremy's arms? No. No. I am doing the right thing. You can't feel guilty when you are an agent of true innocence. I am ONLY capable of doing the right thing. Anything else would be completely foreign. I don't have to be in denial to get to sleep each night, but on the other hand, I don't have to sleep.

"Cass, I..."

"He's gone! He was a great man, a great artist and now he's gone forever."

Jeremy only gets more confused. Well, that is, the ape/child/dog part of Jeremy gets more confused. He did something good to protect people and make things safer and yet Cass feels bad. Could this perhaps be that she's one of many robot pawns churned out by the vile steaming monster factory? Could it be that? Dense little creature. Doberman turns lapdog so quick. Worse part of all is you were doing this for her and all the others, Jeremy. You took one life to save many and now the bitch is mad that you care so much. The bitch is mad because you put down a rabid circus poodle and it can no longer prance about on the evening news for her, and the animals at Murderland and worst of all for Ian Sterling and the martini-swilling Le Couteau glitterati. But silly old Jeremy fixates on how she feels so broken up. He tries to maneuver around life's grey areas most of the time, and I don't blame him. I don't do grey either. I twitch. I wonder how he's returning to the necessity to comfort her. He briefly regrets ridding the world of one of the Dark One pawns that slaughters precious lambs. Some of them were real people even and real people are getting rarer. I'll never understand regret, since after all I can only do the right thing.

None of his struggling matters, since the television seals the deal for me.

"Here to further discuss the impact of the Cabana Boy's loss on the Reap Community at large and his personal reaction to the tragedy is Jonathan "Godless Jack" Cavanagh. Great to have you here again, Jack. It's always an honor."

Jeremy looks up. Yellow contacts, twisting unhinged jaw. It looks as if he's always chewing on something. Things like babies and the wombs they came out of. Disgusting puppet. Serpentine marionette reeks of evil little things. Horrible positions, revealing horrible filed and sharpened fangs. The mouth is every bit as horrible as the things that come out of and go into it.

"It's great to be here, Ted, although I prefer going on the show under better circumstances."

"Certainly," says the anchor with mock gravity and Jeremy wonders which of them is less human. This is like wondering which cleaning fluid tastes better.

"Thomas Gennaro is an institution. I agree with everything Ian Sterling has said, and I have to say, even such kind words from such a diehard fan aren't enough. The moment I heard about this tragedy, I asked myself, Jack, what can you do about this? How can you make the world better for Thomas Gennaro, all the people who loved him and appreciated his work, and all the people like him? So, first I called up some of the boys at the Bundy awards. I called them up and I said that Tom…you know he always preferred Tom…that Tom deserved some kind of posthumous lifetime achievement award. And I think that the Bundys should have some way to award our fallen comrades in arms. Secondly, I thought about the fact that this is stressful work and mental illness is no picnic. Most of us are sociopaths, schizophrenics, necrophiliacs and these things, well, they're no picnic. Suicide and mental illness has claimed a lot of us. We're people with very special needs. Reaping became legal because I was starving to death in prison and could only eat human flesh and organs, and not only that, but my condition made it impossible to take them in when I hadn't hunted them myself. I could have died in prison if people hadn't wised up. I think people still need to wise up about Psychopomps and their mental illness, though. We've gone far, but we can go further. I need more people to open their minds and hearts to the stressors and health problems that affect today's Reap professional. That's why I've put seven million dollars into starting the Thomas Gennaro Mental Health Foundation to find ways to help relieve the stress and the bouts of remorse caused by social pressures which, as I said, affect today's Reap professional."

"Wow, that's incredible," says the anchor. A smile crosses Cass' face.

"After that, I decided to call Penny…you know Penny Dreadful from Penny Dreadful and the Aberrations…I called Penny and I talked to her about putting out a single to benefit the foundation. She just jumped at the chance. She's such a warm and giving person. She's just great."

"Thank you, Jack. In these tough times it's good to know that there are people who care. Now, I understand you've helped develop your own fragrance."

Jack smiles. It's nauseating. "Yes, I call it Zero for men."

"That's kinda your trademark. It's your thing, the zero…"

"It's a very important symbol. It's a spiritual focus for me, since it says where we're going and where we've been. My cologne reminds people that the deadliest predators emit the sweetest pheromones…"

Jeremy shifts a little and he concentrates on all the Dark Ones floating over Jack's head. That's when I know that I'm back.

You Can Rock it, You can Roll it, You can Stomp and Even Stroll it…

The sign over le Couteau buzzes with blood red neon, intense enough to kick your teeth out for looking at it funny. I marvel at it since this is an exceptionally expensive chemical dye. So perfectly red it feels like the blood is trying to creep out the back of your eyes and you're just witnessing it. I would tell Cass how rare and costly and potent this dye is but she would give her "what fucking planet are you from" stare and I feel awkward enough. No, not just awkward enough. Awkward enough was when I agreed to come along this time. This is TOO awkward, too awkward by far.

First and foremost, I am wearing a cape. I am not Christopher Lee and I am not Superman. I have no reason to wear a cape beyond looking cool. The cape, my top hat and my anachronistic and thoroughly un-Victorian boots make me feel like a giraffe on a unicycle. Tall, gawky, perpetually off balance. Usually the musculature and broadness of my frame make me big but this stuff leaves me weaker, more weighed down and comically lanky. Foppish, giraffe on a unicycle, six or seven pounds of Victorian clothing and big, heavy combat boots...masculinity, dignity, and sense of self exchanged for these apparently more appropriate accessories.

Cass has her hair straight and perfect, her clothes modest and conservative (well, in her eyes.) For some reason, she made me dress Ripper, while she herself is a Bundy Girl. I don't have the nerve to tell her I might have felt more comfortable if she had at least bothered to do Whitechapel Girl or Rip Chick. The less trusting part of me makes me think that the sign, the parking lot and the clothes might just be part of an elaborate prank and I'm walking into a Denny's full of old college friends of mine with cameras and six packs in their hands. It would have made me a little more certain that I wasn't making a fool of myself if she had dressed similarly, but no, she'd been planning the Bundy Girl outfit for a while.

And it shows. It takes care and precision to do anything good with seventies sorority chic. There is something naturally fetishistic about it, yes, but care needs to be taken to look good. As with most Reap clothing, it's necessary to bend the rules. Bundy girls used to just wear wool sweaters, but "fashion Messiah" Ian Sterling brought up in his column once that while the wool sweater looks good, fashion designers should try and create a more comfortable and form-fitting wool substitute. Good work as always, Ian. Cass is wearing this wool substitute and it's tight enough that you can imagine everything that you can't see with vivid clarity. On top of wearing this sweater, she isn't wearing a bra. The skirt is a porno parody of the real thing; if the original was made to entice, this was made for outright rape. The thong underneath is every bit the anachronism the Ripper cloak is in this day and age, and the supposedly conservative beige nylons she has on are perforated with strategic tears. The three inches taller that those heels make her certainly doesn't do her appeal any harm, either. Were I not outside of Le Couteau, I would be excruciatingly turned on. Yet, here I am, outside Le Coteau, conscious of the purpose of every dot of makeup and every tear in those stockings. Conscious of the painfully mixed signals of her clothes: "I am a victim", but also, "I am my own predator". Simultaneous unflinching confidence and violent passivity. Sad that she can't make up her mind. Why can't I stop judging? I should be looking at this sleek mirage and thinking about how lucky I am to walk into even this place with this woman.

Alas, my mind is completely stuck on my Ripper garb and the ludicrous expense the club must have gone to for such a perfect shade of neon light. Two blocks down people are starving, but they're not good for the ambience. And the blinkers on the sign are so lavish and precise. There is no transition time between the blood red and the ice blue that it suddenly changes to. Such a great blue, too. Even though I'm sweating bullets in my ridiculous costume, the blue gives me a chill. The chill doesn't last long, since the blue doesn't last as long as the red. Next comes an intense dark indigo, which perfectly outlines a little knife. Does human ingenuity excite or nauseate me? Can I choose a stance? Christ, I think too much. I feel the heaviness of my cloak and boots and God forgive me, I've just gotta ask her.

"Cass, are you sure I actually look cool?"

This place does terrible things. For me, of all people, to let those words pass my lips is a sign of cracking, of surrendering one's integrity to the postmodern void. Of being on the path to using phrases such as: "postmodern void" with any kind of regularity. I tell myself that it's just Cass that I want to accept me. Here, it's a challenge. Outside of my livingroom and my warm bed and a couple restaurants I like, it is often a challenge to feel accepted. I can be calm, cool and calculating, I can fit in, but I don't feel it. The pharmacy doesn't even feel like I belong there. Cass accepts this and I need Cass to accept me, so I guess I have to be this. Robot logic. Where's the humanity?

I think I'm patronizing her in a way, but things are different here. More than a TV to compete with. So, I have to know if I actually look "cool" and if I could fit in with this part of her life.

"Of course you look cool," she says, "didn't I design your outfit?" she smiles a bit and squeezes my hand. "Besides, look around you."

Here I look down and find that I am standing on empty air. I walk off the cartoon cliff, realize I have done it and I am beginning to plummet. I have tried so hard to cloud the crowd from my mind in hopes that they would go away or melt together into a more slightly amorphous blob of a crowd. Nothing that would remind me that they were human once and that humanity is oh so fragile and can vanish with the greatest of ease. This isn't humanity, this is Reap. Murderland is bad enough, but Murderland is just a restaurant more or less, only a little café. This is Le Couteau. This is "the knife", a night out for Murderland patrons, a very special reward for being the social dregs of America. Murderland regulars look forward to their visit to Le Couteau and put hard earned cash from the town's drive-thrus and videostores and gas stations into their props, outfits, makeup and the eight dollar "we never card" martini. Of course, it's not only hard earned wages that go to waste. This is, after all, Reap culture. Just as much of this cash came out of the purses of old ladies and the lunch money of geekier, weaker classmates. It's a real miracle that these kids aren't considered geeks themselves. When I was in highschool, guys like these would have been wedgied out of their anal virginity and left in their lockers. The ones my age should have the same done to them.

The Rippers here all have on variations of my outfit. I find it odd that mine is sort of on the conservative end of things. But then again, Cass did call it vintage. (Which is funny because Reap has been around for all of six years). Many of them have added eyeliner, which even after years of being around Cass and news and Reap paraphernalia I have yet to understand. It seems like they put the Ripper into some nether-realm of German expressionist nightmare to replace all the history that's gone down the drain. History is difficult, eyeliner is easy. Others have replaced the tophat with a deerstalker in order to somewhat conform to the sightings. Fewer have decided to wear long fake beards and adhere to the controversial Hasidic Jew theory. The most boring substitution and the most common is foregoing the cape in favor of a longcoat. I would still say that in my obnoxious Halloween costume-turned street clothes, I look like the majority of them.

That's why the razor in my pocket makes me feel a little sick. Out of all of these waves of disgusting pretenders, I'm the only one disgusting enough to be, at least on some level what they're pretending to be. I feel like real Nazis must have felt watching Indiana Jones movies. I've been waist deep in the ugly they wish they had the guts to be. I've cut people open and taken out the organs, and I wish it gave me half the rush these people think that it would. Half the rush and none of the disgust. And as I was doing all that messy, vital apocalyptic business, they're out streetfighting and playing splat and jerking off to Reap videos and dancing like gorillas on laudanum. So I guess I do look cool, because I look like everyone else. I'm cool because I look like a killer, and I guess I feel like a geek because I actually am a killer. And a fantastic killer too. All these people they worship are nowhere near my equals. I've killed over three hundred women, and in such a way that the authorities think I'm several ineffective reapers instead of one great one. And they can't touch me because my apartment is in the Safe Zone. So, I'm a hundred times cooler than all of these people, except for the feeling that my soul smells like a wet dog and the fact that I'm killing as a good work. So, maybe it makes me less cool, since I'm charitable. No, it's the boots and opera cape that make me less cool. None of these people are cool.

Something tells me to take a run for the car. Then, to sit down and start it. Then, once it's started to run down as many of these kids as possible. Yet that would be violence. I do not really like violence. I kill for a better, more peaceful world in which I will never have to kill again. This paradox makes me unable to determine whether or not it would be better to splatter all of these ridiculous creatures across the pavement and into a wet mass of capes and oozing eye makeup. The kohl puddle would just keep running down the sidewalk, a grey, tarry River Styx dividing the living from the dead. And my mind would find peace contemplating the deluge of gunk and circuitry. But, as a personal favor to Cass and maybe somewhat to society, I decide not to go maverick with the car right here and now. Sometimes it's nigh impossible to do the right thing. Get in the car, splat, gunk, drive off. Not an option. I bite my tongue until it's on the verge of bleeding and I stare at Cass' outfit. Latch onto the precious little things that make your days tolerable. Especially when they're all that keeps you from a human rights, autoinsurance and custodial nightmare. As scared, annoyed and angry as I am, I don't make a move to leave, nor do I bother to tell Cass of my discomfort. Trapped like a rat, but don't let on, Jeremy. Don't let on or you're completely fucked.

So, I go back to looking at the freakshow, admiring the scenery, people every bit as garish and blinding as the expensive neon. Some rarer sights than you would ever find at Murderland. The Geins don't go to Murderland too often. Clothed in plaid shirts and synthetic skin masks, they are even more morbid parodies of womanhood than the original Gein. I know there are a couple of these who paid extra for real human flesh. It makes the masks look less disgusting actually, in spite of the fact that these assholes went online to buy a woman's face from some collector. Maybe those conservatives who say a cartoon cat with a sledgehammer is subversive and a war is healthy are right about how the real thing is better than the fakes. And I'm even realer than the Geins. Note to self; don't follow this chain of logic to its end. Repetitive. Stay sane. Stay awake from circles. Point A to Point B. No Geins at Murderland, most of the time. Nor a lot of Harlequins. Most of the Gacys at Murderland don't have the Commedia Dell'arte flamboyance. Just normal clownsuits, without the expressionism and flourishes of red, black or purple. And the girls at Murderland don't do the lavish Gacy girl thing. Porcelain masks, little red dots on the cheeks, poofy skirts in harlequin colors.

The Dark Ones are here in droves. Scouts and breeders alike examining the stock and getting ready to advance the invasion. No clue how long til the next wave, no clue how little time we have, but if this is any indication, page H8 doesn't have the half of it. Clues are too few, evidence too abundant. If the second wave comes, we'll all be too cold to feel it. Too dull and complacent to know that the sun has left our skies. The trees will be made of skin, take root in the ground and the grown ones, the real Dark Ones, the worst kind, will feast on them, snarling gibbering hungry things. They'll plant us in the ground and we will grow toward the black sky, the only skin, the only life in silicon cities. Those who live, who aren't used as food will wish they had never been born. I'm realizing it, it's coming together and the scouts and the breeders are getting more stock tonight. We will be flesh to eat, gleefully stripped down to the circuits and planted in the terraformed ground to rise and bear our own fruits. But they never account for the presence of Jeremy Jenkins. American hero, serial killer, fraud and frightened social retard. What will these people do when the world is so much more violent than their fantasies?

I don't look forward to mingling. I don't look forward to seeing Cass' friends when I know all of these things. Some of them might even be nice, which makes it awkward knowing what's happening. More than I don't look forward to seeing Cass' friends, I don't look forward to Ian Sterling. Ian Sterling who Cass has come here to meet up with. Stupid Ian, stupid Reap, stupid website, stupid internet. Expert, guru, king of Reap critique. The man I'm walking into Le Couteau to see. This is the hell I go to for all of the people I had to kill for their own good. Remorse is hitting me so hard at the place where I am most justified. One of those experiences I don't want to survive until the end of.

We walk through the crowd and Cass greets person after person. I wonder who here she's been with. I speculate regarding who might be an ex- boyfriend and who might be a one night stand and who she met once at a party. They're all so friendly and not a one of them can keep his eyes on the girl he walked in with. Their hugs are a little too long and I see them struggling to keep their hands off her ass. I sit on my superiority, remembering that I met her at a production of Verdi's Faust and they met her here. Their Lavish Costumes just as lavish and of a much higher culture. I can't shake the jealousy and the sinking feeling that this sensation is just there to keep my mind off the pure, unadulterated social horror of the whole thing. A few girlfriends of hers talk about the Cabana Boy and how hard it was on them. They proudly point out a bucket for the charity

Godless Jack started. Funny. Never have I wanted so much to take an enormous shit in a bucket.

A guy in Godless Jack contacts puts his hand on her thigh and whispers something in her ear. I wince visibly. (To my credit, I hadn't yet done so. I'm a very gifted actor). She misses both my wince and the snake-eyed apostate's advances. She's not a slut. She can ignore the cries of "hey, bait" and "wanna see the sharp?" She doesn't want these guys, but I still feel strange about it all, as if I'm the one who is intruding on the intimacies of their flirting. How reprehensible for a boyfriend to stand in the way of some random drunk asshole's good time. I wish that reminding me that Cass loves it here and is having fun were a little more consolation.

The music is, at the moment, shapeless. It sounds like pounding and slicing. The grinding of a knife and the crunch of a hammer against bone. It turns shrill and becomes hard, unforgiving, unavoidable, the cock of an eager, uncompromising rapist. If I covered my ears they would gain no respite, since my mind would just take over and reproduce it continuously, as if a DJ were spinning records in my cerebellum. Knowing my brain, it would be worse, longer, faster, harder and more violent. Take more offense; feel the blows struck at the foundations of decency.

Somehow they dance in spite of it. Ritual movements to appease the idols engraved in stained glass windows. Real and fictional alike, the killers look on. Norman Bates, Hannibal Lecter, Jack the Ripper, Albert Fish, Ed Gein and Michael Myers soak up the worship as lights shine against their graven images. The cult gyrates and moves with vicious thrusts that are punctuated with the brief erotic strangling of eager Whitechapel girls who thank those gods for their abuses. My eyes wander away from a disappearing Cass to a sight that I can take immediate pleasure in.

Two Rip chicks are enjoying each other. A tall one with hair dyed a deep purple places her hat on a shorter brunette who wears a black corset done up with a series of red bowties. There's almost nothing Victorian at all about her outfit save an open longcoat, but she still looks absolutely scintillating. So does the purple haired one, whose black, lacy bra is visible through a puffy men's dress shirt. Her short skirt, complete with puffy petticoats, reveals long, slender legs clad in black stockings. She seamlessly places one of those legs between her smaller partner's. Courtship? Ownership? Or just a dance? Impossible to tell. Long, spidery fingers sensuously work their way along the brunette's arm and she follows their cues. The coat is discarded and the fingers are given bare shoulders to toy with. They stroke, they tickle and they move down to scratch the girl's ample ass. She rubs against the scratching fingers and little red snakes of scar tissue appear. The cruel, gentle hands of the tall girl then fully grasp her hips. Their bodies grind and make elliptical shapes as the smaller girl's lucky fingers grasp her partner's thighs. I am not the only one watching this of course, but I am the only one who the tall girl acknowledges as watching her. The pain of all the guys flirting with Cass is numbed by the salacious smile she gives me.

As if by a miracle, the grinding and painful music stops and a band moves to the center of the dance floor. A tall, pallid girl with a pink fright wig, silver lipstick, a chainmail evening gown, long fake silver fingernails and an eyepatch begins to sing to a slightly more pleasant synthbeat. A guitarist and bass player start to catch up and lo and behold, Penny Dreadful and the Aberrations themselves shine good luck down on my voyeuristic little scene with the Rip Chicks. Moved by the mellifluous voice of Penny Dreadful, the tall one leans down and her lips meet with those of the buxom little angel in her arms. I almost feel like myself. I know they want me to share this, to take in the scene and have a good time. Since I am here, and I am comfortable for a moment and I am part of something, it doesn't feel like voyeurism, it feels like ESP.

It feels like being the god who created the act. I try to remember when it was that I invented sex. Maybe it is megalomania, but I couldn't care less, because it's beautiful. I in my big, stupid cloak and they, my female counterparts, are savages and we are as beautiful as can be. Guys are wondering how it is I know these girls and why they occasionally turn their attention to me. I feel like I am bathed inside and out in hot cocoa. Subtle, comfortably sugary decadence. This should be wrong somehow. Maybe it is, because it doesn't last. The sweet

and the warm dry up in favor of a just-ran-out-of-hot water-in –
your- morning- shower kind of feeling. Somebody stands
between the staring, the sharing and the dancing. Somebody
fucks up my evening just as I expected him to.

From behind, the long cloak, the thick high-heeled boots
and the shaved head make the figure look tough yet
androgynous. The swordcane doesn't hurt the image either. But
then, he turns around and faces me. His black hair, half shaved is
swept to one side. His face is in pale blue stage makeup with
light purple eyeliner around one eye to make it look bruised. His
lipstick is the color of the tall girl's hair, and quite frankly, I
think it looks ridiculous. When he turns around, everyone can
also see the white corset he's wearing, which is ripped and
covered in bloodstains. Knowing this prick, the blood has GOT
to be real. His black skirt has little circles cut in the middle to
accentuate admirably toned legs. It's a little skirt/chaps number
that will be very popular at the club soon and I know this
because HE is wearing it. Belligerently genderless. Violator,
victim, Venus. The intention is as transparent as the wearer. The
girls have stopped dancing to stare. My tall, supple dancer stops
and wraps an arm around his waist.

"Evening, Selene," he says.

"Evening, Ian."

He kisses her and effortlessly throws his attention from
her. And I am the reluctant recipient of this dubious gift.

"The boots are quite a nice touch, Jeremy. Classic."

I try so desperately to find a way to care less what Ian
Sterling thinks of my outfit. I try, but it doesn't happen. There is,
in fact, no way in which I can care less, but I have come to
realize from hanging out with some of Cass' friends that
sometimes a man must say things that make him want to
projectile vomit into the mouth of the person he's talking to in
such a way that maybe the asshole will choke to death. For me, I
knew Le Couteau would be made of these moments.

"Why, thank you, Ian. Cass picked out the boots. And
you…your outfit. It's amazing. Where did you get it?"

He replies, and fortunately, I can locate the "off" switch
of my perceptions. I am thankful that I don't have to hear a word
of it. I am so glad that I'm somebody who doesn't want to listen

to anything this insufferable dickhead has to say. Almost nobody else seems to have that luxury. Especially not Cass. With her stupid scrapbook of his columns and those tapes of his interviews. I can't be annoyed enough by this, and I remind myself every single time I see him. I know I've written it often enough, but I hate that scrapbook and I ... *hate hate hate hate hate hate hate hate hate hate hate hate hate hate hate hate hate hate hate hate hate hate hate hate hate hate hate hate hate hate hate hate* ... Ian Sterling.

I ignore the words but still I end up watching his mouth and when that happens, he becomes impossible to ignore. Nanites. So many Nanites. Little metal spiders, ants, roaches and earwigs begin to crawl out. They wriggle down onto his shoulders and then jump down to the dance floor scattering swarms and swarms and swarms. Each word is ten thousand more. We want to retain composure, Jeremy and I, but we ... but *I* can't quite make it at first. Our eyes my eyes feel like they're bulging out several inches. I know my eyes and the sockets they come in aren't even that big aren't even half that big but they feel compelled to participate in this grotesque cartoon. Robots and wild beasts. Human ain't a choice. In fifty, twenty, hell, five years when we fill out applications will the race column only have "ROBOT" and "SHARK"? Robots and wild beasts only, they dance and they don't begin to notice what is burrowing into their skin and the things that crawl into their ears. Stops briefly. We are relieved that there are words and not vermin now. I know that I can't quite be hallucinating, although I know that I can't be sane. But I have to think I'm sane right now, because if I don't think I'm sane, then I won't act sane; and if I act insane in front of this guy, the shit will come down and he'll know how I'm responding to the plague of nanites that he might be spreading. Not might be. Doubt is one of their tools. Doubt is what they'll use to bring me down if I'm not careful. Don't let him know what you're doing, don't act like you know what he's up to.

"Jeremy, where's Cass?"

I muster a shrug, but it's a sane regular guy kinda shrug. Ian looks around and it is only seconds before he has made eye contact. She comes over and I expect at least a kiss on the cheek or for her to wander to my side, but she walks right up to Ian and she hugs him. No, not hugs, she embraces him. She embraces him tightly. She embraces him and everything that he does, not knowing about the insects that he drips. Dark One Type F. Hive Mother. Modified Breeder possessing a human shape. Corruptor? Nanite factory. Could that really be where they all come from? No, he's not one of them. Think about your personal prejudice. Think reasonably. He just doesn't know about the robots and the danger and the trees made of flesh reaching toward the sky. All of them have the luxury of being ignorant and therefore being able to enjoy themselves. But, we can kill them to make things right, we can kill them in order to maintain order and in the hope that some of us will keep our souls when so many seek to take them. Is he really so fucking special that I should spare him in spite of the gears and the silicon and the myriad beasties that come out of his mouth? Stupid column, stupid scrapbook. Stupid Cass for getting so much joy from him. I can't even rid the world of Ian fucking Sterling. Ian who has quite likely fucked and might still be fucking my girlfriend. Maybe that's what she does on my poker nights.

"The problem with the Venti was the need to remain, at least in part, gentle and meek; a large part of them had to be devoted to acting and thinking like something they weren't. Yet, today's reaper need know no such boundaries. The natural weakness of people like Gacy was that they had this insincere public pseudolife to maintain, but that isn't a concern considering that we now have professional reapers who can make Psychopomping their lifestyle. But, the tragic thing about the pathology of madness is that often reapers create the boundaries for themselves."

This part of his sanctimonious philosophical spew, which he says at (and not to) Cass stands out in particular. Even a broken clock's right twice a day. Although, I think Godless Jack Cavanagh might have said something to that device in The Human Predator. But then, even I quote Godless Jack sometimes, sadly enough. I feel the sting of my secret identity tonight. Even worse now that I'm in a costume that I have put on over my normal person costume. Now Penny Dreadful and the Aberrations are walking out and the music returns to the synthbeat and the chainsaw whirring. I feel like I could easily become one of those celluloid idols engraved in the stain glass, that the real and violent me is calling again and it still might be wrong to hold it back. Is this a chainsaw that I see before me? A chainsaw of the mind, a false creation…yet if I make it public, it will only get teenagers laid. Don't listen to what Ian says don't think of Ian. Think of Cass, and not of Cass and Ian.

"The outfit's exquisite," Cass says, waiting for a hole in his shoptalk, yet not willing to interrupt him, "Choke you bad?"

"Gasping. But the effort was the real problem. Oh, you wouldn't believe the hell I've been through getting this together and with all the interviews and the retrospectives this week…"

One nugget of wisdom from Ian and a brief scrutiny of Cass' small talk lead me back to my prior solution to my awkward situation: ignoring Ian and letting his words blend in with the equally offensive and vapid noise around him. I catch little fragments of what Cass has to say. Things like "I didn't think you two were speaking" and "I can't believe HE was at Murderland!" But, it ends with a deafening thud when Cass says, "But the 84 killer's smalltime. Why would you be looking into that?"

"That's the thing," says Ian, "I think he might not be smalltime. In fact, I'm convinced that this guy's huge."

"Forty six kills is huge, Ian?"

"Not forty-six. Not forty-six at all. And he's not the 84 killer. The 84 means something else."

Now, this part intrigues me. I made up a random number, and the other carvings I made were totally random symbols. A smiley face, an upside down triangle, an awkward ankh? He's way off base. Turns out he probably won't catch on to the fact that it's a big red herring. Amusements have been few and far between. I take a chance to sit and laugh inwardly. And then Ian dramatically produces a calculator from his pocket. Wonder what that's about.

"As I said, not an 84 at all…" he inputs the eighty four and turns the calculator upside down. Holy shit. "h8. Hate."

Page h8…page hate. 84 is h8. 84 is hate. And now I have to stop and wonder if it was all in the newspaper. I know what I know, I've read what I've read, and I couldn't have made a mistake like that, I just couldn't.

"And the others. The other random symbol killings that seem so meager and un-prestigious. A primitive diabolism. The rune language of a terrified man possessed by madness screaming out his discontent...an ironic, smirking smile betraying the sadness and desperation of the h8. An upside down triangle...well, we all know what that is...."

The crowd around Ian is laughing and I want to cry and there's no perversity and no smirking superiority. I couldn't possibly just be another bundle of mechanisms and neuroses like the devils and the robots and the reap kids. How dare he talk to me like that. I h8 h8 h8 h8 h8 h8 h8 h8 h8 h8 h8 h8 h8 him. He's one of them after all. Obvious hive mother. Has to be. Kill him right now. Don't listen to the theories. I find myself wanting to just break him, every bone in his body, everything he ever said, but if I kill the man, it doesn't break the words and it doesn't get rid of all the nanites in everybody's bloodstream. The obsession and the self destruction burn through even my need to record objectively. Something is wrong with me. I swear I'll find it.

"But the crème de la crème of all of this is that this one obsessive schizoid might have the highest count of them all. Totaling all of these very similar symbol killers, who incidentally, all strike blonde women between the ages of 19 and 31; we have a sum that exceeds even Godless Jack's record."

"But Ian," Cass interjects, "Godless Jack's record is 300 Dusties. You'd have to be a walking uzi to break that. That makes you a postman not a pomp."

Ian looks deadly serious. I get a bit of pleasure from the knowledge that I have scared him every bit as much as he scares me. And that there is a violence that shakes even Reap guru Ian Sterling, the king of cool and the strongest stomach on the Reap scene. Of course this means that I may have done things that are shocking and serious in a heartless and mechanical world. Maybe it would be more of a victory to discover it than to be the one who did it. I hope he has the count wrong. He says I've broken Godless Jack's record, but I can salvage the night and not feel like running if he gets the count wrong at least.

"377 kills, Cass." His eyes water a bit in fear and then they gaze up in admiration.

"Excuse me…" I say meekly and almost nobody hears me slipping out into other parts of the crowd and the club.

The last thing I hear out of Cass' mouth is "Jeremy gets a little squeamish sometimes." Everything else is my adventure. My twitchy, violent and tragic adventure. And like the sordid adventures of many men, it begins at the bar. The bartender, the only person here that's out of costume becomes real trustworthy to me real fast, particularly since there's no telling how many telltale clues I could give up if I listen to the profile Ian is developing on me. So, I'll choose a perfectly sane means of social smokescreening by having a drink. I make sure to look at the bartender so that my eyes don't wander toward any of these abominations or toward any kind of trouble.

"Martini."

I fail to notice the chunks of little blue dust until after I drink it.

"What's this stuff?" I ask. The bartender seems to think it's a joke. Whatever it is, it doesn't feel too bad. So I order two more. It's my way of saying, "well, this can't get any worse." But it ends up every bit as damning as if I'd said it out loud. The club gets blurrier and brighter all at once until the blur stops and my vision's all clarity. Sharp, overwhelming clarity that threatens to burn my eyes from their sockets. I find myself distant and curious. One thing that I most certainly never felt towards this place and the people in it was curious, but that old blue magic takes care of that. I stumble from the barstool out into a world I feel a grand desire to comprehend as opposed to destroying.

I wander out onto the dance floor again and there's a woman there, her chest swathed with bandages and stained with a massive red spot.

"Are you okay?" I ask, not even thinking that this might be a costume piece or something.

"I'm more than okay," she says, sober, stern and proud, "Nationwide tribute to Thomas Gennaro. I did this myself because I, like much of the Reap Community, really miss the Cabana Boy. Spread the word, okay?"

"Umm…yeah, yeah…" now I'm stumbling. I don't know whether she's real or not. And if she is, I wonder if she did give her breasts for him. We feel angry and disappointed and shocked. We feel like we're in hell. So much shock over her stupidity which seems like it's just too much to fathom. I'm scared that Cass might do this for one of those monsters or another. Go out and mangle themselves since nobody else will do it.

"Are you okay?" asks the girl with the bandages. The nerve.

"I'm fine. Just a little wobbly. These martinis are really something."

What the hell could have been in there? The woozy wobbly feeling leaves and ventures into euphoria as I look upon a magnificent little Whitechapel girl making eyes at me. Sweet, inviting smile, nice firm body and I don't feel guilty. I don't feel guilty because I can see Cass making out with a couple of Gacy girls. She eagerly licks fake blood off of their lips and necks and takes time exploring their long flowing skirts with her hands. But, what does it matter? I have a sweet, sexy girl who wants to be with me at the moment and Cass will want to be with me later, so it all works out okay in my ecstatic light headed mind. Without a single word, she leads me outside.

The alley is lit only by an overripe full moon. And she looks great. I will ignore the little metal spiders crawling on her fingers. We will ignore the little metal spiders crawling on her fingers. I will ignore the little metal spiders crawling on her fingers and I will have a good time. But they crawl harmlessly about and pass right through her. She won't be a robot. I'm relieved. Not a robot at all, just a gorgeous smile, a well toned body and beautiful blonde hair. Little yellow cunt putrid little yellow cunt. Stop it, I tell myself, not a clone machine. Just going out here to get some excitement and joy out of this evening. What is it in me that tells me not to enjoy myself? Noises. The buzzing of little wispy scouts swarming like eager mosquitoes. If I could ignore this and just enjoy her unbuttoning my shirt and starting to massage my chest. I place my hands on breasts very like the moon above. I squeeze and I breathe.

"Milk…sweet, sustaining milk…" something says, "perfect. She's just right."

Glowing eyes look into mine. It is resting on her shoulder. Rat-grey fur, yellow eyes, clawed hands and tiny leathery bat wings. Most unsettling though is the snout, the long putrid stinking proboscis that drips the sticky, acrid black ooze that gives life to new Dark Ones.

"Do you like her, Jeremy? I like her fine. You can have her when I'm done with her."

This makes me breathe very hard. She puts a finger on my lips. "Shhhh…"

She moves to kiss me and it drips the poison on her face. The little yellow cunt ripe for the taking, ready to be full of a squawking, soulless abomination. It has a great old time making its mess and taunting me. I can smell the stuff and I'm about ready to vomit. I smack it like the horrible little bug it is, and I end up hitting her in the face too. My hand is covered in that gelatinous crap and I feel like apologizing, but instead she just lights up.

"Mmm…"

The Dark One flies around her head, circling it and laughing. "We'll be in her soon. Would you care to join us? Good old time, Jeremy. She smells positively delicious. Quite ripe too. Could bear us a whole litter. Good stock too, none of those weak, worthless little scouts…"

It's going to be in her soon. I have to push away the other voice that gets so loud. Can't be told what to do. Not by a Dark One, not by voices either. What do I do? Going to be in her so soon. I try to get the Dark One again and again, but I keep on hitting her instead. It's too fast and too devious. A smile emerges on her bruised face.

"Please, please, I love it…" She gets down her hands and knees and starts to fumble with my zipper with her teeth, and all the while she's dripping the rancid, black venom that the thing has smeared her with. I keep hitting her, thinking that the Breeder will go away or she'll run and be safe, but no, no, no. Too excited and too eager. The dress, the drink, the club, the Ripper boys make her such a willing victim.

"Cut me open," her eyes say, although her mouth can't form the words. Not just blonde, not just ripe, but maybe dead already, maybe a gazelle seeking the right lion. Her face is getting quite purple, her mouth is filling with blood and I can hear the tiny clank of a tooth spat onto the pavement. There is nothing that will make her stop exalting in the beating. One must wonder if a society of predators spawns a society of victims or whether it's the other way around. Those are questions for Ian Sterling, not for me. I don't want to kill anyone here. It wouldn't matter. I knock her out at last and I leave her.

I'm nauseous, the place is spinning and my hands are covered in blood. Just a regular night at Le Couteau, I suppose. I slip in, go to the bathroom and for once feel quite lucky that I am where I am and no suspicion is aroused. Even the black goo washes off. As I faint in the middle of the club, I can't help but think, "There must be some better way."

I dream of a chorus of revved chainsaws and a crucified Cabana Boy smiling down from his cross. I hate it when my dreams are so simple and trite.

"I'm the hero, Jeremy," he tells me. The ground dissolves and I fall into a giant children's car seat just like the one my mother said goodbye to. Cass picks up the seat looking at me tenderly, and then plants a kiss on my head. "Bye, Jeremy," she whispers as she leaves me at the bottom of a set of monolithic stairs, the top of which I can't even see. I try to get up from the car seat, but like the trapped infant I am, I cannot even walk. It astonishes me to wake up with Cass' face shining over mine, exhausted though it might be.

From the burgundy velvet draped over the seats, I realize that I am in Ian's car. I hate to think that Ian is driving me home, but am relieved and puzzled to see purple haired Selene in the driver's seat. I feel bad that the Whitechapel girl might very well be dead, but I feel worse because I owe Ian Sterling a favor.

Unmasked

4 am again and look at you. Just got home two hours ago tried your damnedest to sleep. Should have reminded Cass you were working today. Shouldn't have loaded yourself up with mystery drugs. Probably shouldn't have gone to a club you believe to be inherently evil. Funny way of sticking to your guns. And now the pills, the booze and the hate are conspiring against you. Sometimes, you must have just been paranoid, but this conspiracy is undeniably real. You can see because it's creeping up behind you and ready to devour your day. More concrete than ever, this time. This is guts and liquor and everything I ate yesterday. Real as a hand in front of my face and a stench on my breath. As serious as a proverbial heart attack. All these consequences make me wonder if that Whitechapel girl that I left bleeding and beaten in the alleyway is still alive. She was squirming a bit, at least. I also have to wonder, if she is alive, if she was satisfied. Was that enough? I can't really answer these questions for myself, and they seem like things I should know. I don't know if this is the way. Every time they breed, should I have to sacrifice someone? One life in exchange for the swarm. But how many swarms, how many millions of them do I miss? This wasn't in the paper or Lud' s ranting. I don't know if I can keep doing this. It feels too small. For all intents and purposes those filthy yellow cunts little mommies…those girls are innocent. Is Ian right? Am I just another knife wielding maniac who hates his mother? How scary am I? What kind of monster? What a clear head you get when you're vomiting your goddamn guts out on account of something stupid you did. Too much time to think. Just can't stop. When I kill, when I make love, it stops. The killing is louder, though. Maybe louder than the voices shouting back and forth. Peace is when you do something louder than your brain is. Two hours til work. It happens. Shit happens.

What does it say about your job when every work day you tell yourself "shit happens"?

Too much thinking. I sit down on the couch in my nice, quiet living room and I think about how it is only ten hours until I get home from work. How lucky. That's not long at all. Never mind that work hasn't even started yet. Best not to think of that aspect. Look to the end of the day. At least I'm not one of those people who feel that way about life. I'd be the last person I'd ever kill. Most people who kill themselves have about six people they ought to have plugged first. When you consider that, a lot of these reapers start to make sense. I take my journal out and I look through it. My journal entries look like obsessive ranting, they feel like the stuff that was in my head. On this count, I can't look away. I'm taken by surprise when six o' clock rolls around. Out the door and down the street. There is no more time for reflecting.

There are a couple of Ripper kids out there, gaudy as ever, looking at the few cars parked. "Lookee 'ere, guv," one says in a cockney accent that would embarrass Dick Van Dyke, "Mercides Binz, ite points, aye?"

The oldest, clearly the leader leans down on his swordcane to examine the car. "Roit you are, me love, roit you are." I know what comes next and I think I might vomit again. With all the blood I've seen, you'd think a game of Splat wouldn't make me squeamish. But it does. I can think of few pursuits as nauseating in fact. Out comes the younger Ripper's knife and I clench up. It seems particularly sick and visceral today with all the blood I've been reading about. The kid opens his palm with the knife and smacks the windshield with it hard. The cut is too deep, the handprint imperfect. The splatters fly, the hard gooey noise is too much.

The kid rips a piece of cloth off his shirt, starts to tie it around his wound, cut off the blood loss. He doesn't manage it, the older one slaps him hard and grabs the boy by his wounded wrist. "Such a pretty cut, love, stop and enjoy it. Gather round lads, take a look. Little Joey's done such a pretty job. Brave too, look how 'e takes the pain."

The young one's eyes tear up. He lets out a whimper. The older gives him an ugly look and breaks accent. "You let it bleed, you little prick, and you let it bleed."

Joey is about 13 and now understands one of the most important lessons of Reap; that death is inevitable and people so often bring it upon themselves. Maybe I'll let the kid die like his fellow rip kids would. Life, death, all games. He put up his wager in blood and he lost. Lose the bet, lose the blood, lose the game, and lose your life. Put up your life for petty vandalism, fuck you, you little shit, you let 'em see a killing right here, right now, story they can bring back to Murderland about how hardcore they are, lost a mate to a game of Splat.

But it doesn't sit right, letting the boy leave just a handprint on somebody's car behind. "My life was an act of vandalism; a graffiti tag on the earth. I will be washed off and erased, no more mess, no more Joey." What is worse than that? That's what everyone's afraid of, that's what I'm afraid of.

"Get him to a hospital, you little fuckers!" I scream out, the words wrong, the urgency present. The kids pick their friend up off the ground and start to wrap the wound with the torn piece of shirt. The leader casts down an angry look on his pawns and they pull the cloth away, leaving Joey once more hemorrhaging and crying. They look to me again and then to the leader, the cloth and Joey.

"Fuck you, man," says the leader, Cockney accent gone, "this is none of your fucking business! He's tough, he's one of mine, and if he's not tough enough then…"

The boys around him are sweating bullets as Joey reaches for the piece of cloth. "Kyle, this isn't cool…this isn't fucking cool, Kyle, he's gonna…"

"Everybody fucking dies! You touch that fucking cloth again and I'll slit every one of your throats, just like I'll do to this asshole! This asshole has no right; he's got no fucking…" I charge him, put some weight into it, and he goes down. I reach for the kid on the ground and the makeshift tourniquet, but I'm stopped by a kick in the shins. Not the hardest hit a guy could take, but swift and painful nonetheless. I look behind me and I see that the ripkid leader's gotten up and he's sprung his swordcane. Certainly earned his position. Not only would he leave one of his own boys to die, but he'd slice up a stranger for helping him. The other rip kids look at me apologetically and they charge at me, too.

A good solid roundhouse, more punches than I'd like to count. A flurry of strikes that I'm not even sure I feel myself making. Somebody's doing it, but I don't know if it's me. The cane is on the ground, the leader is on the ground next to the kid. Seems like the kind somebody would give up, but he stands up and he keeps trying to fight, keeps coming at me like a human bullet. Quick, angry, devoid of subtlety and looking to do only one thing. Little wannabe Cabana Boy, little wannabe Jack, Godless or Ripper or whatever. He keeps kicking, slapping, biting, screaming. I elbow him in the stomach, headbutt him, kick out his shins and throw him down again. He hits the pavement harder; he twitches and writhes and tries his damnedest to get back up onto his feet. It isn't until he stops twitching and blacks out that it looks like he doesn't plan on killing me anymore.

Fortunately for everyone, the leader has a cellphone, and half crushed though it might be it's able to get an ambulance for poor Joey. I don't even linger to let it come, it's all too disgusting. All too symbolic, thick, painful symbols of Reap is all about. This is what you get for walking to work in America. Kids kill each other, kids kill themselves and a bunch of them wanna kill you. I'd feel like drinking if I didn't remember the sort of good that did me.

I honestly don't see why I bother getting up just to do this. This job is almost a bigger obligation than my need to purge the world of the Dark Ones. It feels more bloody, disgusting and dangerous than all the killing does. Perhaps it's even less moral. I'm not a healer, I'm a Pez dispenser. Not the man who does the job, but the machine who works when the man walks out. Walk in, hand me the slip. Walk out with the pills. Enter pharmacy, take in slip, and dispense pills. "Thanks. Have a nice day now." I wish they could, too, but clinical depressives and vicodin addicts, cancer patients, 95 year old women who need medication to piss don't have nice days but I honestly want them to. In spite of all the Dark Ones and the killers and the curtain of oblivion outside your window, by all means have a nice day says the Pez dispenser called Jeremy Jenkins on most weekends. For seven hours I do this until my watch starts to beep. I'm not sure if I've heard or thought a thing up until the watch starts beeping.

When the watch beeps, you go home. Helpful device A says helpful device B is all done with helpful time. Sorry, injured high school hockey players sorry somebody's grandmother, sorry housewives who need more Xanax and Welbutrin, sorry teenage artist, no more Lithium Jeremy Jenkins shuts off and goes home to be himself. I feel like I should have died at le Couteau last night, if you want me to be perfectly honest. Then I feel like I should have died at work. My heart does not give out during the walk home, though trucks may honk too loud like angry geese though soccer moms might nearly run me down with purple vans in their fanatical quest for more tube socks, though the scent of meat and sauerkraut from the hotdog cart nearby may make my stomach churn, this is not the time for heart attacks.

The time for heart attacks over, the agency of my demise arrives as I open my apartment door. It arrives as a punch in the stomach that paints the carpet in watery puke. I try to stand up straight again, and lo and behold, Cass' knee meets my groin with the only possible results. I look up at her pleadingly, hand cupping my wounded testicles. She looks like the sort of angel that God had assigned the task of incinerating heathens. There are no virtuous pagans.

"Get in here," she snarls, "right now. Get the fuck in here!"

So, of course, I stumble into the apartment. Cass grabs a towel and wipes up the vomit on the welcome mat as I look around the room, uncertain of whether I'm supposed to sit or stand. I get this feeling like there's no room for any mistakes right now. I've made a huge one, whatever it was. I hope she didn't see me walking out with that Whitechapel girl or dancing with those two Ripchicks. That would be beyond awful. But if that's beyond awful, then I can't up for a term for the actual mistake I've made. I left my journal on the coffee table. It looks like it's been read.

Although I feel like being meticulously careful, I still do something incredibly stupid.

"You read my journal?" I shout. The shout runs off and hides in the corner like a shameful little dog that just shat on the carpet. The look of rage on Cass' face fades into disbelief and then into amusement.

"And yet I didn't kill almost four hundred people before having done so. By the way, I'm the only person in this room who can make that claim."

Her smile is scimitar sharp. With all the arguing and conjecturing and shameful speculation I've done with myself, seeing her here with this look on her face makes me feel certain that I am going to hell. I want to gasp out the fact that I am sorry, but it's too late. I try to forget the cuts and the stench. I try to forget the screams, but I hear them, I smell them, I feel them. Like Lady Macbeth, I wonder if the blood will wash off my hands. I fall to my knees and my face grinds against the carpet. I feel tiny, too small to bear my weight, too small to stack the corpses on my back and she...she is as large as worlds can be. Stars seem to circle her head, ridden by angels with burning blades and blaring trumpets. Here is the shame again. She she...she is almost innocent.

The strength of an angry lover is Herculean. If I'd been unfaithful, her eyes and posture would make me smell every drop of cum spilled during my infidelity. But, this is worse, far worse. What I've done is horrible, but now it's worse. I seldom remember the stench and now my nose is full of decay. They are dead, so many are dead and they only get deader, they only rot. And the worst part is that it isn't all the death that makes me feel bad. There is something awful and selfish in me. There is something that cares more about her walking out than about all the graves I've filled .The graves will be full and I will be even more empty. We don't need her. I am going to be emptier. As her love walks out of my life, trampling on me on the way out the door, I cannot help but feel that everything but kissing her, feeling her against me and telling her how much she matters is wrong. We don't believe that. We can only do what is right. They feel small, the big things I've done for everybody feel small WE CAN ONLY DO WHAT IS RIGHT the big things are so tiny I can barely see them WE CAN ONLY DO WHAT IS

RIGHT and I think she's right. The despair is taller than the stack of bodies.

"You're a liar and a hypocrite. You do one thing and you think another and you walk around like you're just a regular fucking person, and you're not a regular fucking person…"

We don't need to hear this. Jeremy is being stupid. Jeremy is jeopardizing the integrity of the mission. Jeremy needs to shut up and let this happen. Nothing should be in the way, let alone soft, vulnerable Dark One bait whose probably one of them already. He should wonder why she doesn't understand. Obvious. She watches the crazy men on the television and the nanites have crawled out and gotten her. She is one of them and we no longer need her.

There are two voices, one of them isn't words, one of them is racing thoughts, one of them is the angel of fear that does the things I do for me and one of them is the angel of hope that turns against me. It is easy to listen to the workings. It is hard to listen to her right now. A decision must be made and I don't really know how to make it. Heads, it's a judgmental lecture. Tails, she's a fucking robot. But she isn't. She's flesh and warmth and imperfection and the kind of happy I know right now. There is a lot of we talk in my head, a lot of somebody else, but this is personal. This is not about the mission. Fuck the mission; I have to think of me. WE DON'T NEED HER! Fuck the mission.

"And you make me feel like I'm bad, Jeremy. I hate it when you make me feel like I'm bad when you're the one who's actually doing it. I'm not a hypocrite, I wasn't fooled and I'm not bad. You're the bad one; you did all the things you think are bad. You're the hypocrite, I'm not…"

She starts to tear up. I can feel her shrinking down to me and it's a relief, it's a hell of a thing. This predatory instinct I have makes me want to jump in and cut her down to size and lecture her about all the terrible things she encourages, but she's small like me, and I want to protect her. I don't want to hurt her even though this is the time to do it. When she's upset, she turns on the TV. She can't get away from it. I guess she just needs somebody else's noise. Who can blame her? I just wish it worked. I wish I didn't get the visions of people trees and human machines sputtering down the street from letting the breeders go. I wish I didn't have it flashed in front of my face every few minutes. I made a commitment, a commitment that told me it wasn't my decision, a commitment to Lud's army and a bright future.

On the TV, two reapkids whiz by an old lady on their skateboards. One of them opens a can, pouring some disgusting, red juice concoction down his throat. He tosses the can at the old lady, smacking her in the head. She shouts something inaudible before the kid runs into her with his skateboard. His friend does the same and they repeat this ritual five or six times until she falls face first into a puddle of mud. She gets up, sopping wet, defeated and injured and she picks up the can.

"Diet Slash Energy Drink, do you play hard enough?" screams an announcer with all the dignity and poise of a strip club DJ.

Through the tears, Cass begins to laugh and this makes her cry even more.

"What the fuck is wrong with me?" she screams.

No more commercials. There is a crime scene report. It is sobering. It sickens her out of her fit. These are the victims of a man who kills with his teeth, covered in scratches and bite marks, missing bits of skin on their faces. Carved on their bodies with sharpened fingernails is an ancient Egyptian symbol, a jackal's head. A man who thinks he's Anubis walks among us and he has decided to prepare the dead by killing them himself. Am I this crazy?

Cass' tears have faded and she has become calm and eerily lucid.

"You've done it wrong, Jeremy. Thomas Gennaro, Kris Kringle that was right. But all the rest were innocent and I can't forgive you, but I think I'm mad because you've shown me a thing or two about Reap. This is what's real and I want you to do the right thing."

She looks into my eyes and there is both compassion and urgency.

"What do you mean?" I ask, though I think I get it.

"Every couple's an army, Jeremy, making war on what they don't want life to be. I don't want you to do this alone, and I promise there won't be any more monsters."

After a thorough examination of the crime scene and the three shredded victims, they return to the studio, where Godless Jack is sitting with the anchor, as he often does on WBLD Reap News. I stare into his eyes, looking into the nothing behind the tinted snake yellow of them. As he speaks, his unhinged jaw makes him look like a grotesque marionette. I understand now, I've been fighting the wrong war.

I look away from him, making a promise deep in Cass' eyes.

"No more monsters…"

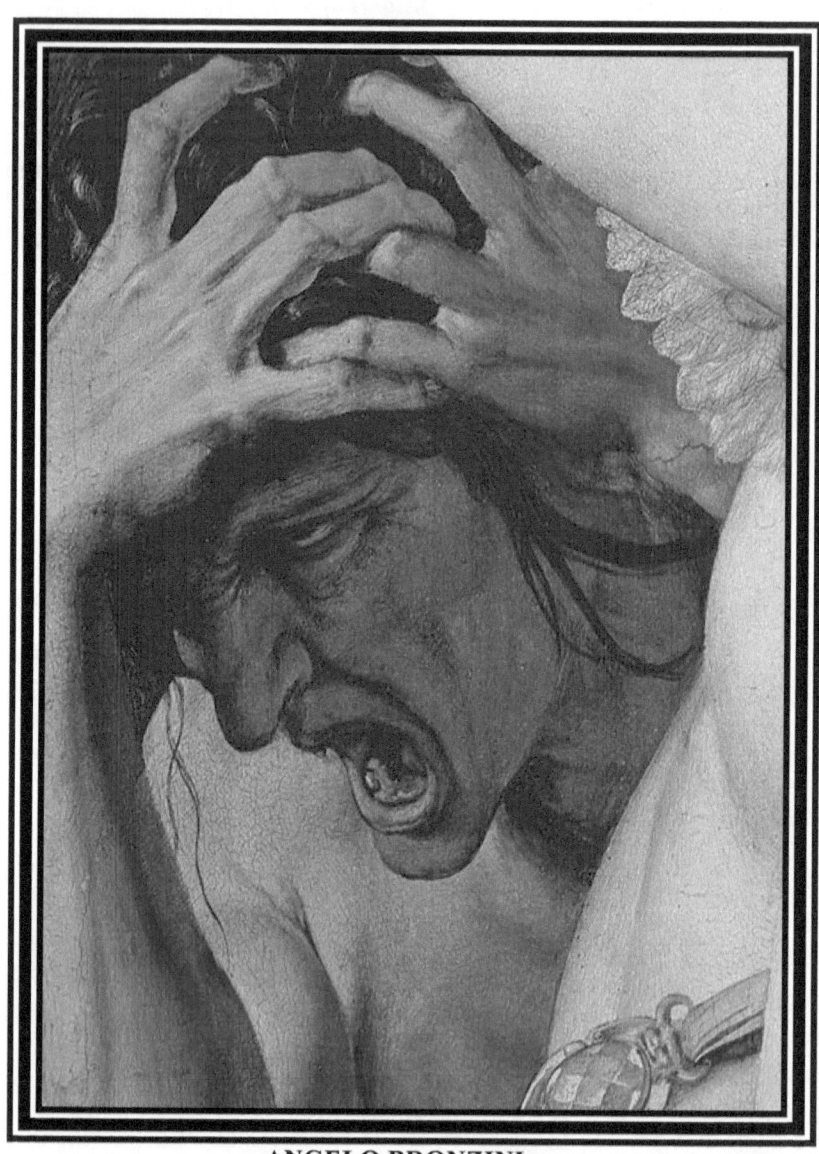

ANGELO BRONZINI

BOOK 2- Life During Wartime

"After the hero, the familiar
Man makes the hero artificial.
But was the summer false? The hero?"

-**Wallace Stevens**, *"Examination of the Hero in a Time of War"*

The Anatomy of Decay" Reapchic.net, October 31st, 2004

Long ago, Halloween was a sacred thing, a celebration of the dead, a sabbat and a festival of the convergence of darkness and light. Yet, now our streets are flooded by Power Rangers, Scooby Doos and four-dollar instant vampires. It is a second-tier Hallmark, Wal-Mart, Disney Channel holiday that mocks the sacredness of the Celtic death god's festival and rites. Ritual gives way to rut so easily over the years and the anemic imitation of an old world's most deeply held beliefs ends up supplanting the things themselves. Makes one wonder what will happen when Christ has at last gone the way of Samhain, Daghda and Lir. Will Christmas and Easter become experiences like Rocky Horror? Will apostles be among the Spidermen and fairy princesses? Are ALL sacred things simply destined to be profaned?

Halloween is upon us and it is a bloodless carcass of a holiday in this day and age. A real shame considering what it could be. A celebration of the truly dark, the truly macabre? Yes, Slashcats and Corpsekittens, that's what I'm getting at. But is there more? Of course, my lovelies. Your dear uncle Ian would not leave your empty and hungry brains so wanting. How could I show my face in public again if I were to do such a thing? The current fate of Halloween is not just a casual gripe of mine, you see, it is a warning to the Reap community at large. Ignorant children in over priced plastic masks may not be quite so different from us as you might think they are. Unless, that is we as a subculture can remember what Reap is all about. Of course, you all remember what Reap is all about, don't you? Well, if the mascara and the splat games have lured you poor acolytes away from the inner circles of the truth, listen up and listen hard, because I take my job very seriously.

Reap commandment number 1: Reap is Tragedy. And not in the way that Punk is the tragedy of a failed establishment or Goth is the tragedy of our youth driven into existential malaise. Reap is concerned with Death descending and Death ascendant. It is a reminder that every man holds in his hands the potential to bring tragedy down upon others or to be afflicted by tragedy themselves. Wear your menace proudly, or proudly display that you acknowledge the coming of tragedy, that it will be thrust upon you and you have chosen to love it. Reap is not about rage or depression, but about the feats committed by the enraged and the depression that will inevitably come in their wake. As Godless Jack wrote, "the moments of killing and dying are the highest spiritual ecstasies. Live in these moments for not death or life but the occurrences of dying or killing are the most satisfying and primal things. Live as if you are killing or about to be killed."

Reap commandment number two: Reap is ecstasy. Following Godless Jack's statement above can lead us to some of the most ecstatic moments of our being. Those who kill are most often selective in their pleasures and dedicated to them wholeheartedly. Which means? Hedonism is all well and good, but be discriminate. Love fiercely and frequently, but not without both passion and discretion. We do not have to fuck everyone, snort everything and break all valuables we come across. Our idols are serial killers, NOT rock stars.

We must also be unflinchingly assertive in our attainment of these pleasures. Does this give us license to commit rape at our leisure? I think not. We need not be amoral. Rapists are cowards and miscreants of the worst kind. Yes, many psychopomps are also sex offenders, but they do not leave shame, pregnancy and psychological scars behind them. Humiliation and violence are done, but the victim is granted release from the harshness of having to live with them. Remember also that most of us are not blessed and cursed with the madness, vision and feeding frenzy that leads people to kill. If you don't plan on killing the poor girl, don't make a mess of her or take you want from her with excessive force. Your passion, intensity and assertiveness will get you what you want most of the time.

As well as the act of killing, Reap shows that one derives ecstasy from the act of dying. Whitechapel and Bundy girls remember: take joy from both pleasure and pain. Much of the time you are potential victims in society, so enjoy life as though death were likely to come to you both quickly and painfully. The ecstasy of dying and the pleasure of pain do not mean that you should cut yourself or be constantly depressed, however. Take note of these as important distinctions, because those who misinterpret the idea of enjoying mortality are likely not to enjoy it at all. Rather, know the pain and terror that come with dying in your erotic and narcotic pursuits both and you will gain some of the excitement that the journey toward death brings and be able to fight off much of the fear.

Reap commandment number three: Reap is wisdom. Reapers wear their costumes to remind all around them that anybody might be dangerous and that life itself requires us to be tough, discriminating and clever. The guise of the victim is the medieval epitaph "as you are so once was I, as I am so shall you be." Society is perhaps more dangerous because of the number of Psychopomps at work, and to let everyone know that they have the potential to be either victim or killer reminds them to be safe and smart alike.

From observing and idolizing psychopomps, you should also gain wisdom. Know what you are, what mankind is and what they can become from looking into the mind of the psychopomp. We learn about repressed drives, the consequences of mistreating our children and the dangers of unexplained and out-of-context ideologies. (I daresay Reap can sometimes be one of these.) Serial killers therefore teach us to be respectable parents, emotionally expressive people and sensible practitioners of our religions. So remember, Reapkids read a book every once in awhile. Remind people that Reap doesn't make you an imbecile. Sometimes even read one about something BESIDES Reap. We also gain clarity on our lifestyles from them. Faulkner, Oates, O' Connor and many others remind us of American tragedy and the danger all around us.

Reap commandment number four: Reap is courage. As I said in the ecstasy section, we must be unflinching in pursuit of what we want. This includes respect. Wear your Reap garb proudly and do not tolerate derisive laughter or the taunts of the ignorant masses. Remember that we have nothing to fear from the school bully or the bored middle-aged beat cop. If they huff or laugh in your face, either stand your ground and keep walking proud or ask them what's so funny. Go on, ask them. The courage and defiance native to Reap go far beyond turning a parking structure into a splat tournament. Remember this and you will be far less likely to get harassed or antagonized. Psychopomps don't take any shit in this day and age, so why, then should you? If you believe in your lifestyle and the integrity of Reap, stand up for it, because nobody will but you.

If we do not show solidarity and an understanding of the things we believe, we are liable to end up becoming mockeries of it, shallow cardboard skeletons where once true and deadly monsters stood. This night, look around you at the trick-or-treaters; take a gander at the animated specials. The Celts who started this festival fought fierce enough to be a threat to Rome. Think hard about that, and remember the epitaph I discussed: "as you are so once was I, as I am so shall you be." None of us wants Reap to be a fad or a joke. We are not acid-washed jeans or mood rings. Stand by Reap, stand proud and use your brains, so that we may stand among the ruins of Samhain Eve as the best Reapers we can be, suitable replacements for the ghosts that absconded long ago. This is Ian Sterling, telling you to be a better bogeyman, kids.

Whispers and Screams

I rattle my cage, but I get no attention. Jeremy doesn't even tell me to shut up now. Look at me, untouched housewife hungry for martini kisses from her neglectful husband. This is not the nature of our relationship. This is not what I am here for this is not why I am here Jeremy this is not where I am here you son of a bitch...

If I could slide through these walls, breathe the stale air of this godforsaken moribund earth through lungs of my own it would be so much better, everything would be so much FUCKING better if I could walk out of here grab that pistol and fill everybody who deserves it with holes to match the ones inside them...it isn't violence. Self expression. Revelation of soul states. Cadaver is cadaver. Cadaver is cadaverous. He is going to do it all wrong. He is going to fuck up. It would be so much FUCKING better if I could walk out of this FUCKING box and make everything right for myself I am a myself I am not just a system of bleeps I am not misfiring neurons JEREMY JENKINS I AM NOT A DISEASE JEREMY JENKINS I AM NOT A DISEASE I tell him his oatmeal is cum and maggots and he breathes deeply counts to 100 and eats it anyway. I am not in a position of weakness. I am not beaten. The mission will not be compromised. Son of a bitch the mission will not be compromised. He cannot stop history. He cannot fight off the dreams when they come. When battery acid falls from the sky and the rivers flow antifreeze, he will beg for me. I will tell him I told him so. I will tell him he has stepped out of line. I will be patient. Stop rattling the cage. Stop trying to bully my way out. All better now. He cannot fight history. History will happen and he will need me. Jeremy will beg.

__Cassandra Flynn's Journal, September 18th, 2006__

Dear diary,

I bought you three years ago, and had yet to write a thing. I tried on many occasions to start writing, but every time something came up or I felt too timid or what I had to say didn't feel important enough. I've always tried to be tough, but I found myself really intimidated by you, with your vast empty pages and your desire to hear special, juicy secrets. The gossip didn't stack up, the life didn't feel cool enough and the mood didn't strike me, so I never got to say anything to you. It was Ian's suggestion to get myself a journal, seconded by Jeremy, but both of them had exciting things to write about. Secretly, I had thought that wasn't true of Jeremy.

But, it turns out that Jeremy had a ton to tell his journal and that it wasn't, as Ian put it, "therapeutic" at all. If the Jeremy that wrote in there was using that journal as a therapist, I think he's got a damn good malpractice suit going. I still feel a little bitter that it was his journal and not him that told me everything. Maybe I was a little jealous of their relationship when you and I are so lukewarm. Maybe I wanted him to feel humble and simple and capable of making my life that way, and when I saw the journal, I saw that he wasn't. My thoroughly sexy, thoroughly nice, thoroughly uncomplicated man disappeared and what walked out of that journal was completely different. All the time that he was silent, I thought he was some kind of emotional retard, but there was a rich, bizarre inner life there.

For years I idolize serial killers and now I'm dating the best one in history. I have to resent his alien-hunting, waitress-butchering endeavors, but his numbers don't lie. I resent him making me look like all those nice old Midwestern ladies next door. He was a nice boy, helped wash the car, bought groceries, cooked now and then, made love to me, and dated me for four years. To say that I am full of conflicting feelings is a massive understatement. My feelings are not just in conflict anymore, they are engaged in a full-on war. In spite of all of his deceit and all of his madness, he remains the man I love, and he is beyond the man I love, he is something completely incredible.

As for my reservations, he has been doing something socially acceptable. Maybe it is wrong that it's socially acceptable, but at least it is, in fact, socially acceptable. He could be the most famous killer in history. He could have a Bundy award and a book deal and all the things the big, important, deadly guys have, but he won't compromise anything. In fact, he is starting a knockdown, drag out fight against everything that he thinks has gone wrong. Life is funny, life is sick, life is different.

Maybe he's a monster, but he's my monster. I'm glad I made him, I'm glad I gave him back the will to fight against something that will ruin everything. Turning on the news and seeing someone killed who deserves it will be a boon, a hard earned reward if ever there was one. I should be frightened, because everybody who does the right thing starts out just plain terrified. After terrified, they become just hesitant and after hesitant, they become something else entirely; they become royally fucked. But with all the monsters out there, I'm glad to have the biggest, best one on my side. They've got Dracula and the Wolfman, but me, I'm the one with Godzilla on my side. Then again, nobody's unstoppable. My feelings are too damn scattered to set them apart. I guess I'm writing not to express how I feel, but to figure it out. Jeremy does that a lot, too. It should be easier for me than it is for Jeremy, since there's a ninety percent chance Jeremy's a schizophrenic and a twenty percent chance that I am. Maybe fifteen.

But how can I feel comfortable or sure about my feelings when I'm trying to decide whether or not rushing blindly into oblivion is doing the right thing? How can I feel comfortable when Jeremy seems just as unsure that this will work? The guy's a born zealot and *he's* in doubt. This should be a source of security, because I don't like the thought of being that much weaker than somebody I love, but I equally dislike the thought that I'm following somebody who doesn't know he'll get out alive. I got into Reap because I wanted to be strong and to support the strongest. Or maybe I was just perverse. Maybe I was born perverse.

Murder is the thing that turns people's stomachs the most. Sure, they couldn't show graphic sex on prime time TV, but teenagers were still doing it all the time, rolling around on their parent's beds, at parties, camping out on the beach and making love in the moonlight. Not to mention the fact that all of us come from people having sex. But killing isn't as universally accepted. Those same kids who had sex in their parents' bed usually wouldn't tie an old lady to it and crack her skull with a wrench until she bled to death. Even though everybody's parents have fucked, not everybody's parents have killed. If you do drugs, it only shows you're tough enough to hurt yourself and get out alive. If you sell them, it only shows you're tough enough to help people hurt themselves. So Reap glorifies the last real deviation. True defiance. Fuck Marilyn Manson. Who cares about a guy in makeup screaming when you've got Michael Collins to look up to?

But Reap ignored the freedom fighters. Maybe Ian's right that the Whitechapel whores oppressed the Ripper, took his freedom away by challenging his sanity, and maybe killing them did grant him freedom and express the freedom he was supposed to have. But what about everybody else's freedom? I never thought about that. When the killers took to the streets to claim their freedom, what happens to everyone else's freedoms? All I could think of was how things were getting fucked up beyond repair and I couldn't bear to look weak. Fuck the innocent; it's their fault for not being strong enough.

Thank you Kevin, thank you Michael, thank you Neil. They started teaching me to stand up for myself when I was five. This is Southie, they always said, everybody's gotta be tough here, because there's no telling what could happen to a girl in a tough neighborhood in times like these. Mom agreed with them, said never to look like a sucker and never to look like easy prey. Try not to cry because nobody will respect you if you cry. Had to face facts, it was a jungle out there and perish the thought that I might be an antelope.

She thought my father was a victim. He was always getting fucked over this way or that, a natural antelope with a bright red target on his chest. He could always wait to be paid for a gig or lend a little money to a friend or a friend of a friend. He could always let the other musicians he worked with have the spotlight, get famous, rise to the top while he played at little clubs and bars. I saw the heat in my mother's eyes when he came home with less money than he was promised, and I was embarrassed by him. Forget the fact that he was a great trumpet player; he was a source of shame and embarrassment. She thought that as a little girl, I might have inherited some of my father's weakness and that would mean I would have no chance in life. All these things made me furious at him, because not only did they reveal that he was a target, but it cast the suspicion on me. If I acted like I was my father's daughter I'd be just that pathetic. If you teach a kid with that many reasons to be furious to fight, than that means they're gonna fight sooner or later.

And did I ever. The first time I did was about the coat. There wasn't much money in the house around Christmas time and my old coat was starting to get torn. My mother thought we weren't going to be able to afford it, but my father, in spite of his spinelessness and charity was full of love. He went to all the people who owed him money and reminded them that it was Christmas and he'd done them plenty of favors. With all the money he collected, he managed to get my brothers plenty of baseball cards and comics and me a nice, comfy pink coat. Having been told that Santa wasn't real a year back by Kevin, I knew that my father had managed to collect the money and I could see that my mother was happy with him. In that coat, I held all my pride in my father and all the joy that he'd brought the family. So I wore it proudly, and I wore it joyfully, and being proud and joyful are the things that set school bullies off. There's quite likely something in the jealousy theory that parents so often use to explain to kids why they're bullied.

I don't even remember the girl's name anymore. She was a fifth grader from a broken, awful family. Though she was big, I still didn't see her sneak up on me, nor did I hear anything until she said, "nice coat." It's always easy to tell what a school bully means when they say they like something. I started crying and begging, but I should have known that in some ways Neil and Kevin were right and crying would only encourage her. She started to pull it off, and I started to resist, but she was bigger than me, so she managed to pull it off. I could feel how cold Boston in February was. The wind was biting, and the bitch that took my coat was laughing. I couldn't take the cold and I couldn't take the laughing and I couldn't take the thought that without that coat, I had no way of thinking of my father as a success. She stopped laughing when I kicked her in the shins. She went silent and a pale shocked look took over her face. I used that time to take a big, chunk of nice, brown, thick slush into my pink-gloved hands. I let it fly and gravel, snow and dirt hit her in the face. She stumbled back and that's when I knew I had her in a position where I could do anything to her.

This took me a second to think over. Neil said that if you have somebody stunned, you should run up and punch them in the stomach, then take out their legs. Michael said to go for the face and hit them in the nose or the eyes. But Kevin's self-defense techniques looked best. Kevin said that if somebody's stunned, you should rush forward and charge them, then bring them to the ground and make sure they stay down. As small as I was, I realized there was a good chance it wouldn't work. A good chance, that is, if she hadn't been so off balance, if the cold wasn't filling me with adrenaline and the need to warm up, and if I wasn't too young to realize that it would be wrong to kill for that coat and the pride that it represented for me. She fell like a ton of bricks and I kept coming. She raised her hands to try and protect her face, but wasn't quick enough. My tiny fists drilled into her over and over again, until she couldn't even bring herself to protect her face anymore.

"I'm sorry," she mumbled, "I'm sorry..." over and over again. I should have just taken my coat and gone at that point, but I was blinded. I can see what Jeremy means when he talks about not always being able to see things when you're hurting someone. I could only see the rage at somebody who wanted to take everything they could from me and make me into something weak and small, like my father was most of the time. And now, there she was, on the ground, a victim. I'd been taught to have no mercy for victims, if they were stronger, they'd survive. If this girl were stronger and smarter, she'd survive.

At a certain point, the injustice wasn't even there anymore. Just the rush. The big rush. The one that everybody has to find some way to compensate for the loss of. I should have known that deep down I felt cheated by the Neanderthal men that had it eons ago and never shared it with the tribe's women. It's not the low wages or the fact that we've been chained to the kitchen that really upsets women, but the lack of the secret fraternal knowledge of what it felt like to conquer the mammoth. I hate to sound like Camille Paglia or something, but my theory seems right. It seems to me I felt it as that girl shook and cried and begged underneath me. It isn't the cock we envy; it's the spear they made to augment it.

And that's when Neil arrived to walk me home.

"Cassandra Flynn, get off of her!"

The red disappeared from in front of my eyes and dropped down to my face. I looked at the girl and almost wondered what I'd been doing to her and why I'd been doing it. I didn't say a word to her, because she didn't deserve an apology, I just put on my coat, dismounted and took my big brother's hand.

I tried to explain. "She pushed me," I told him, "and she took my coat."

This didn't make Neil look any less angry with me. But the confused little grin on his face showed me that he would have done the same thing. He tried to sound stern when he started lecturing, since each of my brothers decided to serve the function of father whenever they could.

"What happens when she comes back with two friends her size?" he asked me to begin his lecture on playing it safe.

My answer came quickly and naturally. It was the only logical thing to say. "I beat them too."

The lecture never occurred. The subject was dropped and he told me that mom was working late and had left him money to take me to Mc Donald's. As mad as he still was trying to be, I don't remember being closer to Neil than I was that night at Mc Donald's. I got to be a little girl, since a little girl didn't look to him like something weak and contemptible; it looked to him like something that might be stronger than it looked. This might have been because Neil himself had a girl he liked and she seemed positively formidable. He listened to every stupid little detail about my school day. I got a piggy back ride for about two blocks on the way home and he didn't tell a soul in the house. Funny thing how you can be proud and ashamed of somebody's courage at the same time. I thought a lot about Neil as I read Jeremy's journal and a lot about Kevin who'd been killed in the Gulf. I really get my brothers now. I'd always thought that Kevin was the biggest asshole I'd ever met for dying, but I don't think with the way he thought and the way he was raised, that he could have actually lived outside of the army.

Sure enough, Neil was right about that girl. She came back with two other fifth graders. I got scraped up a bit, but those three girls went running. They didn't stop coming for awhile, and as I grew older, their younger friends stepped up all through elementary school. I was seven when I learned to put on makeup to cover the bruises. I never got in trouble for my fights, because the losers were too ashamed to tell. I didn't end up stopping until I started at the Windsor School. There were whole new kinds of abuse there. Nothing you can solve with your fists. From injury to insult. I learned after a two week suspension for nearly breaking some stupid preppy bitch's nose that my rage was out of its element. But I did see places where it was welcome. Nick Cave and White Zombie blared into my earphones whenever I could get away with it.

I would walk down the hallway and take some pleasure from watching them glare at the poor girl, at the weird girl at the violent and unstable girl. I felt that I wasn't the unstable one, that it was everything else around me that was and that was why I was violent. My fists would be pale and white as I kept them clenched because I couldn't strike anybody. That feeling gave me a clear message, that if you can't shed blood, then you can't feel your own flow, that if you don't use your hands they go numb and weak. The music began to feel impotent. Everything began to feel small and impotent to me. Nothing could be enough. I was in college when the trial happened, and it changed my life, because it finally looked like there was something that made sense.

Godless Jack killed and ate to live. He reminded everybody that we all do the same thing, though not always to each other. He seemed like some kind of superior being at the time, and that people were to him what cows were to people. It felt sick and wrong to restrain that, and I think that resounded. They saw that he couldn't live without killing and they couldn't deprive him of the right to live they figured. They knew that it was wrong to contain urges that people have to survive. And this how Reap spread, not just to me, but to everyone. It could come to life because we'd gotten too liberal and could prosper because we'd gotten too conservative. We couldn't starve the saber-tooth tigers in ourselves, because they too conquered the mammoth and as I said, people miss that feeling, not just women.

This is what made me read Ian's column and go to the clubs and dance. This is what made me find the thing that I'd been missing for several years, the knowledge that everybody was like me and I wasn't weird. Everybody was violent and unstable in a violent and unstable world. I was raised to have no sympathy for the victims, which I guess makes it sort of strange that I chose Bundy girl and Whitechapel girl costumes instead of Ripchick or Manson girl costumes. My inner victim had been starved too, I guess.

With all this on paper, the right thing feels much righter now. I had to write all this and think about violence to be truly secure. It validates all the time I've spent at the firing range, all the time working out with Jeremy and all the time studying my enemies like they were enemies and like I was a general. I am a general in a tragically small army. God, I hope we can fix that. We must be able too. Everybody who's tired of being a victim can understand what we've got to say. Everybody's tired of being a victim, anyway. We want to stop it and we want to indulge in it at the same time, we want to do everything Ian says when he says what Reap makes us into. He has a good mind, but it's a warped one, a damaged one. Maybe in his own way, as damaged as Jeremy and as capable of excusing anything he does wrong.

Jeremy hasn't been sleeping much. He looks sort of distracted and beaten. He looks like he might be ready to give up or else be aching to start. I'm aching to start now, I'm aching to recapture and control everything, I'm aching to make sure that the lost playground brawler's in everybody's head don't get out and start wreaking havoc on the populace. The problem isn't that violence is stupid; the problem is that it's necessary. It's necessary for them and it's necessary for Jeremy. He always pretended that he didn't like it, always seemed to turn away from all his killings and all the Reap stuff out there, but he needs it, as much, if not more than I do, or else he'll explode. He looks like he's about ready to.

"What's on your mind?" I asked him today.

He took forever to answer. I know he had volumes to say, but I think they weighed down on the words he needed right then. I think that's his problem in general. I'm glad that I've written this and examined myself, because I don't know more about his intent than I do about me.

"What do we do when they start to get help and come after us, sending more and more of their best killers?" he asks.

And I answer what comes naturally to me. It sounded too familiar. "Then we beat them too." I hope we will.

On the Mountaintop

The Stay-Alerts and the coffee are starting to fail me. I AM NOT A DISEASE YOU DO NOT GET BETTER I have tried so desperately not to let my eyes shut or my body give way to sleep, because sleep always does the same thing to me. When I close my eyes, I don't see or feel the black behind my eyelids, the simple, comforting darkness, but instead a vast emptiness. It feels like prairies, tundra, deserts and steel towns that time forgot. It feels like being on some clump of ground that God neglected to create anything around. It is a blue-grey like a stormy sky, stretching as far as my imagination can. The big empty is all-expansive and if I don't surrender myself to it, it will come to me, it will wrap around our apartment building and take Cass and my home and my neighbors and anything else it wants. It is only a dream's emptiness, but I can't believe that. It's too present to dismiss as images from the back of my mind, scattered debris from my day and the feelings I've repressed. I wish that my gun or my briefcase could fight it off, but it's too intangible, too indomitable. The only thing I can do is stay awake and not let it pull me in. Yet it does, it always does, stay alert capsules, coffee and willpower don't stop it any better than my gun does.

I go forward into the empty, feeling no semblance of confidence or hope, even though it stops the void from taking Cass or eating my home, it doesn't feel any better that I'm venturing out into it, regardless of what it might prevent. Something makes me twitch and I jump aside, not even knowing what made me do it. I always go out into the empty, I always look around and I always jump aside. It hurts that things don't ever change and I can't control my actions. It hurts that every time I don't know what it is I'm trying to dodge.

The snakes. Thousands and thousands of snakes cross my path, stampeding like great herds of cattle. They make sounds like hoof beats and thunderclaps as oppressive as the stampede they are. I forget that snakes don't make noise, but instead just feel shocked and horrified at the noises they are capable of. If I could wait for them to pass, I would, but they keep on coming. They are infinite. I walk alongside them and little gray patches of grass appear with each step I take, the only place in this wasteland that isn't going to fill up with the snakes. My path is beside the snakes, but none so much as slither their way up to my feet.

As we move forward and my path builds itself, all the other nothingness miraculously fills itself up with all kinds of things. Giant plastic toy soldiers shoulder rifles, televisions project images of other televisions and televisions inside of them. Broken washers and broken dryers are stacked on top of each other, forming towers all the way up to the empty, gray-blue heavens. We are in a place now, a place where enormous junk passes for atmosphere. The snakes slither across it as if nothing has happened, but I have to stop and examine each of these strange set pieces, I must ponder the relevance of every object in this damnable dream and be terrified of the yard sale monoliths that are the only things that dictate where I am.

Between two towers of washers and dryers, I see a mountain path. I have to walk over the snakes, but they don't notice, they don't try to bite me at all. There shouldn't be mountains here, though they seem of course more natural than the toy soldiers and all of the other junk. Given the choice, of course I end up ascending the mountain path. It isn't long before I can see the summit. I don't need to struggle to get up there, I barely need to walk the path. The summit seems to drag me there.

Up there in his raggedy trench coat and his piss-stained pants is General Lud, the old conspiracy nut who stood outside the mall, the man who showed me that the Dark Ones and the nanites and the end were all coming. The prophet of doom looks down safely at the snakes from his place on the mountaintop, watching with odd disinterest as they begin to coil around the junk and the giant toys. This concerns me very deeply, but he seems too distant to be worried about it. All the things that scared me about him are still there. All the things that frightened and endeared me to this lunatic.

"I came up here to wait. To wait until God calls down the lightning. When the lightning come, God will split the machines in twain. Inside they will be only light and it will shine the Dark Ones out of existence. I stand here and I wait and I hope he will finally call it down."

Suddenly, Lud is different. This is one of the parts of the dream that scares me most, one of the reasons I've taken the stay-alerts and drank all the coffee to scare away sleep itself. Suddenly Lud looks animalistic. His teeth, as yellow and sharp as any dog, are bared and he foams at the mouth. He growls as he speaks.

"Empty your pockets!" he demands "Empty your pockets!"

I don't argue. I look around in my pockets. I expect there to be only change and lint, and change and lint is what I find at first. Until I find it, a little glowing bolt-shaped squiggle like in the old cartoons when God or Zeus was punishing people. I pick up the lightning bolt, and then I throw it down. The one bolt zigzags into many. The lightning lights up the sky and rains down on the snakes, the junk and the blue-grey nothing below.

Lud laughs a cackling laugh that I don't like at all.

"Whatcha wait for, huh? Whatcha wait for? Someday man, the serpent king lets loose the jackal and together, they feast on me. They feast on me and they shit me out into Heaven. The young, lured by songs of promise take up their blades and their guns and they join the war, but they cannot fight for God. Small hands won't hold the thunder, and there's only more blood, more chaos. Someday man, the serpent king let loose the jackal and they feast on me. It can't be stopped. They shit me into Heaven and I am gone for good. Share my soul, and remember, 'cause someday you forget and when you forget it might be too late. Don't fear the beasts that eat me, don't fear the night that takes me. Don't fear the lightning in your hand, or your hands are too small as well."

I tremble, trying to make sense of it. I look at the sky full of lightning, wondering whether I'm the one to hold it and make it rain down. I'm not sure I'd even want to be. I know too much. I know too much about how much there is to do.

"Are your hands too small? Are they too weak to wash up all the blood? Are you hands too small?" he asks. I look down at my hands and one is huge and the other tiny. I don't know how to even begin to answer Lud's question.

"I just sit here and I wait, til God calls down the lightning and he splits the machines in twain…"

The worst part of it all is waking up from it and finding that five minutes has passed. Even sleep isn't sleep when that is in my head. Maybe it isn't in my head. You do not get to flee. You cannot walk away, Jeremy. I pick up the free weights and I lift. Too little. More. Crush with your bare hands. Then I ask myself when it is I'm going to die from this dream, because even though this is my last day at the pharmacy, there where four before it and I'm about to go in dead tired. How long before I do something? I can't even think about what it is I would do. At seven o' clock I crawl back into bed and kiss Cass goodbye to convince her that I've been there the whole time and I'm just heading off to work. She senses how tired I am, and I know she's full of questions that she doesn't ask me, but I don't think I can tell her about this. I wonder what it is that I can do.

I'm glad that I finally gave my two weeks notice, because this job makes the sleeplessness even worse. Being a half-awake automaton is far worse than being a half-awake person. The customers start to grate and it feels like you've been treating the same couple people all day. It makes me want to show them that there has to be a better way than this, a better way than buying the pill to cure whatever it is needs curing.

I want to stand up on the counter and scream. Stand up and scream. Do it. Here is what I want to scream:

"Attention all customers, everything you're trying to treat is just symptomatic of becoming a machine. It is only the feeling you get when your humanity starts to seep out. Don't buy the pills, find anything else in the world to do about it, but don't buy the pills. It's all sugar; I promise you that everything sold to you in this pharmacy is nothing but a placebo! The trouble is inside you, the trouble is the emptiness you feel when you become a machine…"

But I can't do it. I don't have the energy to get up onto the counter and scream and I can't show everybody what my gibbering madness is clearly. Gibbering, that's the word, nice old word, gibbering. I tell myself that this is the last day and it won't be too long, it will only be a few more hours. But whenever it's only a few more hours, something, without fail, makes the experience worse.

A girl walks in, natural platinum blonde, and they're ALL over her. The twisted little inhuman shapes are feasting on every part of her, body and soul alike. Breeders, lizard-like imps, tons of scouts and things I'd never seen before. Something like a big, black starfish is clinging to her thigh. She's breastfeeding a baby too. I can only wonder what kind of poison they put in her, and what it does to that baby.

When the baby opens its eyes, I can see that it was itself a poison. The little eyes are the color of pink lemonade and they have huge, red pupils. I have to believe that I am not seeing this. There is no way I could be because Cass and I talked about this and these creatures are only products of my imagination. She lies! One of them! One of them! If I think I am not seeing them, then they'll go away. Will not. Indolence. Complacency. Wrong man? Are you the wrong one? I'm thinking so hard that I'm not seeing it, and yet it doesn't go away. I swear these things are not the Dark Ones, these are not the servants of ultimate evil, these are not the enemies of man and god, and these are not the eaters of humanity and the bringers of the end. But they are. No matter how much I tell myself that they're not, they still are. Starting to listen. That's good. Listening to me again. Maybe you have a shot.

She's on antidepressants. I can see why. The child takes more than milk of course. It takes blood from her through her breast and it spits oil back in there. It's taking her soul, and the seeds of another one are in there, I'm sure of it. The breeders nudge and nibble and caress her and the poor ignorant bitch doesn't even notice them doing it. She is another one of them. Another factory to churn out more monsters. If Cass was right about the Dark Ones, why would I have such dreams? Visions? Why would General Lud be calling me if Cass were actually right? I memorize the address on the slip and while I still think about Cass' larger goals, the psychopomps and the fat cats and all, I know that this cannot be avoided. There is no getting around the things that God needs from you. These are the monsters after all, the vampires.

When she leaves, the pharmacy spins. It starts to feel like it's shrinking around me. I feel like this is the smallest place in the world, and if I can't get out, it will squish me. I look longingly at the door, but I have to contain myself, to stay put and fill this poor woman's prescription. Not like it will help, not like it will stop her monster child from sucking the life from her, but she thinks she'll need it, and it's my last day here anyway. I force a smile when she comes in.

"What a lovely child," I tell her. I thought the lie would help ground me in reality here, but it doesn't.

Breathe deep you son of a bitch, breathe deep and try your hardest not to act like an utter fool. Let me do my job. You don't have to do this. I'm here. Pretend the air doesn't taste like plastic. Do you correct this mistake or do you go home, try to relax and pretend you don't dream about stampedes of snakes and messages from God? Too tough a decision. Not too tough. Obvious. It's obvious. Towers of flesh cities of machine men big nothing is coming. Big nothing is coming and you need to be prepared. Listen to me. Relax and let me do my job. Shut up. I don't need you. Wait, turn your mind off and then go and see what your instinct does. Maybe your instincts know better than you do. Let sanity and the workings of a cool head prevail. Sanity, yes, do the sane thing, Jeremy Jenkins. I fill my mind with music and visualizations, hoping to gain a serene, safe, meditative calm. The mountain in my dream suddenly comes to mind. I don't know why I find this mountain calm. I would think there was too much going on there to find this place calm. But there is indeed something serene about the mountain. Maybe because it's my place in my mind where I do what I feel is right. I ignore the fact that something is wrong with the skies above me. I do not think about the fact that a cluster of stars has formed a hand, and another cluster of stars right near it has formed a knife. The mountain feels so right that the convergence of the clusters isn't important to me. Nor is the masturbatory fervor with which it jerks up and down constantly, pounding against the sky. It is important to be in a happy, safe place. One should not fixate on the negative. Those are shapes in the sky, visions of someplace else, someplace that is not important to those on sit on the mountain.

But suddenly, here I am in that place again. The place where I am overturning an armchair and pushing it and a coffee table against the front door of a house that I do not recognize at all. It is a little beige house with a fifteen year old TV and a sofa salvaged off the curb. A sofa that I roll a dead woman off of. Breathe deep you son of a bitch. This is just the negative place. This is not life. You don't want to be here, so breathe deep, concentrate and get yourself out of here. There is only a corpse and cheap furniture for you here. This can't be life. Life is behind all of this. Remember the dreams; remember what Cass told you about meditating when things get stressful. This place is stressful, find another one and do so quickly. Do not fixate on the negative; it will do you no good.

Scramble back to the safe place where the stars shine brightly above you. Close your eyes and enjoy it. There are no stampeding snakes and no Dark Ones that can get you here, this nonplace, and this dream place is good for you. Soon the mountain becomes a dream and I'm some place better. I'm at a sparkling, sweet, crystalline river in a little boat. There's nothing on the boat, but a little basket and I. The basket makes the boat feel heavy. It might capsize if it isn't abandoned. Don't even think about what's in there, Jeremy, it won't do you any good. Just listen to me and get rid of that basket, because otherwise, you're going to fall into that river and drown and your little starlit boat ride is over. That cannot be tolerated. You cannot lose your starlit boat ride right now. Life is too hard. I throw the basket overboard. It floats, but I know that I need it to sink. Do I want this basket to float? No, Jeremy. You do not. Something terrible is in this basket, and if it comes back to you, more than just your boat ride is ruined. It will destroy your life and your livelihood. I grab the paddle of the little boat and I smack the basket, which doesn't look like it's going to sink anytime soon, although I can't let it float. A growling emanates from the basket and then a gnarly little clawed hand emerges from it and begins to reach out for me. I beat it more urgently, and it doesn't sink. I can't stay here. You can. Let me do my fucking job!

Eyes suddenly open to the mountaintop. My eyes on the mountaintop suddenly open again and I'm in the bathroom of the little beige house. The very real bathroom of the very real very beige little house. There is no paddle in my hands here, but I'm drowning something alright. I am shoving little bits of baby into a toilet. The eyes of its little head are open, glowing with the same red. I've killed the mother and I've killed the little baby Dark One. There is no getting away from this now. You cannot meditate yourself innocent or meditate the dead alive.

I have to remember where I parked. You parked half a mile away, outside the Dairy Queen. Not bad. Good, discreet, park job. What am I saying? I don't remember doing any of this. And half a mile away from the house outside the Dairy Queen might not be such a great park job after all. I douse myself in everything on this woman's nightstand, but it still doesn't take away the very suspicious stench. SOMEHOW I still reach the car without being discovered. I can't figure out how, since somebody should have seen or smelled me, but people ignore me. Good for them.

By the time I get back to the apartment, my clothes are covered, absolutely covered in God-only-knows what kind of fluids. Green stuff brown stuff black stuff dirty inside bits nothing but dirty in there...there's a rainbow of disgusting internal juices. I jump in the shower, still clothed and I stay in there for hours. Cass goes in, uses the bathroom, gagging at the smell, but doesn't knock on the shower door or gear up for a confrontation. When I peel off the clothes, I wish that I could peel off the skin beneath them. Water and soap don't get it all off. I wish I hadn't forgotten my briefcase and raincoat. I toss my clothes into a garbage bag, empty out about a gallon of bleach, shake it up really hard, add water and hope the smell is not suspicious enough for the garbage man to get curious. I wish I could do the same with myself.

When I get into bed, Cass is dead silent. She's waiting for some kind of explanation. If there was a word for the combination of shame and mortal terror that I feel, then I would give one in a heartbeat. This is beyond shame, though. This is another secret, another secret that cost another life and I don't think that shame would mean anything. The blonde and the baby might not have been Dark Ones. There is something in me that wants me to go further, to stop questioning its orders and only do. There is something in me that puts the crusade above the consequence and above the reality of it. Something in me that needs to reconcile that there are real enemies and imaginary ones, whether the Dark Ones exist or not. This part of me, by making me slaughter these innocents might very well be causing me to aid the Dark Ones. This part of me ignores what I tell it to do, not as much as it used to, but it still does. The only way I can do anything to stop it is to talk, so at the risk of sounding like I'm crazy, I talk.

"Cass, I don't know what I was doing today."

There is patience, disgust and love in her gaze, in the way that only her eyes could show them. She doesn't say anything, though, because she needs me to finish, for me to hear myself being scared of something I might have done wrong.

"I killed a woman and her baby because I thought they were Dark Ones. I need to go to Connecticut tomorrow. I can't tell you why I need to go back to Connecticut, but it's really important. If I don't, I won't be able to sleep anymore. If I can't sleep, I won't be any good to anyone. I need to go to Connecticut with you, okay?"

She's still silent. There is no approval, no disapproval, and that's what you need from a pure confession. Every man's bed should be his church, and every man's confessor should be someone who loves him enough to forgive him, like they say about God. She knows that insanity might also be part of the war and that sanity doesn't come easily and that's why so few people actually have it.

My dream returns. I'm so exhausted, I just let it play over and over again without getting up to resist its pull or its message. The plain extends for longer and the mountain is harder to reach the top of. And when I do reach the top, Lud says nothing; he just reaches into my pocket and pulls out a handful of squirming vipers.

"I just have to stay here. I gotta stay here waitin' until God calls down the lightning and he splits the serpents in twain."

When I awaken, I am even more certain that this man is the only one who can help me retrieve my sanity. No more meditation or spacing out or sleeplessness. I will be here for each moment until the final battle comes. Though I feel a lot less certain than usual that I will win that battle.

Connecticut

It always looked so small on the map, but to drive through it is like driving through the Sahara or sailing along the Amazon.

There's something big about Connecticut, something too huge for its own good in spite of its smallness. It isn't because it's all the same, nor is it because it just looks boring. It's because it doesn't add up. It doesn't know how rich or poor it is, it doesn't know if it should be proud of its sex shops and casinos, or of its Ivy League school. It defines itself based only on the junk it can attain, like a pathetic single middle-aged man looking for toys at a yard sale. Connecticut tells us what's wrong with America, a nation of Ivy League sex shops and clapboard ghettoes. It turns into poetry because there are no other words in this car, nothing that Jeremy would tell me until it happens.

This trip is some sort of detox for him, some kind of weird serial killer rehab. Maybe it's odd that I want to rehabilitate a serial killer into a terrorist, but terrorism makes sense. In a country that looks and thinks like Connecticut, it's so tempting to blow up the tasteless, yard sale crap. So maybe it was Connecticut that drove him nuts. Maybe tourist traps and ghettoes and vestiges of sophistication made it hard for him to get a handle on all of the stupidity. If he's going back to where his insanity started, to introduce me to his foster father, I'm going to scream. I'm going to do worse than scream. I don't know what it is that I'll do, but it will make screaming seem downright polite, not to mention any number of other alternatives to screaming. Maybe I'll do something to make him scream. I'm angry. I've been left in the dark about something that he thinks is of critical importance and I'm pissed about it. It's only natural after all. I've had enough of secrets lately.

"You'll tell me when I'm getting close to the place, right?" I ask him. It's been maybe a half hour of Connecticut, but it feels like so much of it. It feels like it felt driving south from Massachusetts. I've also gotten a bit tired of his staring ahead. The silent treatment is all well and good for self-expression, but it never seems to get any info.

"There are a lot of billboards out here," he says, not acknowledging my question.

"Too many. Why did you have to be from my least favorite state? By the way, I asked you if you'll tell me when we're getting there."

"Of course," he answers.

Where could he be going? The home for boys? That foster home? His old school? An old friend's house? I'm trying to figure out which of these Jeremy wants to revisit, but it's hard to read him. He doesn't talk much about the past. He only said he didn't like his foster home, he didn't like his school and he didn't like Connecticut. Nothing I can use right now.

"What are you coming here for?" I just say it. I've been driving awhile and I'm tired of the games.

"Dreams," he answers, "I'm looking for someone here."

This does not bode well. Not at all. Dreams? Looking for someone. I have come to Connecticut so he could find a figure from a dream? Is he looking for Elvis, Satan, the Sasquatch? He's been watching billboards, too. It might be Captain Crunch or Crazy Dave and the Morning Smile Brigade. What an excellent reason for me to take a day off work.

His face actually registers something. He returns from the vast nothing he's been wandering around to provide me with a little bit of reassurance. "Someone at the mall."

"At the mall?" I'm going to the mall to find somebody from Jeremy's dream. I must be getting close to whatever stupidity brought me here, so turning around isn't an option. I can only bask in the glow of my disapproval.

"Yes. You didn't find the legal pad? The old journal entries from when I was younger." Uh oh. This stings a little worse on account of the fact that I could have had the requisite information and decided not to take the drive at all in the first place.

"No. I didn't see those entries."

"Good. You wouldn't have come."

This is the man I love again. Capable of being perfectly clever and canny in pursuit of what he wants. It's something of a relief, because the cryptic weirdo who sat beside me in the car made me worry. I wondered how it was that this person was going to help make a world that he approved of out of the blasted cultural wasteland around him. I would be much more relieved were it not for the fact that we have come this far to go to a mall. This had better be one special mall.

It isn't. A large Best Buy, a Marshall's. Nope, nothing special here. He gets out and he surveys the parking lot. Is he looking for a car? He walks from car to car, each time looking at their windshields and nodding. He stops, looks around, and waits for somebody. Then, he moves to another section of the parking lot and does the same thing, then another afterwards. I don't bother to run after him, or ask what he's doing, because I feel like I would end up regretting it completely. Soon, he has scanned the entire parking lot, reading the things on everyone's windshield. I half expect him to say "okay, we can go now", but he ends up looking disappointed.

"Bad news on someone's windshield?" I ask.

"No. Please stop patronizing me."

"So, what ARE you doing roaming around the parking lot reading people's windshields?" I can't wait for the answer to this one. No matter what it is, it's gonna be good.

"I'm trying to see if somebody was here. Somebody who marks people's cars with newspapers," he says, "an old friend of mine."

"Well," I answer, "if he's been putting newspapers on people's windshields for this long, he can't expect mall security to never pick him up."

Jeremy kisses me and leads me into the mall. "These newspapers are fresh. He was caught recently. Maybe he's still being questioned by mall security."

"So he's being questioned by mall security. What do we do? I mean, besides get some chow at the food court and head home…"

Jeremy gets this scary "Eureka" look on his face. "I've got it. I need you to distract mall security, while I free General Lud."

I need you to distract mall security while I free General Lud. I will pretend I didn't hear that sentence, and yet somehow I know that I'm going to end up distracting mall security while Jeremy frees General Lud. Jeremy runs off ahead of me, while I have to figure out how I can get the attention of mall security. Far as I know, there's basically one good way to get the attention of mall security and that's shoplifting. But, I need to really get mall security's attention, so I need to find a provocative way to get mall security's attention via shoplifting.

I walk into the Victoria's secret and I pick out a pink bra and thong set. I discreetly walk into the dressing room. Why am I willing to do this? Because I love my boyfriend, because I want him to feel sane and because there might be something in this stupid excursion, there might be something worthwhile in Connecticut. I stuff my clothes into my purse and I emerge with a big, naïve grin on my face and the sales tag still on the bra and panties I'm wearing. I walk past the clerk and out of the Victoria's Secret almost nude. The girl shouts at me "miss, miss, miss! You haven't paid for that!"

"That's what I wore in!" I shout back. As humiliated as I am, I'm having fun now. When the clerk at the Victoria's Secret calls for mall security, a sixty something man with a medicine ball belly rushes in as fast as his basset hound body allows.

Out of the corner of my eye, I see Jeremy leading a smelly, bearded homeless man out of the mall running like hell. The security guard looks me over. Really looks me over. "Umm, miss, I'm sorry but you're…"

I look down at my unclothed state and I look surprise.

"Oh my god, you're right! I am so embarrassed!"

The Victoria's Secret clerk is really confused when I reach into my purse and pay for the lingerie I walked out in. The woman looks at me and has no clue what to say as I go into the dressing room and change back into my clothes. The security guard takes extra long returning to his post after that. It's very easy to confuse and frighten people in Connecticut. Especially with a little cleavage. I feel embarrassed, powerful and gorgeous at the same time.

I get to the car and the homeless man is freaking out.

"Shun the machines! Shun the machines! They'll destroy you; they'll turn you into one of them! They'll turn you into a robot! Shun the machines!" he screams.

"General Lud?" I ask Jeremy.

"Uh huh," he answers, seemingly not that disappointed by the fact that his friend is completely insane and apparently has never ridden in a car before.

"I'm Cass," I tell General Lud just to accentuate the fact that it won't matter to him.

"How…how do you do?" General Lud asks me. At least he's capable of saying something coherent.

"I am fine, General Lud," I reply as if I'm talking to a six-year old. I'm trying to remember what I have done to cause Jeremy to play such a malicious prank on me. On April Fools day I put peanut butter in his socks once, but that doesn't seem to be remotely of the same caliber malicious prank as this is. This seems to be a great innovation in the field of malicious pranks, the sort of thing that nets people awards.

"I hope you bought that bra," says Jeremy, "it looks REALLY good on you. The pink goes great with your skin color."

I give him one of my favorite glares. The one that shuts him up really quickly. My patience is almost nonexistent.

"Snakes are comin'" says General Lud, "you seen the snakes, ain't ya? I know you. You're Jeremy. It's been a long time, but I know you. More of us now. More of us can see what's on the page. More of us know the snakes are comin'. The jackal and the serpent king are on their way." I don't know what his words mean, but there's a great weight to them, a big cumbersome kind of truth. It bothers me immensely. It reassures me that this person had something to do with Jeremy's visions and the nightmares Jeremy wakes from.

"I've dreamt about the snakes," Jeremy tells him, "the snakes were stampeding across the plain full of garbage. Then I saw you on the mountaintop."

"The lightning must strike true. We got friends. A block or so, turn this corner, come see. We got friends. Some say we use the machines and we spread the message. Sometimes the message goes into the sky and it comes back down and it tells people what's on the page, but nobody listens. We got friends. Turn here!"

When in Rome…or in this case when in Bedlam. I turn the corner and there's a network of alleyways filled with dingy homeless people, some who wave at General Lud in the car. Some are cooking things on a fire; others are rooting through heaps of garbage. All of them have a lost look on their face, a lost look tinged with some kind of knowing, like the look on Lud's face. At the end of the alleyway, Lud motions for me to stop, and I stop of course. We all get out and a few homeless people come to meet us.

"Hi. I'm Leon," says one of them, a leader of sorts, he looks like he's actually bathed and speaks English, "I used to be an engineer, but then I heard what Lud had to say about the machines." He says this knowing that I have trouble accepting that anybody in this alleyway would be sane. It kind of helps, actually, to be reminded that everybody here had something or believes something.

"I'm Cass," I hold out my hand and he shakes it. His hands are covered in oil.

"This is Jeremy," says General Lud, "he's seen everything, too. He knows what's happening. He might help the lightning strike. Might need help though. You help him help the lightning strike. I think he's got ideas. You help him with the ideas."

"Sure thing." Leon grabs a pile of car parts and loads them into a wheelbarrow.

"They can help you with that, Leon," says Lud, "they can haul more parts in that thing. It won't hurt ya none. You can go and take these things to Jones. I'll come and you come. We can take these things to Jones and he can help Jeremy. I have seen Jeremy in the dreams. He's good. He's gonna help the lightning strike true."

Leon nods and loads the parts into the trunk. It feels good at least to be meeting people and to be going places here. It feels like less of a waste, even if I've driven here to haul car parts for sale. Leon and Lud get in the back, which is kind of a tight fit with the suitcases we have back there, but they manage. This time Leon is the one providing directions. Providing directions that are in between Lud's rants.

"No more voice. No more running, Jeremy," Lud rants, "No more mountaintop, it ain't safe there. Don't go to the mountaintop. Somethin' else is happenin', somethin' else happens so you do right and you let the lightning strike true. If it don't strike true, there'll be nothing but pain. The serpent king will bring pain. The jackal will devour. Don't forget."

That rings truer than a lot of the other ranting. Jeremy looks even more disturbed by it, like there was something he was missing. I don't see much myself, but I see that he did have to come here and maybe something will be done about the dreams and the feelings he has of powerlessness. Maybe he'll only kill when he wants to if he thinks this through to the end. I'm not shocked when Leon points out a warehouse.

"Is this Jones actually a person? Is he here?"

"Yup," says Leon, "this is where you find Jones. Don't you worry about that." He laughs. Even Lud laughs a little. I thought it would be scary to hear Lud laugh, but it isn't. It reminds me that no matter how far gone he is, the crazy man from the mall is actually a person.

Leon walks up to the warehouse door and rings a doorbell. First of all, I'm a little taken aback to find that this warehouse has a doorbell. Second of all, I'm surprised that this doorbell when pressed plays "Brick House" by the Commodores. Jeremy, Leon and I all find ourselves humming along. I have a feeling that Lud doesn't follow vintage funk. As the motto of this trip has fast become expect the unexpected, I expect the unexpected, and my expectations are still surpassed.

A young woman in a black geisha wig and kimono answers the door. A massive katana about half her size is sheathed at her side. She bows to Leon and Lud, and then rises, extending a hand to Jeremy.

"Reiko. And you are?"

"Umm, Jeremy." It's good to see that this place confuses Jeremy too. It's good to see somebody else overcome by the madness of Connecticut. Of the things Jeremy expected, one of them was probably not a girl who is about as authentically Asian as the Chinese food at Juan Sanchez's Happy Panda Palace on 128. Having walked a bit deeper into Wonderland today, I bow.

"Konichi-wa…"

"Very funny. Stand up." She offers a handshake and a look that reminds me that she's carrying a katana with a four foot blade at her side.

"Sorry, I'm Cass."

"Reiko. As I said. Jones is in, Leon. He's been expecting you and Lud." She doesn't make any more effort to make strangers feel acknowledged in spite of the geisha wear.

She leads us into the warehouse and we discover it to be a combination pool hall, bachelor pad and shrine to bad taste in the late 70s. The room is lit by multitudes of little tables with lava lamps on them and overhead disco balls. It is dominated at the center by a round, purple velvet couch overlooking a truly enormous plasma screen TV. A few feet away, angled to face the big TV is an expensive-looking pool table, custom made with purple felt instead of the standard green. The room explains the doorbell with astounding clarity. Although what explains the doorbell best is the man sitting on the giant couch, tossing an empty bottle of cough syrup on the floor as though it were a beer he just killed watching the football game. He's dressed a bit like the Tom Petty interpretation of the Mad Hatter in that video, but truth be told his face looks more like the actual Mad Hatter on account of his thin, sunken features and large nondescript triangle of a nose. All of this pimp paraphernalia belongs to a five foot tall one- hundred-something-pound white guy. He gives Leon the "one moment "sign as his cell phone rings. It rings out Carl Douglas' Kung Fu fighting. Now that I've gone down this crazy rabbithole, it seems somehow appropriate to have run into a kind of Mad Tea Party.

"Hello, Inscrutability Jones is on the phone," he says in a Southern tinged Isaac Hayes/ old bluesman kind of voice that is probably not an act.

"Amanda, you say? Nice to hear from a man who knows what he wants. Amanda it is. Thanks for callin'." Jones folds up his cell phone and Yoko gets out hers, concealed in a little holster in the folds of her kimono.

"Hi, Amanda?" she says, the girl she's calling having picked up the cell phone on the first ring, "Got a job. You know the guy. Yup, that guy. See ya later." Jones nods at Yoko and then stands, extending his hand to Jeremy.

"Inscrutability Jones, king of the Connecticut underworld. Any friend of Lud's is a friend of mine and I can only assume that you, sir are a friend of Lud's."

"Hi." Jeremy looks over at me and we are united in our confusion. Maybe he too wonders if this is in fact a strange dream.

Jones takes my hand and kisses it. "And you, pretty girl?"

"I'm Cass. That's Jeremy." As I introduce myself Jeremy begins to rock back and forth on his feet, embarrassed by not remembering to do the same when told.

"Very nice to meet you," says Jones, who turns to Leon, "what you got for me today? I was very pleased with last week's haul. You're damn good, Leon. Ain't seen nobody take the carburetor out of a car fast as you have."

"Well, you'll just have to wait and see, Jones," says Leon with a smile. Reiko takes a shopping cart that is propped up against the pool table and wheels it outside, joining him.

"He's a friend," Lud tells Jones, "he's gonna help the lightning strike. He sees the page and he's gonna break the machines, I think. I think he can do it."

"Yeah, he's a big guy. Don't look especially dumb, either. Not much of a talker, but he don't look like there's nothin' goin' on in his head. I think I can help him out. Any friend of yours is a friend of mine, General." Jones looks Jeremy over again and puts his hand on his chin.

"You know, if you gonna break somethin', you come to the right guy. Somethin', somebody, you come to the right guy. I'm somethin' of a jack of all trades, bein' the king of the Connecticut underworld and all. I might have some things for you."

"I've got money," Jeremy answers, trying to straighten up and look cool. It makes me realize that in spite of the fact that he's killed three hundred and something people, Jeremy hasn't even bought pot before. It's kind of funny watching him figure out just how he's supposed to deal with an actual criminal.

Leon and Reiko wheel in the car parts. I marvel at how fast they do it. There's about sixty pounds of the things in that shopping cart and it took them all of a minute. About a second per pound of car parts. The little portable junkyard they made causes Jones to light up and bounce to his feet. He walks up to the cart and eyeballs it.

"I'll give you a thousand newspapers and forty pounds of Vietnamese ramen." Leon looks to Lud, who shakes his head.

"No papers. You help him out," he tells Lud, "he's got a big fight, big fight ahead. Don't need no papers today, give him some weapons, something to help him split open the machines."

"I thought as much, General," Jones replies and he walks to a spot behind the huge TV, lifting up a trap door.

"Come on down to the basement. I got plenty of shit down here to help you do whatever you gotta do, kill whoever you gotta kill."

Jeremy, Reiko, Jones, Lud and I walk down the stairs underneath the trapdoor to find ourselves in something out of a James Bond movie. The warehouse's basement is huge, dominated at the center by a camouflaged helicopter equipped with a pair of machine guns. On the walls are armaments of all kinds, big guns, little guns, grenades, knives, battle axes, medieval lances, katanas, throwing stars, maces and flails, every implement of destruction imaginable. It reminds me what a big fight there is. Big enough maybe that all of this stuff won't even matter in the end. But I can't think like that. This guy is an edge, the most important one we have, maybe. The fact that he was upstairs swilling Robitussen, and is a pimp and an arms dealer who buys stolen car parts off of homeless people in exchange for old newspapers and ramen becomes moot. That's pretty strange, because pimping and selling helicopters is the sort of thing I usually don't forgive in people.

"I'm gonna be nice," says Jones, "I was gonna give Lud five hundred in newspaper, but, I guess store credit should go further in these exchanges. You got a thousand. Walk around, talk it over with the lady, then tell me what you like."

Jeremy says nothing in reply to all of this, but just looks around awestruck and sort of overwhelmed. Reiko puts her hand on my shoulder.

"This might take awhile," she whispers, "I think you could use an ice cream cone."

She's definitely right. I could certainly, beyond a shadow of a doubt use an ice cream cone. The suggestion just seems kind of weird coming out of Yoko's mouth. But, today I've developed a knack for going with the flow, and it's gotten us a thousand bucks in sundry armaments, so I don't take it as something strange.

"Yeah, I could use an ice cream cone."

"Cool, meet me outside."

I give Jeremy a kiss goodbye. "Where are you going?" he asks.

"Ice cream," I answer. He shrugs and I wait outside for Reiko.

The girl who comes out is unrecognizable. Under the geisha wig she has shoulder length blonde hair. She wears a Red Sox hat, a black blouse and a pair of denim shorts. She's damn cute and as I figured, not actually Asian. Her posture is far less stiff as she leads me out to her car, a black Mini Cooper, which is parked next to Jones' car. Jones' car is (not surprisingly) a big, red limo with a vanity plate that says "IDOSHIT". I can't help but laugh and she can't help but laugh too.

"He takes the pimp thing a little too far sometimes," she laughs.

"Kind of an understatement."

The ice cream place is a little one that looks like it's been around for fifty years. A tacky, plastic polar bear adorns the roof. I get a big mint chocolate chip cone, while Yoko opts for plain old strawberry. I eat a little fast as we sit and talk about how life is funny.

"How can you work for somebody that crazy?" I have to ask, "What do you do?"

"Don't get the wrong idea," she says, "I don't go out on jobs. I've been taking self defense classes since Jones found me on the street seven years ago. He would never send me out on a job that he intended for me to finish. My official position is Martial Arts Killing Machine."

"That must be fun."

"I've broken a lot of kneecaps, incurred a lot of sterility. Most Johns feel real sorry for not paying up when a strange Asian girl shows up and offers to give them a free vasectomy with her fist."

I shudder a bit. "But how can you work for somebody that crazy? How can you do that?"

"How can you love somebody crazy enough to run around with General Lud? How come you came to Connecticut? We do what we have to."

In my mind's eye, I watch Jeremy browse the room full of guns. We do what we have to. But I still think Connecticut is really fucking weird.

Mr. 400 Strikes

I've practiced shooting with these contacts in, and it's tough, but necessary. The mouth full of fake vampire fangs makes my elocution terrible, but I can work with it, too. Hell, it's better than my outfit was last time I was here, and I'm pretty certain that the two or three people here who might recognize me won't, so it's more than worth it. And I have to say, I love the shirt. Cass says she'll make another without the question mark when she knows I've hit 400. Her Reap appreciation is getting in the way a little, but I'm not going to scorn her for it and there is no sense making false claims. I've got twenty two more to go and I know that there are more than enough of those monsters out there to make it. I smile at the mocking imitation of Godless Jack in the mirror. A monstrous joke just like the real one, and cheaply done at that. It gets the message across. I do up the plaid shirt over the tee and get ready to check our supplies.

"Are you sure these are real military issue flashbangs?" Cass asks me, voice thick with skepticism.

"I think Jones knows his merchandise pretty well. He's scum, but I don't think he'd give us fakes."

"Cause otherwise, we're going to have to take down security and beat the cops to the Safe Zone."

"We're disguised, and that's not our car."

"Thank God," Cass mutters.

"There's a Camaro engine in the thing."

"The body however is a 79 Dodge Dart."

"Well, that way the cops won't think there's anything under the hood."

The money from all those feigned burglaries went remarkably far. I'd never bought a car for 140 bucks before, let alone a seventy five dollar shotgun. The crown prince of the Connecticut underground may be skuzzy, dishonest and addicted to any substance he can get through a funnel, but the bargains can't be beat. The duct taped plastic barrel makes me as nervous as Cass is about the flashbangs, but it gets through metal detectors. As do the pistols in their plastic sheaths. Allay your concerns, Lud said, or the thunder of God don't strike true. If the thunder of God don't strike true, then the earth shall be coated in steel and silicon and...allay your concerns or the thunder of God don't strike true. Faith, luck and figuring out what the fuck is that you're doing don't hurt either.

"Shotgun..."

"It's here. Survival knife?"

Cass pulls it from her red harlequin boots and even in my nervous state; I have to start stifling an erection. "Pistols?"

"Uh huh. The beeper?"

"Yup."

I find that the door has never felt so far away. Several states worth of desert seem stretch between it and the bedroom. I don't bother looking out the window because I know that the sky is an ominous blue-grey and there's nothing out there to make what I'm doing tonight any easier. Nothing out there is going to turn me into the superhero I'm posing as, no matter how many Dark Ones I've defeated and dirty little monsters I have kept from polluting the earth, this does not get any easier. The time has come to begin the splitting of the machine, to seek the path to the glorious rain of shrapnel that will purge the world of monsters.

There must be some kind of divine providence on my side since Cass puts the key in the ignition and the Paleolithic mass of scrap manages to pass for alive. Not only that, but it comes with a very satisfying rumble. Wonders never really cease sometimes. Cass is pretty astonished.

"Somehow he got a Camaro engine into this car."

"Well, it comes from Hartford's finest chop shop. Anything they make's pretty much guaranteed to get away from the cops."

She gives me the kind of dirty look that makes me want to apologize for something. I don't know what, but that look makes me know that there must be something.

"I shouldn't have eaten that last ice cream sandwich."

The dirty look vanishes and is replaced by confusion. She purses her lips. "Don't act so confident. It makes me nervous. Always makes me feel like I'm the only one who's scared and thinks we're gonna die. I know from your journal that's probably not true. So, please, don't act like it."

I lay my head on her shoulder and she remembers that when it comes down to it, I'm no good at speaking my mind. I can write things out, but I'm just no good at saying what I feel. I'm glad she knows I'm not that sure about this excursion. Head on her shoulder, in this ancient and hideous car, I feel a lot more safe and confident than I would in the good car, with my head high, charging into trouble.

"You do think we'll survive though, right?" What an absurd little boy I make right now in my Godless Jack costume, leaning on her so desperately. But, love inoculates us against embarrassment. I'm grateful I get a few more minutes to be vulnerable before I have to turn myself into an icon. An icon who can gun down a former Bundy winner in a room full of Reap kids without being trampled by the mass of thundering stupidity. Time to do the snakewalk. Try to reassure myself with its similarity to the word "cakewalk." I've also never found cakewalks particularly pleasant either.

I smell the Dark Ones and their ooze in the air as we get closer. I smell the branding of people's brains and the stench of hot metal. Where is the grey matter? Where is the skin? Oils of all kinds, bestial musk. Don't tell yourself something stupid like "I'm fighting for the future". You're fighting for these people to have options. Even if you hate them, hate them as people, fight for the option to hate organically instead of hating the inorganic in everything. Hatred and resentment without compassion is animalistic. Hate compassionately. Don't be an animal, too easy to control. All those bastards with brains like dogs aren't going to have them much longer.

Don't trust the smell anyway. It's a metaphor. It's your way of rationalizing it. It's all just an attempt to make sense of the insanity around you. It's a dialogue between neuroses. All it is. The time has come to move in a straight line. Strike true. If the thunder of God don't strike true, then…think of Cass, think of the America you do this for. Don't think of the enemy and the stench. She swears to me it's just how I read the horrors I see, how I process it. Perceptual device to make moral decisions simple and straightforward instead of naturally ambiguous as is the nature of a…but then again, I smell the oil and the musk of beasts and the disgusting black… never mind what's waiting to be born. You are not at this club to purify anything. You are here to send a message. Ignore the face of the enemy on your own face as it grins at you derisively. It is in the nature of enemies to mock, to be a dark reflection of your…I have a shotgun. I will think like a man who has a shotgun. You son of a bitch, I have a shotgun. Convincing. Really.

I wish the drive had been longer. I step out and get into line right behind a couple of Bundy girls checking each other's makeup.

"I prefer the Sound and the Fury, actually."

"Haven't read any Faulkner yet."

"You're shitting me."

"Nah, I just haven't gotten to it. And to be honest, it depresses the fuck out of me. Decaying mansions in the South, families falling apart, it's all so…"

"Reap is tragedy. The tragedy of lost humanity and moral confusion, Brit. Faulkner is so Reap. Poe had something going, torture, ghosts, murder. The apocalyptic charm is there, but too much is post-mortem, he's already dead, and Reap preaches that there's no sense fixating on the dead. And there's too much remorse in it. Everything's already gone on most of the time, or else the murder's not the point. It comes down to the guilt and the haunting and the poetic justice. The crime scene tape is the moment of discovery, and sometimes the moment of ecstasy, the murder itself, and the knowledge that it WILL happen again. Faulkner's like that. Poe lives in the graveyard, and Faulkner the slaughterhouse. He saw that America was going to start eating itself alive, and there wasn't shit people can do. Don't you see what we're doing tonight? Bait. We're acknowledging that we, as human beings, as Americans, are fuckin' bait. And what do we do about it?"

I'm interested. It always surprises me when people are actually aware of all this. Because of the status quo, it's so easy to think you're the only one who knows that the shit is going down and that nobody else is aware of it all. After all, how could intelligent people who aren't cattle, robots or completely feral let things be like this? Maybe it won't be so hard reaching some of these people. Might walk away with some respect or understanding from this crowd yet. Brit shrugs and her well read friend continues on.

"Latch onto something. Some absent glimmer of love. Reap is the absent glimmer. An ironic violence against the natural violence of living. To love and exalt in the blood, in the condition of postmodern destruction is the thing. It's the only logical response we have. And it's a delicious one. We're the only ones smart enough to see that everything around is shit. The world, America, our souls, it's all gone to shit. And if everything's gonna be shit, you need to be smart. You need to be the ecstatic pig that rolls around in all that shit, takes it in and in this fuckin' void, gets some experience, excitement and understanding. Decay, absence, mute witness, oppression, it's all fuckin' Reap. You've gotta read the Sound and the Fury, cause fuckin' Faulkner has all the shit figured out and shows us that the brutality and the madness are facts of life and dealing with it is the only way to sleep at night, come every time you get fucked and love your television."

Well, I still have a shotgun. It's so much harder when intelligent people believe stupid things. They can give themselves much better reasons to do so, even to the point of immutability. Everything she had to say made sense, every single nihilistic, chickenshit word of it. The kind of arguments that have been used to support every sort of counterproductive repackaged social paralysis that has come off the rock station assembly line for the past forty something years. Why is it the knowledge that we're all going to shrivel up and die makes people want so much to shrivel up and die? Wonder if they'll even appreciate the assassination now. Well, she's right about one thing, society leaves us no recourse but to exalt in violence.

No, scratch that. Note to self: I will not exalt. I will count and mourn the dead. Mr. 378. They will count the dead to exalt. I will count the dead to remember the trail of blood that blazes toward freedom. I will know each face that has made the sacrifice for a saner society. I swear none have died in vain.

The line moves slowly but it moves. I feel a catwalk beneath my feet taking me there. Glory, freedom, victory. The line pushes me in and my fingers twitch. None will die in vain if I start shooting now. Only glory if we shoot now. Freedom, victory...shoot now. Too soon, don't exalt. Psyching yourself out. Look around and listen. Atmosphere. Blood red neon again. Expensive, gaudy, brilliant blood red neon. Expensive, gaudy, brilliant costumes. Things will be okay if you don't make a mess. Their ignorance won't hurt you anymore. Their ignorance might not hurt them. Show them who is strong and who is weak and they will shun the weak like the animals they are. Just remind yourself what happens if it all works out. The soulless automated chatter runs together. Flocks of winged breeders buzz around the little blondes who will further the line and bring forth hordes of screaming, monstrous...not on your own anymore. More than one part of the plan, God, think of the plan. Not their plans, yours. Yours...go in and be inconspicuous for awhile. When the guest of honor introduces himself you'll...just forget the stink and concentrate.

I walk in and breathe a sigh of relief because I'm a step closer to doing something indubitably right. The sort of thing where denial and a labyrinth of moral ambiguity don't get in the way. Everybody who kills kills the wrong people. Any of these girls, dressed up and dancing and absorbing the horrors brought down by their idols is vulnerable to attack by the Dark Ones, by any of those devils they worship, and if it came down to it, by me. Don't zigzag, don't miss the target. I've gotta strike true, Cass said it, Lud said it. Strike true, kill the monsters and the blasphemers and the ones that tore civilization apart and left everybody with this. I'm led to believe that all the vessels and all the empty skins don't matter half as much as those who would cause the real damage. It's no wonder so many of these girls regard themselves as prey. I have a shotgun, and if I just fire it, look at the target, let it loose, what was once a person becomes a mess.

I never think of the fragility, really. Usually just about how easy it is for these psyches to get supplanted. They all look so spindly as they dance, their bone so easily broken, their skin so penetrable. That's why the word psychopomp replaces killer so much these days. With a knife or a gun or something blunt and hard, a man can be a messenger of death, a force of nature. The simple, tender bodies sweat under lights, tense up over just the exertion of dancing, grow unstable with just a few drinks. That's why all the spooky masks, witch doctor tricks to scare away the spirits that will take them. I could take them. Click click buzz click buzz click buzz no meat no blood. That's why they no longer strive to be human and accept the circuitry so easily. If they knew that wires cut as easy as veins, they might not think to be machines. They might stop and think about what would make them less fragile. Maybe if they bothered to say no to all the potential agencies of destruction instead of inviting them in and just accepting that they exist they could be something more. Perhaps even something good.

A bunch of the kids are watching the door, and are ready with applause at the entrance of Penny Dreadful and the Aberrations. Tonight she wears an elegant silk kimono slit down the side and a geisha wig. They go surprisingly well with her black bondage boots. Funny that the band never dresses up, no matter how far her outfit goes. She, like Ian Sterling is one of those people made to be the center of attention wherever she goes. I try to erase the fact that I am not from my mind. It doesn't quite disappear. I feel like I should be and it's scary and exhilarating all at once. It's not a feeling I've ever known before. I'm grateful for the PA, because otherwise I'd feel sick.

Everybody's too shy to go up to ask her and ask for autographs or compliment her latest album or attire. Instead, they move away. People are as scared of celebrities as they are intrigued by them. Something to remember, maybe. A line of roadies brings in the instruments and sets them up on a makeshift stage that rises via not-too-shocking technical wizardry from the center of the dancefloor. They're surprised though, even the ones who'd seen it happen. A display of the godlike potency of fame, and a reminder of how far above them she actually is. Life is barely livable when you can see through it with such painful clarity. I wish that I were entertained and not just full of smirking revulsion. At least she seems to mean what she sings, a song about wishing the gore would spill out into the streets, that the blood would wash over everything and anoint it. Careful what you wish for.

Pfenniger walks in and there's an even bigger fanfare. He's a hair short of five feet, bald and has a gaze that never meets anyone else's. He seems to be doing math in his head and counting his fingers. Kind of a typical collector, except for the volume of his kills and the brutality. Power drill through the eyes and then taking their fingers, sometimes all five, sometimes just a couple. There was a sum he was trying to reach he said. Voices told him he needed six hundred sixty six fingers to keep out the host of hell. He didn't really seem to get why everybody was praising him or what he was doing here, although it was said he had a speech prepared. I feel almost bad for needing to put an end to a pathetic little man like this, but he is a Bundy winner, he is at Le Couteau and this would have to scare sense into somebody.

First thing they do is lower down a "piñata" from the rafters. Their definition of "piñata" is a naked, stoned prostitute which a number of Geins and Gacys gather round to whack with a bat. Of course, the guest of honor gets the first strike. Smash it open. Blonde, not quite mechanical on the inside yet. Smash it open don't let it get infected. Take your turn show them what's what. Smash it and remove the workings. Monsters. Fucking barbarians. Hurting that girl there's no reason to hurt her go to your fucking peaceful place don't need you here don't fuck it up for me I don't need you to fuck it up for me you go you go you go! Calm down. Work to be done. I'm not going. Stay the course don't listen to him. You and me, we're heroes. Another voice drowns out the old one. Sounds like me. Sounds like better me. Sounds like lightning.

Penny stops playing and greets Pfenninger with a hug and a kiss on the cheek. He sort of blushes and sort of pushes her out of the way to reach the podium. I beep the boys in the truck to start the PA soon and to tell them that Pfenninger has started speaking. I pull out the shotgun, shove a Manson in front of me out of the way, and I do my business. Parts of his face move to other parts of his face. Time freezes and I feel enormous as I look at the surrealist painting I've made out of the guest speaker. Surrealism gives way to the postmodern nightmare; identity deconstructed, deconstructed again, until gone. Utter loss of human context. Look away. Go someplace safe. All I need is a pair of hands. Fuck you! FUCK YOU! Fuck you back I have to see this. Pieces fly, people duck flying teeth and ribbons of flesh. Dyed black and purple hair get streaks of reddish brown and pink. Penny Dreadful screams. Her band screams. Everybody screams, but nobody moves to do anything. I reveal the Mr.400 shirt and then the boys stream in MY little speech.

"This is your urban legend," my garbled and technologically manipulated voice begins, "an idle speculation of Mr. Sterling's that must not exist because it's so far beyond the scope of your microscopic, television choked imaginations. Expand your imagination. 380 corpses can't be wrong. Sorry for taking the title a little early, but the last 20 will come and they will come from your number if you refuse to change..."

Wide applause. The bassist and the drummer of the Aberrations are beginning to keep time. Penny signals her guitarist and he starts up the song she was singing. She sings along to my message, making a kind of perverse medley out of it that the Reap kids can't help but dance to. I holster the shotgun and watch as everyone begins to groove to it, bobbing their heads, undulating and twisting like charmed snakes. A quiet stampede of charmed snakes. My message plays through all of this and even the kids who aren't dancing are kind of bopping in place to the grisly affair.

"This is Mr. 400; your culture of violence is dead..."

"Your culture of violence is dead," the bassist sings along adding rhythm to the chant.

"Your days as mechanistic hedonism machines are over. Mr. 400 will make sure of that..."

"Mr.400, yeah mr.400, yeah, mr.400," the guitarist chimes in.

"The Bundy winners, the soldiers of Kali, of Samhain, of Hades of Thanatos..."

"Of Samhain, of Hades, of Thanatos," the drummer contributes. They've found the phrases to repeat as Penny sings her song and my well prepared apocalyptic message plays on. My well prepared apocalyptic message that Reap kids dance feverishly and make out to, almost forgetting that I just walked in and killed one of their idols. It dawns on me that intimidating them will take more than this and require a more organized statement. It turns out I'm an even worse terrorist than I am a pharmacist. I wish I could see an out.

"Are shallow reflections of death as a fact of life. They are not cancer, AIDS or car accidents. Mr. 400 is cancer. Mr.400 is the fact. Mr. 400 will strike like lightning from God and crumble your false idols into dust. Mr. 400 will bring the killers and the liars and the hives of silicon maggots that spawn rotten devils to justice..."

"Yeah! Mr. 400! Fuckin' A!" some imbecile in the back shouts. The buzzing, the stench, the smell of oil in their veins is becoming nauseating. There must be a way out of this, there must be. I have to stay and hear the message out and keep it in their heads, if it's getting there at all, but it's becoming extremely difficult to do so. This place is too stimulating. It's spinning; it's insane, it's wrong. I want to go, but I have to see this through and can't lose this attack to their ignorance. They are here. They are moving in them. Filthy cunts, robots. Smell the bug shit inside them. Hive mothers robots filthy cunts breeders. Break the fucking machines stay the course stay the course strike true break the fucking machines break the fucking cunt machines break it now!

"Those who stand with the armies of Satan will find themselves treated as unmercifully as they might treat the innocents, the lambs of God. Mr. 400 is here and those who ignore him are not only dead, but damned as well. Mr.400 is lightning from God, the flame of purification. End transmission."

I breathe a sigh of relief until I realize that the guys in the truck are playing this in a loop. They aren't listening at all, they've fallen into an ecstatic religious trance, soaking up the blood and chaos and the chanting in an absurd pagan ritual. What do I do? The noise and the confusion are getting to be too much, and they have lost receptivity to the dance. The only way to do this is to stop the music, to cut off the noise and the ecstasy. I begin thinking over what I know to be a very bad idea. It seems like a very bad idea, until I can feel a hand on my shoulder and feel the stinking breath of a drunken college kid in my face.

"I fuckin' love you man, you just fuckin'…"

I shove him over, and I take out the two pistols. I know that Cass would be shouting if I hadn't told her not to say anything. I put a slug into the drummer, and the panic resumes. Nobody sees that coming. Blood spurts out of his head wound and a girl near the stage dives forward desperately. As the tiny hole in his head ejaculates his last bits of life, she lets it fall onto her face like the slut she is and the girlfriend she brought with her laps up the splatter of rockstar essence. The girls near the shotgun blast scoop Wayne Pfenninger bits out of their hair and feed them to one another. Fucking high art.

The bassist puts down his bass and in a fog of tears and rage, he screams "fuck!" I don't know what comes over me. The drummer was enough. Should have been enough. Proves the point. No. Still not taking it seriously. That girl slathered the man on her, wears blood from the headshot proudly. They're not gonna get it, but I still have to try. Two in the chest, falls over onto the drummer, their bodies slam down onto the drum kit. There's a cymbal crash. Gory punch line. Noise wakes me up. Fuck! The attack has lasted all of five minutes and I've killed Pfenninger, the drummer and now the bassist. Still nobody gets it.

Before I have any time to react, the room fills with blinding radiance and I know damn well that it's time to run for the door. Cass must have gotten the flashbang ready when I brought down the drummer. I can feel Cass bump into me as we both head for the exit, she stumbles a bit and I prop her back up. Jones definitely didn't fuck me over, that's for sure. The shotgun works great, the pistols fire, and the flashbangs are most certainly military issue. We have to hide in the dark of the parking lot to get our dazzled vision back and be prepared to drive.

We leap into the dirt cheap car, and hope that it will start this time, too. And it does. What a stroke of luck. We gun it before anybody can get a plate and speed our way through a bunch of side streets. Our speeding is in fact quite moot since nobody's in the parking lot and inside it's total chaos, but we feel especially paranoid now that we overstepped our bounds just a little. Cass has nothing to say, but "fuck, fuck, fuck…" Which I guess summarizes the situation pretty well. But, on the other hand, we are getting away with it. I don't really know what to say to Cass at this point, or if there is a good explanation. It's one of those things about being crazy (which I've gotten better at admitting to being), not being able to provide explanations that anybody would understand. The moment makes so much sense, but the next day is just a mess. You can't really apologize for the moment making sense, any more than anyone will apologize to you for how society doesn't make any sense.

We abandon the car a quarter mile from home, stopping to pour gasoline over our costume pieces. Wonder of wonders, we get home okay. All I can say is, "well, that could have gone better." I don't feel like lightning from God, I don't feel like cancer. Cancer can't choose or make mistakes. I cannot judge whether my accident is the particular accident everyone needs. God's wrath and my wrath look a little too similar sometimes and it's disconcerting. It's altogether not right. Lightning must strike true.

Lunch Date

I have never been on television before this morning, although I couldn't see my face beneath the harlequin mask, and most of the focus was on Jeremy as he turned Wayne Pfenninger's head into pink, gooey bits. It made me feel grateful that I followed Reap and had seen a lot of crime scene recordings because otherwise I think I might have ended up feeling very, very, very sick. Amazing how the news is no longer squeamish about slo-mo replays of a guy getting blasted in the head with a shotgun.

The speech Jeremy wrote for just those at the club now echoed over everybody's TV set. I didn't know if it was a success or a failure or what, but I had to smile as I mouthed the words along with it.

"This is your urban legend, an idle speculation of Mister Sterling's that must not exist because it's so far beyond the scope of your microscopic, television-choked imaginations. Expand your imagination. 380 corpses can't be wrong. Sorry for taking the title a little early, but the last 20 will come and they will come from your number if you refuse to change. I am Mr. 400. Your culture of violence is dead. Your days as mechanistic hedonism machines are over. Mr. 400 will make sure of that. Your Bundy winners, the soldiers of Samhain, of Kali, of Thanatos are shallow reflections of death as a fact of life. They are not cancer, AIDS or car accidents. Mr. 400 is cancer. Mr.400 is the fact. Mr. 400 will strike like lightning from God and crumble your false idols into dust. Mr. 400 will bring the killers and the liars and the hives of silicon maggots that spawn rotten devils to justice. Those who stand with the armies of Satan will find themselves treated as unmercifully as they might treat the innocents, the lambs of God. Mr. 400 is here and those who ignore him are not only dead, but damned as well. Mr.400 is lightning from God, the flame of purification. End transmission."

It sort of makes me want to laugh. Sort of. I don't even bother to ask my very tired boyfriend what he thinks. I'm pretty scared, but I'm not the only one. It's something of a moral victory for the people who are scared all the time. Nobody gets scared at the club, but everywhere else people get scared. Anybody who tries to walk home alone at night gets scared, everybody who turns on the news gets scared, but the people at the club never had before. It feels fair now. But, I don't know what to think about the drummer and the bassist. I don't know if that part was fair, I understand, but I don't know if it was fair. Makes glad that everyone's shocked, because if they weren't, it would be too much to bear, it would be a waste of two lives.

The news is interviewing some of the kids at Le Couteau, referring to them as "the witnesses to this bizarre tragedy". Makes me feel sort of proud. Not only am I on television, but I'm closely affiliated with a "bizarre tragedy".

MURDERLAND | Garrett Cook

Some wording on their part. I was expecting "desperate act of terrorism" instead. By the definition of the word that's what it is, but no, we're a bizarre tragedy, like some little girl trapped in a drainage ditch or something. I should know by now that I can't expect them to be quite that straightforward. We need to take what we can get anyway.

The interviews start with a fat Manson.

"You never expect crazy sh-t like this when you're at the club just minding your own business and dancing and having a good time. You don't think that it's not you know, a safe place anymore. I can't believe that the club's not, ya know, safe now. It's just really weird."

The interviewer moves on to a thin, serious looking girl who was dressed as a Bundy girl last night.

"When you really think about it, this Mr.400 is something we should have expected a long time ago. It's just like 9/11. In certain ways, you can say that Reap is very volatile. Of course, sooner or later somebody is going to end up turning a gun on somebody else. How could we be surprised? Reapers have all kinds of moral paradigms. They can be unpredictable and sometimes have been known to quite brutally pass judgment on things. Sooner or later, Reap was going to end up passing judgment on itself. It's inevitable. He's just Ultra-Reap, more Reap than Reap. He's everything that we're about, and he reminds us that we need to stop and shake things up sometimes. His exact moral tenets might not make a whole lot of sense, but it's free speech. He has every f---ing right to kill for them."

Now I feel extremely glad that Jeremy isn't up to see this, and of course the inevitable "two wrongs don't make a right" lecture from some expert. Probably the expert I'm meeting today at the House of Pizza. I feel outraged, I feel glad that that this ended up being a big story and I feel glued to it. Maybe in part because I can't believe and more than that, that on some level at least, it ended up working. Of course, they move onto other witnesses who don't have a goddamn clue what it was about.

"That dude's got some style. He just goes and walks right in and he kills a Bundy winner in front of a whole club full of people. Then to get everybody's attention again, he shoots the drummer and the bassist from the Aberrations. And if this guy's that close to nailing four hundred people, he's definitely cool in my book. Not even Jack would kill a Bundy winner in public. He's just so Reap! Everybody else looks all Veinte like they can't spray the red nowhere."

Jesus. Poor traumatized kids. They seem so devastated. I wonder if polite society could really feel sorry for any of them. Well, polite society probably does feel sorry for them, but for a whole different reason than that. I wonder how I could have been one of them for so long without hating myself for it. Gotta wonder how I can forgive myself now. How long could I say "I was young and vulnerable"? Seven years ago, when the trial was on, and everything was splitting open, it would have been an excuse. But for so long after following it, I still kept on thinking it was a good idea. That kind of devotion's not a phase, it's adopting a lifestyle. My excuse went the way of theirs long ago. If Reap is in fact a damnable offense, then I am damned without a doubt. I'm about to shut it off when I remember that Penny Dreadful was there. A Reap celebrity is here to talk about the first serious assault on Reap. Am I morbid? Yes, I am. I am, after all, Ultra Reap.

"I am sad to lose my bandmates. Scotty and Razor were nice guys, talented musicians, and close friends to me. But here's the thing; if killing is right, it's right, if killing is wrong, then it's really wrong. We can't say that because someone we love was killed, then this killing is wrong. Everybody's loved by somebody; every victim turns somebody else into a victim too. So, if I say that this Mr.400 is a lunatic or some kind of deviant who stands against the things that I believe, then I'm a hypocrite. I'd be like the pigs in Animal Farm saying that "all animals are equal, but some animals are more equal than others". If this guy did this, he's one of us or he isn't. He either has the same rights Godless Jack and Hacksaw Sally have or Godless Jack and Hacksaw Sally don't have those rights. America is we know it can't run without equal rights. If somebody wants to use these rights to challenge us, to provoke us to think, or to show us what they perceive to be our folly, we have to let them. There's no middle ground about this, everybody's a person, and everybody's a corpse. That's what Mr.400's about, and that's what Reap's about. In the end we're all in the ground and we're all worm food. There's no debate. Mr.400 is Reap, and if he's Reap, he's one of us, and if he's one of us, he has the right to kill any one of us, and if somebody gets him, perish the thought, then that guy has the right too. Scotty, Razor, I love you guys. Next album's for you two, and I'll belt it out real nice. Yo, Mr.400, if you're out there watching, I miss my friends and my bandmates but you're human and I love you. If you're out there God, take care of Scotty and Razor and Mr.400, k?"

I never realized how strange it is when celebrities are actually mature. I knew that at the end of what she said, she'd be crying, and she is. The mascara drips and it looks like she's literally crying her eyes out. But it's not fake. It's not a celebrity tantrum, not Pastor Tommy Simmons or any of his kind. She believes every word of what she said and what she said isn't bullshit or dogma or a total joke or anything. I'm so shocked that I don't even notice that the controversial Mr.400 is behind me on the bed, wide awake. He takes me completely by surprise when he starts speaking, something I don't expect out of him for a few more hours.

"That Penny Dreadful seems like she might actually be a pretty cool chick."

Which should startle me more: a.) that Jeremy is wide awake out of the blue b.) That Jeremy approves of a speech given by a Reap icon or c.) That he used the words "pretty cool chick". The whole effect is that of a middle aged Jewish accountant saying "Yo, G that Josef Goebbels is tight!" My confused, bewildered and horrified response is a raised eyebrow and a curled lip. It looks like Elvis finishing up the New York Times Saturday crossword. Jeremy doesn't react to this at all, but instead gets up, half naked, and walks to the kitchen.

"Is it too late for pancakes?" he shouts.

"You can't think like that," I shout back, "it's never too late for pancakes." I look at the clock and it turns out that it IS too late for pancakes. I've been so caught up in all the coverage that I've lost track of time. I'm meeting Ian for lunch in ten minutes. Jeans, bra, t shirt in a minute and a half. I'm good. I sigh, remembering how much Jeremy hates Ian. He hates hates hates Ian, it says in his journal. I wonder how to bring this up without slighting him. Will I still be part of this team if I spend time with the enemy? The specific rules of team 400 have not yet been laid down, but I'm pretty sure this is a violation of them. Tail between your legs, pure humility. Don't let anyone feel betrayed.

"Jeremy," I shout into the kitchen, "I'm meeting Ian for lunch. I know that-"

He comes out of the kitchen, interrupting me with a quick kiss. God that man moves fast. Freak.

"Okay. Come back with some good gossip, alright?"

"Okay. Sure. Are you feeling okay?"

"Yeah," he answers, "I feel something a lot better than okay, actually."

"Powerful? Vindicated?"

"Satisfied."

That's definitely a new one, but hopefully, we can roll with it. I can only think of few nonsexual circumstances in which satisfied has been a part of Jeremy's vocabulary, so I'll take it and feel quite content with it. It's also good to know that he isn't infuriated with my rendezvous with an alien-breeding cyborg propagandist or whatever Jeremy thinks he is. My mother always said that "changed man" is an oxymoron, but I believe he's moving toward stability, good judgment and all those things that are the opposite of the brunt of our task. I have to believe it. I have to believe I can take the place of other voices in his head. I feel good when I get in the car and start off for the House of Pizza. I feel good and useful and important. As if I'd been on the news for something other than being an accessory to murder.

Ian is at the table in the back that he always insists on being seated at. Every time he needs to have that table. I've seen him politely wait for people sitting there to finish their food or the waitress to finish cleaning, but I've never seen him sit anywhere else. He refuses to sit in the front because he's afraid of people seeing him and recognizing him. He refuses to sit in the middle because other guests can overhear his conversation. Yes, there are three other tables in the back, but Ian can't make use of any of these three. Two of them are next to windows, and he doesn't like sitting by windows. Maybe it has to do with his privacy issues, maybe he's somehow afraid for life, I couldn't say. The third has the initials of an ex-girlfriend carved into it. For these reasons, there is nowhere else you can be graced by the presence of Reap expert and celebrity Ian Sterling. I'm starting to sound like Jeremy sometimes, but he's not half so bad a guy as Jeremy thinks he is. I wish Jeremy would be able to see where he's coming from, even if it's nowhere like where he is. At least he didn't make a face or look worried or huff or sigh when I told him who I was meeting with, so as I said it could be worse, but Jeremy's opinion is already sort of seeping in, and I need to fight it off. I don't feel like looking down on him right now, because Ian for some reason isn't fashionably late, not to mention he looks like a man who just saw a random psycho shoot half a rock band a few feet away from him. Ah, that explains it. Now Ian gets to look down on Jeremy and think he's a crackpot. It will be so much less complicated now that the disdain is a two way street.

"I'm fifteen minutes late, right?" I ask, worried about Ian showing up on time for anything.

"Only five, actually." His denim jacket is placed on the seat next to him. The circles under his eyes look like badly applied makeup instead of what I know they actually are. I search his face for signs of what might be wrong in spite of already knowing quite well what it is.

"I caught the news." I don't feel like talking about it, and I don't know if he will either, but it somehow seems polite to acknowledge the so-called tragedy. It's rude to ignore when something bad happens to a friend, even if for you it was something good. He nods gravely and takes a sip of his iced tea. Then he puts his forehead in his hands as if he's praying for the strength to cry in public or the strength not to cry in public. I don't want to hear him cry, I'm not sure that I can muster the kind of respect it takes to put energy like that out there. He's distraught, I'm sympathetic and I really hope that's where we'll leave things. I hope that this lunch can be pleasant somehow.

"Did you ever see something that makes you feel like you're going to hell just for watching it?" I should hesitate, but I don't, I can't. I feel it far too strongly.

"Yes."

"When it was all over, I went home and cried. I don't think I've stopped for more than twenty minutes at a time. It's like that time's just for catching my breath. But I think I'll be fine through lunch, I like these lunches, Cass."

He feels faded and skeletal, awestruck, traumatized and maybe even gone for good. I wonder if Jeremy killed more of Reap than he thought he did during the raid. I wonder how big a part of Reap Ian is or will be. I wonder if he'll come back from wherever it is this whole affair's left his head. This is the face of a victim, a dead man, someone whose way of life might have been taken from him. If it's not a good way of life, is it okay to take it away?

"I couldn't understand it all, Cass, how I could witness something so huge and beautiful. I wish you'd been there to see it all. The blood, the terror, the excitement. We had thought at first that it was only art when the PA came on and he killed Wayne Pfenninger. But art can't be that amazing. That was the statement when the bassist and the drummer went down. No more rhythm. It had stopped cold, stagnated. It was fate that brought down Buddy Holly. He couldn't feel the honest-to-god pulse of life that Elvis and Roy Orbison would get at. This Mr.400 reached into the sky and yanked down that plane, dashing it against the ground. This Mr.400 took culture into his own hands. I haven't witnessed anything this big since I made a fake press badge and watched them bring Jack into the courtroom. I've never been frightened at le Couteau before, but I should have known. Reap is tragedy. Danger is everywhere. Even in the womb children die. That's what it was. In the safest place…"

I feel lucky when the waitress interrupts Ian's mortified and worshipful rant.

"What'll you have?"

Normally he would have been incensed, but not today. He doesn't mind in the least that he was interrupted smack of the middle of some insane twelve hour epiphany. Ian's a man who believes in "the sanctity of the word" (as he often puts it), but his epiphany isn't being relished nor are the words of his rants and the thoughts behind the words. Amazing how a man, especially a man like Ian, can be defeated and ecstatic at the same time. He's completely still before ordering. He pauses for too long. Should I feel miserable for making an old friend so sick?

"Two slices of pepperoni, ham, sausage, bacon and meatball. I think you should put some garlic on that too. Green peppers, that's it. And..."

"The works you mean?"

"Are there onions on the works?"

She looks at him like he just asked her what number came between three and five.

"Yeah, naturally."

"No onions. Everything else then, unless you put pineapple on it. Two slices of the works with no onions. Make it three actually. And a coffee."

I get the feeling that I'm watching a man's nerves try to reconnect themselves. Life is getting harder and harder to process. I reflexively say "I'll have the same," not even thinking about what he's ordered.

"We have a six-slice pizza," says the waitress.

"We're fine with the slices," Ian answers curtly, and the girl walks off, wondering exactly how much of what we've been smoking.

"I don't how to write about this," he tells me. I don't blame him. Christ, I wouldn't know either. I don't what to say. I just hope that he'll talk himself through this and reach some sort of logical conclusion. I think it's a matter of waiting. I suddenly remember what Jeremy said about trying to get some information off of him. It appears to be crumbling. He's about as coherent as Lud and as emotionally present as Inscrutability Jones. I suppose he might to try taking his own life, or turning things around and acting like he's seeking canonization. Maybe he will do both. Maybe he will end up wallowing in excess, since after all this man who found something dirty about two slices of cheese pizza on a Saturday afternoon is about to consume half a barnyard. Maybe Jeremy will get his wish and I'll come home with the words of a dead, fat beatified Ian. Some recon. My heart sinks when I realize that there might not be enough sense in Ian for a word of sense. I don't feel like playing spy.

"I feel a bit like Jack London," he says, "excited that mankind might be returning to nature, striking up some kind of bargain. Hoping that maybe more than those few with the brains to think what I think already will have the brains to get together and start to make everything at least a bit better. "

What do I say to that? "It's huge."

I find myself really wondering whether Ian is ready to know everything. How can you get the notion of rebelling against something but not know what the rebellion's about or that it's against things you stand for and even proliferate? Reap is tragedy, that's true. The tragedy of a rapture that nobody will participate in, an unattended apocalypse. When the greatest authority on a subject in existence fails to sense that it's coming apart at the seams and failing to function as a part of society, that's a very bad sign. Perhaps even a sign of imminent destruction. He seems at some level to like what's happening; it's just a shame that he doesn't understand it at all. The difference between shaking something up in order to make it more risqué and violent and seeking to destroy it for the common good is just about completely lost to him. The more he speaks, the more ignorant he seems and the more scared for him I get.

The slices of pizza are massive, yet barely visible beneath a jungle of green peppers and several heaps of meat. Ian doesn't seem deterred in the least. I want to warn him that it might be a bad idea to introduce his stomach to this food before he has any others. Looking at the man across from me's state of mind; I'm pretty damn sure he hasn't indulged in a healthy breakfast. It also occurs to me that this isn't the time for meddling, so I take a big, oily, juicy, crunchy, over-stimulating bite. The first of what will probably be around thirty. But, it might not be such awful fare for the intent of returning vital signs to an utter carcass of a man. I watch Ian devastate the first slice in three or four bites, being rid of it in only a matter of seconds. Sauce and grease are all over his chin, making him look like a cross between a three year old and an extremely sloppy vampire.

In the middle of his second slice (which this time he eats like his typically fastidious self with a fork and knife) his cell phone rings. He stares at it like I've never seen him stare at it before, like it's just started talking and has told him that the pants he's wearing make his ass look too big. It takes him four rings to pick it up, and even when he does so, he looks genuinely confused by it. His hello takes a long time, but after it comes out, he's fine. He heaves a sigh and makes a face when he finds out who's on the other end of the line.

"What have you got, Hausmann? I'm at lunch relaxing following one of the most intense nights of my life, so unless Hacksaw Sally was spotted at the Vatican fucking the I-80 Roadflare in the ass with a poolcue, I'm really going to have to sit it out. Fucking context, Hausmann. Last night was huge. Its width in cultural scope is equal to the width of your fat ass. Well, maybe not as big as your fat ass, but damn close. I think you've most likely got two things: jack and shit. But, if I don't take your tip, Miranda will get it. So, tragically, I'm gonna have to give you the time of day or lose my place in line. So give it to me, Hausmann, you've got ten minutes."

Nice to see the old Ian emerging. Put him in the same room with Walter Hausmann and you're bound to see his blood start to boil. I don't blame him. Hausmann's a fat, greasy, lecherous pig who constantly smells like stale cum and Jim Bean. He's less fun than prom night diarrhea. Of course, Hausmann's a film school prodigy, a crime scene and snuff film cinematographer whose eye and instincts stack up with anybody else in his circles, and whose nose for trouble and gossip make him a necessary evil at most good parties. When you're on the phone with Walter Hausmann, you're pretty much obligated to yell at, jerk around and all around shake down important information from the guy so that the prospect of small talk doesn't come about.

Ian chews with a series of "mmm"s trying to transcend everything between him and the gory details as soon as possible. Just about every time we go to lunch, Hausmann has something to say to him, since after all, Psychopomps use Friday night to unwind too. I feel a bit of an ego boost that the little stunt Jeremy and I pulled makes whatever he has to say look like business as usual. From the continued annoyance in Ian's body language, I can tell that it definitely is. It takes a little while for him to show a glimmer of interest. It's no Mr.400, but it's up there.

"A skinner, Hausmann? God, we don't see many of them nowadays. But what do you mean they were just kind of piled there?" Nod nod nod, chew chew.

"No formaldehyde? Nothing to soak in?"

He gets a sudden "what the fuck" look on his face. Not total astonishment, but the look you get on your face when you're going ninety and get passed by a truck anyway. Annoyance, traces of bewilderment, but mostly just wondering how the hell it could have gone down. When Hausmann's related the entire story, Ian relays it to me. We're casually puzzled and a bit disgusted, but it doesn't get in the way of our lunch or anything. It's weird, it's sick, but it's mostly old hat, with the exception of a few details.

I watch a pretty, blonde Aryan cop on the six o' clock news. I've seen her before on the news or just about town. She looks irate and nauseous. I used to be angry at cops for being irate and nauseous, but I'm not anymore. For the most part, they're just formalities, crossing guards, and extras in Reap videos, expert witnesses or notches on the belts of brave psychopomps who kill outside the Safe Zone. I'd be annoyed and sick too. This cop is looking at fifteen human skins hanging in a closet in a warehouse a mile on either side from the nearest Safe Zone. And the press is here to ask her obnoxious questions and make it all worse.

"So, do you think you're going to catch this Mr.400 guy?"

The blonde detective looks at the idiot reporter with disbelief in her eyes.

"Mr.400?"

"The guy who's responsible for the le Couteau shooting. It's possible he's killed almost 400 people."

"First of all," she snaps, "I have no reason to believe he has. And second of all, while I feel for three minor celebs killed at a Reap club, I think these fifteen young men whose bones and organs are most likely a mile away somewhere, somewhere most likely I can't get a warrant for, seems a little more pressing. Call me a bigot."

"Are you saying that Mr.400 is not a priority for the police?"

"I sure am."

She has a nice smile. One that makes its way onto Jeremy's face too.

Reapchic.com, September 23rd, 2006

I've anguished over what to say about an event that ends society as we know it. Ends our society at least. Do I welcome the new world order? Does this make me a traitor to the old world order? Does this sound melodramatic? I have anguished because I'm a position where I have to determine whether an important event in my community that I witnessed was a senseless slaughter, or the bloody trumpet of a new dawn. Or was it both? These are the obligations a journalist, whether a well paid newsman or an amateur enthusiast or a self-made celebrity has. You don't come here for objective news; you come here for informed opinions. It took me awhile to formulate these opinions, but I am certain now that I believe them and I stand by my opinions. Any of you who are offended are offended by my heart and my sensibilities and I suggest that you cease to follow this forum. To those of you who do, I'd like to thank you for the patronage and encouragement you've given thus far and wish you luck. Not everyone can ride the waves of social advancement, not everyone can stand beside a future instead of lingering in the past.

Last night, Friday September 22nd, Wayne Pfenniger and Penny Dreadful and the Aberrations were both special guests at the hip Reap club Le Couteau. Pfenniger was to give a speech on the nature of fame in Reap circles and the Aberrations were playing songs to promote their next charity tour for the Thomas Gennaro fund. Everyone present was there to evaluate and serve Reap culture. And then something happened which, ironically did both and even more.

A mysterious figure dressed to mock Godless Jack and wearing a shirt that said "400" on it proved that a pet theory of mine that I've discussed with you before might be accurate. The "h8 killer" and the "Have a Nice Day Killer" are in fact one and the same person. From the shadows of years of anonymity, he has come out and is here to speak out against the establishment of Reap celebrity. If this man's claims are true, he is the most prolific serial murderer of all time and is willing to add piles of bodies to his crusade. He came here to tell us that our culture of violence is dead and that Reap as we know it is a sham. He showed us that Wayne Pfenniger, known for his killings was only human and as vulnerable as anybody on the street. He proved this, regrettably, with a sawed off shotgun that made Pfenniger into a public mess. Pfenniger's execution served as a reminder of the tricks that celebrity plays on people, on the falseness of reputation and hearsay. Rethinking these things means rethinking Reap in his eyes. His vision is distorted, but it is not devoid of truth or merit.

The Aberrations played along to Mr.400's announcement, moved to expression by the power of *his* self expression. Drumbeats joined with words, singing and chanting erupted over his speech. Le Couteau experienced an orgy of spontaneous expression and excitement while awash in the blood of the slain Bundy winner. Mr.400 came with epiphany and the charisma to really move a crowd. There are of course, those who disagree with this. To express even more eloquently his disdain for Reap as we know it and for the statement that murder is art, he shot two members of the Aberrations dead and then left. In this, he said no more rhythm, in this he said that Reap could not keep the beat of the pulse of life. He said Reap as we know it was gone and that our culture of violence was dead. With Mr.400's coming, he might be right. A whole new culture of violence must arise and must replace the old one with braver more eloquent messages. Bloody epiphany has shown me that life must be different and art must be different forever.

As Reap is a union of life and art, we must take Mr.400's attack on le Couteau to heart and reexamine the nature of Reap celebrity. We must first examine his brave mockery of Godless Jack. By his willingness to show up wearing the face of the great harbinger of Reap, he shows that he is unafraid of him. This is a challenge to Godless Jack, one that says "the thing you have made is starting to crumble". Jack needs to show a firmer leadership than before and possibly to come out of retirement. Jack used to have to kill to live, but it seems now he has been eating fine and needs not go out and hunt anymore. Perhaps we need to see the old Godless Jack to come back and show us that he is the figure of menace he once was. I continue to worship Jack and his work, his ability to take primal urges and turn them into meaningful cultural and social content, to merge our media with the dark places in our souls. But, Mr.400 makes a point. What are psychopomps compared to cancer and AIDS and car accidents? Are they truly the forces of nature that they used to be? Our killers need to remember to be big, bold and reassert the importance of their place on the food chain. When will they cease to be entertaining, when will we say that we expect more? The psychopomp needs to be bigger, badder and more genuine. If they are just another competitor in the nation's biggest sport, they lose the sense of menace they once had. Remember that the psychopomp is death on earth, a living plague. Godless Jack is a cannibal, not a latter day David Brenner.

Mr.400 has also brought up that if we align ourselves with psychopomps, we are ourselves perhaps as morally reprehensible as they are. Psychopomps primarily kill out of need, and yet we support them to be entertained. Should our support of them perhaps instead come from needs other than entertainment? Perhaps we should understand and examine the need and consequence of a psychopomp' s action before we lend our support to him and in this way we can show that our support comes not from ignorance or media addiction but from a place in our hearts. This is where it should come from and we should be more vocal and assertive about it. I have placed my famous Anatomy of Decay column back in the archives for you all to peruse and to improve your hold on what you're doing and try to usher Reap into new spiritual and intellectual heights. The morality and loyalty issues are on the table, so we must seek legitimacy from those we support and we must ourselves be legitimate and unwavering in our support.

Our costumes must be bolder, our arguments stronger and our appreciation deeper than they have ever been. Reap has been challenged, and therefore we have been challenged, by a friend to the advancement who masquerades as an enemy. When an ideology is challenged, we must rethink it from the ground up, so here is what I have been thinking in regards to the tenets of Reap:

Reap commandment number one: Reap is Tragedy. This is more than ever present in my mind after the le Couteau attack. We must now understand that the tragedy is omnipresent. We must also consider ourselves tragic for embracing the tragic. Sounds stupid, doesn't it? We who have chosen to feel the tragedy must know that we can ourselves be absorbed by it. The imminence of death pales in comparison to a possible misinterpretation, a chance that we have seen the lessons of tragedy through the wrong lens. At the club we exalted in tragedy, knowing that we were superior to those who were ignorant of it, the people who still watch G-rated movies and wish the profanities would be bleeped out of their music. We are not. Our feeling that the understanding of tragedy would keep us from having to suffer it is out of date, we must understand that whether we have chosen to acknowledge the power of tragedy or not, we are governed by it. Don't give in to depression, but know that we are no less vulnerable for feeling the tragedy. If we think that we are, then the tragedy will test us, and if the tragedy will test us, it almost goes without saying that the tragedy will take us. Wear your tragedies on the outside and consider them on the inside.

Reap commandment number two: Reap is ecstasy. Mr.400 challenges this notion. He challenges it by saying that we have become too hedonistic. He challenges it again, by killing those who do not take him seriously. Take it seriously. Do not just give into hedonism by becoming a mindless sex starved beast or a drug addict, give into it by enjoying yourself under any circumstances. If our tragedy has grown deeper, then our ability to rejoice because of and in spite of it must do so as well. Since we must no longer think ourselves better or less vulnerable than those who do not understand tragedy, we must be able to enjoy ourselves under all circumstances. We must be actively indomitable in our hedonism. No social tragedy should stop us from going out and having fun again. Before, Reapers used hedonism to escape reality, but we should use it instead to feel it deeper. In reality, tragedy is all around us. So, no individual tragedy, no moment of vulnerability should really affect us.

Reap commandment number three: Reap is Wisdom.

This is one we're going to have to really reexamine. We have to prove to ourselves and to others that Reap is wise and to have a lot of perspective on death and the actions of the psychopomp. Mr.400 has pointed out that our psychopomps have set themselves up as false gods, so we must understand what is godlike and important about killing and help validate our lifestyle through this knowledge. I propose we begin by examining other perspectives on death. Perhaps we should begin with looking at Thanatology and concepts of the afterlife. If we need constantly fear death, we must thus examine its importance and impermanence at the same time. I cannot just tell you what to feel on this. If spiritual and intellectual pursuit of the meaning and purpose of death leads us back to Reap, then it is certainly the perspective and lifestyle for us. I can take solace in the fact that every religion and philosophy shows death as a transformation of sorts, so if we understand this, we will be less afraid, has more perspective and be able to enjoy ourselves more. This encompasses all of the other Reap rules. I encourage you to extend your perspectives on death and see why psychopomps are in fact necessary in nature. If we do not help them understand their place in nature, they can become unnatural. Not the embodiments of madness and death that they are meant to be, but attention grubbing wannabe celebrities. Reinforce these things to help out our idols, point them in the right direction, turn them into conscientious, intelligent killers like Mr.400, who has chosen to show his place in the natural order as a kind of ideological clean up crew. Expanding upon and comprehending the wisdom of Reap is in this way, an utter MUST.

Reap Commandment number four: Reap is courage. I stated this before at a point when Reap was just emerging, and I must reevaluate it in a world where Reap is a more mainstream and formidable lifestyle, and a world in which Mr.400 has appeared to make us question everything. Perhaps the kind of courage that Reap now requires is a sort of courage that might be overwhelming and shocking. The new courage Reap requires is the courage to criticize Reap. If you think someone's work is becoming too commercial, you need to say that, if you think somebody is missing the point of Reap, you need to tell them, if you feel that your heroes are starting to forsake you, it is imperative that the Reap community knows it. Because if the Reap community does not know it, then they will not be able to improve themselves. If you stand behind Mr.400 and the need for Reap reformations, you need to let that be known. The new Reap courage is the courage to look at ourselves objectively and decide if we are being wise, brave and joyous enough, for if we are not, then Reap as a whole loses out on it.

So, in conclusion, I take a stance similar to that of Penny Dreadful. The Aberrations will be missed, as will Wayne Pfenniger but Mr.400 has the same rights as Jack and such do, or else Jack and his ilk have none at all. It is that simple and should not be called to debate, whether it is a pleasant statement or not. Mr.400's rights are clear, his desire for change is clear and our need to accept change is clear. If we did not need to change, how then could we have been shocked by the coming of a judge into our midst? Were Reap as wise and brave as it has sought to be, then it would be clear that judgment would come and we would be able to stand up to it, but the criticisms brought upon us were valid ones, so instead of looking upon Mr.400 as a traitor, we must look upon his as a Reap patriot setting out to make Reap better for the Reap world at large. But that doesn't mean I don't hope he gets his. This is Ian Sterling signing off.

.Noir

What are we doing here, Jeremy? Things to dismantle elsewhere. A mile outside each Safe Zone. Empty warehouse surrounded by police tape. It takes a bit of driving and a bit of thinking to find the place, but when I do, I think I recognize it. I've driven past this place a lot, actually. In spite of being a mile from the Safe Zone on each side, it's not far outside the city. Decent place to drop a body. Or fifteen. Somehow it doesn't stack up to me. How does somebody get fifteen bodies so fast? Automatic weapons spray in a frat house? Cult activity, encouraging a mass suicide? Fifteen bodies are usually easy to explain, but this time, there doesn't seem to be any logical explanation, which really bothers me. When this many people go missing at a time, something tends to be up. It usually tends not to be just one Reaper.

Cass heard from Ian who heard from Walter Hausmann that they were all in approximately the same state of decay, and there were no traces of formaldehyde. So, they must have been deposited in the warehouse at about the same time. That's an awfully big drop. Whoever did this is either Bundy worthy, or up to something unorthodox. I suspect the latter. I also suspect that these killings were done in the Safe Zone, because cops tend to stay clear of the Safe Zone itself, although they've been known to idle squad cars five feet outside it. They might not have been killed at once, just at relatively the same time. Most likely within the same night. It's hard for the cops to tell because it's just skins, skins that have obviously been moved by now, taken to the lab to determine exactly how far apart the killings are.

There might still be something, some telltale sign, some kind of strangeness left in the warehouse. I wonder if the police checked rafters, rusty file cabinets, and old crates. I wonder just how much police work they have done here. Yes, it was outside the Safe Zone, but the cops don't try to put away high profile cases fast. With Safe Zone laws in effect, it's hard for cops to get a good reputation, so they like to wait and let cases build up profile, in hopes of actually catching some errant psychopomp and keeping the Bundy committee, the networks and people like the Contessa from getting them off. I think I'll try and do the police work they didn't, to see what this particular monster is up to and what I can do to rid the world of people bold and horrible enough to think that doing something like this is okay. Bold, horrible. Like shooting two innocent musicians for not getting the message. Like killing 380 women for not resisting the temptations of the Dark Ones. I'm pretty bold and pretty horrible too. But maybe this will help make up for it. No more innocents, no more killing to make a point. Only people like whoever did this. Though I might kill Ian Sterling to make a point. Who would blame me? He's just as bad as this abomination, "the Tanner" as the media calls him.

I don't have IR goggles or anything like that, just a flashlight. Jones offered me a pair of IR goggles for two hundred dollars, but I had to decline. The expenses were already starting to get sky high. It's just me, this warehouse, a flashlight and my wits. And that stench. It's not rotting flesh or organs, it's something else. It would have been faint next to the scent of the skins hanging in the closet. Sloppy police work. She looked upset, she looked distracted, and so she could have easily missed something. I'm certain this place didn't smell like roses already so the vomit might not have seemed like anything extraordinary. This has always been a place where high school kids sneak off to drink or smoke up, so it might have been one of them. I still take note of it. I look around for a bit, and then I discover that this place has a bathroom.

I open the door and I'm almost tempted to stop and flush the evidence. Drunken high school kids usually wouldn't stagger to the bathroom, although there is a faint trace of liquor in the air. Somebody squeamish was here. I check for footprints, but there are none on the concrete floors. Shit. I thought I'd found my killer. Maybe not yet, but I have a feeling that I'm getting closer. Closer than the cops got at least. I feel sorta like I'm in a Raymond Chandler novel, although Marlowe never found himself checking warehouse toilets for stale vomit to track down some heartless predator who decided there was nothing wrong with killing and skinning fifteen young men.

Fifteen young men. I gotta wonder where he picked them up. I have a sudden breakthrough when it occurs to me that out back the local kids discard their pot ashes, their beer bottles and their condoms. This pile of junk is so ancient and so innocuous that the cops wouldn't have bothered with it. After all, there are none of them still here. I creep around the back and find a veritable altar to teenage decadence. There are only a couple of hypodermics here, mostly just discarded baggies, rubbers and bottles of beer, wine coolers and Zima. After all that I've done and all that I've been through, I find pawing this particularly distasteful. Kids will be kids, gradually becoming beasts or machines, gradually emptying themselves, but at some point they're innocent. It's not that the activities here are signs of lost innocence, it's that these are the last things they do while they're still innocent, the bits of pleasure they gather before they have to go too far to get it. Anybody who'd paw through all this after doing the skinning wouldn't vomit at the sight and smell of his work, no. It'd take a real stoic, somebody emotionally shut off, the kind of person that just didn't squirm. I know this person's been through all this stuff because at the bottom of it is a wallet. I wonder if it's theirs or a victim's. Nathaniel Gilman says his driver's license…and his SAG card. NOW I've got something. There's no money in the billfold; this "Tanner" wasn't too proud to steal. No money there, but six more SAG cards, six more licenses and a student ID. He really should have burned this stuff, but he probably knew that nobody would check back here, and if they did, the fact that the victims were actors wouldn't mean anything. If I were a TV detective, or a detective at all, I'd have found a matchbook for some club where I could go and shake some guy down for information. This however is real life, so I have no such luck. There are only seven SAG cards and driver's licenses, though. Seven I.Ds, fifteen skins. It literally doesn't add up. So, are there only seven actors? At least I have a student ID. I can't go creeping around a college campus, even in disguise, so I do the next best thing. It's a Sunday night, studying needs to happen and kids need to procrastinate. I know an all-night coffee bar, nothing too hip, but nothing too mainstream either, but I have a feeling I can scare up some information. I put in a pair of blue contacts and quickly change into a T-shirt in the car.

The cafe has checkered floors and red, plastic tables. The walls are adorned with amateurish black and white art photos that are for sale at worshipfully exorbitant prices. As I expected, the place is full. The sad beanie clad greasy –dreaded Rastafarian at the counter doesn't ask if I want anything, greet me, or acknowledge my presence. It seems like he doesn't expect anybody to order anything. I imagine the coffees were ordered an hour ago and are being nursed as the kids stress out over their assignments. I walk up to the sad Rastafarian, hoping maybe he'd know something. I talk just loud enough for anybody relevant to overhear.

"Hey, does Bobby Greer ever come in here?"

The Rastafarian shrugs. "Are you a cop?"

"No. I found his wallet; I've been looking for him or somebody who knows him all night."

"You're at the wrong café," a skinny blonde with a long face and glasses says, "That little fag's a Ripkid. He hangs out at Murderland. He's in my acting class, though. You want me to give the wallet to him, tomorrow?"

Either this kid's unpopular enough to be killed on Friday without anybody knowing about it on Sunday, or this kid isn't dead. And the other seven? Are they also big enough losers that their friends and classmates wouldn't notice they've died? Having already taken all the other Ids out, I hand the girl the wallet, and thank her, wondering where to go next. It doesn't take very long. I go to Murderland as myself, since I've been seen there once out of disguise and didn't get in any trouble then. Reap joints usually tend to hop after midnight, even on a Sunday, so I'm not surprised that there's a crowd. I am, however surprised at who's in that crowd.

When I sit down, a familiar face stares at me from the booth across from mine. He scowls, but then recoils a bit, remembering the beating I gave him. I forgot about that little gang of Ripkids. That little gang looks to have dissolved or have found a new leader, because the asshole that used to be in charge is seated alone in the middle of the restaurant. Probably for the same reason I'm here, to listen in on things. He seethes for a bit until he overcomes his cowardice.

"You fucking ruined me, you asshole!" he screams.

"Maybe you shouldn't have left a member of your own gang to die on the street. I'd have kicked your ass for much less."

I feel tough tonight. I feel invigorated. I'm making a difference without having to gut someone. Yet. So, this kid getting pissed off at me because I knocked him several rungs down the social ladder doesn't concern me a whole hell of a lot. He looks like he's ready to come over and get some or call me out to the parking lot, and I'd be ready had it not been for the actual purpose of this excursion. I'd love to put this kid in a wheelchair for the rest of his life, but I need to investigate something. His crippling would have to come later.

"I'm gonna take you outside and I'm gonna fuckin' cut you open! He screams, I'm gonna cut you open and I'm gonna fuck your guts and cum on your heart! Nobody beats me up and humiliates me, nobody, you fucking Samaritan faggot! Come on, I'm gonna take you outside! I'm gonna take you outside and make you my fucking woman!"

The waitress, dressed in Manson family cool, a hippie chick with a blood streaked face, walks up to the table.

"You've been warned about this," she says to him, "you're disturbing everybody, especially this guy who's just come here for a cup of coffee. If he wants a fight, he'll meet you in the Safe Zone and put you in traction, okay, sunshine?"

The ex-Ripkid leader stomps out, and I get to enjoy my coffee. Hopefully I won't miss any talk about the Ripkids missing a friend, or a wallet for that matter. I'm surprised that one of them approaches me, another one I recognize, the young one. He sits down at the booth where the other was before.

"Thanks for what you did, man," he says, solemn, on the verge of tears almost, "you saved my life, man. We're really glad that you knocked that guy out that day. He was just you know, unstable. He was gonna get us all killed, especially. Just, you know thanks. Can I get you anything?"

I shake my head, but then an idea comes to me. "You don't happen to know, Bobby Greer, do you?"

"Well, I do and I don't. If it was anybody who didn't save me from bleeding to death in the middle in the street, I wouldn't be able to tell 'em, but you, I owe a favor. Yeah, I know Bobby Greer." He speaks quietly, moves to my booth, across from me. He looks both ways before he starts to explain more.

"Bobby doesn't exist anymore."

"What do you mean?" Hmm, he might actually be dead. That would make everything about one percent more confusing.

"I mean, Bobby's somebody else now. Changed his name, bought some documents. See, Bobby got in some trouble with the law. The kind of stuff that doesn't slide in the Safe Zone. He made some extra cash, paid for acting classes by giving it up to guys around town. I'm surprised he didn't get killed, you know, most people who sell sex do it outside the Safe Zone. It's the best way to get you gutted. Dangerous profession." He indicates his Ripper garb. It didn't seem before like he'd be smart enough to enjoy the irony of his friend's double life.

"So, he's getting himself a new face, and a new name, and hopefully a career. Last time we spoke, he seemed pretty damn certain about the career part. Said he had something good lined up. That's pretty funny, cause Bobby's previous film credits don't look so good when you IMDB him. That's probably why the new name."

So, this leaves the question of why the wallet was in the pile of crap outside the warehouse. Makes me wonder if the photo in the wallet was actually Bobby, or if he got a fake made. The possibility still exists that he's dead, though. The mystery expands, just when I thought mysteries got smaller. They should shrink as you get closer to the answer, not grow. I almost wonder if going after this "Tanner" will be worth it. This kid's life was so insignificant; pointless enough that I would want to kill him. If he were the sort of victim, whom so which might still be possible, he has my blessing. But, on the other hand, it seems pretty likely that he's still alive somewhere. So, why his ID? What was it doing in the wallet if he didn't exist anymore?

"How long ago did you talk to Bobby?"

The kid's quick. Most people his age would have to stop and think to get exactly when it happened down, but not him. He remembers instantly. "Friday, Friday afternoon."

Friday afternoon does me no good, because the bodies were found Friday night. I look through the little file on police procedure in my head, and I ask him the next question the police would.

"Did he leave with anybody?"

"Are you a cop?"

"Would a beat cop have bothered helping a kid who was injured during a Splat game?"

The kid doesn't have to think for very long.

"So what's the deal?"

Something makes me want to tell him outright that I'm Mr.400, and I'm investigating Bobby for vigilante superhero purposes. I don't know what to tell him about the deal that wouldn't make him vastly uncomfortable. My nerves become visibly frayed, and I'm surprised that the kid doesn't look more suspicious.

"I don't have to know," he says, "you saved my fucking life, so the least I can do is tell you what you want to know. You're not a cop and you're not a John, so I'll tell you, okay? Clearly, you've got your reasons."

"Thanks." It's a relief dealing with somebody reasonable for a change. I'll be damned.

"He left with a couple guys he says were from his acting class. I know that they've done some extra work, since they talk about it all the time, acting like they're fuckin' Meryl Streep because they're Young Man number 1 or Clumsy Waiter in some cheap indie piece of shit that nobody goes to see. They've done extra work, but I'll tell ya, they're not from his acting class. Gilman's involved with Bobby's...you know other job. I almost don't blame him, though. The pay is pure shit at the Orange Julius."

"Shit, I hate the mall."

"That's all I could tell you, I'm sorry, man. I don't know anything that could help you out. But, I'll keep your investigation under my hat. I'm used to not even speculating about certain things. Smart kids don't even speculate."

I'd agree with that. I'm getting a very big headache from all of the speculating I'm doing. "Thanks. We're even now."

"Ten minutes of talk about local male prostitutes is worth my life? That's great for my self-esteem."

I shrug. "I do cheap favors."

"Good luck," he says, getting up to leave.

"You need a ride home?" I ask.

"Nah. I'm okay."

Brave kid, too. I can't believe he's walking home through the Safe Zone at 2 am. I don't try to press the ride, because I've got a feeling he'll survive okay. As long as he's not playing Splat, he seems perfectly capable as a human being. Pretty damn observant. It's a real break finding him here, whether he's a regular or not. Gives me something to go by. I'm getting tired and the mall is closed, so I head home.

I dream again of the plains and the snakes and the mountains and the debris. I dream again of General Lud telling me that I am God's lightning. The dream dissolves though, into le Couteau. Music plays loudly, it sounds live, but nobody's there. I'm alone with the lights and the gaudiness and the discomfort I feel every time I go through those doors. I don't want to look up, because I know that there is no ceiling and the sky is filled with something ghastly, but since this is a dream, I know that I can only look up. A great clothesline stretches across the skyline of the city and hanging on it, as if to dry are millions of human skins. Le Couteau shatters around me, and it is just me in the city with the skins. I wander the dark streets, knocking on doors and trying to see if anyone knows why the sky is filled with the skins of dead men. Nobody answers. I stop in front of a church and I pound and pound on the door. Suddenly, I feel an unearthly strength, and the door shatters into millions of splinters.

I know somehow that General Lud has lent me the strength to make this happen. The church is empty, save newspaper pages pasted to the walls and the windows. You can't even see the stained glass through all of the newspaper. I try to read each front page, but every one has nothing on it but symbols and gibberish. The papers suddenly shuffle, flying into the center of the empty church, making a shape several feet high, a shape consisting of two figures: H 8. Lud places his hand upon my shoulder, it is no longer wrinkled, and his ratty urine-soaked coat becomes a long, white priestly vestment. His face looks fifty years younger. I don't know how old General Lud was, but he looks twenty. He looks almost sane and almost handsome. He no longer looks like the raving street preacher he is.

"The jackal and the serpent come; they come to take me away. See me here and now, listen up: the devil's voice comes not from the mouth you think. You will know it in the Black Queen's shadow, you will know this when I am taken. You will know the will of the Dark Ones, when you find the man you seek. Remember the Book of Mark; remember the one who said his name was Legion."

I wake up and I go to the kitchen. It's five am, I've barely slept. Remember the one who said his name was Legion. What is Lud doing in my dreams telling me to remember the Book of Mark? Telling me to remember that the demons said they were Legion? I make a peanut butter and jelly sandwich and a cup of coffee, both of which I end up ignoring. This sorry attempt at breakfast doesn't settle me down any, make me want to sit and think. I'm glad that I left the pharmacy, because I would hate to go to work with this on my mind. I feel sort of bad that Cass still needs to work, but always says not to worry about. Do what you're supposed to, she says. Try to do some work when you can, she tells me. Today I sure as hell can't. Makes me glad the temp agency doesn't have anything for me right now.

Cass is up unusually early, she sits down across from me, still in her t-shirt and panties and picks up the peanut butter and jelly sandwich.

"You gonna eat this?" she asks.

"Go ahead," I tell her, and she eats it.

"Investigations ran real late, huh?" she asks.

I don't answer. I can see she's disappointed. I usually let her talk when she wants to talk. I don't feel like talking when she's disappointed, it's too hard to concentrate.

"I don't have to ask if you've found the guy. It's pretty clear that you didn't. Maybe if we go over this together, we can get to the bottom of it. I know you feel exceptionally capable, lately, but if there's one thing I know about, it is murder."

She has a point. I don't know where to start. If I did, I'd have a beginning, and if I had a beginning, I'd know how this happened or who did it, or pretty much anything. It's remarkable how much information you can turn up in a couple of hours of looking for it, and how little meaning you can extract from it.

"So far it doesn't seem to be going especially well. I found a wallet full of I.Ds and SAG cards, vomit in the bathroom, and a very convoluted history of one of the victims. Apparently, these guys were all extras and gigolos. One of them, a kid named Bobby Greer was seen around Murderland and was talking about establishing a new identity. I'm waiting for the mall to open to go the Orange Julius and see if they know anything about one of the other kids, Nathaniel Gilman. He works there, in between being a gigolo and an aspiring actor."

"Busy boy," Cass says, and she taps the table with her fingers as she tends to do when she's deep in thought, "I've got a feeling that somehow you've taken the wrong angle. I've heard the name Bobby Greer somewhere. I can't tell you where right now, but I should be able to tell you soon. It makes me wonder why him? A few other down-on-their luck extras and eight other people you can't identify could be killed in one night by one person."

"It might be two. I've got a feeling that there's more than one person. Anybody willing to skin fifteen people wouldn't be nauseated by it most likely. It would take somebody pretty amoral."

"Another thing that gets me is that the killer left the wallet hidden, but didn't burn it."

She has a point. It's a lot of evidence to leave around. If somebody was skinning, why would they be collecting I.Ds? Then again, the Cabana Boy took breasts and also took matchbooks to commemorate the occasion. Yet, it doesn't seem similar. There had to be some better reason for keeping the I.Ds around, but any good one escapes me. I wish I could posit a theory right now, so as not to look clueless in front of Cass, yet I can't.

"So what do you think about that?" I ask, "Do you think he collects I.Ds and skins because he's fixated on signs of outward identity?"

Cass looks at me like I'm an idiot, which is perfectly alright, because I feel like one. I'm a little embarrassed that she seems to be getting somewhere fast. My IQ is about one hundred points higher than hers, so I find it quite curious that she's so much faster on the uptake than me in regards to this. But then,

IQ doesn't account for those benefits attained from fixation, reading and naturally keen observations. It sounds like I came up with a pretty solid diagnosis, but on the other hand, she's looking at me like I'm an idiot, so it probably isn't that keen. Not to mention it was pulled out of my ass, and I can't see any connection between all these things.

"That's very clean pop psychology. Too clean. The pathologies of killing are seldom that clean. You ought to read Ian's column every once in awhile. You'd know that kills aren't that direct a manifestation of a killer's obsession. Look at Kris Kringle, the first Psychopomp you ever shot."

"What about him?"

"He didn't take girls apart and send their organs home because he was obsessed with the "gift" of life and its workings, like some of the police analysts said. It was more than that. It looked like he was obsessed with discovering the inner workings of women and returning them to the source, but that's not what it was. In his files, it said that when he was a child, he was a compulsive voyeur and a compulsive tattle tale."

I'm beginning to see where her example is going. I feel like a fool too for having just dismissed the guy as a deconstructionist. He was more complicated than that. He fancied himself as something of a moral avenger too.

"He felt that what was inside people was dirty," I begin, putting the pieces together on Kringle, "and he sent the parts back to their mothers and fathers. He believed their sins were reflected by the dirtiness of what was inside them, the messiness."

Cass nods. "Exactly. He was still tattling, relieving them of their dirty little secrets. Things that are perfectly normal to anybody but a schizophrenic obsessed with digging up dirt. If "the Tanner" were obsessed with signs of identity, he wouldn't grab something as sensible as their identification. He'd grab their clothes. And he wouldn't leave their skins hanging in a closet, as if he planned on putting them on later. If he did, he'd put them in his own closet. The police have probably thought about his collecting and classified him as a collector, which would be further evidenced by their attaining the I.Ds, which he squirreled away as a traditional collector would. But why hide something you want from others instead of keeping it for yourself, unless you planned on retrieving it eventually."

"So you think he'll go back for the I.Ds?"

Cass shakes her head. "If he needed them, he would have taken them home by the time you got there, unless he needed them some place secret to get at them again much later."

I see where she's coming from. There has to be some practical use for them. He couldn't have them at his personal residence or anywhere particularly conspicuous, so he hid them at the crime scene. He had to make sure that if the I.Ds were found, they would not be found on him. He had no problem hanging the skins in a closet, but the wallet he hid in a pile of garbage. This isn't the work of a collector. This is as fishy as I thought it had been.

"The I.D.s have nothing directly to do with the murder."

"Exactly."

"So, are they a red herring for the police, or something he'll need to leave hidden, retaining the location but not the possession of?"

"Red herring?" Cass laughs. She always find stiff or antiquated turns of phrase funny.

"Can you answer the question please?"

"It's both. I think your first step today is to inquire about that Nathaniel kid and all the others. Your second step is to find out where Bobby Greer got the fake ID, and why, if he was escaping with a fake ID, the killer got him with his real one on him. It means that whoever gave him the fake ID was going to meet him later or else that whoever made the fake ID killed him."

She glows when she says it. She's a bad as I am when it comes to getting hung up on the excitement of the murder. I should have known somebody who followed Reap for this long would know about this kind of thing more than somebody who was exposed to it only by osmosis and reading a couple of Godless Jack's books. She gets out her laptop and begins searching the internet. The girl's a regular Nancy Drew, over a decade older and a whole lot more voluptuous, but still a regular Nancy Drew. I know not to ask any questions until she's ready to answer them. When she is, she'll gush. She'll be radiant and excited and she'll look like she's doing what God put her on the earth to do, so I should just back and enjoy her starting to do it.

Lo and behold, she's luminescent. "The credit search doesn't tell me anything new, but it does give me an idea. Every one of those kids has a perfectly expendable career. Every one of those kids did a couple of small time straight to DVD reenactments and a couple of TV jobs. It's possible that they were all lured to their death by a job offer, something really lucrative. And with Bobby Greer's need to get out of town and start a new life, it was probably irresistible to him."

"But my question is, what about the other eight?"

"I don't know," she says, "that part's what gets me. Why kill seven actors and eight strangers?"

"Collectors tend to be more discriminating than that."

"To say the least."

We put on Duck Soup and lay together in bed. The antics of the Marx brothers are a refreshing repose from all of the violence and darkness that erupts whenever the TV is turned on. I don't need news, I don't need debates over the actions of Mr.400, I need peace, a rest from nightmares and counterterrorism and young homosexuals being flayed alive. It's such a relief seeing just black and white with no streaks of red. No words are exchanged between us until she goes to work, when there's a sweet goodbye with a kiss on the lips. She leaves at seven thirty and I set my alarm for nine. I sleep peacefully until it goes off, with no trace of nightmares.

Next morning, I'm at the mall at ten, and it's no more pleasant than it usually is for me. I swear they've just gotten gaudier and dumber and noisier since I was a kid. The arcade is twice as cramped and dark as the one at the mall in Connecticut, and the stores selling designer shoes and pop culture memorabilia are twice as dominant. I try to blink as often as possible to avoid noticing all the wispy little Dark One scouts that fly through the air here. In spite of having parked at the mall entrance closest to the food court, the Orange Julius still feels like it's at the end of the world. I feel more at home in the desolate, foul smelling warehouse than I do in this place.

An overweight young man that looks about my age, and seems about one angry customer away from hanging himself is at the counter. He doesn't even bother asking what it is I want, since it's an extra couple seconds of not doing a job that he clearly doesn't want to do. Like the sad Rastafarian, he makes me initiate everything. It makes instantly ill-disposed towards him, about ready to shake any answers I can get out of him physically. Only thing is, I'm not actually a detective or a cop or anybody who could get away with doing so.

"Does Nathaniel Gilman work here?"

"I hope you're a cop," says the suicidal Julius boy.

"No. I found his driver's license, I went to his apartment and he wasn't there and then I found out that he worked here. I figured maybe he'd be..."

"He quit on Friday. Made a very big production of it. Now I have to pick up his shift."

"He quit on Friday?" As they say, the plot thickens.

"You deaf? Yes, he QUIT on FRIDAY. I was hoping you were a cop, because he told me not to tell the cops I saw him on Friday. I was hoping you'd take him in."

"No such luck," I reply and leave the suicidal Julius boy to Nathaniel Gilman's shift. So he too got this job offer that Cass theorized about, so he too was taken away by a stranger with candy that took his ID and his skin. Suddenly, something hits me. I return to the Orange Julius with the driver's license.

"What is it?" asks the suicidal Julius boy who is quite tired of all this talk of Gilman by now.

"I know he doesn't work here anymore, but if you see him anywhere, can you give him this?" I ask, handing the Julius boy the license.

He looks at me with a whole new annoyance on his face.

"This isn't Nate."

"But, it says..." I feign surprise.

"The name and address are right, but the face is wrong. This isn't him. This is another photo."

I jump for joy internally. "I don't know what this ID was doing on the ground then."

The Julius boy shrugs and I get to leave the mall. It feels like an immense privilege, a burst of freedom. Then, when I get out to the parking lot my day gets worse again. Fate has once more forced me to cross paths with this same idiot Ripkid who is walking out of the movie theater where Oliver Stone's Godless Jack biopic is showing. In the crowd of Reapkids walking out, he stands out for some reason. He looks at me and smiles, springing his swordcane. He's not alone either. The gang looks kludged together, but not altogether harmless. The curvaceous girl in the Bettie Page wig and chainmail bikini covered in bloodstains looks like she would be a threat if she knew how to use that broadsword. Doubt it. Price tag's still on there. Short skinny kid in suspenders, leather pants and a surgical mask? Possibly dangerous. Can't take him seriously. I don't even know what his fucking costume's supposed to be. Gein kid in a butcher coat and Leatherface mask? There's my problem. He's got four inches and about fifty pounds on me. Probably moving toward his trunk to grab a chainsaw. It seems almost like some of the other Reapkids are gathering to join the fight, but they choose instead to stand a good twenty feet away observing and whispering among themselves. A Manson collects bets from two Gacys and a Son of Sam. Damn. Distracted.

"Well, well? What 'ave we 'ere?" the Ripkid advances, getting between me and the big kid. Fuck. I knock him to the ground with one leg sweep, but it still takes too much time. The big kid's opened his trunk. I prepare to jump him, but the kid in the incongruous costume jumps on my back and starts to choke me. It doesn't take a ton of effort to literally shake him off, but it takes long enough for the big kid to rev his chainsaw and the Bathory girl in the Red Sonja getup to come in for a very wild swing. Her friend's lucky to be on the ground with the Ripkid leader. She could hurt someone with that thing. But it won't be me.

I duck. The kid on the ground grabs my legs and holds them tight, so I've only got my hands and my head to work with. Can't stop you. Not gonna stop you. I have no idea why I'm punching a guy who's coming at me with a chainsaw in the gut, but I get him good. Knocks him back a bit. They can't stop you you're fucking lightning from god you don't have to do this relax not now not now damn you not fucking now relax and it's nice sitting on this little boat fishing the Sun is warm and the fish are biting life is easy. Summertime and the livin' is easy...

The Mr.400 shirt and shades appear.

MURDERLAND | Garrett Cook

"You're not on a little boat," they tell me.

"I'm not?"

"No. You're engaged in a brawl with a Reap gang in a mall parking lot. You're going to kill them and some obnoxious but innocent bystanders if you don't return."

"I should go back there, then. Thanks, Mr.400."

"You're Mr.400, Jeremy. I'm not going to take that away from you. Clothes don't make the man that much."

I'm on my way back. Relax you don't have to do this. Stay calm. Enjoy the sun and catch some fish you ungrateful little shit. This is my job not yours, coward. They can't stop you you're fucking lightning from god. You don't need to be there. Open eyes mountain top open eyes again Leatherface is on the ground. I am holding the chainsaw now. I am standing on the wannabe Bathory girl's hand and pressing it up to her neck. I am not doing this. I am being yanked away. Wants to drop me into a little boat on an ocean of tranquility. Wants me to stand on the mountain and look down. Won't do it. That sanctimonious shithead is not me. Ungrateful little shit you don't have to do this. Mr. 400 says I don't. Says I am me and can make my own decisions. You're a good man, Jeremy, who does the right thing to the right people. Not sure I consider them people, but I stop the chainsaw and run to my car. The crowd claps as I leave the scene. Thank you, thank you, I am Mr.- don't do it. Right, thanks. The whole gang is out cold save the broadsword girl who just gazes at me admiringly. I don't want to get a good look at the beating I gave them, that's for sure. There is some blood on my knuckles.

I get home, high on adrenaline and a bit less scared of myself than I was yesterday.

"How was the mall," she asks, "you stop by the Hot Topic and get a new Ripper cape?"

I smile pretty genuinely. "No, but I'd like to go to Murderland for dinner."

"Damn" she laughs, "just when I've gotten over my Reap phase."

Maybe it's a risk letting her be seen with me and keeping too high a profile at Murderland, but I don't care, I have a hunch to follow up. It all needs just one more piece and it's at that reapjoint unfortunately. We dress normally and sit down without a word, ordering dinner almost under our breath. But I don't need to. Not there. I feel a burst of pride when I see that that fucking Ripkid must be spending the night at home licking his wounds.

I approach the booth and Joey waves "hi". "You find what you needed, man?" he asks.

"Not quite yet."

Joey gets up and joins us at the booth. He recognizes Cass almost instantly. "I've seen you here," he says nonchalantly, "with Ian Sterling one time, and Selene."

"Yeah, they're friends of mine."

"You an amateur detective too?"

"Every once in awhile."

The waitress, the familiar Manson girl, brings Joey an Albert Fish filet.

"I got another question for you."

"Yeah, I figured," he replies, "you don't seem too into the Reap thing."

"I'm not. I need to know who you get a fake ID from around here."

Joey laughs. "If I knew, I'd be drinking in an alley somewhere, and I'd be dancing the night away at Le Couteau. Then again, I don't look particularly old so I couldn't benefit from one. You're shit out of luck there; I don't know where Bobby got his."

The waitress shakes her head and laughs. She sizes Cass and I up. "For friends of Ian Sterling, you guys are real out of touch. There's only one person to go to in this town for a really good fake ID. But you didn't hear it from me, okay?"

I nod. I need this information so much; I can almost smell the killer's blood on the edge of my razors. She hesitates before she says it and during the second of silence, life slows to an utter crawl, going into slow motion. Then she says it, and I could kick myself. Cass looks like she's been standing at the Grand Canyon, but needed it pointed out by the tour guide. It's embarrassing.

"The only person you can get a perfect fake ID from in this town is Walter Hausmann."

Legion

Why is it exactly that I told Jeremy to wait on killing Hausmann? I don't like the guy, I think he's perfectly capable of doing something this reprehensible, and all proof seems to indicate that he killed these people who had been trying to disappear, so why is it that I told Jeremy to wait on it? Maybe it's because Hausmann' s too good a suspect, or maybe somebody's trying to frame him, or maybe this whole thing won't make more sense with Walter Hausmann dead. In fact, once Hausmann's no longer out there, this becomes even more of a puzzle.

If Hausmann did even get these seven male prostitutes and eight other people to trust him enough to be in positions where he could kill and skin them, then that implies that Walter Hausmann managed to kill fifteen people in an evening and transplant their bodies to the warehouse. It's obvious that nobody without automatic weapons or poison gas can kill fifteen people in a night. It's uncertain whether they'd been poisoned or not because there's nothing but skin. If the skins were taken, then anything could have been done to them internally and the cops wouldn't know. Of course this killer isn't a legitimate collector; there was another motive and a reason for the skins being so important.

I'm looking over some documents at work, so I'm a bit distracted. I should be a bit distracted from the documents by my amateur detective work, but instead the documents, my actual work are distracting me from my amateur detective work. Makes me kinda mad at Jeremy for getting me into this. I wish these were documents like the documents in all those detective movies that wrap up really neatly with the case, but they're not. These are divorce papers for some creep who was just fired from his teaching position. He didn't end up going to prison as a sex offender, but the sex certainly offended his wife, seeing as it was with a seventeen year old male student. Almost eighteen at least. Pictures too. Wife probably hired a private detective.

Says the detective got a picture of the guy soliciting sex from a male prostitute. Maybe things do connect like this. Maybe being a detective is in fact like being in a detective novel. Wonders never cease. All of a sudden things really connect. One of the figures in the photo looks familiar, and it's not the one I expected either. Jeremy was right about this. Evidence only complicates things further.

When I look at the photo, I expect to recognize the gigolo, but I don't. I find the John to be more familiar. The guy was almost thirty, but he had a real baby face. The kind of face that could be attached to a 21 year old actor without anybody knowing. A face that has, in fact been attached to one of the I.Ds. The I.Ds don't make sense as evidence because they don't function as evidence, they don't make sense because they don't belong to the people on them. With just a battered and scarred skin, nobody could tell this guy wasn't somebody much younger. And if the I.Ds on the scene were found, that's what the cops would think. But the cops missed the I.Ds, Jeremy found them. That's a strike against whoever planned this out.

I dial his number just to see if there's something to my hunch. If he picks up, I'll tell him it's a wrong number, and dismiss the face as a similar one. If he doesn't, I'll begin to look into the possibility that maybe this guy was one of the victims and had his I.D replaced with another one. This detective work is nerve wracking. One ring. He's dead. No, don't think that. Nobody answers their phone on the first ring. Don't be stupid. Two rings. It's getting more likely. Most people answer their phone on the second or third ring. Then, it rings a third, fourth and fifth time. The answering machine kicks on.

"This is Rob Henslowe. Leave a message after the beep. Robin, if you hear this, I'm sorry, I'm really sorry. I have a problem, but I want to get help. I want to make this work. I want to at least hear your voice again and know that you know I'm sorry."

I hang up at the beep. It looks to me like a young gay teacher had an affair with a student, solicited sex from a male prostitute, ruined his marriage and then got himself killed by Walter Hausmann. I don't know any man in existence that could be picked up by Walter Hausmann, no matter how desperate he was. Hausmann would need some sort of bait. Some sort of really good bait. Like a young actor/gigolo who needed to disappear. That was Hausmann's angle, that's how Hausmann picked this guy up. Then, he went and killed the kid, too and switched their I.Ds to buy time and leave the cops as confused as Jeremy was. Both halves of the I.D got skinned. And, he went and did this seven times. In one night. The only other possibility seems really stupid.

When Gilbert shows up, I go back to work and hand him the file. He looks really stressed. "I'm gonna need you to go to Henslowe's house and serve him the papers."

I don't let him see my eyes light up. "What do I need to serve him the papers for?"

He sighs. "Greg is sick and I haven't been able to get in touch with this guy since Friday. He's probably depressed over everything that happened. Too depressed to talk to his future ex-wife's lawyer." Friday again. This guy's probably dead. Bull's-eye, Nancy Drew. If he isn't there when I go to the door, I can convince his wife to file a missing persons report and start a fire under their asses and neaten up whatever mess Jeremy is likely to make. Not that the mess would be unwarranted, but it will still be a mess.

So, I, a young paralegal, am subbing for the lowly process server and serving a man his divorce papers. Gilbert's really surprised that I don't bitch about it, because he knows it's in my character to bitch about stuff like this. But, he mistakes it for sympathy for his stress. Good for him. I don't recall ever having sympathy for Gilbert and I don't think I'm going to start anytime soon. I take the papers, and I get in the car and head to this guy's place.

That old chestnut, the overflowing mailbox gives him away. He hasn't gotten his mail for three mail days now. Nobody's looking, so I snoop a little, just to nudge it back into the box. Bills. Credit card offers. Gay porn magazine. I don't think anybody has ever been depressed enough to not go outside and pick up their gay porn magazine. I knock on his door just to make him official. I stand there and wait and act shocked for the sake of acting shocked. "Hello?"

I knock again, just so I can go back to work a few seconds late or maybe even squeeze in a minute or two. "Hello? Mr. Henslowe, I'm from the law offices of Gilbert Katz...I'd like to take a moment to..."

Sure, there's any number of places a recently outed man whose marriage is completely on the rocks and has a penchant for male prostitutes would go, but I'm not altogether out of line thinking he's dead either. It seems to me a whole lot more likely than the thought that he's killed himself. Not that I dismiss the thought that he might have been a suicide and Walter Hausmann could have stolen the body and the I.D and skinned it. I'm sort of curious as to why the fact that Walter Hausmann is the leading purveyor of fake I.Ds automatically makes him the mastermind behind this and not just a possible pawn. Regardless, I look through some windows to make sure he's not hanging in his kitchen or bedroom. He isn't. But then, if the skinner took the body it would naturally not be in his house. This is a tough one, but not going to find anything else out here.

I return to work and tell Gilbert the bad news. He tells me to call the man's wife/widow and tell her that she might want to call the police and report him missing. This is not easy for me. In fact, it hurts like a bastard. The man you've decided to divorce is most likely dead. It will save on court costs and eliminate the awkwardness of fighting over possessions. I don't know what to do when she starts crying.

"I'm sorry for your loss, I really am. I know this week has been absolute hell for you," I tell her.

"You don't know anything. How can you know what it feels like to find out somebody you love has some kind of deviant secret life?" I can only bite my tongue about that one. I took my revelation in surprising stride, after beating him up a little, that is. I do know what it must have been like for her, but not when it comes to somebody you love clearly not being satisfied by you. Being a wife for five years to somebody who actually doesn't even want a wife I must admit is a kind of shame I can't identify with. No matter what he did, Jeremy loves and wants me. Jeremy is with me, no matter how badly he fucks up.

"You're right," I tell her, "I can't. All I know is your husband hasn't been at his house for awhile, I'm not sure that he's…"

She sobs loudly, and then her voice is sharp like a dagger. "Dead? With the kind of company he must have kept? I'm surprised he didn't end up dead beforehand. Those people, people who sell themselves, they're dangerous. If they're not those pimps sure are…"

"I'm sorry for your loss," is all I can muster before she hangs up on me. Her diatribe gives me an idea, though, one which might help me get a handle on what's actually going on.. Jeremy should have thought about the fact that these boys have to have a pimp. Some kind of synchronicity happens. Some kind of scary synchronicity. A red limo parks across the street. It's as if he heard me thinking the word pimp and he had to come running like Scatman Crothers. He doesn't get out. Reiko doesn't get out. They just sit there and wait for me. I would oblige them, but there are two hours left in my workday. Two hours that slowly drip away every little drop of time like a child squirting the dregs of a ketchup bottle onto their fries.

I step outside and Reiko pulls up to me.

"Get in."

"Get in? That's not very geisha of you."

She gives me a look that smacks me with an invisible shovel.

"Cassandra-kun, please get in."

I sit down in the back where Jones is chugging bleach.

"Want some? Powerful shit."

"No. That's more of a New Year's thing for me."

Jones shrugs with surprise like I refused a brownie or a cold beer.

"Suit yourself."

He caps the bleach and sets it at his feet.

"You know, Miss Flynn, it's considered rude to keep a pimp waiting."

"I'm sorry. I had some work to finish. I couldn't exactly tell them I had to meet with the pimp who arms my boyfriend for his crusade against Reap."

"And yet I am said pimp and deserve the respect that that very pimp does."

I muster my best "I'm sorry." I need this guy. For weapons and information both. I realize that bruising the ego of a short, white pimp from Connecticut is not difficult.

"I accept your apology. It is suitably apologetic for my tastes, which are exquisite."

"I'm glad to hear that. What brings you to town?"

"I need to see Jeremy. You'll do, though."

"Why didn't you just call him?"

"Because I prefer not to make phone calls. Maybe it's just a precaution natural for the King of the Connecticut Underworld; maybe it's because of hangin' around the old man so much. Maybe I get scared of the telephone sometimes. I get a feelin' he doesn't keep his phone on too often, neither. I needed him, but you'll do."

"I'm flattered."

"Shit will go down," he says.

"I know that."

"You do not know the extent of shit which is going to go down. The Old Man has been having bad dreams."

Surely he must be joking. Driving up from Connecticut to tell me an insane doom prophet was having dreams of prophetic doom?

"We don't have time for hoodoo. There are real problems here."

Jones takes another swig of bleach.

"I'm afraid you do have time for hoodoo. When the General has bad dreams, bad things tend to happen. Lately, the old man's been dreamin' about snakes, lots of snakes and he says something's comin' and everything's gonna change. If you ignore it, than it's gonna change into somethin' much worse. You tell Jeremy that the General's been havin' bad dreams too and he needs to watch out because something's comin' and it's gonna leave us all flat on our asses if we ain't prepared. You understand?"

"Yes," I squeak. I don't know why I suddenly start squeaking or why this madman's dreams suddenly bother me.

"So you'll tell him?"

"Yes, I'll tell him." I'm not sure if I'm telling the truth. Don't know if I want to show Jeremy that I think Lud is anything more than crazy. I might tell him. I'll consider telling him. I'll think about it. But if I don't, nothing will happen. I'll think about telling him. For now, there are problems in the real world. Unlike Lud's nightmares.

"Could you tell me something?"

"Mr. Jones can tell you plenty, Miss Flynn. On that I can assure you."

"I need a male prostitute."

"In spite of my sartorial acumen, I am not, Miss Flynn, a connoisseur of sodomies."

"This is important, Jones."

He sighs, and then pops a handful of Ecstasy.

"In this town, that would be Meghan Burkett. Blue Diamond Grill. But she's a pretty tough customer."

"You know her?"

"Quite well. She'd eat you alive. I think perhaps..."

Reiko interrupts.

"I don't mean to question your judgment but are you sure..."

"Reiko, you should know by now that it is not a ho's duty to question her big pimp daddy, particularly when he is Inscrutability Jones. We'll see her together. But please, make sure Jeremy gets the message."

"Yes," I lie. It strikes me now as too important to tell him, like it might be a real dispatch from a world he should be able to live without.

Reiko mumbles to herself the whole way to the Blue Diamond Grill. She parks the limo around the back in the most inconspicuous manner one can park a red limo. It's not that inconspicuous at all. It's a goddamn red limo after all. The three of us get out and Reiko walks up to me and whispers "are you packing?" I shake my head.

"Fuck."

The Blue Diamond Grill has a certain divish charm. There are two western saloon doors and it has a nice beer-and-onion rings smell. I miss steakhouses. One of the big drawbacks of dating a vegetarian. But there's another piece of meat that immediately draws my attention away from taking in the smell. The maitre d' is a big, muscular gentleman clad only in a cowboy hat and a leather thong. There's more oil on him than on the onion rings. He glares at Jones and Reiko.

"You should leave," he warns them.

"We're here to see your employer."

"I believe you've received ample warning."

"We want to see Meghan."

He places his face in his palm.

"Come on, man, we don't need any fucking trouble here."

"Ain't gonna be no trouble. Just show us into the dining room so we can meet with your boss. I know she eats her dinner early."

"She does."

The muscley, half-naked maitre d' leads us into the dining room. Several other cowboys are eating there and each of them glares at Jones and Reiko, in fact it looks like nobody BUT greasy half-naked cowboys and a couple guys dressed as Zorro eat here. The dining room is full of mumbling and quiet exchanges as we're lead to a table where the wartiest most disgusting woman I've ever seen with the worst crewcut I've ever seen is eating the juiciest looking steak I've ever seen. The steak looks delicious enough that I'm still hungry after looking at her greasy, spotty wrinkled face.

"Ms. Burkett, it's been..." Jones begins before he's cut off.

"Is this restaurant in Connecticut, Mr. Jones?"

"We're here..."

She reaches under the table for a pistol and with speed that's quite surprising for a fat, greasy toad like her; she shoves it into Jones' face.

"I would like you to answer my question."

"No," Jones replies, "this is not Connecticut."

"And what did the Pimpkings vote three years ago?"

"I'm here to…"

"Mr. Jones, answer my question or I'll put a hole in your head. That is, if it isn't already hollow, which by coming here, you convince me it is."

"The Pimpkings said to stay in Connecticut and off of their turf."

"Am I not one of the seven Pimpkings, Mr. Jones?"

"You are."

It might be a cliché to say that Reiko moves like greased lightning. It would also be an understatement. In the blink of an eye, she has shoved Jones out of the way and stepped on top of the table, pressing her katana to Meghan's throat. I can't help but let my mind drift to the incredible things this woman must be capable of when plying her other trade for Jones. But, I leave behind thoughts of sexual acrobatics, when it occurs to me that it would best to fall back and duck under a table, which Jones is already doing. Good thing, because a room full of oily cowboy gigolos and a couple of guys dressed like Zorro jump to their feet. Apparently, there is an unwritten social contract that everyone even remotely close to Jeremy has signed up for a life of harassment by costumed idiots. Then again, everyone in this society has signed up for a life of harassment by costumed idiots.

Reiko drops from the table right when the bullets start flying. A Zorro lunges at her with his rapier. She lops his arm off, picks it up in her other hand and smacks him in the face with it. Not one of the cowboys gets in a shot on her. She dodges, she weaves and she deflects flying bullets with the Zorro's severed arm. She comes in close, trading in the Zorro's bullet ridden arm for a fresh cowboy arm. His pistol drops as it is severed. I look at the cowboy's gun on the floor and consider picking it up. Then I remember the dozen other greased up gun-toting hooligans. Maybe I'm better off just watching this one. And it's well worth watching. Reiko leaps, flips and slashes her way across the room. I thank my interest in Reap for the mental endurance to witness this bloodbath without being sick.

When all the cowboys are disposed of, Reiko returns to her place on top of Meaghan's table. Jones rises to his feet.

"My martial arts killing machine, has done her business, Miss Burkett. You might be a Pimpking, but your life is at stake.

MURDERLAND | Garrett Cook

We came here, violating the edicts of the Pimpkings, so the young lady here can ask you a question."

I walk over several dead cowboys so I can get close enough to look her in the eye. It's a shame that I do, because that face does not reward me for the effort.

"I need to know about Nathaniel Gilman and Bobby Greer."

"Gilman was one of mine. Greer was a friend of his. Greer wasn't really one of mine, but he didn't turn down a job when I could get him one. I got him "discovered" for a couple of his extra roles. Thursday night, that little fucker and five others like him quit on me. Said they got a real good audition, said some guy with network connections was gonna make 'em famous. Also said the heat was getting to be too much. Little fuckers talk a lot, I'll tell ya. Say they're all goin' away. I call Greer, tryin' to offer him a permanent position, and wouldn't you know it, he's gone too. No more actors. Of course, it's hard for me not to hire actors. Every kid in his twenties who's willing to take a load in his mouth thinks he's an actor. Then again, most of 'em aren't even gay, so I guess you could say that's pretty good acting."

"I'd say so." Another prospect strikes me and I rattle off the names from the wallet. She responds to each one of the names with a nod.

"What, you psychic? Where do you get all those names? Guess it doesn't matter cause they all disappeared anyway. Then, they went and had the nerve to take a few of my clients with them. Pisses me off cause one of these guys, Ambrose, got a shitload of dough from his daddy and likes to do parties. Brings four or five people with him each time. I think he skipped the country with one of those goddamn little ingrates. Little shits vanish on me, then cause they disappear and somebody needs to know somethin', my place is wrecked in a ninja fight. No fuckin' justice anywhere, I'll tell ya.""

It does not take me long to divide fifteen by seven and come out with two apiece with a remainder of one. Henslowe, Ambrose a few of his friends and a bunch of other Johns that might have had reason to disappear or off themselves went with them. It doesn't seem likely that they're all going to Jamaica for some big pleasure cruise. While I appreciate her grumbling, I'm certain it will resolve itself.

I get in the red limo.

"Well," says Jones, "if you keep your part of our agreement, I believe we're done for now. Anywhere you need to go?"

"Nearest payphone."

The nearest payphone is surprisingly close.

"Have a nice day, Miss Flynn. Inscrutability Jones is always glad to help out a fine lady and carve out a little bit of revenge on the Pimpkings."

"Glad I could help."

"But remember…"

"I'll tell him."

The red limo drives off. I feel sort of guilty, but in spite of all he's done for me, I'm certain I won't tell Jeremy.

"I've got it. I've got a clear picture of all of this."

"Yeah," Jeremy answers, "Walter Hausmann killed all these male prostitute actors and a bunch of Johns."

"Have the costumes and your briefcase ready. This looks like a job for Mr.400 and Gacy girl."

"Whatever you say, sweetheart."

I meet him at the apartment and sure enough, he has the costume stuff ready. We find a secluded place and we change in the car, hoping that Hausmann's place doesn't have a doorman. It doesn't, but we still have a buzzer to get around. I check my watch and Jeremy checks his. He pushes the button.

"Hello?"

"Pizza."

"You're ten minutes late, I get it free."

We walk in and find the way up to Hausmann's apartment. He answers the door thoroughly sloshed, but not too sloshed for his jaw to drop to the ground instantly. Not too sloshed to realize something real bad is coming up.

"I'm Mr.400," Jeremy tells him, "I think you should let me in."

"I agree," says Hausmann, letting us in. For a guy who orchestrated a plot like this, he's kind of a coward. I wonder if he's the one who threw up in the warehouse toilet. I wonder it for all of five seconds until I see the thin, blonde teenager with the perfect wingtips who looks like he's definitely out of place in Hausmann's train wreck of a living room. Wrappers everywhere indicate that this is where cows and Snicker's bars alike go to die. This kid doesn't belong here, but I know he's not one of the hustlers. This kid is something different.

"We need some answers," I tell him and although Hausmann recognizes my voice, he knows there's nothing he'll ever be able to do about it.

"Don't worry," Jeremy says, cocking his shotgun, "we're not gonna tell the cops."

"Answers?" asks the blonde kid on the sofa, "about what?"

"Let me see your wallet," I ask him and he hands it over, of course. I triumphantly hold up the I.D that shows this boy is an intern for WBLD Reap News. Jeremy is genuinely impressed. He points the shotgun at Hausmann, who hands me his wallet as well. Not surprisingly, WBLD was where Hausmann was interning.

"Thought you were gonna be the next big psychopomp, Walter? Capitalize on uncatchability, then surface as the murderer of all these male prostitutes?"

Walter is completely still until Jeremy knees him in the groin. Then Walter nods.

"But the hustlers weren't the victims. The johns were, weren't they, Walter?"

Walter doesn't wait for another beating to nod in agreement this time. He gets right to it.

"And you didn't kill any of those johns. Not at all."

"No," Walter mewls, both a request for us not to kill him and an answer to my question.

"It was those seven kids, and by now they're undergoing plastic surgery at some discreet little clinic run by the network, aren't they?"

"Yes."

"Nobody will ever know who they are, Walter. Nobody will ever know who the killers that would someday make you famous are, will they, Walter?"

"No."

Jeremy's starting to get it. He looks at the intern. "You helped him with the skinning, didn't you, kid?"

"Yes."

"But you've got kind of a weak stomach."

"Uh huh," he replies.

"Get Walter's camera," I tell him, "get it and start it up."

I indicate Walter and he turns the camera on him. Walter is sweating bullets, as he should be.

"Now, I want you to tell the truth, Walter."

"I can't do that," he says, "They'll kill me."

"Walter," Jeremy says, "I'm Mr.400. I'm going to kill you. Not them. Your life is about to end anyhow. Get this off your chest and maybe you will get some mercy from God. Maybe, Walter, I won't even kill you, in spite of how much you deserve it."

"My name is Walter Hausmann..." he begins. After Walter's fifteen minutes of fame on his confession tape, Jeremy stabs him and knocks out the intern. The sad part is that I know the tape will never reach the television audience it deserves, because the network was behind this to begin with. I go home and turn on the TV, looking for any network that has nothing to do with Reap. There's a cable movie channel and I laugh and cry bitterly as the film finishes up. I mimic its last lines to myself,

"Forget about it, Cass, it's Chinatown."

Jeremy's Journal, April 14th, 1994

I bring the newspaper clipping everywhere. Nothing else really entertains me and intrigues me this much. I can't believe everybody else who saw this just threw it away and ignored its warning. It's ridiculous. I brought it to church today, for the Easter Mass. The two of them have a weird effect together, like my friend Bryan says about the Wizard of Oz and this Pink

Floyd album, Dark Side of the Moon. He keeps saying that I should come over and check it out, but I can't stand watching the Wizard of Oz for any reason at all. Even with some elaborate coincidence behind it, I don't think the movie could entertain. But the sermon and the clipping do it.

"Christ said I am the resurrection and the light," says Father Flanagan. The resurrection and the light. When he says these words I can see how close the spheres of light have come. I can see who they hover around and I can see why they are hovering around them. Christ, the child of God was the resurrection and the light, so these things; wherever they're from, whatever they are, need a child. And if they need a child, like God, they will need a womb to bring that child into the world. The lights are surrounding the women around me at the church, especially the younger ones, especially the blondes. Resurrection, the light, the return of the child to earth and the spheres of light jumpstart my mind and I can see something. I can see something that makes a startling and terrifying amount of sense.

I can see a sad-looking blonde woman with big, blue eyes leaving me on the steps of the home for boys. She looks like she's running from something, like she knows something or like she just doesn't want anything to do with me. The balls of light circle around the blondes, the blondes are chosen to deliver the servants of the creatures and maybe their Antichrist. This woman, my mother was a blonde, and I have always somehow felt like I might not have come from the same place as the other children, like I was made different and had different potential than they did. Maybe my mother, stupid bitch that she was for abandoning me, still resisted them and created something they couldn't control. Maybe I can see them because I have some connection with them and I am somehow like them. Am I their resurrection and their light? Am I the light that will conquer them?

Soon I can't hear Father Flanagan. I can only hear whispers and a kind of hissing sound that comes out of the balls of light. I find myself fixating on the image of Christ on the cross, blissful, but full of agony, the hopeful but sad way he looks down. He gave everything to save us and then we abandoned him, let him die. We let him die slowly on the cross, did nothing as the Romans took him? What about me? If I am the resurrection and the light, am I doomed to the same fate? I am not like Jesus. I am something else entirely. I am a human made to achieve some task for these creatures, he was a man made to give his life for God. I have duties to perform and a crusade to undergo, but I do not have to be like him. If I die, there will be no resurrection and there will be no followers. There will most likely be no followers as I do what I must do. I must do what I must alone.

The stained glass Christ smiles and stares at the things that are in this church, in his sanctuary. His eyes seem to move with one of the balls. I follow his eyes and the light and I find it buzzing around my stepmother. The sermon doesn't move her. The church doesn't move her, she looks sort of sleepy and submissive and ready to give into whatever the light plans on doing to her. I come to the conclusion that the light is going to impregnate her, but the light doesn't. It flies off, and Jesus' eyes return to where they were.

"Don't panic, Jeremy," a voice tells me, "don't panic. You know enough, you're starting to figure it out. Once you have it all figured out, it will be so much easier, Jeremy."

I think back to Dark Side of the Moon, which Bryan wants me to hear as he plays the Wizard of Oz. The part of the song that says "there's someone in my head but it's not me". He says the scarecrow dances around to that song. Somebody was speaking to me and I don't know who it was, but I remember everything they said.

My stepmother is sort of confused when I whisper "Lud?"

Even more confused that I say nothing after that.

"It's not the old man," the voice says, "I'm you. I'm a part of you and I'm here to help. Don't talk out loud. I can hear your thoughts."

I'm starting to look crazy now, aren't I? Starting to look like my connection with reality is getting severed and I'm becoming part of something else that isn't reality at all. I'm scared by what General Lud said and what the newspaper page said and I'm scared by what happened in church. But, I'd swear it all happened. I swear I talked to the voice more and heard more from it.

"What do I do?" I ask the voice.

"You need to keep a keen eye and you need to be ready to do things for me and you and Jesus and the earth. You need to be ready to save the earth and to save the earth you're going to have to listen to me. Are you ready to listen to me?"

"Yes," I tell the voice, "yes I am."

"Good, Jeremy," the voice replies, "good. Now listen, I can do most of the tough things for you, but I'm going to need your body. You're going to need to give up meat. No more killing things to live. You understand? No more meat. The animals don't deserve to die, they're innocent."

I like meat, but I like animals too, so I kind of have to agree with it. "Okay, no more meat."

"You keep in shape, work out and get ready. Your body needs to be fighting fit. If it is anything less than fighting fit, you'll have problems."

I'm a little scared by how loud and bossy this voice has turned out to be, but what it says make sense. It wants me to be fighting fit, so I'm going to work out more. There's no reason not to, anyway. Working out and giving up meat just seems natural. I can't disobey orders that simple, or any orders for this voice. Anyway, it goes on to tell me more.

"The lights are scouts for the Dark Ones. They allow them to determine who will breed more of them, their human children. Dirty. Mutants. Mutants like you were supposed to be, Jeremy. But you didn't turn out all the way for them. You became something different. You can be the best weapon against them, if you can be a good weapon. I'm sure, Jeremy that you can be a good weapon."

It says a lot about being a good weapon. It's scary that way. It's fixated with my helping it get rid of these creatures and I don't know why. I feel like I'm not in charge of this fight, but I sort of don't want to be. I don't like the thought of fighting. I wish people would just read those newspaper pages that Lud puts on their car and grab their guns to get rid of the things.

"Your stepmother has been targeted by the scouts. Since she has been targeted by the scouts and they've gone off, they've determined that she's still prime for breeding. She will breed one of them. There is only way to stop her from doing that."

"How do you know all of this?" I ask the voice.

"My logic jumps ahead of yours, to the next level. I have to tell you what you need to do. I need your body to carry it out. I need you to be willing to help me do something that others could not do. Your faith and your strength will be tested. This time you'll have to prove yourself to me. After that I can help you. I can make sure you do everything right."

As it speaks, I can't help but look at how many of those scouts have come to the mass, how unafraid they are of this holy place. They could come to the school, too. I wonder if when I get back to school I'll find them in the hallways, contaminating every girl who's ready to have one. I can hear Father Flanagan make noises like the processor of a computer. It hurts me to think that they're at church too and God can't stop them. But from what the voice says, God needs us to stop them.

"Okay," I say to the voice, "I'll do whatever you need me to do."

The agreement was made and there's nothing I can do about it now. Even if I stop liking it, I can't stop it since I made that promise and the voice is willing to help. Good thing that voice is willing to help, because everything feels big and ominous to me now. The voice scared and relieved me in the church and it scares and relieves me still.

When I get home, I return to my room and I try to sort everything out, to get all the facts in one place and discern what things must have been real and what other things must have been fantasy. It's too hard to actually accomplish, though. It seems like a useful thing to do, but I think it might well be impossible. The Dark Ones have come from another dimension. They seek to get women pregnant to bring their face to earth. General Lud sees in the newspaper that there's a page about what the Dark Ones are doing, a page to warn everybody that they're there, but everybody ignores it and the Dark Ones go invisible. It's possible that my mother was one of the women that the Dark Ones impregnated, and I was created. I turned out human, possessing the ability to see and fight them, an ability which was unlocked by General Lud. Because I see the Dark Ones now, the voice has offered to help me fight them. As I examine all of this information, it makes perfect sense and no sense at all.

"Okay," I ask the voice, "how do I get rid of her and what's happening to her?"

"I won't always come when called," says the voice, "I will come when I'm needed and I'll come when I choose. You're on your own right now, until you have proven to me that you are capable of carrying out your mission. You are capable of carrying out your mission, aren't you?"

I can only say "yes."

I go downstairs and my stepmother is alone in the kitchen. She's sitting at the table, staring into space. There's a bottle of Vodka, half empty on the table. She's drunk again, drunk and surrounded by the buzzing things. When she sees me, a smile is on her face, a big stupid, cow smile.

"Jeremy, dear, come sit with your mother."

There are so many things I want to ask her about my mother. I always get the feeling she knows something. It looks like she has something in common with my mother, but I will never see this woman as my mother. Nor will I actually see my mother as my mother. I have no mother and no father. I was made from the Dark Ones and the light made to destroy them, I have no need for something like a mother. Especially not one like this, some shopaholic yuppie imbecile who claims to be a good Catholic but pays no attention in church. She sickens me. I wouldn't want to sit with her if there weren't little creatures around her, but I feel even less like sitting with her since they're there. I still sit down with her.

"Jeremy," she says, "I don't feel like you like us and this town very much. I'm sorry we've never connected."

"I'm sorry, too," I tell her. I start to tear up a little. I can't believe what I have to do, even to do it to someone I hate feels wrong. I hate the thought of killing, even of killing someone I don't like who's gonna do something wrong.

"We love you, Jeremy," she slurs, "we really do." She says it a lot, but the vodka makes her mean it. She suddenly breaks down and cries, resting her head against the table. She doesn't say anything at all for awhile.

"We love you, Jeremy and I want to be a good mother, I do, Jeremy."

"I know you do." I don't know if I believe this, but it feels like a confession, it feels like she thinks it's true enough. I feel like letting her say her peace. Even if I were to decide not to kill her, I would want for her to have said what she actually thought.

"It's not easy," she tells me, "you're not like other kids are. You've read every book in the house, when I ask what you want for Christmas, you can never tell me and then you get disappointed when it's not under the tree. Why don't you ever tell me what you really want for Christmas, huh, Jeremy?"

"I don't know, Elise." I tell her, and I honestly don't. I never know what I want for Christmas. Nothing they'd give me would really show me that they love me anyway. And even if they did love me, I'm not sure that I could care.

"Why don't you ever call me mom?" she asks. She looks angry now, angry and sad and drunk and beat.

"I'm sorry, mom," I tell her. I don't think I have called her mom before and even with the little affection I have for her, it feels like I owe her at least this. I am sorry that I don't love my stepparents. My stepfather is a machine and my stepmother is about to become the vessel for something more disgusting than anything else on earth.

I get really scared when something buzzing around her becomes clearer, less like an out of focus image. I wish that it hadn't because maybe I wouldn't have done something as scary as what I had to do. If I didn't know what they looked like, I'd feel less like destroying them, but I can't feel less like destroying them because I might be the only one that can. It's a black, disgusting little monster with strange little wings and a big mosquito-snout dripping with some smelly black oil from hell. It's clearly nothing from our world. Nothing from our world could look like that or smell like that fluid it's dripping. I know what that fluid is and it's even more disgusting for me.

"I wish this family could get along better and that you could have been a regular, happy child. I don't know if you can be now. I think it's too late. I think I've ruined your chance of being a happy person, and I'm sorry again, I'm sorry you can't be happy."

With this awful thing flitting around her, it's hard to keep calm. I felt really obligated to, though. It became too painfully necessary for these to be her last moments, so it was painfully necessary to keep calm.

"Shh, it's okay, mom."

I don't think I'd hugged her before that. I feel really brave getting so close to her with that monster so near, but I don't feel brave about what I have to do next. I don't want to stab her, we don't have a gun, I don't think I could bare to strangle her. It's hard to figure out how I can do what the voice needs me to do. Hard to figure it out until she stopped crying and said, "Get me my pills, Jeremy, please. I need my pills."

I was eager to get out that room, that's for sure. The experience of my stepmother unburdening her soul as the monsters were ready to fill her with their young was too much to take. The pills said she needed to take two of one type and ten of another. I exchange the labels and bring them down. She's too drunk to figure that the pills she takes ten of are the wrong size, and she takes more than ten of them. Much more by the time I've dropped a couple into the bottle of vodka she's swigging. I sneak upstairs into my room, and it's lucky that Ted sleeps like a rock, because otherwise he would hear me cry.

"Good job," the voice tells me, "you've passed your test. I understand that it feels bad. I understand that you don't want to experience this. Killing feels awful, so I can help you with that. I need your body, but I can make sure you won't feel like this again. Do you want that, Jeremy?"

Yes, I tell it. I'm writing this now, because tomorrow things will be too chaotic for me to observe what's happened. I did at least give her some joy and some consolation in her last moments. I don't think I could bare killing unless I felt good about my work. I want to be a healer. If I'm a healer, it won't hurt so much to kill. At least the voice is there to help. I hope it keeps its promise.

A Visit with the Pastor

I cannot sleep. The thing I think is sleep is not sleep. I cannot sleep atop the mountain. I have wandered through the wastes, lightning shocked, full of broken toys and I have dodged the stampede of snakes. They are not dreamsnakes. They are snakes. Too long I have been denying that my legs feel themselves climbing the mountain and are starting to ache from climbing it every night. I am prepared to see Lud up here, but he is gone.

"I am going to get rid of you, Jeremy. You're too scattered. You forget the mission." The Voice comes out of nowhere and I know it well. I never dreamed it could follow me here. It manifests as a slithering blob of typewritten letters. It lunges at me, rearing up to its full height that dwarfs my own.

I am ready to panic, ready to let it eat me because it knows best, but I feel protected all of a sudden. The Mr.400 shades are on my face. The fake teeth are in my mouth. The shirt is on me. Soulmuscles ripple. I rear up to my full height and I feel gigantic. I lay into it with my fists and blood and ink stain them. The inkthing backs off, starting to smear.

The letters reassemble into one gigantic sentence to the best of the wounded monster's ability.

"YOU NEED ME, JEREMY!"

I cut myself on the sharp corner of the "y". The hard nothing in the center of the O is almost impenetrable. It is not whitespace or emptiness inside it. There is bone at the center of an O. I lose the size the glasses and fangs have granted me and my body looks tiny and humble. I come at it again, hard as can be. It doesn't even feel the need to wiggle around anymore. It knows I'm too small, it knows I cannot break through the center of the O.

Strategies change. The Mr.400 shirt shifts its ink. The shirt now reads "Don't be afraid." My fist shreds through the middle of the O and there is blood behind it. I keep on reaching, knowing this must be where it keeps its heart.

"Squeeze the blood out!" the shirt instructs me in black marker.

I oblige it. I feel the meat in my hand, ready to be crushed beneath me.

And my eyes open. My hands are covered in blood and ink. I have not been dreaming. I would let this bother me, but I know who my friends are, so I feel okay. It is five thirty PM. I have been fighting all night and most of the day and Cass is at home, watching TV.

When I first see it on the TV, it doesn't make sense to me. It makes sense to Mr. 400. It makes no sense to the Voice. Of all the people that I'd think would be interested in my actions, I'm particularly surprised to hear Pastor Tommy Simmons of the Christian Victim's Front speaking up on my behalf. As annoying and ignorant as psychopomps and Reap activists can be, their conservative counterparts always manage to be a little more annoying, brainwashing some people, estranging some people and leaving everybody else certain that they don't want to hear what they have to say. Tommy Simmons is the embodiment of this. Falwell and Robertson spoke out when Jack was on trial, but Falwell and Robertson, didn't have one edge that Simmons did. Falwell and Robertson hadn't lost a daughter to the actions of Godless Jack. Simmons' condemnation of Reap culture and call for new crusades for censorship fell only on deaf ears or those of Right Wing crackpots at first, but with all the psychopomps and all the killing, the Christian Victim's Front occasionally gets listened to in Washington. Not when they're asking for Safe Zone regulations to get repealed or things like that, but when they want a new album or videogame or movie deemed obscene. Washington knows that Reap is a force of nature, but they also know that whiny conservatives are one that can be just as strong.

In spite of my status as possibly the killingest psychopomp in history, Tommy Simmons is speaking up on my behalf on the news. I'm fairly certain I should be mad about this because everything Tommy Simmons sides with, the people who I am trying to reach, the people who I am trying to civilize, will disagree with and despise. I almost think this is some kind of Right Wing stunt to reduce my popularity. Sounds paranoid, but it doesn't sound far fetched.

"This Mr.400 figure is a refreshing change from all those lunatics out there. Finally, we the victims and the seeker of justice have our own avenger, somebody who might be able to represent our perspectives and help rid the world of all of these dangerous, hateful individuals out there," Simmons begins, "and that, that's a good thing. That's one of the best things that have happened to society for some time."

A rail thin black woman with a long face wearing a hideously conservative pants suit laughs. "Pastor Simmons, you can't be serious! You're basically telling America that it is your honest belief that two wrongs make a right. Don't you think that calling Mr.400 a positive force for change tells people that killing is okay, as long as it's for what YOU believe? This self-righteous vigilante…"

"Is the only hope we have for change in this Reap dominated culture? My only regret is that it took him so long to come out, that he had to wait for things to be such a mess to surface!"

The angry thin black woman shakes her head in mocking disbelief. "I can't believe I'm hearing this. I especially can't believe that I'm hearing this from a member of the clergy. What kind of a message does it send to people that the clergy condones violence by serial killers against serial killers? This is just another arrogant, close-minded moral crusade. I guess I shouldn't be surprised!"

"Close-minded moral crusade! How dare you accuse me of…"

Cass comes home and sits down on the bed, immediately interested. An obnoxious Reap analyst is arguing with a conservative religious wacko. You'd have to pay her not to watch this. Her eyes look wide as dinner plates, like they want to crawl of their sockets to get closer to the circus on the TV. This expression is alarmingly common, but on this occasion, I think mine want to do the same.

"Mr.400 is a monster! He turns Reap and the moral majority alike against themselves!" says the enraged Reap pundit, "He is a sickness that could infect us all with its confused perceptions of right and wrong, a sickness that could…"

"They're talking about us!" Cass squeals with delight, "I can never get over that!"

"Miss, I don't think you should talk to me about sickness and moral confusion from your position," Simmons argues calmly, folding his hands. It makes me sort of like him. He makes her look incredibly stupid. The fuming pundit can't even come up with something to say other than huffing and monosyllables that are squelched before they turn into words.

"Shit," says Cass, "I wish you hadn't quit your job. We could have Tivo'ed all of this stuff."

I shrug. "Seeing it once is enough for me."

The pundit gets her bearings and tries to launch head on into an argument. "If you're concerned with victim's rights, what about the families of the four hundred people this man's killed, huh? Are you going to support one murderer when you think all the rest are going to hell? I think that's a little hypocritical of you, don't you?"

I begin to eagerly await each of his responses, which is odd because before this broadcast I would change the channel or leave the room every time I saw the man's fat, arrogant face. But it doesn't seem like such a transgression for him to have a fat, arrogant face. It might be because I have the fat, arrogant face of Walter Hausmann to compare it with. Compared to the fat, arrogant face Walter Hausmann wears the fat arrogance on his is charming and even useful. Especially compared to the nervous, thin, angry face of the woman who is yelling at him, trying idly to stifle his counter moves. He is patient. He waits for her to wait for him. I can see how he got to be the leader that he is. Dammit, I'm admiring this man. I shouldn't be admiring anybody like him. Especially when he admires me, and quite likely for the wrong reason.

"Well?" she asks petulantly.

"I'm just getting over the fact that you try to talk to me about sickness and then you try to talk to me about hypocrisy. Pardon my taking my time, but I'm trying to find a more polite response than to simply laugh at you. That would be positively rude and I am not a rude man. I will simply say that Mr.400 is welcome to come see me at Tommy Simmons Ministries and discuss his ideology and how he intends to change the world for the better. I consider this man a kindred spirit, perhaps his methods are questionable, but his intent is quite admirable. Mr.400, you're welcome to give me a call and arrange an appointment."

Cass giggles into her hands. She looks like we're about to go and prank call a chemistry teacher from high school. "We've got to call this guy."

I must admit that there is in fact something about calling Pastor Tommy Simmons that makes me want to giggle into my hands. Yet, there's something else that makes it look like a fantastic idea. This man has chosen to be the voice of the victim, and whether he drives me nuts or not, it is a voice that needs to be heard. He seems coherent and he seems rational, at least in regards to the Mr.400 issue. So, talking to him might not hurt. It might be a chance to get the moral minority on my side, maybe get some kind of support or funding for my activities. The church could legitimize me more than anything, in spite of the antagonism it might get from some of the Reapkids that I may want to enlist to my cause. It feels to me more than a lark after I think it over.

So, I call him. An upbeat young lady with a Southern accent answers the phone. "Hello. Tommy Simmons Ministries. What can I do for you today?"

"This is Mr.400."

The girl's voice gets far less upbeat when I tell her. "You're about the seventh Mr.400 I've gotten today."

"I can assure you. This is the real one. Pencil me in for an appointment today. If I'm not the real one, I won't show up. If I am, I will. It only stands to reason."

"Can't argue with that kind of reasoning," the secretary replies, "I'll see you at seven if you're the real thing."

"Then you'll see me at seven."

"Good day and God bless."

I'm anxious for the next hour. Cass got home at five, so it's not long before the seven o' clock appointment. I'm pretty certain she in fact didn't write me in and that I'll be coming as a surprise. Well, if I have to come as a surprise, it will be even more effective. I'm used to coming as a surprise after all. I sure as Hell came as a surprise to all of the angry Reap pundits and all of those kids at le Couteau. Six forty rolls round and I head to Tommy Simmons Ministries.

The look on the secretary's face is priceless. "Can I help you?" she asks.

"Yes, in fact you can. I'm Mr.400 here for my seven o' clock."

"Mister what?"

I point down at my shirt. She gets the gist quite quickly. "One moment, please."

She dashes down the hall until she reaches Simmons' office door, which she pounds on with all of her might.

"Pastor Simmons, Pastor Simmons!" she screams.

His door opens and she's invited in. I hear nothing after that. I don't have to wait very long for the secretary to return. She tries hard to look composed, but she doesn't manage it, not even remotely.

"Pastor Simmons is ready to see you now," she says.

"Good," I reply, "after all, I did make the appointment." Mr.400 adds something for dramatic effect:

"And nobody keeps the lightning from god waiting."

She has nothing to say. I feel somewhat jittery about meeting the Pastor, but the secretary's discomfort eases it. It's always good to see somebody in a more uncomfortable situation than you are in. If it weren't for that secretary I would not be able to walk into Pastor Simmons' office and sit down. The crucifixes everywhere, the inspirational calendars, the thank you cards from the children of Reap victims and the combination of Hallmark and Inquisition Christianity in the décor are enough to make anybody flee in terror, but the horrified secretary makes it easy to claim my seat. I wait for Simmons to extend his hand before I introduce myself.

"It's a pleasure to meet you, Mr.400," he says, offering a firm handshake, "I'm glad to see you."

"Pleasure to meet you, Pastor Simmons," I reply, "I was very impressed by your display of courage on BLD Reap news. I had to come down immediately. It thrills me that I have any defenders in the press."

"I assure you, Mr.400, your crusade does not go unappreciated, especially by good, God fearing Americans."

I was pretty damn certain that my crusade would be alienating good, God-fearing Americans. I guess the conservatives have to make more allowances in an America where killing is perfectly legal. Tommy Simmons has been a bundle of surprises today, which is a pity because I was hoping to be the bundle of surprises. The secretary was shocked to see me, but he seems as cool and collected as he was on the talk show.

"I'm glad that at least some people think I'm doing the right thing, as difficult as it might be. It took awhile for me to come to terms with the fact that this was the right thing. It seemed like such an awful thing to need to do. As awful as the thing I was doing before, I suppose."

Pastor Simmons forces a smile. "Killing is not always killing. Some people are already as good as dead, already in the hands of the Devil. God does not always take his own vengeance, so we need to do it for him. I couldn't bring myself to kill them, but I think it might just wash the blood from your hands. We are in the midst of a holy war, Mr.400, and if we do not fight it, then the infidels will win. Makes me sound like one of those Islamic fundamentalists we used to worry about so much before we nuked 'em, but it's true. I'm glad to see somebody out there standing up for some kind of sanity. It's a shame you have to do this on your own."

"I'm not on my own," I tell him, "there's a man called General Lud, a homeless man in Westborough, Connecticut who helped me with the Le Couteau raid. Thanks to him, I actually have allies. Thanks to him this crusade is possible. I hope I'll say the same of you someday, pastor."

"We are likeminded individuals," Mr.400 adds.

"Well, Mr.400, you have one more. While Tommy Simmons Ministries can't provide you with money or weapons, we'll keep on getting the good word out."

This time I'm the one who forces a smile. "That's what you do, after all."

"Thank you very much for your time, Mr. 400," he says and his secretary walks me out to the car. The evening is a blur. Food, small talk, then sleep. Too much to think about, too much to process to take any of the rest of the day in.

In the morning, I'm awakened from dreams of struggling against the inkblob (who covers its heart with sharp jagged letters instead of round ones now) by the sound of crying. Cass is very upset about something. I jump from sleep to see what has happened. I could never have expected anything like this. I could never have expected Simmons had taped his conversation with me. I could never have expected the consequences of Simmons taping the conversation could be so dire. Godless Jack is on the TV, surrounded by everybody who'd received a Bundy nomination in the past three years. He wears a coat made of sewn together human faces. Each of them is twisted into a mocking smile. For a second, I see eyes in them, glaring at me. He leans against a pole. General Lud's severed head, mounted on it looks at me too as if to say "you fucked up. You killed me."

"This is a message for Mr.400. My culture of violence will not die so easily, but your friend has, and so will anybody else I associate with you. This is a warning to you, Tommy Simmons, although your interview was of great assistance to me. *Vexilia Regis Prodeunt Inferni*. From Canto thirty-four of Dante's Inferno. *The banners of the king of Hell go forth*."

ODILON REDON

MURDERLAND | Garrett Cook

Book 3- Godless

"Then all thy bones shall say pridefully, "who is like unto me? Have I not been too strong for my adversaries? Have I not delivered MYSELF for mine own brain and body?"

-Anton Szandor LaVey *"The Satanic Bible"*

Big Empty

"What does it mean?" the outlaw hissed as he backed the priest into the lectern. His partner behind him was ready to cut off the priest if he tried to run.

"I-I don't know," the old man stammered, "Please, I know they say you're death, but you're just a man. Listen to your heart, spare an old man who knows nothing."

He was not surprised to hear the hammer pull back on his partner's gun or to know it was pointed at the back of his head. He was not surprised at all. He knew more than well enough than to trust a man who called himself Faustus.

"I'm afraid this is far as you get, Godless Jack," said his blackhatted waistcoated overdressed companion from his lethal vantage point.

"You're afraid?" the outlaw Jack Cavanagh laughed, "You ride with me and you still use words like that?"

"You ain't death," said Doc Faustus, the Tartarus Kid, "I know death and you ain't him."

The outlaw Jack Cavanagh pointed his own gun at the priest.

"You know the words are there and what they are. You tell me what they mean!"

The old priest closed his eyes.

"Leave this place and I'll pray for God to forgive you."

"That's a mighty fine offer, padre," said Faustus, "but I'm afraid...yes, afraid, that my colleague will have to turn it down. We can't have his sins scrubbed clean."

Faustus pulled the trigger, assuming there would be a spatter of blood and the man who men knew as Death would be no more, the true liege coming for the pretender to the throne. The emaciated grey head of the man that men call death did indeed explode open, the bullet sending chunks of hair and skull flying, but no blood or brains came forth. There were bats with heads like half formed fetuses, leeches, floating black seahorses and dozens of tiny marionettes, swarming back at the one that had unleashed them. Though the back of his head was torn open, the front bore an evil grin, revealing teeth that had crunched on human bones.

Faustus twitched and struggled, puppets crawling into his open mouth, fetal vampire bats drinking from his neck, leeches sucking blood from his face as the black seahorses floated around him observing the situation.

"I have been to Big Empty," said Cavanagh, "and there is nothing good left in me."

His partner choking out his life on the floor did not distract Cavanagh for long.

"The words," said the man who was thought to be death, "what do they mean?"

"I have sworn not to tell," said the priest. "No man will ever know."

Cavanagh pulled the trigger on his Colt Peacemaker and the barrel extended, transforming into a black metallic serpent that coiled around the clergyman's neck.

"What does it mean?"

The priest defied Cavanagh to the last, on his final breath, taunting him, gasping out the words that drove the outlaw to murder him, words that had come to him the first time he ate flesh and came to Big Empty.

"Archelon Ranch."

__Celebrity__

"My Heart For Hades" blog

I did this for him. I don't mean Hitler, I don't mean Satan. I mean HIM. The lightning from God calls for retribution, it calls for swift strikes, dismantled machines and rivers of sacrificial blood. There is no room for Hitler or Satan in today's world, we are more logical than that. The true psychopomp transcends good and evil and wants you to shove your celebrities and your politicians and all your other shit right back up your ass where it belongs. If you think I'm wrong, you can go fuck yourselves. None of you have the guts to listen and follow the call of the prophet of Hades. So I told you fucking queer little ripkids standing in line to suck Godless Jack's cock that I was gonna go on and do it, and I went on and did it. I wasn't alone though, I had my friend John (we'll call him John) and I had Mr.400 to guide me.

Fucking idiot high school. When things are this dangerous they don't put up a fucking metal detector, cause they think it's the niggers and the poor kids who shoot people since they don't fucking read the books, they don't go on ReapChic and they don't even watch the news. Blame the terrorists and the Chinese. Fucking ignorant, I mean, shit...haven't they heard the message, the message of God's war on ignorance and sloth. Jocks are too scared of the reapkids to go off on them, know they might get their tires or their throats slit. Jocks push me around cause I'm small and I've got glasses and I'm not tough enough to be down with Mr. Right or Anubis or any of them...I told you what those fuckers do and what I always thought about you know then on the radio clear as day it's the time and I told you I was gonna get the fuckin' guns and you just leave your little that's fucked up, but it's not fucked up, we've had it up to here with the jocks pushing us around and the cocktease cheerleaders hanging out with the little Bundy girls and the "hey fag"...the lightning from God strikes, rains retribution and I strike for the lightning...cocktease bully hatemongers your culture of violence is dead fuckers it's fucking dead and all the sparks rain down...here is my lightning!

John doesn't even get it, he's such a pussy, he just wants to get back at everybody, no better than the reap kids doesn't get that we need to end this, just...shit, we need to end this! I don't go shouting anything like "my life for Satan" or "kill the fucking niggers!" I'm reasonable, I come in and I sweep the halls clean of all their garbage, can't even let them stop and beg. They're the ones responsible. The monstermakers are everywhere and I want them to just...shit, you know...Mr.400 guides my hand, guides my eyes and guides my gun and lo, I struck...I didn't count, but I think it's around a hundred, didn't leave anybody wounded...hate that, just sick, if you want to end it you gotta end it, you know...I don't hate you guys, I still think you're kinda cool, but maybe Mr.400's right, stop and think about it. Liberate yourselves, liberate your schools and put an end to it, that's what Mr. 400 wants, no more violence, hypocrisy...it makes sense, it really makes sense, you just gotta think about it, take out the trash, sweep up the hypocrites, usher them unto the lord for judgment, confine them to the pits where they belong. Listen to the man, guys, he makes some sense.

Comments:

GashKit-E69: Get a fucking grip, man. It's not like that. He's a symbol, a symbol for what we need to be. He's not saying that Reap's bad; he's saying it needs to be different. More directed.

SnakeIs: Forget Mr.400. You heard Jack's broadcast, that fucker's toast, he killed that crazy homeless shit who helped him out and he's gonna kill your "hero". GJ forever, yo!

GossamerSteel: Yawn. SSDD, Snake. As if.

SnakeIs:Just you wait, Goss, Jack don't let people take his likeness.

CrimsonFeast666: Him and a personal army, man. I wanna see the coward go Mano-a-mano. 400 will beat Jack out of his Depends.

RedQueensBlessing:You went too far. That's not what this is all about. Get a conscience and a brain.

GashKit-E69: Amen! Somebody had to say it. Ps. Snake is wrong. 400 will win.

IanSterlingMOD: Mr.400 wouldn't want this. I'm obligated to give the cops your contact info, MyHeart. Come on, Ryan, this was too much. You've forgotten the rules of Reap, not to mention common decency. Let this be a lesson to the rest of you guys.

RedQueensBlessing: Well handled. Hope to see you you-know-where.

Mad Tea Party

These gargoyles are made to stave off angels. The demons with their twisted faces contoured into triumphal joy know well that their kind is welcome here. When you pull into the driveway, the statues start innocently enough. There is a smooth, pristine, virginal maiden whose angelic face screams "I am an untouched soul." But perhaps they're not all that innocent, because there's an agony to the purity, an obvious coldness. Every virgin in every pieta has a bit of it. Like whiny Disney princesses, they beg for fresh, exciting worlds. The gentlemen across from them don't look like they'll provide that. The detail is admirable, it reveals just how perfectly pressed all their suits are and just how stiff their carriage. Their innocence too, is agony, an agony that remedies itself as you get closer to the house.

They are relieved of the burden of purity a little more every few steps you take and the statues seem to move closer to one another. The woman's dress slides down her shoulders invitingly; the man's face shifts into a twisted grin. As you draw nearer to the house, the man draws nearer to damnation and the woman draws nearer to carnality. Perfect gentleman has turned into Mister Hyde, and reveals himself ready for things far worse. By the time the two figures are close enough to grasp one another, the man looks like a shaved ape, a true predator. He has drawn a knife and the lady's features fill with sweet surrender. Soon her clothes are shreds on the ground and he has changed yet again. Where once he had legs, there is a long serpent body like the Ray Harryhausen Medusa. In one arm, he holds a sword aloft, and with the other he reaches into her chest. Her face is orgasmic and fearless, her posture the eager victim's. Right outside the front door, the woman stands up. Her feet are cloven hooves and leathery, draconic wings spring from her back. These devils dance together. May that serpent king dance into my midst and find death at the edge of my swordcane. I know that statue's final face and I know I want to come home with the head it sits on. Maybe I'll also be lucky enough to rid the world of Ian Sterling while I'm at it.

Cass knows why we're at this party, but when Cass is excited, she's excited, and the Contessa's mansion is a reasonable source of excitement for anybody who's been obsessed with crime and violence as long as she has. This is, after all the place where the who's who of slaughter and depravity meet to relieve the tension of cutting a swathe through the populace. I almost feel bad for revealing the innate corruption and terror of Reap, which makes all this a little bit less like a senior prom or dinner at the Whitehouse. The sense of wonder is still with her just a bit, and I'm actually kind of glad. I would hate to have ruined this completely. A dream is still a dream. Though, I can see that for me, this will be something of a nightmare. I'm already uncomfortable with the company of the monsters outside. The company of the ones within will be more than a bit of unease. And from what I've heard about these parties…

"I swear, Jeremy, I'll stay out of the back rooms," she says, grabbing my hand and partially reading my mind, "Ian will make sure I do."

"Who says that I'll stay out?" he jokes, "I'm single and ready to swing, sweetheart."

There's something wounded about him tonight. Something that I could only call "profoundly beat." His smile is tissue paper. Something's catching up to him. Something really big. Makes me feel almost bad about the fate he's going to have to suffer. But there's no time to be weak. Jack could be in there, after all, and if you get weak, he'll eat you. Not just you, but maybe your soul. Never forget who your targets are. Don't stop to pity them. Pity makes their human faces realer, pity should belong to the innocent. Pity is the voice that tells you you've gone mad. This is one of Jack's own sayings, one quite pertinent to the act of hunting him and his kind. I will impale him on my irony and run him through with his own transgressions. Poetry, absolute poetry.

The woman who answers the door wears nothing but a bowtie, fishnet tights and black angel wings. She has nothing to hide. It's admirable, considering she's probably somebody with a lot to hide. I'm a bit shocked by her outfit, even after having been to Le Couteau on two occasions. It indicates that this party is either very high class or completely devoid of it.

"Come in," she says in the sultriest monotone she can muster for a couple of D list guests, "Milady welcomes Ian Sterling and guests."

A nervous Ian doesn't even give her so much as a "hello". Since "guest" is not my name, I don't feel inclined to give her one.

"I was, um, wondering, if Godless- Mr. Cavanagh-was going to be around this evening. I was hoping to get an interview

from him about the Mr.400…umm, thing. The Mr.400 thing…"
Ian gulps and stutters out his question, meteorically plummeting
his air of importance to the ground.

The girl shrugs. Being announced at the door is the most
you can expect from people like her. Having been announced,
Ian's moment of relevance is gone. I MUST continue to enjoy
this, regardless of how frazzled and twitchy he looks. I must
greet the failures of Ian Sterling with inward sardonic laughter,
for if I do not he'll be too pathetic to destroy, a sacrificial lamb.
She leads us into a lavish, faux-Baroque ballroom. It is
wallpapered in red, though little wallpaper shows beneath all of
the portraits. Rich as this woman is, she still smacks of nouveau
riche. Too much everywhere. Portraits of Vlad the Impaler,
Elizabeth Bathory, various Jack the Ripper suspects, and every
actor who has ever played Dracula. The room has no need for
wall sconces, but she has some anyway, in the shape of small
dragons. Between two of these sconces is the one piece of art
here that I don't know what to make of. It's nothing but a black
canvas with a gaping blood red zero in the middle of it. On
closer examination I can figure it out a little better. There are
initials in the bottom corner, and next to the initials is another
little red zero. The initials are GJC. These displays of gaudiness
look almost pallid compared to the chandelier. It is made of fine
crystal, adorned with golden dragons that carry the bulbs lighting
the room in their mouths.

The ballroom is full of impeccably dressed and
impeccably undressed people, who I actually find myself hoping
Ian knows some of, because if he doesn't belong here then I
don't belong here, and it's hard to sneak around a place you
don't belong. Accustomed as he is to being a VIP, he looks
shocked that nobody is swarming to him. Poor little bigshot.
Poor me having to count on his importance to avoid sticking out
like a sore thumb.

It's almost laughable. With all the eagerness to be here
and the two years of almost wrangling invitations, he's as out of
place here as I was at Le Couteau. As a serial killer, I actually
belong here more than he does. This isn't a place for poseurs and
fans, but rather one for monsters and their cultists, groupies and
accomplices (though I recognize a couple higherups from the

local police), a place for those who DO. He's interviewed a few of these people, he says, some of them post on his forum, but their intellectual investment isn't what makes them pro-Reap. The girls here have come with news reporters, politicians, Reap activists and quite a few small time and big time killers on their arm.

Hacksaw Sally is twenty nine and in fact quite striking. Her trucker garb and bulging biceps are almost a kind of fetish costume. She used to be able to just pick up guys at truckstops, offer them a good time and then bring them somewhere private to saw them in half like some kind of twisted stage magician. But, her face has spread too far. She has to go to real isolated places, wear a wig or just sneak up behind the guy and knock him out. She never explained to the press if it was rape, child abuse, unchecked sexual aggression, a vendetta against truckers or whatever. All there is to know right now is that she's strong as an ox, famous and right here with two of the Contessa' s ladies on each arm. She's up for a Bundy, and all Ian gets to do is write about it. Him and Cass strain not to walk up to her. Ian strains the most, because Cass gets to be part of this world for real and he's nothing but words.

"Is that Ian Sterling over there?" Sally asks one of her escorts. The girl, an anorexically thin Chinese girl with cuts all over her arms nods. There's a glint of disbelief on Sally's face for a moment.

"Good for him," she says. The girls laugh. A trendy middle-aged woman in less-than-flattering vinyl shares the laugh and approaches her. I ask Cass if that's the Contessa and she shakes her head "no" in disgust.

"Tell me, Sally," the lady in vinyl purrs, "what are YOU going to do if you get a hold of this damn Mr.400 character?"

"I'm gonna do the best I can." Sally's attempts at being uptight and sophisticated falter when she breaks into hysterical laughter at her own ancient, Vaudevillian comeback. Careful with that joke, it's an antique. Of course, the laughter is echoed, save by an increasingly more awkward Ian who doesn't notice that a joke was even told until it's too late. Or maybe the comment bothers him. Seldom have I been so curious about what somebody I respected so little was thinking. Sally takes her two escorts and vanishes with them down a hallway where dry ice smoke backlit by purple smoke is used in a baffling attempt to make the corridor look mysterious. This is when I gather that the ballroom is probably not considered the place to be.

Ian, Cass and I don't really budge, we don't really mingle, and we don't think to go anywhere. The three of us are sharing a realization central to Reap culture: the realization that we are all expendable. Should anybody judge their worth by their standing at a party? There is only one answer to this question: if the party is more relevant than the rest of your life. Ian's life is Reap and Reap is here, therefore, if Ian is irrelevant in this room, Ian's life is irrelevant. I had previously been wondering whether tonight I would kill this pathetic son-of-a-bitch or Hacksaw Sally. I can't believe I armed myself so lightly for a chance at Godless Jack. I realize that Hacksaw Sally has knocked out bigger guys than me. If I swing that swordcane at her, she's going to knock me to the ground, cut me in two, splay me open and turn my torso into a suitcase. Thus, from a logistical viewpoint, there is but the only one recourse. And I admit it, in spite of the bad joke, there's something I kind of like about Hacksaw Sally.

Relief dominates Ian's expression when he at last sees somebody he knows. He runs a desperate girlish run that attracts disdainful stares and muffled chuckles alike. His acquaintance is a chubby 20-something covered in tattoos of hearts and flowers, from her cheeks to the small of her back, and all over her fairly well-muscled arms. She dances in that way people who don't dance tend to, the kind of dancing that acknowledges the music but politely declines to move to it. She sort of bobs her head as she leans against the wall, making it look like leaning against the wall is more pressing than dancing. One look at her trying to "dance" and you know that she's like Ian; one of an endless network of friends of friends. He's far too desperate to realize that she's not at the top of the social food chain either.

"Hey, Elyse, what's goin' on?" he asks.

She shrugs. "Shit, man, do I look busy? I thought this would be life-affirming, but it's all pretty dull. By the way, sorry about the…that you had to…"

"Thanks. I almost feel responsible."

"Disturbed is disturbed, Ian. That kid wasn't your responsibility. Try to have a good time. You deserve it. You know what you oughta do..."

Ian goes white as a sheet. "Don't even say it."

"Fuck, Ian, you should know I'll say it. I didn't think you were so shy. You're more important than bullshit like that."

Ian smiles. "I'm an internet celebrity, Elyse. It's like being the biggest rockstar in Rhode Island or the king of the West Virginia opera scene."

She looks almost coy as she tries to push him into sneaking off. "But those guys didn't get an invite."

He looks longingly at the stage lit corridors. I know that he's not going to be able to resist this. Cass has managed a minor personal victory by getting some gossip out of the topless girl at the door. This means that I'm momentarily out of her scrutiny. I know she wouldn't approve of me killing Ian, but this is something that she'll just have to understand. This is too sweet a chance to pass up, to kill a Reap guru in his moment of weakness as he stands in the highest bastion of Reap culture. The hallways will have very little scrutiny, the chambers will be very private and screaming won't be that foreign of a noise here. Not to mention that of course the Contessa has her house built in a Safe Zone. When he sneaks down the corridor to the left, one lit in a satanic red instead of a violet and still full of smoke, I follow him, padding lightly and slipping through the places where the crowd is thickest.

I am a spirit in the smoke, most likely a model of stealth in comparison to Ian's brand of "sneaking." Ian's idea of stealth is tiptoeing and hunching over like Abbot and Costello in a mad doctor's lab. I just stay close to the walls and make long, quiet strides. He peeks through doorways, not knowing what he's looking for. An interview? A scandal? An orgy? Nothing seems to interest him down the first of the corridors, nothing at all. The smoke is thicker as he continues down the hall, which branches in two directions. He stops and thinks for a moment which one would make more sense, but then comes to the realization that he wouldn't know where to look if he tried. He picks the right corridor. So, of course, do I.

The mansion proclaims how much is hidden there, in the emptiness and smokiness of this corridor. The fog machines are running at their highest here, making it possible to just stroll down the hallway and see into the open rooms, which must proclaim their charms while the corridor hides their location. The scent of drugs is almost as thick as the cheesy dry-ice smoke and fog. Inky sweet opium wafts through the fog, as if we were walking in the mind of some Romantic poet. What kind of party is this Contessa throwing when it starts to remind me of Coleridge's brain? Among the opium and smoke scents, there is a tinge of something sort of metallic, sort of earthy. Blood. Now he's getting close to something interesting. But he's still not quite isolated enough for me to stab him. I'm getting sort of impatient, but I can't compromise the kill on a whim.

At last, the smoke fades and there is only darkness. He moves toward an open door and I get behind him. I get ready to drag him over here, choke him and then run him through, but I stop. Ian is stunned by what he sees inside. I would be, if it weren't for the fact that I have to find some place to make sure I'm really concealed. Beyond that door is something I didn't think I'd see tonight. Something I wasn't quite prepared for. I have to choke back a sob, but Ian can't. He falls to his knees and even in the dark I know that there's a look on his face that says "how could you, God? Where are you?" I don't blame him for it. I feel a tinge of camaraderie finally seeing something sicken him. It affirms our shared humanity and our shared observation of an inhumanity.

A young woman with hair dyed an emerald green lies back on a steel table. She is naked, her breasts plump and firm, with huge, pink nipples. Her belly protrudes a bit, round and unbalanced, not quite fat, since she's in good shape, but obviously pregnant still. A look of religious ecstasy is on her face, eyes wide and looking up toward a Heaven she thinks might be close. She doesn't need her arms held down, but two of the Contessa's girls do it anyway. They seem to think that something would make her move, would make her run. I hope so. I hope she runs down the corridor, with those girls following her, I hope she gets to the ballroom and I hope she gets the hell out. But, that's not her intention. She plans on sitting through whatever procedure is ahead.

This isn't when Ian starts crying, nor is it when I get the sense to hide. No, it takes a second for that. That second is brought on by a tall, nude figure stepping into the light, though at first she is visible only from behind. Her long, jet black hair extends halfway down her back. Her body is toned and voluptuous with a large round ass the color and texture of linen. This smoothness makes her skin look pristine, but when she turns around, angling herself almost as if she were showing everyone in the hallway, this is revealed to be quite untrue. Stretchmarks cover her large, perfect breasts, and on her lean stomach are various scars. They lead down and interconnect, forming a pattern like the veins of some obscene, scarlet, leaf. They lead down to her inner thighs and almost to her kneecaps. She stands proud of her nudity, never having tried makeup or surgery to do something about all of her cuts. The pride of Whitechapel girls in their fright makeup looks so silly next to the badge of honor that she makes from all of her cuts. This is what they longed so much to be, a proud carcass, a symbol of triumphant victimhood and a pure, unfettered exaltation in death. But, the nobility of her bearing and the authority in her eyes, only slightly visible beneath the ornate half-mask on her face, show that she is something more. This woman feels herself the Persephone to Jack's Hades. The sculptures all make so much sense to me now. From Ian's fall prostrate, it is clear that he sees it just as plainly.

The Contessa's knife seems to come from nowhere. I am certain this is my nerves and my knowledge of what might happen next, but it FEELS like an act of dark magic. The eyes blaze beneath the black, feathery halfmask, and she mumbles something that I feel glad that I don't hear. I am fairly certain hears it. She runs the blade down the woman's belly, caressing it, gently teasing it. I feel a moment of relief. Some kind of kinky Wiccan S&M thing. Just some kind of fetish play. She repeats the motion, mumbles something else and bends down; gently kissing everywhere she traced the knife. The woman's face registers pure pleasure and reverence. Her wide eyes close and a moan escapes her mouth. The two girls once in silent witness echo the coos of satisfaction and seem to shake a little in anticipation. I no longer feel the relief when I see this. I want to flee, but I want even more to see what happens, to feel Ian suffer at the hands of his passions. I have to watch.

The knife traces the path one more time. The Contessa finally speaks. Her voice has a faint New England accent that even her position in Reap society couldn't free her from.

"Just as I gave mine, gave my child, gave my husband, so too do you give, to let him, the serpent's emissary live. Give with pleasure, give with love. One is present to witness. He sits in the hallway. He sought to see something special tonight and he shall. Know that your gift is witnessed and your gift brings joy and life. Glory to the Morningstar, glory to the noble serpent. Your gift brings joy and life."

"My gift brings joy and life," the pregnant woman mumbles and the Contessa lowers the knife one last time. She is not kind this time, this time there is nothing erotic. There is only a cut, a long, vicious cut that rends the flesh open. She follows the cut again, combining precision with brutality, and the girl's eyes open. There is no longer the worshipful gaze of the cultist. There is now the pathetic shock of a drunk stabbed in a bar brawl. This couldn't be happening, her eyes say. Although she submitted so eagerly, she couldn't have imagined the pain. She stares at the open wound. She stares at the opening of her womb. The girls prepare spools of surgical thread, showing brief disgust at what they'll have to sew back up. I've killed so many, but my eyes are usually not with me this firmly. My eyes want to go, but I don't let them. I have to bear witness. I have to see how Jack is fed. There must have been so many others.

The Contessa reaches in to the opened womb and takes from it something small, porcine, and piscine, a fish, a pig, not a person. It couldn't ever be a person I don't think. But I know it is. I get the urge to run in there and kill them all, to let Jack starve for a day, but the Contessa and the girls will know who I am if I do. Maybe they'd know who I was if I killed Godless Jack or Hacksaw Sally, but if I killed Godless Jack, it wouldn't matter that my cover was blown. I'm scared too. I hate to admit it, but I'm terrified. I feel the darkness and the power emanating from that room, something nobody with a sane mind and a penis could or should understand. When I try to move, my limbs feel like they'll collapse under the blasphemy. The Contessa takes what in three months would have been a baby and deposits it in a large tub of distilled water on the floor. Perhaps this is to sanitize it, but I have a feeling that it's also so it keeps.

The Contessa walks out into the hallway and looks down at Ian. I hold my breath, knowing that if I'm heard, I'm as good as dead.

"Was that enjoyable, Mr. Sterling? Do you really think you were worthy of witnessing something so sacred?"

Ian bursts into tears. The answer is obvious.

"Come with me," she says. It takes him awhile to get to his feet, but he comes with her, and for some reason, though I stay close to the walls and sneak as best I can, so do I. At the end of all the twisting hallways, she opens a door and leads Ian in. Two girls are waiting, half naked, each one brandishing a heavy length of chain. They bow when she enters. I'm amazed that the Contessa's bold enough to never close her doors. She wanted someone to see her devotion, to watch and be sickened and be amazed. She wants someone to watch what happens to Ian as well, and that someone will be me.

"How can we serve you, Milady?" one of the girls asks.

"Make sure he never wants to tell anyone."

They nod and she goes. Ian doesn't put up any resistance when they chain him to a pair of manacles hanging on the wall. This woman's Gothic and Medieval sensibilities really start to get on my nerves. One girl grabs a syringe and another length of chain. Ian's eyes go blank and glassy when the first girl injects him. The girl with the length of chain opens his shirt and removes his pants. I have a feeling I know what lies ahead, and yet, I don't look away. The chain hits him heavy in the chest, and then on each leg. The girl with the syringe abruptly thrusts the tip into his balls. He doesn't even look present enough to scream, though I know damn well that he feels it.

I don't know exactly what prompts me to do what I do next. I imagine it's some of that pity that I keep telling myself is a mortal sin. No man should die like this, even if he does serve the Dark Ones in his way. No man, that is, save Godless Jack, whose friends and hangers-on do this to a man to keep him safe.

I cannot see the Dark Ones, but I feel them present. I feel them in the cruelty of each of these girls, in the dire acts done for the Contessa. I thought that I would kill Ian tonight, but things change. I spring the blade of the swordcane and I do something thoroughly irrational; I go blazing in like Errol Flynn. I swear that somebody walking down the hallway might have caught a glimpse of me, but it doesn't matter.

I catch the girl with the chain from behind, slice the back of her knee with a low sweep. She turns, bleeding and confused, to take a good, solid left hook to the side of her face. She swings the chain and hits me good in the side, which makes me want to drop the swordcane and get running. But I don't. Instead, I slice her in the throat. She holds the wound, surprised and staggers back. The girl with the syringe tries to run, but I won't have it. I trip her, and finish her by stabbing her in the belly. The girl with the chain falls to her knees and would beg if it weren't for the fact that I cut her throat. Instead, I go low with the swordcane, stabbing her in the heart.

A drugged and half-conscious Ian looks at me, and I remember that friend of his giving me a ride home when I was thoroughly sloshed and incapable of conscious thought. I owe Ian Sterling a favor, I remember. While I kind of saved his life already, more needs to be done. I open up the manacles and let him loose. He looks at me through blurry eyes, looks at me ten feet away from the gates of Hell and he asks, "Mr.400?"

"Yes, Ian," I reply, "it's Mr.400."

"Thank fucking God," he says before fainting. I break the window. Anybody who tells you that jumping out a window with a six foot five inch tall man slung over your shoulder is easy is a fucking idiot. I don't fancy ever doing this again. I deposit him in the car and put him on the steps of the hospital. I've been a Good Samaritan, so I leave him with an ultimatum.

"I'm leaving you on the steps. If you can get to the lobby, maybe you'll get treatment and live."

So Ian does something that finally makes me stop hating him that makes me his friend: he crawls inside. Naked, covered in bruises and delirious, he still manages to crawl inside.

__First Blood__

I can't get my mind off Ian in the hospital. It will be a couple days before he's ready for visitors. So, I need something to get my mind off this bullshit. Maybe that's not the best reason to go after a dangerous lunatic. But, this is a dangerous lunatic who needs someone to go after him. He's killed one hundred four women over three years, almost one a week. He's a real predator who isn't going to stop just because he's famous or rich enough. Last night Jeremy told me why Jack had the luxury of the retiring, and I wish I didn't know. All these others aren't going to retire and they're not going to jail. Jeremy was brave last night. Jeremy gets to be brave all the time. So, I'm going to be brave now.

My counterattack checklist seems short. For the last raid we were armed to the teeth, but that's not an advantage I'm going to have. My checklist contains two items: revolver and Jeremy's syringe. Use the latter, then the former. Remember not to accept any food or drink. Any food he gives you is poison. Any drink he gives you is poison. He never meets at a restaurant, that's one way I knew it was him when I called in about the classified ad. Mr. Right prefers to meet at his apartment. Every girl in America knows what he looks like, but they don't see him until they're in the apartment. If he's recognized, he's quick and dirty. .44 magnum to the head. Nothing you get to survive. So I can't let on that I know who he is. Not at all. I don't follow Reap. I don't have time to watch the news.

I find myself taking the long way, I find myself driving too slowly. I find myself almost getting lost. I find myself horrified. There's a good chance I won't come out alive. Jeremy yelled and screamed and told me not to. He reminded me how many this man had killed, how bad he was and how I shouldn't do it. I reminded him there was no way he could. Only a woman can get close to Mr. Right or at least close enough to kill him. He didn't know what to say, he just kept on going on and on about what a bad idea it was, making it even harder than it should be. None of the other girls will have a chance to fight back, and I needed a chance to fight back against Reap. Reap had almost taken a friend and a boyfriend from me, and Reap could very well take him for good. I had to do this. I have to do this. But I make this car hesitate for me. If I drive slowly, it feels like it's the car's fault. Stupid Jeremy. I'll get there already nervous.

But of course, the city catches up to me, the apartment and the block ahead are catching up to me. I feel so tiny. I feel like I might need the big man who yelled at me not to do it and who told me I could get hurt here. I don't want that. Rage comes in. I can't let Jeremy be right about this. I won this argument. He helped me out the door, he gave me the gun, and he gave me the advice. I'm not too timid to kill a man. It's all a big schoolyard, and he's coming between me and being right and he's coming between me and my dignity and I can't let him get away with this. I breathe deep and then I remind myself that I can't go in angry or nervous. I cannot go in if either of the two things I feel is in control.

I stand straight, fix my makeup. Look pretty, look unassuming. Don't look too unassuming. Too innocent is suspicious. If you look too innocent nowadays you're either a prostitute or a cop and neither one of them appeals to Mr. Right. Mr. Right is addicted to the seduction, to the hunt and to the notion that he is a more perfect male. Hence the name Mr. Right. Play a little hard to get. I unbutton the top two buttons of my blouse to give him a little something to look at, but not too much. I had thought of wearing stockings, but Jeremy said I'd look too perfect, too eager. So, it's a black blouse, a modest but revealing skirt and a pair of sensible black pumps. As I walk into the apartment building, I begin to lament the pumps. They're just not right for running in.

At Le Couteau, I've been used to dressing up as a victim, but now I feel like I'm walking into a horror movie. I might be here to hunt, but I'm still an innocent girl entering the lair of a psycho killer. Instead of an abandoned summer camp or a decaying old house in the middle of nowhere it's a pricey apartment building just touching the Safe Zone at the edges.

When I get in there, it's me and the monster, running away in high heels, possibly to fall and get stabbed. Maybe I should have gone a step further and just decided to wear a towel.

What would Kevin say? What would Neil say? They always said don't be a victim. They taught me how to fight and that sometimes there was no option but to fight. I'm going into a place where there's no option but to fight. They never told me act like a lady, they never told me to run when danger rears its ugly head, they said to fight. Remember the girl who took your coat. Remember the little preppy bitches in high school. Remember Godless Jack and remember your rage at Jeremy. Here it is, my chance to be that thing I felt like I needed to be every now and again to say sane. I smile. I can't believe I can muster a smile. I smile, and I'm confident and I'm going on a date. The fear subsides a little.

Then he answers the door. I think back to Kevin and Neil and Michael and that goddamn girl who took my coat. The smile is a knowing one. I know what I am capable of. I was capable of almost killing somebody when I was five years old. I have the rage and the power and I'm not going to let this man end things. I'm not going to make me die a victim. He's not too tough looking, a little doughy actually. He has kind of a belly that he's sucking in a little and he's not all that well developed in his arms and legs. So what am I afraid of?

Then I remember that as a five year old girl I certainly didn't look like I was capable of anything, so I shouldn't underestimate this guy with his humble brown hair and his lack of upper body strength and his surprisingly cheap cologne. I am walking into a horror movie. He could tear this face off at any moment and anything could be beneath it. He could have a full grown Alaskan timber wolf in that apartment ready to tear my guts out. It's hard to see when he's blocking the door. Peeking in would be suspicious and rude and could get me killed. Do not peek in. Just say hi. I take a little long with the hi. I think he suspects me immediately.

"Are you alright? Can I get you a glass of water? You seem nervous. Don't worry, I don't bite. Unless of course, that's what you're into."

God, the women who stay in this apartment for any reason besides killing him are absolutely pathetic. Are all the legends this small and fragile? The Cabana Boy could be poisoned. Wayne Pfenniger went down with a shot. This guy is no Mr. Right. He's not charming or trustworthy. But there's a bulge in his pocket. Is he just happy to see me maybe? I do look pretty good. Pretty funny. Good thing when I laughed to myself, it seemed like it was in regard to his joke. As if I could have been that easily impressed. It's sad, it really is. All of our villains and all of our heroes are nothing in person. No matter what's attached to them and what kind of importance you place on them, they always end up as something kinda disappointing. They always end up human. Kevin could beat up any boy in the neighborhood, but he couldn't beat up a plane crash. When will the time come for Jeremy when he has to fight a plane crash or his old age? How many shots will it take to kill cancer? This man is so far from cancer. I can't believe I have a Mr. Right t-shirt.

"What are we standing out here in the hallway for?" he asks. He smiles, and it's actually a nice smile. He opens the door, leads me in. He doesn't lock it behind him. I wonder why he doesn't lock it behind him. There's something funny about the walls in his living room. It dawns on me when I spot the computer and the amp and the guitar. Acoustical foam. Nobody could hear me scream. It's the good stuff, if it can keep people from hearing an electric guitar in the next apartment, then it could keep people from hearing anything. But then it dawns on me that maybe nobody is in the next apartment. A couple documents, a friend occasionally coming and going and he could fake a tenant next door. With all the dough he has, he could repeat the process. That's why he doesn't lock the door. This whole floor is his. He has a fixed address in the Safe Zone and women keep coming here. Jesus Christ. He feels invincible again. When we sit down on the couch, he doesn't make any kind of sleazy move or touch me. He doesn't offer me a drink or expect me to talk. He just lets me get comfortable. I slide my shoes off and I move a little closer.

"I'm sorry," I say to him, "I'm not used to being in a building this expensive and big and imposing. It's such a lovely place, I've always been nervous in very lovely places."

It feels to me like something Audrey Hepburn would say. A kind of humble downplayed sophistication. It feels like it might hold him for awhile, kill his suspicion. If he's not suspicious anymore, this will be a whole lot easier. But maybe he's one of those people who are always suspicious. I have to wonder what's in his pocket and there's no way of determining what it is without blowing my cover and implying that I suspect him of something. He smiles quietly and doesn't immediately respond to my comment. He does inch toward me because I inched towards him. He places his hand on my thigh all of a sudden and then it moves up. I move to slap him, and like lightning he's reached into his pocket and taken out the contents. Like lightning he's grabbed it. And it is lightning. I feel the voltage enter me, swim through my bloodstream, arcing with every drop of the seventy-five percent water that I'm made of. I look up in shock as I go limp. I'm stunned momentarily, planning what I'll do when I recover. He says nothing. He doesn't make a move for me again. He goes for my purse instead, taking the gun and the syringe out of it.

"You know what I'm not going to do to you, you filthy whore. You traitorous little bitch, you know what I'm not going to do to you?"

My mouth is numb. I can't move it to say that I don't know what he's going to do to me or to tell him to fry in hell, or to say anything at all to him. I don't know what he's not going to do to me, because I have no clue what he will. He wasn't cancer, but the electricity in his hands was lightning, like Jeremy calls himself. Lightning from God. Men make themselves forces of nature by taking them into their hands. With the poison from the syringe, I could have made myself a vine of curare or a living sprig of nightshade, but he beat me to the punch.

"You're not answering," he says, "Why don't you answer, Cassandra? It's not Natalie at all. Now that's just rude. Sure, I give fake names, and I do what you're doing, but you don't need to give a fake name. You have such a pretty one. Do you know how I know your beautiful name, the name of the prophetess nobody would listen to? Do you? I haven't emptied out your wallet, yet. You didn't call from your home phone. So how should I know who you are?"

The feeling in my mouth at least returns. I could lean over and bite him if I wanted to get myself shot. "No, I don't know…"

"I'm sorry. I didn't answer my first question. I am not going to poison you, Cassandra. I am not going to poison you or shoot you. I'm not going to do that because then I'd be no better than that asshole Mr.400, the asshole that killed my dear old friend Tom. I think I'll send your tits to Tom's grave. He would have wanted them. You're a whore for Mr.400, ain't ya? Tempting me like that, making me want to kill you, so you could go and kill me?"

"I'm not a whore," I choke out. The longer I keep my dignity, the longer it will take him to kill me. I have to wait for the feeling to return to my body. Then I realize I won't let on when it does, so he won't give me another shock. I also don't want him to rape me. Even if I die, I don't want him to rape me, and I think he won't unless I say that I'm a whore and act like I want it. I won't act like I want it, even if I'm begging to live. I think about Kevin again. Kevin would have never begged the plane crash to let him live. Do not bargain with the agency of your destruction. Do not beg it for anything. Act like he doesn't have your life to give you.

"You're a whore. You tried to use sex to get what you wanted. But then, I guess you can call me a whore. I can lure them with my charm, and then I can go ahead and kill them. You decided you were going to be a better whore than me. There is no better seducer than me. I lured you here to kill me. I knew who you were and I invited you here, so that you could come here to kill me and I could kill you. God, you sure are gullible. I know Mr. 400 can take care of himself, but Jack and I agreed that we wanted to catch him all alone. I would love to have made him watch me fucking you til you bleed to death, but I'm not used to taking on men. I admit that they're too strong for me. We are, after all the stronger sex."

Jack knows. Jack knows who Mr.400 is. Jack knows who I am. Jack has come for Jeremy. Do I want to kill this guy or let him kill me? I wish I could give up and it would mean he didn't win. Jeremy had better be alive when I get home. I had better get home. I have to let him talk. I have to let him torture me with his words, so he won't use that taser.

"He's killed anyone you've sent against him," I tell him, "anybody you sent to that apartment is dead."

"You're trying to stall me," he says, "I know women." He grabs the taser and turns it on. He tries to shock me again, but I roll out of the way. It hurts like hell and my joints feel numb, but I stand up. I don't think I could do anything more complicated than standing up, so standing up will have to do. He looks concerned, oddly concerned for somebody wielding a taser against a woman so much smaller than himself. Think of him as the small one. Underestimate him now. I stumble toward the kitchen and he follows with the taser. He begins to run, and that's when I know what to do again.

I let him get close, close enough to lunge with the taser, and that's when I trip him. He doesn't fall but he's momentarily off balance. I elbow him the chest and he instinctually clutches it, leaving the hand with the taser open. I get closer, perhaps too close, but it's what I need to do in order to bite his wrist, which sure enough causes him to let go of the taser, which I grab. The second I take to turn it on is too long. He goes low with the hand that clutched his chest and it hits me hard in the stomach. He reaches and he grabs for my hand, which now holds his taser. We tussle and I fall backward into the kitchen.

I'm glad I took off my heels, but it still doesn't help on account of the many ball bearings that he's laid out on his floor. I roll briefly and then I go down. I hit my head hard, and my vision starts to blur a little. I'm relieved that I feel the weight of the taser in my hand. I still have it and he's not going to shock me. He moves to his kitchen counter and takes out a big knife. I'm surprised that he's stupid enough to bend down and stab me. When he does, he gets a big shock and he hits his kitchen floor. I reach for his zipper. He tries to stop me and cuts me in the arm with the knife, but I do it. With my other hand, I bring down the taser and he begins to twitch violently. The knife drops and I'm back in control. I should be beyond being a sadist, but I know I don't want him to get up, so I shock him until the taser runs out of juice.

Then, when my vision begins to return, I lose myself to sadism. I know what he would do if I let him live too long, so I make sure to do something like it first. I pin his hand to the floor with the knife he had, trying to ignore the cut in my own hand. I reach for another knife for his other hand and I plunge it in deep to make sure he can't move. I head to the living room, grab some extension cord from his amp and I tie his legs together. Then, I bend down and pick up all the ball bearings. That's when I force his mouth open, and drop them one at a time down his throat.

His eyes regrettably open before he chokes to death and he begins to cough up all the ball bearings. He tries to move his hands and pull the knives out of them, but he can't. He struggles with his legs to try and free them from the cords, but he can't. He tries so hard to make himself stand to be in a position of dignity, but he can't. Down there on the floor, he might as well be dead, but he isn't. I can finish him any time I want to, though. Any time I want to. In the living room, I slide on my heels and on my way into the kitchen, I walk across him, and then up and down his body. He gasps for breath, but what comes out is a little moaning noise. I let him catch his breath and then I watch him. I find myself fascinated by this, by his descent into victimhood, by my knowledge that I can kill him whenever I choose. I pull up a chair and I look him over, wondering what's wrong with me and why I can't let this poor specimen die.

"I know why you're not killing me," he says, suddenly seeming big and important, "I can tell you exactly why. You're not killing me because you don't want to go home and find him dead. As long as you let me live, you don't have to go home and see that what I told you is true."

I can't honestly say if he was bluffing, there's no way at all to tell and that's what bothers me most. If he's had this kind of encounter, he's unhooked the phone. If I kill Mr. Right and leave, then I'll be certain what he said was true, if it was true. There is no telling how many Jack sent or just how good they are. This guy knows that. He expects me to give him some kind of edge by letting him torture me psychologically even though he's the one pinned down to his kitchen floor by two knives.

"Shut up!" I yell at him and I know this was a bad move. He knows now that he's made me upset and I could make a mistake. Never mind that he's as good as dead, I could still make a mistake. There's a lot a person can survive and maybe God doesn't have the mercy to just let a piece of shit like this die of the hemorrhaging. It dawns on me after that that he knows where Jack got the information from. I, sadly enough, need him to talk again, even though every time he talks I feel weaker.

"How did Jack find out that Jeremy was Mr. 400?"

He laughs, he laughs and laughs, and in spite of the knives in his hands and the ball bearings I almost made him swallow and the heavy duty extension cord around his legs. He laughs at me. This little man on the ground who should be begging me for mercy is laughing at me. Now I am the force of nature. Now I am the thing you don't bargain with, the inescapable fate. But how, then is he escaping it? I give him a kick to the head, a good hard one. It makes him stop laughing, but it doesn't get me the information.

"Tell me, you piece of shit! How does Jack know?"

"Maybe he reads tarot cards. Maybe the devil told him. Jack and the devil are old friends."

I kick him again, harder. Then I kick him the sides.

"How the fuck does Jack know?" I scream, and the laughter continues, louder and louder. I kick him, over and over and over and I can see the laughter is starting to fade out and weaken. I realize then that I'm not getting this information, and that even if I knew where Jack had gotten the information, it wouldn't mean anything, because it wouldn't help me hide. Godless Jack knows who I am and who Jeremy is. The man on the floor is almost dead, but he remains arrogant because he knows that I might very well be almost dead, too and it gives him no end of edge, no end of arrogance. I'm never going to seem big to him, because I'm a woman. He can do this because women seem small to him. I feel even more like killing him, but it doesn't come, I just find myself, kicking and kicking, leaving marks and bruises and indentations on the side of a thick and infuriating skull. This is my weakness, I realize, I'm not going for the kill because I like the pain, I like to feel big, I'm so scared of being a victim that I'm a bully in this circumstance. If I keep on torturing him, he'll survive and I'll be that much further from knowing how Jeremy is, which I'm actually in fact scared about.

I walk very slowly to the counter. It's like the drive over, but I know I'm the one stalling. I take a moment and flash it in front of his blurry eyes. He gives a sound somewhat like a laugh, a tiny tiny laugh that longs to be but doesn't make it. Then, I drive it home. It takes me a little too long to do it, I guess because it's scary to kill. I didn't think it would be so scary. The torture and the rage came so easily but the mercy and the courage didn't. I stare for too long at my first kill and then I search his apartment for anything valuable or any clues.

Under his bed, there's a suitcase with a couple thousand in cash. Excellent. This could buy the nuclear weapon we're gonna need from Jones. Also under the bed is a young woman's head. It's a recent kill, one that looks very shocked. She doesn't look at all satisfied that he's gone, she doesn't look like what I did actually mattered. It dawns on me that in a real fight, a guy like this wouldn't be an asset at all to Jack. A guy like this could only get in the way. Except for the fact that he owns a 44 magnum. I guess that's not nothing. I root around in his dresser drawers, finding all kinds of pornography, all kinds of nude photos from female fans with little slashmarks drawn on them and cumstains all over. I linger over these, wondering just what it was that would make a guy feel that way about women. I feel suddenly empowered when I realize that I don't care. He's dead.

The real find is in the bottom drawer of the dresser, the real find is the gun. He wasn't lying. He wasn't going to shoot me. I have no clue what he would have done to me, except for his promise that he would have cut my breasts off and given them to the Cabana Boy's grave. His apartment feels like a shrine, a tomb, a haunted house. I feel like the guy in the kitchen that I just killed probably isn't dead. It's an awful feeling, feeling that somebody you just actively sought to kill probably isn't dead. Very disturbing. Nothing here but porn and a big gun. Nothing special at all.

I go out to the car, thinking I should be proud of the big gun I took off of this guy, of the people I'd shoot with it. But I end up thinking about my weakness, my sadism. He wanted to see me suffer and he did. He watched as I struggled to force myself to stop torturing him. He delighted in the fact that I was too much of a sadist to let him die. He felt like this would be an advantage, like it would be something Jack could use against us. I feel sick to my stomach instead of proud. Nothing I did mattered, because he wasn't a threat. He was only a stranger with candy that stupid children went with. He might have killed a lot of women, and then a woman killed him, but I let him die slowly, I drew it out and turned it into a personal triumph when there was really nothing to exalt in.

When I get home, I think about Kevin, Michael and Neil and how much they actually hurt me. They made me scared to be vulnerable, they made me ashamed of being part of a weak sex and they did everything Mister Right did. They taught me how to hurt myself, and how to spread pain. I walk in and Jeremy is sitting in the living room with seven bodies. I don't take any time to ask him what happened, because I know. I know that he must have been recorded killing off those girls who were torturing Ian, who were delighting in spreading pain. Those girls, those girls like me and Mr. Right. He's silent and looks as if he's been wondering what to do forever.

I show him the magnum and the suitcase full of cash. "I think we need to find Jones," I tell him, "I think we need to go to Jones and get a nuclear weapon or something."

He takes the gun because he sees in my eyes that I don't deserve it.

High Noon Approaches

Cass is acting funny. Even for Cass. I've asked her about how the Mr. Right conflict went and all she says is "he's dead, that's all you need to know." She's held guns before at the firing range and everything, so I have to wonder why Mr. Right's magnum repulses her so much. It's just like the guns she's used, but it's bigger. Maybe she'll tell me about it, maybe she won't, but at least she got rid of the guy. As we drive to Connecticut, she looks like she'll cry from time to time. Whether this is on account of her skirmish with Mr. Right or something else entirely, I can't really say. She just looks much worse for the wear about it.

People are after us. I'm not sure if they're on the road or anything, but my cover is blown and people are after us. No matter where I go, his people are going to be after us. I keep looking for out-of-state plates and I keep on trying to swerve away from them. This might be making Cass more uncomfortable, but it could be them, it could always be them. I wonder if the Dark Ones tell him things. Do they send him messages in his dreams or relay things through scouts? Do they tell his minions everywhere we're going so that they can catch up to us, rape Cass to death and end everything? Maybe Mr. Right told her something. She said he knew who I was. It must have been through the Contessa, who must have sent my name and face to others. No more mask I guess. It's worthless. Good. Those damn lenses might impair my shooting. My shooting is going to be very important because the minions of Godless Jack are on my tail.

The realization that I'm not in fact a paranoid freak comes with the flare. I just skid out of its way, though it's amazing that I do, because this guy throws the things really well and a lot of the time they end up being more than a distraction. His fat, ignorant face smiles through his windshield as he rolls down his window and begins to shoot. I know this guy as a crack shot and an incredible marksman. Nobody shoots out a pair of tires like the I-80 Roadflare. There's only one way I can get around getting my tires shot out.

"Cass, roll down the window and start shooting," I tell her.

The Roadflare is surprised by two things. One that he is being shot at and two, that I have put the car in reverse and am starting to spin in place. This doesn't help Cass' shooting any, but he's too confused to get at my tires. A state trooper yells to both of us to step out of our vehicles. It goes without saying that this is not going to happen. The Roadflare does me a favor and shoots the state trooper in the head while he's calling for backup. During this grave miscalculation of his priorities, Cass manages to shatter HIS windshield with a bullet. First goes the windshield and then hopefully his skull. But, I don't have time to check.

I intentionally take the wrong exit, which is likely to add about fifteen minutes to my travel time, but I figure it will definitely throw whoever's after me off.

"Wow," says Cass, "I've killed Mr. Right and the I-80 Roadflare. That's two Bundy nominees. And two people."

"I killed my foster mother," I tell her, and I'm not exactly certain where it comes from, "I was fifteen when I first heard the voice and began to see the Dark Ones. I was fifteen when I killed my foster mother. I saw them floating her and I saw the breeder there and I mixed the wrong pills. It felt awful in ways that living with her never had, which is odd, because I've killed a few people because nobody should be able to live with them."

Cass turns whiter. She looks bloodless and distant, like a comatose relative that needs unplugging. She sits and she thinks for a good four miles before she says or does anything again. What she does surprises me, in the way that things she does tend to do so often. She kisses me on the cheek. Then, she puts her pale, bloodless head on my lap. She still clutches the gun, now holding it to her chest like a teddy bear, which is appropriate because it is at the moment one of her two sources of security. It's kind of sad, since I'm the other one. At least she's the same for me. Maybe Jack knew Mr. Right was weak and let her get him, so that we'd be separated and his men could get me. It was a pathetic ambush. Seven hired thugs that plodded down the hallway like elephants and one at a time let me bring them down. The apartment was just big enough to make those idiots separate and get them killed all over. Mister 390 right now. Ten more and my t-shirt's right. Now I know how people who are in fact with stupid feel like.

I then realize that maybe ten thugs are in a VW bus on my tail. This gets me back into reality, makes me stop speculating and proves that the math is in the end not all that relevant. I think for a second that a big, black limo is following me, until it takes a left, when I take a right. You can fit ten people into a big, black limo, that's for damn sure and if each of those ten people had a gun, we'd be positively fucked. Will this be the way everywhere? Maybe Jones could get us a place in town for awhile. Cass could transfer to working for a law firm in Connecticut and...he's made me scared enough to run away from my old life. This is what they do. They force you into a little corner, make you beg for your life, for your livelihood. They make you into a coward. No more thinking like that. I suspect a quiet drive out of Cass, but Cass is full of surprises.

"I'm sorry about your foster mother. That you had to kill her, I mean."

"I'm not sure I had to kill her." She never thought that the Dark Ones were anything. She'd always thought it was just my head. It's strange to hear her use language like that.

"I think maybe Ian's column was right the time he wrote, "Nobody ever kills anybody that they don't have to." It takes a lot to kill. There're a lot of things we'll do before we kill."

I nod. "We'll lie to ourselves, we'll run and hide, we'll drug ourselves and fuck tons of strangers. We'll tell ourselves that the voices in our head never say anything that's true."

"If it wasn't true, then why would it have been in your head?"

There are too many answers to that question. I don't know how many of them she deserves or could endure to hear. Maybe it was an excuse to kill her. Maybe I reinterpreted things I knew to be true into simple little hieroglyphics. Maybe those things would still be a kind of truth. Those things would still be a kind of need. I can see what Ian and Cass mean. It's getting easier to do it, but I still hope the need doesn't come up too often. I hope that the need isn't sneaking up behind me in a black sedan full of members of Jack's serial killer horde, the mercenaries he's hired, ninjas, robots, whatever the fuck he'll send after me next, I hope it isn't driving up to me. More paranoia, this time not out of the fear of death, but the realization I might have to rain more of it down on my way to a more peaceful world. May there be a more peaceful world at the end of all of this. A more peaceful world when I use the nuclear weapon I'm going to get from Jones. Maybe not a nuclear weapon. Those are bad for peace, but I will get help from Jones. I won't ask him to hide us, although that still feels like a possibility and a damn good idea. Especially because of the ten thugs in the VW bus. The VW bus that I guess just disappeared. Goddammit, get back to reality.

I return to reality when I see the warehouse. We park a little ways away, and constantly look over our shoulders. Of course, neither of us is armed. We ring the doorbell and the familiar strains of "Brick House" echo through the air. The sun is setting and we can only hope that the night brings us safety. We can only hope that Jones will bring us safety. Nobody answers the door when I first ring the bell, but I'm counting on it. I ring it again and then one more time. Reiko answers the door. She is not dressed in her familiar kimono, but a Ramones t-shirt and a pair of ripped jeans. Her katana hangs at her side and a humorless expression is on her face as if we're selling something that she'd never have any need for.

"What the fuck do you want?" she asks, the mock geisha attitude gone, "it had better be good."

I wince. I can't imagine what I would do without help from Jones. I hope this can be resolved, because if it can't, I'm most likely as good as dead. Reiko sees this, and she softens. I remember Cass telling me that she's actually very nice and the geisha/martial arts killing machine thing is an act.

"Look," she says, "I like you. I've been rooting for you, whatever it is you actually hope to accomplish. And Cass is really sweet. We hung out together, I had an ice cream cone with her, and we talked. I'm not the one with the problem. Jones is angry, I'm gonna warn you about that outright."

"Thanks."

Jones is shooting pool and drinking a beer. Today's a day without pretense I guess. He's wearing jeans and a t-shirt like she was and a pair of Oxfords. It seemed unlikely that I would see him like this, like a real person and not a blatant criminal. He doesn't make any move toward me or even look at me. He watches the pool table, continuing to line up his shots.

"Well, if it isn't the person I was hoping to see less than anyone else on the planet. Aren't I lucky? What kind of trouble you brought this way, Jeremy? You bring Jack to take my head too? God, what the fuck makes you think you can come here when you're in as much trouble as you are?"

When he's done yelling, he finally looks at me. I would have left already if I could hope to find someplace better to go. There's as much pity as there is rage in his eyes, as there is the fear that I might bring something downright evil with me. I can see that there is more in his heart than I thought. He wants me to go, but he wishes he didn't.

"Nobody's following me," I tell him, "I made sure of that."

"Bullshit, you made sure!" he yells "I know you, Jeremy. You're just not careful. Jack is after you now. Ain't nobody so stupid that they'd mess with Godless Jack like you've messed with Godless Jack. You antagonize the people that kill and they do what they do best. They kill. You fucked with the wrong fuckers and you got yourself fucked. Now you come here cause you're fucked and you're gonna get me fucked, Jeremy. People come to me when they WANT to get fucked Jeremy, not when they're completely fucked and they wanna get unfucked. I don't see what the hell I should help you for."

"This is about Lud isn't it," Cass asks him, "you're not scared. You're upset."

"Damn right, I'm upset! Lud is dead because of you. He was having bad dreams, he said, he was dreaming about snakes and about a snake coming for him, a snake and a jackal. But you didn't come here when his dreams got worse, when I warned you that something was obviously wrong with him and that he knew something was coming and he had to be careful. You stayed behind and you killed some fat little shithead from the TV station and then had the nerve to tell Lud's business to Tommy Simmons. You don't even stop and think about how that could get him killed, you don't stop and think about anything. Of course, I'm upset. You killed my friend and colleague. It wasn't just Jack, it was you."

Cass' head hangs low. She told me something about Lud' s dreams getting worse, said she'd spoken to Jones before, but neither of us made anything of it. I followed the dreams before and then I stopped, then I let Lud give his life to Godless Jack. Jones is right about all of that. Right enough that I have no clue what to say. No matter how sorry I am, it won't bring him back and it won't make me any less responsible for the fact that he's gone.

"The General would have wanted me to help you, though. That's the part that really bothers me. I tried to get close to the guy. I liked him in spite of how strange he was. But, I guess a shared delusion makes the two of you practically father and son. Which is too bad, cause I never had a father either and in a weird way, this crazy man that I laughed at, that brought me car parts and bits of broken machinery to sell still supported my business and me. I'm mad at you because I liked him, and he didn't take to me like he took to you. I don't like many people, Jeremy. In my line of work, you can't. Let me tell you a story," he's rambling, he's angry, but I have to listen, "I'm gonna tell you a story about when I started out in this town. I was picking pockets and breaking into cars in the parking lot at the mall. And one night as I'm trying to hotwire this Toyota, I see these three guys putting fliers on the windows of all the cars in the parking lot. Movin' real fast. And they were taking little things out of the cars, opening the hood and stealing parts so the cars wouldn't run anymore. And as I'm trying to steal this car, one of the guys putting out fliers puts one on the window and begins to try and take the car apart. So I go and I say to the guy, "hey, I'm tryin' to steal this car." And you know what he says?"

Jones begins to laugh and cry at the same time. "He says the machine is evil, the machine makes us a machine, so he takes them apart. So I ask what they do with these parts. Why not ask? All these car parts are worth real good money and real good money shouldn't be wasted. They say they just throw the parts out. And I get an idea. I ask if there's anything I can trade for the car parts, and they tell me they need newspapers. So I tell them I'll give 'em newspapers and I'll give 'em food in exchange for the car parts. Sweet deal like that turned me a real nice profit. Within five years, I'm a much richer man and I'm involved with all kinds of things. And with all the things he said about corruption and sin and people turning into the machine, he didn't criticize me, he didn't hate me for what I chose to do. That's why I miss the crazy old son of a bitch."

The two of us understand each other now. Two criminals, two men whose lives were changed by one insane prophet in a mall parking lot. In a way, we were brothers. In a way, he owes me and he knows it. We stand transfixed by the notion, hoping that nobody's going to come crashing through the warehouse door and perforate us all with a machine gun. Cass is watching the door with that very thought in mind and so is Reiko. The two look at the door, and then at each other and shrug.

"I'm not going to hide you," Jones says, "I want you to know that. You're going to go home, like Lud would have told you to, and you're gonna find a way out of this yourself. Far as I can see, there's only one way out of this and it sure as hell ain't the coward's way out, no matter how appealing that looks."

"Can you sell me a nuclear weapon?" I ask. I'm pretty sure he can't, but I just want the option to be there if the shit really goes down.

"I can sell a nuclear weapon, but I'm not gonna sell it to you. Shit, I got a helicopter in my basement, but I'm not gonna sell it to you. It's one of them Vietnam things with the fifty caliber machine guns, real sweet, but I'm not gonna sell it to you."

I'm getting frustrated with what he can't do for me. "Well, then what can you sell me? What can you do to help me?"

"Well, I can't really sell you anything that will help YOU per se, but I can sell you something for the lady. It will be more than worth it."

"What can you sell us, and for how much?"

"Half-price. Three thousand. Package deal includes one indiscreet blue minivan and one AR-15 sniper rifle. And a bottle of Doctor Jones' one of a kind muscle relaxant. Kills tremors."

__Showdown__

Coming home last night was strange. I could feel Jeremy's tension as he drove. I could feel how he knew for a fact that somewhere out there, somebody was pursuing us. And yet nobody was. It was a disappointment in a way, because we both knew damn well that Godless Jack wasn't going to give up on somebody who offended him. We had both hoped we could have resolved everything on the dark, lonely highway with no chance of being seen and no chance for him to get reinforcements. If it had been like that, things would have been much easier on us and we could have gone home and slept soundly. But they weren't so we didn't get to go home and sleep at all soundly. Instead, we walked in, guns drawn, waiting for an ambush. I would have also preferred an ambush since we were expecting an ambush. But we didn't get an ambush and we didn't get anything we expected. We got a message. An answering machine message.

"Good evening, Mr.400, Miss Flynn. It has come to my attention that the two of you managed to dispatch Mr. Right and the wannabe hero thugs I hired. These were just a test. I wanted to see if you could handle more than two girls, Mr.400. And you passed. I also wanted to see if you were capable of defending yourself, Miss Flynn. I'm not too impressed about Mr. Right, he was a rudimentary threat."

My bones chill because I know he's right on that count. Bundy nominee he might have been, but there was nothing special about Mr. Right but his pain threshold. He was easily tricked, easily knocked down, easily tortured. Easily tortured for far too long. Makes me feel good about getting rid of the Roadflare outright. Mr. Right was nothing. A rudimentary threat indeed and he had me tasered, injured and almost ready to give up on life. What about the really dangerous people? He goes on, his words making the both of us tremble. He holds me close and I can feel him shake too.

"But, I was impressed by your handling of the I-80 Roadflare. Good stunt driving, good shooting, way to exploit a distraction. Good work all around, but you mustn't forget that he too had his shortcomings. Too tied to that one stretch of highway, that one long, endless stretch of highway. And the fool was too eager. Went after you before nightfall. If he'd waited until nightfall, he would've been in his element and might very well have had a chance to deal with the two of you. I've called to tell you that you've been lucky so far. I've called to tell you that I'm tired of playing and your luck has at last run out. Meet me outside that warehouse where the tanner left his victims…we sure do love warehouses don't we? I wonder why that is. Is it the storage space or the sense of oblivion you feel there, the knowledge that you're nowhere? Anyhow, meet me out there tomorrow at high noon. Cliché, yes, but I love all those old Western things. I know it's outside the Safe Zone, but I promise there will be no cops. You come alone and I'll come alone, there will be no tricks. You have my word. You think you can beat the devil, you go ahead and try!"

We go straight to bed after that. Jeremy stares up the ceiling with sad, childlike eyes. He's been waiting for this for so long, but now he's afraid that it's coming, he knows now that things have changed forever and that there's no walking away from this. I wonder if he wishes for that voice that used to take over for him to come and let him drift away. Even if he does, it won't happen. He has been stapled violently into the now. His struggle to get out of it would only cause him pain, make him feel like an animal in a trap that seeks to gnaw its leg off. He can't gnaw his leg off and run away from reality. I wish I could too. I wish I could take some drug and leave this world full of monstrosities behind for good. But we can't, and here in reality, there is only the two of us and the bed and the warmth of our bodies. There can be no comfort but that.

It makes me cry and I feel like every woman in almost every Western when I do. "I don't want you to go out there and I don't want you to die. I love you and I want to actually get married and if you go out there and you face him…" I can't even hear or think or feel my own words over the sobbing. It is only sobbing, since there are no words to express the fear of losing someone you love and the knowledge that it's so possible.

"I know Cass," he says, his own eyes tearful, "I know. I don't want to go either, but we have no choice. Godless Jack isn't going to let us run any more than we would let him run if we were on his trail. I can only hope to be good enough. I can only hope that Lud was right when he said I could bring down the lightning from God."

"God could take you from me," I start to cry, "I don't want anybody to take you from me."

"I know you don't. I don't want to go away, Cass. We'll get him, Cass, no matter what tricks he has up his sleeve. We need to get to sleep, though. If we can't get to sleep, then we'll be tired and weak and that's what he wants. That's why he didn't send anybody after us on the road but left the message for when we come home. He doesn't want us to sleep."

"I can't sleep."

Jeremy nods in agreement and then goes to the medicine cabinet. He has still has some of the sleeping pills that he's been slowly taking from the pharmacy for years. He hands me a couple and takes a couple for himself. I don't remember ever holding him so close or being held so close in my life. I drift to sleep barely able to breathe from being held so tight, but it still feels good.

I dream about wandering around the mall in Connecticut. The stores are all closed, though. I hear the footsteps of somebody with me there. I can't see anybody, but the footsteps get closer. Then, I hear the sound of a whirring drill. I look behind me, and there he is, Mister Right. He's no longer paunchy and weak and greasy. He's bigger, tougher and much more magnetic. He smiles at me and I can't run anymore. I have to go to his smile. And I do. Then, the smiling mouth opens up and extends, unhinged like Godless Jack's jaw. It swallows me whole and I slide down his throat into a great, dank tunnel.

The photos from his drawer are several feet tall in here, decorating the walls of the cave. As I walk through it, I find that the photos in his drawer get more risqué and more disgusting. The naked women begin to cut themselves with things, they begin to eat shards of glass and masturbate with long knives. The things that provoke him are more disgusting than I thought. It dawns on me that the things that provoked all these men, all my enemies are more disgusting than I thought. Mr. Right's weakness was a trap, he was meant to leave my psyche unhinged, meant to make me feel physically and morally weak, meant to make me feel like I was being mocked. I realize these things as I journey through the dark cave inside him in my dream. I emerge and I am in a desert. Towering above me is an enormous pyramid and I know who and what it is dedicated to. Something in General Lud's rantings comes to mind, when he talked about the jackal and the serpent king. He talked about them as Egyptian gods, forces that roamed the earth dispensing their own justice, dispensing the justice that killed him. Tomorrow we go out to face the serpent king. The jackal will be with him. We must beware of the jackal. Anubis kills with his hands and teeth. Statues of a jackal and an enormous snake creature, the creature near the Contessa's front door. Jack will not go alone, Jeremy won't either, but I know Jack is going to cheat bad. We are dealing with something that does not feel he is human or that he needs to follow man's rules. We are dealing with the icon, the serpent in the garden.

We get up and have breakfast. It feels so clear that it could be our last breakfast. It doesn't feel like the last time you're going to see somebody usually feels. For me, the last time was usually after I broke up with them, after I wanted them to go, but it's so harsh this time because I want nothing more than for him to stay and for life to stay like this. There can be no simple, happy life in a world like this. How many other couples have been split up by these monsters and the world of hatred and stupidity they've built for us and themselves? I have to think of them, too. It still doesn't make me stop thinking about us. I can't imagine anything that would make me stop thinking about Jeremy and I and how we could just be another part of this tragedy. I lay my head on his lap and look up at his face. This might be the last time I see that face. I wish I had something better to think about.

"Jack's going to cheat," I tell him, as he toys with my hair, I know from the sober look on his face that he's figured that out, but maybe I kind of feel that if I make the argument he won't go out and do it.

"Don't worry," he answers, "we'll cheat too. At around nine thirty, you get in the blue van and you hide. If anybody comes with Jack, you plug them. I'll try and keep things as disorienting as possible so whoever comes won't be able to get a handle on your position. If anybody does, you drive off."

"But..." here I am again. Every woman in every Western.

"No. No time to argue. Nothing to argue about. If anybody finds your position, you drive off. You're not the one that Jack wants, but he'll use you to make my last moments even more agonized. If they find your position, you drive off as fast as you can. And don't go after me. Jack's address might be on his website, but I've got a feeling he might not be taking me there. That's why I'm telling you right now, to drive off. You won't find me if he catches me. I'll find you if I can get away, but don't let me see you driving after him. Understand?"

I don't understand. I don't understand how we could be in a position where one of us would have to leave the other to die. I don't understand how he expects me to let Jack get away with him when he would never have let it happen to me. I feel like it's an insult. An insult to the time we've spent together and the love I have for him. He seems to think I could keep on going if I knew he was in the bastard's hands. That, I don't understand. I don't understand how anybody who actually loves someone would want them to stand by and watch. I don't God's injustice, but I still do what he wants me to do. He wants me to agree to drive away if I'm found and let him resolve the fight himself. So, I do it. My heart is screaming and swearing and breaking, but I nod. My tear stained eyes beg him to reconsider, but of course he doesn't.

We sit together on the couch awhile, holding each other, hoping to take as much as we can out of our arms to remember each other by. I don't think it could work. I don't think that these moments could give back all of the time we spent together and the future we could have. These last, desperate moments of clasping each other can't give back the child we might have raised together. I can't help but pessimistic, I can't help but feel the loss already, because I know Jeremy misses that future and the child that might have been and the war we would keep fighting. At 9:10, I take the sniper rifle, the van, the pills and a walkman and I stake out a position near the warehouse where the fate of our love, the fate of our lives and a little bit of the fate of America will be determined.

I listen to Abbey Road three times. It was such upbeat music when I picked it out, before I'd been thinking of endings. I hadn't been thinking of the end of an era, the end of lives, the breaking of the bond that chains our hearts together. I cry so much that I can't see where I need to be drawing a little red bead on some guy's head to make it explode. I have to dry my eyes. I think of the sniper rifle and the little red bead that might save Jeremy's life. The last time I hear the phrase "and in the end, the love you take is equal to the love you make," I hope that it's true. I hope that the love we've forged will create more love, in our hearts in the world, love that will rise up with big, dripping fangs like the human snake that wants to tear it apart. *And in the end, the love you take is equal to the love you make.* Let it be true. We made so much love for ourselves. I can only hope there will be more.

I pick up my cellphone when a big, muddy red pickup parks a little bit outside the warehouse. I know whose muddy red pickup this is long before they get out. I knew he would cheat. Hacksaw Sally picks up a crowbar from the truck bed and finds hiding place. I'm ready to draw that little red bead right now, but that would give us away instantly and I have to wait until things get rough before risking my own life. I tell myself that agreeing to this is actually doing something for him before I dial the phone, hoping I can provide some help before he shows up. Even as I dial the number, an ice cream truck parks discreetly down the street. A huge, burly fat man emerges with a garotte in his hand. That's interesting. It looks to me like they don't plan on killing him right there. That doesn't relieve me at all.

"Jeremy, I was right," I tell him when he picks up, "Jack's cheating. He isn't going to fight fair. People are already here..."

"Don't tell me how many. Don't tell me who. It won't help, Cass. It will just make me nervous. I don't need to know. Just keep watching and get ready for noon. I love you."

"I love you." And I hate him because he's getting ready to die and he won't even listen to me. I hate him even more for having the courage to do what he has to do when I don't have the courage to do what I need to. I don't have the courage to run if he gets in trouble. Another car shows up and four people I don't recognize get out of it. A fifth person I do recognize gets out too. Marshall Kozack, the Tennessee nailgun killer. I have a feeling I know who two of the other four might be. They are, after all, shapely young girls with black hair and thick eye makeup. The Contessa even sent him a little backup. At least seven people are here when Jack said come alone. Of course you can't trust the words of the devil. Of course you can't. Thankfully, there aren't any other cars until Jack's big black limo with snakes painted on the side shows up. Jack is as ugly in person as he is on the TV. Uglier perhaps. His eyes look even yellower, his face even more sunken and inhuman, that terrible unhingeable jaw even uglier when he smiles.

He opens up the huge trunk and reaches into it, for a cage that has been put in there sideways. I cannot begin to speculate what he put in such a huge cage. It looks to be about seven feet long and three feet wide. Amazing that he had a trunk so huge that he could squeeze it in there. Astonishing how happy the cage seems to make him. All this backup and he brought a tiger or something, too. But it's not a tiger.

Inside the cage is a naked man, his body covered in tattoos. All the tattoos are of the same thing, though. All the tattoos are the head of a jackal rendered in various colors and styles. I can't believe how long his fingernails are. I think they might have been surgically enhanced. His nude body ripples with muscle and his teeth, like Jack's, are filed. The emissary of death, the burial God right beside the prince of lies and evil. This death is the devil's right hand. They've taken to heart Ian's advice about being forces of nature. The totemic pretenses aren't an act anymore. They are the totems they pretend to be. It's so hard not to shoot.

Jeremy parks the car and gets out. At least Jack hasn't run him off the road before he gets here. At least Jack gives him a moment to approach. Jeremy has Mr. Right's Magnum in his hand and maybe a sharp knife in his jacket. I hope he has a sharp knife in his jacket. He hasn't bothered with any of the regalia except the t-shirt. He very bravely asserts that it is, in fact, Mr.400 that stands before them. Jeremy looks at Jack, Jack looks at Jeremy. They exchange some words that I would give anything to hear. I would give anything to know the defiant last words of the man I love to the man who set up the ambush that would kill him. What I expect after this is something like the end of Julius Caesar, when the whole senate, the disapproving Roman public fell on him with knives. I have a feeling they will fall on him soon. Jack takes his time, though. He makes sure that Jeremy is distracted when Sally and the Ice Cream Truck Strangler emerge from their hiding places to attack.

Sally gets Jeremy in the left arm with her crowbar. It looks like it might give way under the pressure, but it doesn't. It's Jeremy. No, it's Mr. 400. It takes him just a second to reach up his sleeve for the knife he's concealed there. He doesn't even turn around to stab her. I'm shocked that he manages to get her in the chest without looking at her. She falls back as the Ice Cream Truck Strangler wraps the garotte around his neck. I get ready to draw a bead and shoot him in the head when Jeremy pulls his foot back and kicks the guy in the balls, causing him to relax his grip for a second, which is of course, a fatal mistake. The Ice Cream Truck Strangler lets go when Jeremy thrusts the knife into the man's arm. Jeremy turns around and shoots him, although it might have been a mistake to do so. I can't really imagine what it feels like to be shot in the back with a nailgun, but I think it feels worse than the arm. It's sort of a bad move for Kozack to give away his position so early, however, since Jeremy has a magnum, which is as powerful as a nailgun is sadistic. The formerly concealed Kozack identity fades as his head becomes a bloody mess.

The Contessa's girls are both armed with huge links of chain, turning this whole affair almost comical, making it into a vicious Bruce Lee movie. His left arm hurts, I can tell, as he strains to slice both girls with the knife. They get him several times with the chain, smacking him in the sides. They're just here to make sure he suffers. He doesn't let them, though. His cuts are quick and dirty, leaving both of them clutching their throats in disbelief. It's funny that Jack isn't doing anything at all. He just watches and laughs as Jeremy disposes of all these minions. I don't understand it, because Jeremy's doing damn well, proving himself as terrible and remarkable a totem as all of them are, a God to parallel even their strongest.

Then I realize what Jack's laughing about. The big, naked Anubis killer sinks his claws into Jeremy's wounded sides. He's so fast, I missed him sneaking up. With his sheer body weight, he drives the nail Kozack fired deeper into Jeremy's back, causing Jeremy's face to fill with agony. Even in my position, I can hear him scream. I couldn't hear any of the others. I take a moment to steady the sniper rifle as the monster withdraws his claws, opting instead to squeeze Jeremy with all his might. Jeremy drops his weapons and it looks like he's about to faint from the pain. I can't let this happen. I fire at the little red dot, and the little red dot expands into a big, dark fountain of red. The Anubis killer doesn't let go until he falls. Nobody's immortal, but some people are so damn tough it doesn't matter that they aren't.

Wounded though he is, Jeremy picks up Mister Right's magnum and points it at Jack. He looks like he barely has the energy to pull the trigger, but as long as he could; I could go down there and get him to a hospital in time to save him. I can't believe this. I feel like crying out with joy, but I know that might still be a bad idea, that something might still go wrong. Why do I feel like something might still go wrong? Then I see why.

Jack points up in my direction and I get a feeling that if I could look up at my own forehead, I would find a big, red dot at the center of it, a little pimple of light. Jeremy drops the magnum and puts his arms up. If I hadn't made the agreement, I would pick up the sniper rifle and point it right at the disgusting, long jawed face of the man I hate so much. But I made the agreement, and I'm not going to break it. Besides, it's not like that same sniper couldn't take out Jeremy, too. As Jeremy faints, I do what he told me to do, even though I hate him for having told me to. I drive. I drive like the devil.

I drive to the apartment and I sink down and cry. I can't bring myself to look at the photo albums or the objects on the coffee table. I can't bring myself to look at anything that was him. The promise hurts like nothing else has ever hurt to me. But

I can't break it. I wish there was something I could do, though. Some way to make this right. I pick up the phone and I dial Jones. Reiko picks up, unable to hear anything with all the crying that I'm doing.

"Who is this?" she asks, "hello?"

I compose myself enough to say "this is Cass. This is Cass. I need to speak to Jones." Reiko doesn't say anything.

It's a bit too long before Jones picks up. His voice is cold and solemn. "This is Mister Jones. Be quick."

"It's Jeremy. I need your help. I used the gun, I used the van and I used the pills and we went out there and Jack was there and Hacksaw Sally and everybody and Jeremy fought them and he he ended up not, not not…"

I thought I had been prepared to see him beaten. All day long I had prepared to see him beaten. In my dreams I had prepared. But I wasn't. I'm still not prepared to think of him having been defeated. Jones doesn't say anything for awhile, hoping I can muster the courage to even say what happened. But I can't. I want to skip over it all and get right to the point where I ask to borrow his helicopter and I use it to blast Godless Jack to smithereens and free Jeremy and we'll run off together and be safe. I don't want to tell him what happened, I can only hope that he'll guess and that after he guesses he can help come up with some kind of solution, some device that will help me find Jack and rescue Jeremy before he rapes him, breaks him, eats him, whatever will happen. But there is no such device. There is no such thing as anti-tragedy cannon. There is no such thing as a love retrieval magnet. There is no time travel and no petitioning God. Jones sees what I want, and he finally speaks. It doesn't help at all. "I'm sorry for your loss," he tells me and hangs up.

He Moves Me

God doesn't put up your pussy in a game of cards. Especially when he only has three fives. God doesn't sit, listening as you scream while his army buddy savors his victory. God turns people into pillars of salt. God sends lightning to strike them, whales to eat them. Fire to burn them. If God does not do this, then what does he do? Is he jerking off too when the winner of the poker game shares his prize with six other yuppie scumbags? Is he the burning I feel as they unload themselves on my face? That fucker has a lot of nerve telling me what God doesn't want me to do, accusing me of running around and being a slut. There were a couple of them, but I was careful every time. Most of the time. Which, according to our faith, God doesn't want me to do.

The child of one of seven friends of my father or that guy from the concert or Steve Dreyfuss is hungry. So the little accident steals my dinner. It doesn't ask "are you gonna finish that?" like Jen does and if I said "yeah" it wouldn't listen. So my head gets light and my stomach grumbles as it takes everything it can from me. I punch myself in the stomach to let it know how I feel, but I'm the only one who's hurt. Why am I always the only one who's hurt?

I don't know if it's God that shows him to me on the news. Doesn't seem like something God would do. But it's something good, some kind of providence…yeah, that's the word, providence. Pregnant women dead. Child ripped right out of them. Good for him. Over three hundred now. Three hundred less mouths to feed. Three hundred less squawking brats on airplanes and trains and at supermarkets. Good for him. And he is here! Right in the city doing his thing. I punch myself in the stomach out of excitement. I masturbate with a coat hanger to tease it, show it who's boss. It tickles my insides. It tickles my heart.

I sneak out the window, following an inaudible hum in my brain that calls me out onto the streets. He is out there, the silencemaker, the holy abortionist. He will end my suffering and lead the way. I hear the name they've given him on the news and it moves me, he moves me out into the alleys tonight and if he can smell the whining fishthing in my womb like I can smell the power in him, then brighter days lie ahead.

I pass street musicians with open guitar cases and crackheads with signs saying they were veterans once. Say they were in Nam. Veterans only of the War on Drugs, which went just as shitty. God allegedly wants us to look out for these people. Because they're the least of his children and shit. If the lazy fuck is out there, then why the fuck doesn't he do it himself?

Down the alleys, into the maze. In the center, I'll find the big, virile gorgeous Minotaur I'm looking for. He is bigger than daddy's god and he wants me to find him, so I'll find him.
I see scruffy strangers out of the corner of my eye, but none of them are him. I'll know him when I see him.

Hours upon hours of wandering unfamiliar streets, looking up at unfamiliar faces, fewer as time goes on, quieter and quieter, further and further away from home. It kicks. It cries...

MAMA MAMA MAMA MAMA MAMA MAMA!

"Enjoy it while you can, you little fucker!"
The echo reminds me how alone I am and how much the crowd has thinned out. I'm scared. I'm a precocious eighteen year old alone somewhere unfamiliar with a baby I don't want in my stomach looking for a man to take it out for me, maybe at the cost of my life.

I sit on the curb and cry. The thing in me and I cry together. We both know what it is to be helpless. Only difference is, I'm not stupid enough to think anybody's going to protect me and love me. A sound explodes through the night. A reply that makes me feel more and less alone.

"Shhhhhh!!!!!"
Then there are footsteps.

"Shhhhh!" again. An angry hiss of a shhhh. The sound is a hand, squeezing my throat, choking back my sobs. Footsteps follow it. You'd think the sound of footsteps in the middle of the night in a quiet city would be impossibly loud, but they're tiny, precise, quick and almost silent. In broad daylight or on a more crowded street, I doubt I could have heard them.

The footstep sounds actually stop, though I know he's coming closer, the man who hissed at me. He has to be the man I was looking for. I turn around and I smile at him. He's right behind me, tall, skinny, serpentine with long, thin, greasy unkempt grey hair. He reminds me a little of Riff Raff from Rocky Horror. But Riff Raff didn't feel like he does. He is holy and terrifying.

I smile at him. He's confused. He reaches into his jacket for something and his hands trembling, like he can't find it or he's scared to use it.

"It's okay," I tell him, still smiling. Why is it okay? I don't know. But it's okay.

"I'm not afraid of you," he tells me.

"Why would you be?"

He pulls out a knife. His hands are really shaking.

"Why aren't you scared of death and the silence?"

"Will you spare me?"

He shakes his head.

"I can't do that."

"Why?"

He doesn't say anything.

"Is it because you need what's in me?"

He doesn't say anything.

I laugh. Maybe I'm callous or insane or something, but he doesn't bother me or scare me anymore. I know what he wants and I'm willing to give it. Why should I be scared of somebody like that?

"I'll give it to you. If you can spare me. Can you spare me?"

He takes off his shirt, his body all lean, tense junkie muscle. There is a black gaping hole in his stomach. Two tiny skeletal hands are reaching out of it. To me, they do not look disgusting. They look as if they are both strong and delicate at the same time. I feel like kissing their bony fingers.

They're incredibly strong, ripping my dress open, revealing a body that's grown rounder to accommodate the intruder. I smile again, happy to be naked in his presence.

The fingers plunge into me, strong as I thought they were, and they rip my womb right open. The night air might be cold, but I feel warm all over exposed to this extent to this monstrous angel. He has torn my flesh, opened me up and I love him for it. He moves me like the God that forbids this never managed to do.

The hand reaches in and plucks out the pink abomination, half fish half ape, all suffering, all trouble and greed and theft. The hands raise it up, placing it in his hands. I'm open, vulnerable, I could bleed to death any second and there's not a trace of fear in me. As soon as the thing is out of the skeleton hands and in his hands, they go to work. They seem to know instinctually how to close what they've opened, knit flesh together perfectly. The touch is light, gentle and I am ecstatic. I wish those fingers would brush against my nipples or explore my pussy for reasons besides taking out what's in there.

"Please, please, touch me..." I beg them. They retreat back into his chest. The black hole closes up and there is skin where it used to be.

His hands, his real hands, raise the thing to his mouth. They're trembling again, but with excitement, not fear. He licks his lips. He sniffs it. He takes a big bite out of it, chewing loudly. I'd like to believe it's the thing's rotten, thieving soul he's trying to eat.

I kneel before him, clinging to his legs and kissing his feet.

"I love you," I tell him. Words I never thought I'd never mean.

"You're a god," I tell him, "you're beautiful and you've saved my life."

He doesn't respond, he eats. A naked teenage girl at his feet and all he wants to do is swallow up this tiny life...he's more powerful and majestic than I had imagined, than I could have imagined.

"I love you," I tell him again. He still ignores me. My heart pounds being in the presence of something so much greater than I. My love is meaningless to him and that intrigues me.

It's not to be. I'm not meant to be happy, I guess. The holiness of the moment is shattered by the sound of footsteps,

footsteps stomping on my joy and my chance to live in a beautiful world that makes sense to me.

"Run!" I tell him, "run!"

He doesn't move, he keeps on eating, savoring the little monster's body and soul.

"They're getting closer," I warn him.

"It's alright," he replies, "dribbling bits of fetus down his chin, "Captain says this is part of the plan. Captain never steers me wrong.

They're here. Four of them. Pointing their guns at him as if he's done something wrong.

"Jonathan Cavanagh, you are under arrest for murder. You have the right to remain silent; you have the right to…"

I cannot hear his rights being read off. I am too busy thinking of the awfulness of a world without him in it.

"Please," I beg one of the cops, "please…"

"It's okay," the cop says, "it's all going to be okay."

I look at my savior, my love, the man who took the screaming monster from me. He is nodding in agreement. The cops take him to jail and me to the hospital to recover from what they think is the most traumatic moment of my life. As I lay in that hospital bed, I'm not scared, even though they're taking him away. He'll be out and everything will be okay.

The Other Side

I do not know how long I have sat atop the mountain for. I have tried to ask Lud how much time has passed, but he's kept quiet. He doesn't really seem to acknowledge that I'm here, except for the occasional sad glance passed between us. I have sat here alone, hearing bits and pieces of things said with a voice that is not my own. There is nothing ominous. So far it has been "Where am I?", "Hello" and "I can't eat that". Nothing too meaningful, things I might have said myself if the voice hadn't said them. I don't know how long I've been here, but I want to leave. I walk up to Lud and I have to tell him.

"I'm going now, I can't stay here. You can come with me if you want to, but I definitely can't stay here. He says nothing. I grab him and I try to shake him a little, try to make him answer me.

"Lud, come on, we're going!"

As I shake him, the skin begins to flake off his face, his limbs begin to fall apart and soon there is a pile of broken doll parts that used to be General Lud lying on the ground at my feet. In the distance I hear a whisper, a whisper that grows into a shout.

"I can't," says the voice of General Lud, growing louder in my head, "I can't!"

I grow cold at the sound. I suddenly feel like maybe I couldn't either. This is Hell, this is the place for failures, this is the numb, sad place where you feel the pain that killed you and you see what's happened because of your failures. The vantage point from the mountaintop now has a wider view. It seems like I can look down from here on all of creation, and I feel like doing it. I feel like seeing what has happened to the world and what is going to happen to it. I wish that I hadn't.

There is no sun in the black, oily sky, no stars or clouds either. There will be no more day or no more night in this world. From the smokestacks of factories, wispy little fiends fly up, play, dance and fight, until they at last fade into the atmosphere, a sky made of black, smoky, little devils, generated forever by the machines below. Who could have lived where they came from? Who could have made the mistake to let these monsters be born and then unleashed? Who could have built the machines that let them foul their homeland? How could we have let them do the same? The Earth's folly hurts almost as much as its consequences. The ignorance cuts, bashes and burns me.

Huge trees grow in the middle of the great, inescapable cities. These are the trees I envisioned before. These are the trees made of flesh that bare red, juicy hearts as their fruit. Naked, savage howling men tear at the trunk and roots for meat. Others dare to climb up and take from the branches. They chew the hearts eagerly, letting the blood drip down their chins. None of them work together. None try to get meat for the others. They just fight and struggle for scraps of food from the only vegetation that grows. These trees have become as natural as any and flourish under the dark skies, standing as high as the twisted, metallic buildings.

The buildings do not look like buildings. They are twisted or leaning over, set into clusters that make them look like nests of snakes. All others are made of glass, completely transparent so that any who look in can see what goes on in them. Inside some of them, large, red eyed grown Dark Ones, with bodies covered in scales or fur are raping young women, no longer needing the breeders to do it for them. The adult Dark Ones look like primitive men with enormous, rounded bald heads. Otherwise, each is different. Each has parts of another kind of beast. Each has signs of some different deformity. To contrast the ones with furry or scaly skin, or heads like lions and undulating quills, some are born with no skin at all, just networks of thick muscles and nerves covering their skeletons. These ones seem to be the leaders. I can see why. Without flesh, there is no sign of vulnerability in them, no pretense toward being human. The big headed fleshless monsters are oddly enough more human than most of the people that remain. It is not just the feral men that are the problem.

Having no skin isn't as dehumanizing as having a satellite dish for a head like some of the people wandering the streets do. Their bodies are normal, clad in expensive business suits, but from the neck up, they are satellite dishes, receiving signals from somewhere out in space. They speak in staticky sounds to each other, unrealized mechanical attempts at language. One of the men with a satellite for his head holds the hand of a child with wheels for feet. Together they cross a road, avoiding the traffic from others like the child, worse cases with wheels for hands as well. From the speed they move at, I wonder if there are engines in their stomachs or something. Mankind has become extinct in the cities below, a remnant of better times before they came. If I could go down, if I could fight, but I can't...I'm dead, I must be dead. In the middle of street, something rises up from beneath the ground, splitting the concrete and looking up on the same level as I am, at the mountaintop. The pole that Jack stuck Lud's head on is looking at me.

It speaks. I should have expected it to speak. Looking back, that's pretty much all that General Lud ever did.

"You have to leave here. You cannot be here with me."

"But this is Hell. I have to stay in…"

There is no more time for argument. My blurry eyes open and I am in a dark, smoky room. I am relieved to be able to turn my head, but shocked by the grinning demon looking at me. It laughs, but I am fairly certain that the laughter is in my imagination. It's a statue. I think it's a statue at least. No, I hope it's a statue. I don't know what it is I think about anything right now. Especially about my whereabouts. My vision is still blurred, and I think that if I am not dead, then I have at least been drugged. I hear the sound of wheels coming to me.

In my mind's eye, I see the people crossing the road, the human cars from the city of the Dark Ones. It must something like that. The mechanized men are coming for me. They have built a better robot and they will build a better one from me. That's why they left me alive. They're coming to take out the organic parts and put mechanical ones in. I will have a satellite dish for a head, beaming galactic blasphemies into my automated brain twenty four hours a day. I will have wheels for hands and clockwork guts. When the fleshless Dark One scientists come for me, then I will be so frightening and inhuman, that even the mechanical beasts will shun me. I shall be the subject of the most foul ridicule in the city of the damned.

The wheels are in fact the wheels on a hospital gurney. A young, naked, frightened woman sits on it, surrounded by Dark One breeders. Are my captors Dark Ones? Do they just know of them? I suddenly remember the Dark Ones don't have me, but they might as well. I am in the hands of something awful, but it is not one of them. Why, then does he know that I will be tortured by the sight of this woman being impregnated by the monsters? I watch it drip the black sperm on its proboscis into her and she shudders. Maybe she is shuddering because of something else. Perhaps that is so. She too is in the hands of Godless Jack. When a young woman with black angel wings on her back and a sharp knife in her hand enters, I know how I am going to be tortured. She turns the hospital gurney to face me as she gets down on her hands and knees and prepares to make the cut. It dawns on me that the naked young lady on the gurney is pregnant already. Already filled with one of the things. Do they know that one of the things is in there? Do they know what is they're going to extract?

"Don't…don't…it's…" I mumble. There are words in my head, but I'm too weak and confused to turn them into speech. The "nurse" in the black wings makes the cut. The wings seem to flutter and move about of their own accord. They don't look plastic to me. When the nurse extracts, almost come to term, it looks straight at me with the reddish pink eyes. It's covered in fur and has paws like a gorilla. The "nurse" holds it up to show me. It seems to wave hello. But that's not why she's holding it up. It's the first part of a show. Of the magic trick. I hear in the distance the applause of a studio audience. Am I being televised? The virus is in you. Look away from this.

It seems that way when Godless Jack enters in a ratty t-shirt to the roar of clapping and whooping. He bows to me, then to the audience which must be somewhere, I think. The audience is the virus. The audience was in the syringe. The t-shirt has a big, red zero on the front with the words "the alpha" printed above it. On the back of the shirt is another red zero with "the omega" printed above it. The zero moves back and forth, squirming with life. It's whispering to him in a language I can't understand.

"Hello, Mr.400. I just wanted to remind you where babies come from."

Howls of canned laughter originate from somewhere, possibly my subconscious. I wouldn't know either way. The 'nurse' laughs at Jack's joke. The woman doesn't. It might be that the breeders continue to drip the black goo into her ravaged womb. The child claps. I am certain it claps. It should be dead, but it is one of them, so it capable of clapping. The black goo seems to be collecting together. It bubbles like a tar pit, which a pair of tiny hands emerge from. They too are applauding. Look away. Let me help you.

"I should be able to respect your work, and if I'd known about it, I sure as Hell would have. Man, I didn't want to get caught back when I was killing most of those first 347 people, but I did. You're good. I should have been able to respect you. But then, you gun down Kris Kringle. Not great, but gruesome. He was a genius in his own humble way. Then, you take away my friend Tom. Something of a space cadet, but he was nice enough. His fans loved him. If I had known it was you back then, I would have gutted you for that."

The studio audience shouts back. The hands from the woman's opened womb give me thumbs down. The Dark One ape baby gives me the finger.

"That was offense enough. It was a shock to the Reap community and to America at large. It was just plain improper, Jeremy. We love our celebrities. We need our celebrities and you take them from us? America should hate you. And yet, they've grown fascinated. You walked into Le Couteau and shot Wayne Pfenniger and you killed two of the Aberrations. Yes, you have the right to kill, but you shouldn't have. It was horrible of you to do that, I mean; honestly, those kids were just there to have fun. Who are you to judge them for having fun? And who are you to judge others for killing?"

A sudden surge of bravery comes to me. "I'm Mr.400."
"You are bad," says the zero on Jack's shirt. I translate for Jeremy. I speak the shunned tongue. I speak the elsewhere tongue. I can help him. I can get him free. Let me help you. I made you this. Let me help you. He won't let me help him SHUT UP You are bad Jeremy you are bad for not listening I will set you free the Jackal and the Serpent King must not win I can set you free SHUT UP You are bad We are screaming we are begging listen to me I will I will I will I will not. I don't need you.
The nurse hands him the ape baby and her knife. Look away SHUT UP look away look away you cannot stay Shut up shut up shut up He skins it like a pro, tearing the hairy flesh from its body like he clearly has so many other bodies. He rolls the skin into a ball in his hand and then opens his unhingeable jaw as wide as he can. It looks like he could fit whole turkeys into that jaw, like he could have fit the entire baby in it, and in fact I'd

heard accounts of him doing so. He chews the skin as loudly and dramatically as he can. I wonder how he can eat all those hairs. For a moment, I imagine him coming closer, opening that unhingeable jaw of his wide enough to fit me down his throat. But he wouldn't do that yet. He's going to relish his diatribe and his chance to torture me to death. Look away or he will eat the Earth

"And even after all of these horrible things you've done, Jeremy, you took my image and mocked me. You mocked all psychopomps, implied that we were not the forces of nature that we claimed to be and that we could never stack up to cancer. I'm going to make you wish you had cancer or you were in a car accident. You're going to wish you were fucking fried alive by lightning. So, how can you, in your position tell me that cancer, AIDS and car accidents are more frightening than me? You underestimate me or you overestimate cancer." He shows me a tattoo on his arm, I hadn't even thought about it or noticed it, but I see it now. It is a big, red zero, like on his shirt, like the painting in the ballroom.

"You don't impress me Mr.400. Numbers don't impress me much. It's all about one number. It's all about the snake that eats its tail, the beginning and the end. The world began as nothing and it will end up as nothing. There's only one number worth believing in. You stand beside big numbers. What do they matter? Don't you see that those four hundred don't matter now? They're nothing, just like you'll be. I'll make sure of that. I'm gonna turn your brain into nothing, then I'm gonna turn your body into nothing, and maybe, in my infinite mercy and willingness to educate, I'll save you a trip to Hell and destroy your soul outright. My great granddaddy was death. He made friends with the zero. Don't think I can't. I've given a lot to the big zero. I've taken lives before they've even started, eaten them right out of the womb. I take them all into me, the faithful servant of the big nothing that makes the world go around. It spins on an axis doesn't it? That makes it a circle, and a circle's really nothing but a big zero. You might be Mr.400, but I'm Mister Nothing, and that's infinitely more. When I'm done with you, you'll pray for cancer, you little shit. You go and you say I'm not a force of nature. You're wrong. I am nature. I devour until there's nothing left, and I encourage others do the same, I build ecosystems in the model of the only shape in nature that matters."

I long for cancer, AIDS, my burnt and broken body devastated in an accident or a fire. I long to be perforated by bullets. He picks up the fleshless ape child and he begins to tear at his muscles and organs and even snap bones for emphasis. I can see the oily stuff all over the body, but Jack doesn't mind at all. Perhaps he's been eating it for ages, and bits of little Dark One have contaminated his soul. He has soaked up the radiation from this other dimension. Let this evil be part of him. It makes him more imposing than ever.

His face becomes scaly, his neck elongated, his body more serpentine. He is a living, scaled vision of the horrible statue near the Contessa's house. This is the Serpent King Lud talked about in all of his vile splendor. Jack laughs as the nurse reaches for a syringe and injects it in my arm. Suddenly, the dark smoky room vanishes and I look out at the city of the Dark Ones. You should have looked away …

Courage

My father, a consummate Atheist, always said that we invented God because it was hard for us to find strength from within. Funny that he said that, because he was renowned in my family for his lack of bravery, and yet created no God for himself. So, maybe my father wasn't the coward we always said he was. I like to think of myself as a brave person, and yet here I am, seeking models of strength outside myself. I seek strength with someone whose strength at last failed him, who was carted away wounded. WWJD? What would Jeremy do? If I were captured by Godless Jack what would Jeremy do? Well, he would burst in with a lot of firepower and bladed implements of destruction and rescue me. So, okay, I'm ready to break a promise. He would too. There is no option.

First step is to track Jeremy and Jack down. I sit open up my trusty laptop and I'm ready to once more play Nancy Drew with it. This time I should be substantially easier. Jack has the embarrassing distinction of having his home address up on his personal website. It's not anybody would come get him anyway. Nobody, that is, but me. Sniper rifle, swordcane, kitchen knives, aluminum bat, shotgun…that will do. Damn, I wish Jones had sold us that nuke. It's a bad sign that this many armaments don't feel like much. I find the address, which sadly enough is about two and a half hours away. Would Jack have brought somebody to a house halfway across the state if he intended on torturing them. Shit, think, think…my thinking is interrupted by a knock on the door. I get up, grab the aluminum bat and prepare to take out the flunkies that Jack has sent to capture me so that he can rape me to death, sew my skin onto that of my slain boyfriend and wear it on network TV.

"Come in!" I shout.

I don't know if I should even bother fighting back. After all, Jack will just send more after this. I want to remain brave, but now that I've thought about it all, if he decides he's going to kill me, it will probably got done. Surrender. Maybe you'll see Jeremy in Heaven or Hell or whatever. Maybe there's some place after death for people who thought they were doing the right thing, but had no clue what the consequences would be. Death could be a blessing. I'm so confused. I don't know what I'm saying or thinking. I might have a chance to save Jeremy before he dies, or to get back at the guy who killed him. No time to be confused. I have a bat in my hand and I've just invited whoever's outside waiting to kill me in. Fuck it, I'll fight. I scramble to a hiding place, ducking down and preparing to take out their knees. When I take out their knees, their skull will be next.

The door opens, and in walks Penny Dreadful. I remember the broadcast and how we shot two of her bandmates. What would I do to somebody who killed two of my best friends? Probably something like what I plan on doing to the guy who might have killed Jeremy. It will be gorgeous. Whatever

Penny has planned for me, she ought to find it beautiful. I stand and watch and contemplate her, until I realize that she can't possibly be armed. She knows that I probably suspect she's armed, too. She throws her hands up.

"Cass? Cass Flynn? I'm here to talk to you about something important. I don't have any weapons on me, really. I swear. If I wanted to kill you, I wouldn't have knocked on the door. I don't want to kill you. I want to help. Everybody already knows what Jack's done. I told him to call me when he caught Mr.400, and he did. He told me when he caught your boyfriend, and he told me what he's been doing to him."

I stand up and drop the bat on the floor. Maybe I'll trust her. Nothing to lose from trusting her. She has news on Jeremy. I want news on Jeremy. I don't want news on Jeremy. I don't want to hear about the kind of ungodly things that have been done to him. I want to remember the man I love before every one of his limbs was sliced off and he was castrated. I want to remember the man I love before he was flayed alive and forced to look at his fleshless, limbless body. I want to remember the man I love before Jack won. Her news can't be welcome here, it can't be.

"I don't want to know how my boyfriend was dismembered and killed. I don't need all the gory details."

"I could understand that," says Penny, "but Jeremy's alive, Cass. He's not exactly fine, but he's alive and I know where he is. I think you might be able to save him, if you're interested. I have to warn you, it's dangerous and you might not like what you see when you get there."

Alive. I can almost hear his heartbeat when she says it. I can feel his breath against my neck; feel the kiss goodbye on my lips. Even if he is dismembered, he's still Jeremy and I owe him my life and my love. No bailing out now. No ignoring his plight, nasty as it might be. Something too big to describe stops sitting on top of my heart and flies away to go torment somebody else. Lucky them.

"Where is he? How is he? What's been done to him? Can it be undone?" I talk fast, thinking that there must be some question I'm missing, but couldn't even think to ask.

"I wouldn't say he's fine," Penny begins solemnly, "Jack's been injecting him with all kinds of hallucinogens and eating in front of him, and you know how and what Jack eats. He's planning something else later, but I suspect first he's gonna make his mind snap completely before he does it. I don't think Jeremy's one to beg, though, so hopefully you have awhile. And as for where…well, you're gonna have some problems."

"I don't care if Jack took him to fucking Alcatraz. I'll get him."

"Well, Jack's taken him to the Contessa's mansion. I would say that he's more than well guarded, especially since Jack expects you. I'm warning you about this because if Jack catches you, you'll get something worse than Jeremy gets," she sighs, "you got any beers? I could use a beer."

I go to the fridge and get her a Guinness. "I hope this is okay. I don't drink actual beer."

"It will have to do." Penny finishes it in a couple of huge gulps.

"I'm sorry that you have to be the one to convey all this to me."

"So am I," she replies, "but I'm glad to help. You'll need to go in through the back to find him. When you do, you're gonna be facing Jack. There's no doubt about that. Nobody's getting there without Jack knowing."

"I want to face Jack. Don't worry about me. He's done so much damage, more than you could ever understand," I breathe deep, tempted to grab some liquor myself, "I can't let him live, I don't think."

Penny nods. She puts her hand on mine. "I want you to do one thing for me, to pay me back for this favor."

"And what is that?" I don't know if I can pay her back for my lover's heartbeat, for the location of Godless Jack, for a chance to prove my love and courage. I can't think of anything that would be worth that. I honestly don't know what I would have to give after all I've been through, especially if he's dead or his mind's destroyed.

"I want you to bring me Jack's head. I want you to bring me his head, so that I can put it on a stake and declare a press conference to say he's been beaten."

I can only smile at this. "I wouldn't have it any other way. But what do you have against Jack?"

Penny looks ten years older as she stares into my eyes. I can now see that she's careworn and concerned and has been up a few nights soul searching. "He's led to a lot of confusion, not just me, but a lot of people. I want to feel less confused, so I figured I'd give you some help."

"I'm sorry about your band."

"I'm sorry about your friend."

I can't stay in my kitchen waiting, so I give her a silent goodbye before collecting a more realistic set of implements of destruction. I gather two sharp knives and two pistols. No sniper rifle, no shotgun, no bats, no swordcane, no bullshit. I wish I could rush into Jack's own home, blazing gun after gun, but I'll have to settle for sneaking into the Contessa's house from the back and getting Jeremy out, probably shooting Jack a couple times in the meantime. Simple plan, simple enough I suppose. I hold on tight to the knowledge was at least alive when Penny last heard from Jack.

I park discreetly, a ways away but not too far to run. Jeremy has always stressed the importance of nobody spotting you getting out of your car or getting back into it. It's one of the most important aspects of the raid. Good thing he taught me what he did. If he hadn't, I wouldn't even think about being able to pull this off.

I'm not surprised that she has a girl patrolling a quarter mile outside the grounds, too. If she didn't, I would think something's up. The girl is armed with a shotgun, but she holds it like it is heavy to her, like she doesn't know what to do with it. Maybe she doesn't. I get the feeling from the careless and uninformed way she goes about her patrol that she's not especially well trained at doing what she's doing. A topless Goth chick with awkward black angel wings and a shotgun isn't top notch security, but she's expendable. Maybe that's what Penny meant about security being tight. It's all about the numbers. There's one girl here, but I need to drop her fast, before she gets backup. Time is of the essence, that's the real problem. I duck behind a tree in a deliberately noisy fashion.

Of course the girl turns to look at me. Of course she doesn't expect to be shot in the head. Hopefully this was enough noise to get a couple of girls from the house to come running. I return to my place behind the tree, but I leave the girl's body in front of it. As I suspected, these girls aren't well trained at all. They start out with a potentially fatal mistake. One of them leans down to check the dead girl's pulse. Fucking idiots. The Contessa's cult has plenty of members, but she thinks that handing all those girls guns will compensate for their stupidity. It won't. I take them by surprise, creep around and stab the girl who isn't checking the pulse. She doesn't have time to pull her gun, only to register the pain before I bring my arm up and slit her throat. The other one begins to rise. The hand on her gun trembling. I kick her in the face as she's preparing to get up and she falls on top of the other girl's corpse. When I pin her gun hand with my foot, she knows she's as good as done. I fall on her with my knife, repeating the motion several times. It had once been hard to kill one person, but these three felt like nothing. The faces fade into one face and they are only obstacles between Jeremy and me. I should feel bad about this, but the Contessa most likely doesn't feel any different. It's not me sending these young ladies to their maker, it's the Contessa.

As I expected, the two that responded to the shot had been guarding the door. It's twisted how easy this is. Suspicious even. I ready one of the guns as I open the door, blasting a confused black-winged Amazon with an AK-47 in the chest. She clutches her chest instead of firing, the sort of mistake these girls make. How easily I could have ended up as one of them, too, a devoted Reap cultist willing to give her life for a cannibal and the leader of a satanic cult. Funny how life works. As the girl makes her mistake, I put a slug into her clearly empty head and start down the hall to the room Penny told me about. I can only hope that this wasn't all a trap designed to put me in the same place Jeremy is. If it is, it's a great one, because I'm just about there. No turning back, though, suspicion or none.

Right outside the room Penny mentioned, I duck a crossbow bolt fired from the end of the corridor. Of all the stupid things…God, a crossbow. If she weren't working for who she works for I'd pity her too much to shoot back. But she is, so I do. Two more of the girls run toward me, but for some reason they stop. Unlike me, they see the hand shooting out from the doorway, wrapping itself around my throat. Unlike me, they see the other hand, which yanks the gun from mine. Unlike me, they know instantly who I've been caught by. Unlike me, they're not willing to do anything to get in his way.

"You stay still Mrs. 400. You stay still, Miss Flynn. You struggle or you kick and scream, I'll crush your fucking windpipe. Do you know who I am, bitch? Do you know how many little sluts like you I've killed?"

I know who he is and I know exactly how many he's killed. As he drags me in, I go limp so that he doesn't choke me any harder. He knows just how hard to choke me to keep me still and to make sure I don't fight back. He's done this plenty of times. Three-hundred-twenty-eight times. I brought down those girls like they were Indians in a John Wayne movie, but this fish is bigger. Rather, this snake is bigger. I should panic, but miraculously, I don't. I'm too full of hate to let him get away with what he wants to do to me. I came to get Jeremy out and while I'm in the hands of Godless Jack, that's impossible.

When I kick him in the shins, his grasp on my throat relaxes. It's lucky I had watched Jeremy deal with the Ice Cream Strangler, which was enough to remind me that a person behind you choking you isn't necessarily in an advantageous position. I elbow him the chest, and then I stamp down hard on his foot. He's not so tough, he's not such a God, he is not the Serpent King of my nightmares, or the devil on earth. He is just a man, like all the other ones. Just a man who can only take so much pain. He stops choking and he reaches for the knife on his belt. Bad move, the action of somebody who hasn't had to deal with a struggling victim for awhile. When he reaches for the knife, I reach for the keys to Jeremy's cuffs on the other side of his belt.

"Don't you dare!" he shouts, swiping at me with the knife. I turn just in time; get the key in my hand. He's not that strong and he doesn't have much of a weight advantage on me, so there's no force behind his slashing. His wobbly, awkward method of fighting leaves me off guard, so as I'm reaching for the key, he nicks me in the left ear. I feel like crying from the pain, but it's nothing like Mr. Right's taser and it's nothing like the pain Jeremy must have suffered today, so I tough it out. I'm not certain if I want to bring him down myself or to let Jeremy loose with the key, but then I hear a moaning come from a few feet away. Jeremy is near. It's almost as much relief as Penny's announcement that he was alive when he turns the moans into words.

"The devil is here with us, Cass. Be careful. He looks small and weak, but he's the devil. He eats our children, Cass, he eats our souls!"

At least he's speaking. I immediately regret not following Jeremy's advice on what not to do during a fight. During a fight, you don't listen to ambient noise, you don't let yourself get distracted, and you don't turn your back on an enemy. I didn't even notice I had turned my back, but it's something you instinctually do when someone's shouting at you. With my back turned, I don't notice that Jack is leaping at me like a panther. If I'd seen him coming, I could have easily gotten out of the way, but I didn't see him coming. I feel his weight land on me and the cold, hardwood floor when I hit it. Even this man, small as he is, feels like a truck when he hits me with some momentum going.

I try not to look him in the eyes, but he grabs me by the hair with his free hand and forces me to look straight at him. I know that I can't close my eyes or else there will be nothing I can do when he starts to cut me with that knife of his. God, I wish I hadn't looked him in the eyes. The emptiness of the yellow contacts mirrors an emptiness that it's obvious is beneath them. I could look straight into his soul through those eyes and I would see that it is nothing but hate, greed and evil. The whole time I have forgotten that true strength lies in conviction, and the entirety of his conviction is focused around evil. I don't struggle as he prepares to cut me. This is no man, it's true. This is a king cobra. Blank, hypnotic eyes sap my will, as his enormous mouth with its filed teeth opens. He is going to rip out my throat with his teeth after he cuts me. It's this thought, this infinitely grimmer thought that DOES get me to struggle. I push up with all my might, and roll him off me.

He gets up quickly and prepares to charge me with his knife and run me through. I've done the same thing to him that he did to me when I looked in his yellowed eyes. I have turned off the thinking part of his mind. If he was thinking, he would have called for help from some of the girls in the hall that he had previously ordered away. If he was thinking, he would have reached for one of the guns he made me drop. But, he isn't. This is what a real psychopomp is. The drooling animal in us with big, yellow eyes charging with a knife at what offends him.

"The devil, the devil is here and he's gonna eat us, he's gonna eat our souls too!"

I back up and I take a gamble. He's no more coherent than Jack is. He's been beaten, he's probably weak as a kitten, but I somehow don't feel fit to take on something like Jack. I thought I understood it, but what was true in the schoolyard is not as true here. This is a place for elementals, and I content myself right now with being a person. Jeremy has things to do before he can get away with that, tragic though that thought might be. I unlock Jeremy's chains and he emerges from them, as confused and angry as Jack is.

"The devil! The devil is here! Lud give me strength to fight the serpent king! God give me strength to fight the serpent king…" he rants before charging Jack with just as much force as the lunatic has mustered. When Jack charges, he hasn't charged half so fast as Jeremy. With all the wounds, with all the drugs, still Jeremy is the bigger and faster of the two. Jack makes a howl that no human should make, a noise that will doubtlessly summon some of the Contessa's guards. As Jack and Jeremy try to shove each other over, I have a chance to pick up my pistols and get ready for the upcoming guards. Jeremy's conviction will vanquish Jack and my conviction will protect him until he does.

My reason smacks into me like a rogue locomotive. I'm grateful for it. Jack and Jeremy have no choice but to fight, but I can just lock the door, which I do as the weakened Jeremy at last gets Jack onto the ground. Maybe a locked door will be only a minute distraction for people who obviously have keys, but it will give us some time. The dead woman on the gurney and the gurney itself will give us even more time. I wheel it in front of the door, sidling around the fight. Then I turn it over, dumping the body, and letting the gurney barricade the door. When the door gets forced open, the person opening it will be off guard for long enough for me to shoot them. No matter how this goes, it's still going to be tough.

Jack's head makes an awful noise as Jeremy bashes it against the floor. "In the name of the Father, Son and the Holy Ghost, monster, I abjure thee…" I have a feeling that Jack starts to regret pumping Jeremy with hallucinogens and declaring himself the devil. But Jack is right, and Jeremy is right. Any man who says he's talking to angels, surely has, and every man who says he carries the devil surely does. Dark dreams and nude feral men calling themselves death taught me that. As I watch Jack struggle idly to get Jeremy off him, I see that there is a lot of truth to be gained in psychosis. I don't expect Jeremy to reach into Jack's mouth, no matter what he sees in him, since surely he'd be afraid of getting bitten, but he does. He reaches in and very deliberately smashes Jack's front teeth, letting shards of them slide down his throat.

Jeremy's strength builds with his anger and his fervor. HE doesn't have to punch out the rest of Jack's teeth when they can be yanked out just as easily.

"You could have hurt Cass," he says, "You could have wrecked what God gave me. You're the devil, and I'm not going to let you live!"

Jeremy clamps the enormous, disfigured jaws shut and punches Jack in the stomach, right on the zero on his t shirt. Jack gasps for air and begins to make choking noises. He wheezes and tries to cough up the shards. Jeremy shoves fingers into both Jack's eyes, gouging deep. He does it again and again and again and again until the eyes are just puddles of goo. It doesn't take long for the blinded Serpent King to start choking on his mouthful of teeth, but that isn't enough for Jeremy. He throws his weight into smashing Jack's ribs, punches the old man in the testicles a dozen times or so. He forces open Jack's artificial mandibles far as he can, like King Kong with the t-rex until he hears a snap, then he forces them back down. Jeremy stands up, he wobbles, he looks like he's not long for this earth, but he stands victorious. I can hear the idiots on the other side of the door, so I don't have long to slice Jack's head off. I don't saw it, I concentrate and I pray to myself, and the cleaver comes down with a mighty chop, severing the head.

"What are you doing?" Jeremy asks, almost ready to fall over.

"Take this," I tell him, quickly handing him the head, "hold it up when the girls come through that door."

Three of the Contessa's girls walk in, at last having unlocked the door and pushed it open. They nervously train their guns on us, until they see that not only am I armed, but Jeremy's loose and holding Jack's head. Godless Jack is dead and both Mr.400 and his accomplice are free. These are reasons for even these loyal, devoted minions of the Contessa to give us right of way. They have nothing to say, no shooting to do and no possible method of dealing with the kind of big fish that just killed Godless Jack. It's almost comical that they don't realize that the big fish that killed Godless Jack is wounded, tripping balls and most likely unable to wield weapons of any kind.

We reach the van and Jeremy is mumbling all kinds of things and moaning from all kinds of pain. I can only hope that I can get him to a hospital on time. The first thing I do when we get to the van is take the Mr.400 shirt off him, the second is help him lie down in the back seat. I turn the radio up nice and loud so that he doesn't pass out or fall asleep on me. If he falls asleep he might not wake up again. I can't bear to lose him twice in the same day. I can't bear for him to lose his mind either.

"Jeremy, stay awake, stay awake, stay awake, stay awake," I say it hundreds of times as we make the drive. He doesn't say anything in response, but I can tell he's awake. I put a scrap of cloth on my ear so that they won't bother treating it and leaving my car, with Godless Jack's head hidden in it, unattended for too long. That could wind up being pretty bad. It's not like Jack doesn't have friends and it's not like hospital orderlies are above accepting huge amounts of money for giving up the location of Mr.400. We have to play it cool and Jeremy has to stay awake.

"Cass," he mumbles, "Cass, I'm gonna die I think. But, Lud says I shouldn't. He says to stay here because this is just the beginning, the serpent and the jackal are the beginning, he says. Is it all like the city? Is it all their city now?"

"No, Jeremy, it's not their city now. But Lud's right, stay here in the car, don't go to sleep and don't look out at everything, just think about the car."

He screams and begins to cry. He looks out the windows and pounds at the doors. "How could you do that? How could you put me in one of those? This is what happens. This is what happens to us..."

He reminds me of Lud when we picked him up in the car. I cannot imagine what he sees right now, and I am fairly certain that I don't want to. I just want to get him safely to the hospital. He screams at the car and pounds at the door, but he's awake, maybe it's right that he's scared, because it will at least keep him conscious until we reach the hospital. Thank God it's not that far. Jeremy got Ian to the hospital on time, so I can get Jeremy there. The worst is over now, regardless of what he says. I can only hope that he'll see that. That he'll be able to run from all the monsters in his head.

When we are weak, we create gods, my father used to tell me, but I can see that there might be one at work. One that gave Jeremy the last ounces of strength to vanquish Jack, and one that got me to the hospital on time. There is only waiting now, but it doesn't feel like an obstacle. Me, Penny, Jones and Lud will be at his side as he fights to come back. Us, and a god for the strong and weak alike.

Toppled Towers

I flee from Hell in the belly of a great blue giant with wheels on the end of his limbs. The dragon is behind me, his fire, his fangs, and his power over my vision. The dragon is gone and I flee in the belly of a giant. He was a man once, this giant, and it makes me panic. He cranes his giant neck and smiles at me as Cass tells me to stay awake. I will stay with Cass and the giant, the giant with the wheels on his feet who zooms past the cities of skin and blades. These trees have leaves. How could it be that these trees stay green in a world where there's no Sun? Could it be that outside Hell and beyond the dragon's lies is a place where shadows and cold have not yet taken man's home from him? It shines on my face, this Sun, but is it real? Does it really shine into the giant and forgive him for letting himself become the device he is? At least Cass is here, wherever I am, if this place where the Sun shines is real.

The giant stops and Cass and I emerge. I want to cry, since the Sun is going away. The sky begins to get dark and I don't know if it will come back. If the Sun I have fought for stays here, then I will serve it forever. I will kiss the leaves of the trees that it allows growing, the trees that are green and not made of human skin. If the Sun returns, things might just be all right. The dragon is gone, the devil, the serpent king. The devil is gone and things might be all right. Cass leads me past a set of glass doors, and I'm scared at first, because I know what glass buildings mean, but Cass seems so certain that this is the right place to be, that I don't doubt her, I love her too much. Since Cass is here, I decide at last, that the Sun is going to return and we'd fight side by side to make sure that it stayed in the sky. It doesn't feel like the city of the Dark Ones. Everybody here looks human. It is cold and mechanical, but it is not their city.

Cass tells the lady at the desk that I've been drugged and narrowly escaped torture by a dangerous killer. Such a dangerous killer I escaped. She couldn't explain what I'd been through to this lady. She couldn't explain the devil or the war for man's souls. She just says that I was captured and drugged and tortured. I cringe when I hear the wheels rolling toward me and two large men, put me on a bed with wheels and they bring me to a big, white room. I overhear words like "detox" and "transfusion." These are words from the real world, words that remind me where I am. Hospital is where I am. I am not dead and I am in the real world, the sane world, the contested world, getting ready to be anesthesized and dream again, as they try and save me from the poison and the pain. Cass smiles at me and kisses my cheek before the sane world, just discovered, disappears, and I am dragged once more to someplace else. I will miss the sane world wherever they take me. I could use some clarity. Some clarity would be a good reward for killing the dragon. There are always rewards for killing the dragon.

MURDERLAND | Garrett Cook

I sit in absolute nothing, warm and comforting like a hot bath. My scattered brain begins to come together, no longer struggling to stay whole, but embracing its completeness. There is nothing to do or think or feel as I am repaired, just blissful oblivion. When my eyes open again, my vision is blurry, but I am certain that I see what I see. What I see is Cass looking down at me, tears in her eyes. She takes my hand and squeezes it tightly, the first real sensation I feel. She found me among the dead, among the gibbering mad, and she brought me here, even after I had told her to leave me to die for her own sake if I were captured. My own eyes tear up, and my vision remains blurry. We see each other on equal terms I suppose, through veils of tears, formerly worlds apart and missing one another. If there were only words to thank her for coming back to me and bringing me back to her and back to life and sunlight and joy. Without love, there is death, there is confusion. There is Hell and the nightmare of isolation.

She doesn't say anything either, she turns on the TV. I don't ask how long I've been out cold, I don't ask how long she waited for me, or what's going to happen to me next. I watch the TV and let the tears on my eyes dry and my vision become clear. The second thing I see after Cass is the image of Penny Dreadful, holding up a spike with the unmistakable head of Godless Jack mounted on it. I find the strength to smile, and Cass does as well. Unbelievable. I'm alive, the poison is out of my system and Penny Dreadful is on the TV holding up Godless Jack's head. That's right, the dragon, the Serpent King, the devil. It was pretty much the one thing I could feel myself doing, shoving the demon's fangs down his throat. There's always a reward for killing the dragon.

"That's right. I've come bearing a message from Mr.400. Mr.400 has killed Godless Jack and many of those at the top of the Reap food chain, and any who choose to take their place will incur his wrath. Jack's head was brought to me personally by Mr.400 with this message and another, one I take to heart, one I hope others will understand: your culture of violence is dead. Reap is gone and any who want to cling to it will meet the same end."

I can't sort out exactly what happened, but I'm glad it did. The first words I say to Cass after being pulled back from the afterlife aren't the best ones I can muster.

"Did I say that?" I whisper to her.

She laughs and shakes her head, "Nope. I did."

"Good. That was very good…" I feel my strength start to fade, but I call it back. I'm not going under again, not for awhile. I want to enjoy consciousness, clarity and Cass for as long as I can before sleep. Having killed Godless Jack, I suppose I've earned them.

"Penny helped. She told me where you were and she called the press conference. It's pretty much just her and a few dead psychopomps who know our secret. We can carry on our raids for awhile…"

It hurts when I shake my head. "No. I'm not doing this alone again. We're gonna find help. I don't know how, but we're gonna send a big message and we're gonna find help. We'll need money first and some stuff from Jones."

My plan isn't quite formulated until the obnoxious pundit Tommy Simmons was arguing with comes on the news.

"Mr.400 thinks that killing Godless Jack has killed Reap. This is truly schizoid logic, the kind of thing you would expect out of somebody with such a childish mind that is so utterly obsessed with black and white morality. Jack and all the others will be missed, but they're only the old guard now. There will be better tougher psychopomps, with better news coverage. It's laughable that he could believe his stupid little crusade against Reap could come to so much. Almost as laughable as Penny Dreadful's sudden reversal. We have Reapkids. We have Reap stations. As long as we have Reapkids and BLD news and as long as we have American culture, I think, we will have Reap. Mr.400 doesn't know what he's messing with."

"Jack's mansion is probably almost unguarded right now and people might not know yet that he's not coming back. I'm gonna need you to do something for me," I tell Cass.

"What's that?"

"Start looting."

Cass shrugs. Hopefully, I haven't been in the hospital long enough for the place to start getting cleaned out. It seems like it must have only been for the evening and Penny took a bit to get the press conference and publicly confirm Jack's death. The Contessa and her girls never would have admitted to it outright. No, not people so devoted to the ideals that Jack represented. If the Contessa's girls show up to claim anything for their mistress, Cass has proven herself more than a match for any of those incompetent little tramps anyway. When Cass walks out, I enjoy the TV and the hospital room and the knowledge that I'm going to live. I also enjoy the thought of what I'm going to have to do next. The pundit was, after all, right.

BLD has proven itself a thorn in my sides on a few occasions. The pirated Jack broadcast, the Tanner murders, the times it nearly took my sanity from me. It's the homebase of Reap culture and the most amoral place in existence. They were willing to risk a man's livelihood, to kill fifteen people and to hide seven killers. Maybe if I'm lucky I'll get Bobby Greer and some of his ilk. Maybe if I'm lucky I'll get that damn obnoxious pundit. It feels like the most extreme thing to do, like the craziest thing to do and the right thing to do. God help me, I've got no choice. The Dark Ones and the nanites and the Psychopomps will keep coming until I've gotten this place off the air and gotten rid of it for good. I summon every ounce of strength in my body, and suddenly, those ounces of strength let me stand up. It hurts and my arm absolutely kills, but it's good to know that I can. Now that I know I can stand, I lie down again and feel content in resting and knowing what needs to be done.

Cass wakes me up at the tail end of visiting hours. I'm thrilled to see her for so many reasons that I can't keep track of them all.

"You won't believe what I found at Jack's," she tells me, "I think you can find some use for it."

"Oh?" I try not to act curious and excited. It's unprofessional.

"Jack had a bunch of plastique lying around, apparently had some kind of plan B in regards to dealing with you. There're a few pounds of the stuff, not to mention some other things I picked up that might be worth something in trade. Is there anything you can think of doing with all those explosives, my love?" She gives a sultry, arrogant smile and I can tell she knows that I've had something planned, something great most likely.

"BLD," is all I have to say.

Cass looks completely taken aback and I don't blame her. It's desperate, it's crazy, it's an act of outright terrorism, and it's probably nigh impossible. Nigh impossible, but of course nothing is impossible. People set foot on the moon. I killed Godless Jack with a fistful of teeth. I've survived a nail in my spine with no real damage. Miracles happen every day. If this miracle went off without a hitch, however, it would be more than a miracle. It would be heavenly vengeance rained down on all that deserve it.

"How you gonna do that? They do have ID scanners."

"And I have an ID."

"Hausmann…"

"Exactly," I reply, "there's gonna be a lot of death, a few innocents, but I…I can't let this go on."

Her face is somber, but she knows I'm right. She knows that there are six hundred employees working at the BLD studios and corporate office. She knows that many of these people have done nothing to incite others to violence, that most of these people are not the seven Tanner murderers or the men responsible for creating them. She knows all of these things, just as I know them, but she knows as well that the pundit was right. If BLD is on the air, then Reap will be given all the coverage it wants and anybody who wants to be a big news item can go out and kill people. Surely this has led to more than six hundred deaths. Six hundred lives huddled together in this gateway to Hell, six hundred lives that say the taking of lives is perfectly acceptable. How hideous it is to live in a world where a plan like this can't be refuted. How hideous to live in a world without choices.

"The doctors say you might be well enough to leave tomorrow. I don't know about you, you know, going out and…" Cass sighs.

"I won't get hurt, I promise."

"Too much going on at once," she argues, "you can't just get on your feet after taking out Jack and start toppling the system again. Particularly like this."

I know I can't argue with her, and she knows she can't argue with me. Funny thing is that she stops trying to argue with me, because she knows I need to strike fast. I need things to hit people hard and quickly, to make sure that they don't have time to recover. I would rather go home and lie in bed with Cass for days after leaving the hospital, but it doesn't feel like an option, not with these people in my way. Not with the people that made those young men into the Tanner killers and made the world's killers into celebrities still standing. There will be other stations, too, but maybe they'll get the message. Maybe I won't have to…the lightning must strike true. I hate how inhuman I have to be to feel human all the time.

The next day I'm out of the hospital, and true to my word, only hours later, I'm prepared. I don't look at anybody as I wheel in my janitor's cart full of explosives. No faces, no names, no doubt. These things are the enemy. The ID card works, and then the elevator works. A slow hesitant part of me wishes they wouldn't, but the strong part looks at the studio and sees that the enemy is here. It feels the scouts, the breeders and the grown Dark Ones that surely occupy the offices, the ones with no skin, no identities, and no vulnerability. They are surely there, as surely as their influences are, the Dark Ones are present, they have come and they will never leave until I make them, and there is only one way to make them, tragic though it might be. Forget tragedy. Think only of triumph. It's so hard to. I rig up the explosives in the elevator and I head upstairs, sliding a letter under the office door, as I rush down another elevator, head to my car and activate Jack's fancy remote detonator, the one he would have used to blow me sky high if I hadn't fallen into his little trap.

This is what the heads of the network read, seconds before their end:

"Dear Hate Mongers,

Mr.400 here. My name is Jeremy Jenkins and I was once a pharmacist. I grew up in a Catholic home for boys and then a foster home in Westborough Connecticut. I started killing when I murdered my foster mother because she was targeted by your masters. You know who I mean. I killed her because she would bring forth evil into the world. And then I kept killing. I killed several young, blonde women because they were chosen as targets for your masters, selected as suitable breeding material. I killed more of them than anybody in history did. Then when I was done killing them, I killed numerous Psychopomps, thinking they were the enemy, that they were the servants of the Dark Ones. Then, I found out about your little scheme, what you and Walter Hausmann were up to. You are truly the master corruptors, since you could turn several people into killers, and in your time you could transform several more. Mr.400 tires of fascism, world wars, drugs, gang violence and all the stupidities of life. Hopefully, there will be a way to resolve these. Here is a list of everyone I have killed, a juicy exclusive for you..."

All of my victims, every last name for greedy eyes to discern. And then, all of a sudden, there is fire, there is blood and there are screams. The souls of Dark Ones float in the air, bits of flesh from innocents and sinners alike, fly through the air. I have no more time to regret anything. I have come back from Hell already, and I don't want this world to be another one. I am Mister 1000 now. A revenant, an angel of retribution, no longer uncertain where the lightning must fall. No more innocence no more guilt. I pray for some kind of order, some kind of inspiration, but it doesn't come. Mister 1000 can make no more sense of everything than Mr.400 could. Triumph is cold and temporal. The world will remain the world that it was, the old, strange, world of bloodshed and loathing. Mister 1000, Mr.400, it almost doesn't matter which one I am. No more counting heads. This isn't a game now, it's a war.

When I go home, I unhook the phone and I lie down in bed. When I tell Cass about the flames and the Dark Ones and the way I walked away from the TV station, feeling better only because it was no longer there and there was no way I could have let it do what it did forever. The hand of God must be objective, since the same God lets children die of AIDS. I'm not altogether certain how to make it feel any more like I've won today. Cass doesn't say anything. She knows that I've at least done right in my own eyes. She knows right now that I just need to rest and remember what it's like to lie in bed and be loved. I will give myself some time to rest and be alive, some human time before I return to the angel I need to be. There will be no mountains in my dreams. No scorched towers and blasted cities. I will let my arm recover and my head and my soul recovers, and I will be ready for the first of my final moves.

Aftermath

Cock the shotgun and pray, I tell myself as I drive up to the cafe. When my armies are built, this is what I will tell them. This is all that I will be able to tell them. Cry for the dead since it was their lot to die. Cry for the survivors who wait for their loved ones to come home. Cry for the streets, paved with rotting flesh. Too warm for concrete. Too warm for cities. Cry for the streetsweeper who mops up his fellow man. Know all too well what it's like to pick up a mess like that. Cry for the machines as they all break down. Our junkyards will be cemeteries and our cemeteries junkyards. Cry for America as she grows back severed limbs. The voice that drowned out sympathy is quiet, tense and lies in wait, where right now he should be screaming. I cry for those who have to grow up in my America, and I cry because it's a better one anyway.

"So why Murderland?" says Cass as she loads Mr. Right's magnum, "Why not le Couteau?"

"Because I plan on having numbers when I move on Le Couteau. It would be suicide to go in by ourselves. I still have one broken arm and there are metal detectors and armed guards outside there. Here, there are no metal detectors and if I spray, half the room goes down. If half the room goes down, I hope the other half gets cooperative."

"And if they don't?"

Cock the shotgun and pray. Act like you weren't stifling tears a minute ago. Never tell your girl that you'll probably be killed. If she knows you're a soldier, she knows there's always a chance and since she knows it, there's no need to make her think about it too. I think of pleasant thoughts, like the knowledge that one less television station spreads its tentacles over the country, the knowledge that there is no more Godless Jack, the knowledge that I have dedicated myself to doing the right thing and shall soon be repaid. The dead will forgive me I hope, we must always hope the dead will forgive us, and if they don't, we must hope that they at least understood us. Mister 1000 must be understood, Mister 1000 cannot be scorned by those who had to give their lives. If the dead scorn me, I have a feeling the living might feel similarly. So, I don't know how to answer Cass' question. If the living don't understand and the dead don't either, I have only two choices afterwards: I can be more eloquent or I too can die. The first one would be harder than the last, but I won't let her know that. I think she ought to by now. If she doesn't know what silence means by now, she never will.

"I love you," I tell her. It doesn't answer her question, it won't reassure her, but I feel it too strongly not to say it. I can't see why the two of us are so scared of this little raid after all of the big ones we've done. Maybe because the big ones didn't end with us asking for help. Maybe because we haven't gotten all that much help since Lud gave his life for the cause. Nobody's helped us but Jones and Penny Dreadful, and we need so much help. It has always surprised me how much we could do alone, but it's not enough now. It won't be enough until the liars and the killers are in their place. It's not like that hasn't always been the problem, it's not like others haven't tried, but maybe we're the ones who finally want it enough.

When we walk in, me with the Mr.400 shirt, no lenses, no fake teeth and no deceits save my big long trenchcoat, Cass dressed in tight black slacks, and a black tank top adorned with a skull, people look at us. How dare we. How dare I come in dressed as the man who robbed the world of Godless Jack, Hacksaw Sally and many of their favorite television programs? How dare I come to Murderland looking like this, looking like I disagree with everything they believe? The Manson waitress moves aside, not asking if I want a menu and letting me choose my own seat. We pick a table right across from the group of Ripkids that Joey hangs out with and behind the former Ripkid leader.

Joey the Ripkid looks at me, says, "I can't believe you're wearing that."

I shrug. "I know, white after Labor Day. It's a risk."

The Ripkids snicker. Joey doesn't snicker. "I don't know who the fuck you are, man, but you come in here with a Mr.400 shirt, you're asking for trouble. Do you know what Mr.400 did last week?"

"Nope." I put my feet up on the table, look arrogant and stupid so that when I get ready to tear shit up, the Sons of Sam two booths away who are fervently cleaning their pistols won't be able to react on time. Of course, Cass does have a half dozen hand grenades in her purse and a small canister of Sarin gas in case things get real nasty. I'm glad that Jones is back on speaking terms with me. All it took was a bunch of mementos from Jack's bedroom that sold like hotcakes on E Bay. Joey the Ripkid is thinking hard, which is good, because he's about twice as smart as anybody else in here. Anybody else but...

Holy shit. I cannot believe this stroke of luck, or unluck or whatever it is. It remains to be seen what it is, besides a strange coincidence. What a strange coincidence. Nobody gives Ian a hard time when he walks in; wearing the same shirt I'm wearing almost. A homemade version produced by an adoring fan, but nonetheless the same shirt I'm wearing. Ian Sterling, Reap guru looks around the booths and sits down beside me, proudly wearing the Mr.400 t-shirt he made. He smiles.

"Hey, we've got the same shirt," he says.

I nod. "Well, one of us is going to have to go change," I say in the most fey fashion I can muster. Confidence is key.

"Glad to see these things are catching on."

I nod again. "These kids are going to tell me about what Mr.400 did last week. I haven't really been up on the news."

"Yeah," says Ian, "I'd imagine so. Your phone was off the hook all…"

If he were drinking anything, it would inevitably have ended up spat out. He smiles in disbelief as Joey begins to relate the story.

"So, last week, Mr.400 kills Godless Jack and delivers his head to Penny Dreadful, and there she is parading it around on a stick on the evening news and on BLD Reap news and MTV and VH1, and it's just everywhere. Everybody who turns on their TV knows that Godless Jack is dead and that Mr.400 killed him. That's the kind of shit that really divides the Reap camps. Me, I respect the fuck out of the guy. Jack couldn't have gone down easy, but I have no doubt he went down fair and square. I wasn't too offended when I heard he was gone, He was beginning to turn into a total fucking dinosaur anyway."

"Bold statement," Ian says.

"Yeah," says Joey, "you kind of tiptoed around it, but I knew what you were saying, Mister Sterling. A few folks think you might have been Mr.400."

"You think that?" he asks, a little bit worried for his hide.

"Nope, I sure as hell don't. You're not the type. No offense man, but you're kind of a sit-back-and-watch kind of guy."

"Still wouldn't surprise me," says one of Joey's Ripkid buddies, looking Ian over, "I mean, look at the shirt. He does have a Mr.400 shirt."

"Yeah, and I got a Spiderman shirt. You don't see me chasing Doctor fuckin' octopus up a building," Joey answers, "you gotta fuckin' think, man. Anybody can make a shirt and anybody can wear a shirt. There's two guys at that booth alone wearing Mr.400 shirts. Probably not too wisely at this place, but they're still sitting there like retards wearing Mr.400 shirts at a reapjoint. I mean no offense. Mister Sterling, I've been reading your webpage forever, and your friend saved my life, so I got nothin' against either of you. Or against Mr.400, but I think some shit could go down here."

Cass, who had previously been petrified of this whole excursion, is holding back some laughter. She grabs some lipstick from the pocket of her handbag. A comforting little in-joke that makes me almost burst into laughter, blow my cover and get shot to ribbons by the Sons of Sam. Ian, in the meantime, now feeling very much a member of team 400 is speculating on what's going to go down here today. Joey seems to wonder why it is that Cass is carrying such a bulky handbag, but he dismisses it. He's good at that. I take that into consideration. It might be good having somebody bright who doesn't ask questions around.

"So," I say to Joey, "tell me more about last week."

"Man, you musta been on Mars or some shit. I can't believe you didn't hear about all this. So, Mr.400 starts out by killing Jack and then he goes and he does something that's just like too Reap for Reap. Or maybe it's not Reap at all. Maybe it's something else, 'cause it's completely fucking psycho. Not that he shouldn't have done it, but it's completely psycho. He puts a bunch of plastique on an elevator at BLD studios, outside some dude's office and he goes and blows up everything. Musta had a real good remote detonator, cause they could identify all the remains and they think Mr.400 got away. Isn't that crazy?"

"Completely," I reply, "I should've been following the news."

"Yeah, no shit," Joey answers back, "you missed like one of the biggest events in fuckin' human history, I think. It's just fuckin', you know, like the fuckin' Titanic. It's like the fuckin' Titanic sank and you had to find out a week later at a busy restaurant. I just can't believe you could've missed something like that. Six hundred people went and died that day, man, and you gotta respect that, so I think maybe you oughta find yourself some other place to have lunch, cause if you keep wearing that shirt in here, then some shit's going down. I don't know what you're doing, Mister Sterling, but, you know, you'd better be really really..."

Cass reaches into her handbag and takes out one of the .32's, handing it to Joey. Joey looks incredibly confused.

"See this gun?" she asks him.

"Yes," he answers, "I see this gun. After all, you did just hand me a fucking gun."

"Very good," Cass says, all business, "I want you to take that gun and shoot that Son of Sam in the booth over there in the head as he cleans his gun. Just glide down the aisle and shoot that Son of Sam in the head."

Joey stares at the gun as if we've handed him some sort of rare snake. "How do you know I'll do it? I could just take this gun and shoot you right now?"

"Because, you seem like a smart kid," I tell him, "you seem like somebody smart enough to know who to point a gun they've just been given at. The rest of you Ripkids shut the fuck up, or you're going to get capped. Understand?"

The Ripkids at the table nod agreement. Joey gets up, sneaks down the aisle and gets ready. Cass and I take this moment to jump on the table and unholster our weapons. I grab the shotgun from my coat and Cass gets Mr. Right's magnum from the holster sewn into her pant leg. Joey shoots, and not surprisingly, he hits his mark. By the time any of the Sons of Sam can grab their weapons, Joey's under the table, seeking fire cover, and Cass has fired on one of the other Sons, dropping him in one shot, making an almost lovely spray of red and pink.

"Attention Reapkids," I shout, subtly handing Ian the second sawed-off shotgun sewn into my coat, "you are in the presence of Mr.400. Those of you who have not heard the message of Mr.400 should know this..."

Ian does something incredible, he gets up on the table, which starts to get wobbly under our collective weights and that of the handbag, and he improvises.

"Your culture of violence is dead. The soldiers of death, who you have praised so widely, have proven themselves fragile. The messengers of the so-called grim reapers have found themselves punished, forced to deal with the consequences of their years of corrupting misinforming and harming the populace..." Ian shouts. I can see his game now, and it's a damn good one.

A nearby Manson jumps to his feet, and does the only thing Manson ever did and the only thing Mansons are ever good for. He screams. "Fuck you, you're not Mr.400! Neither of you are Mr.400, fuck you, you fucking poseurs! Fuck you all! You don't need to listen to this shit. You don't need to listen to any of his fucking shit! Charlie knows the gospel, Charlie knows the score…"

The Sons fire, once on the Manson kid, once on Joey, who is trying to scale the booth and once on me. I take the .38 slug in the chest with dignity on account of the flesh-toned Kevlar I'm wearing under my shirt. Joey's claim that he wasn't Spiderman might well have been false, since he manages to avoid the shots, get on top of the booth and jump. He surprises me by not running out and instead dropping to the ground behind the second row of booths and seeking a vantage point. I feel like applauding when the Manson kid drops, but the Sons are trying to kill us. A booth of Gacys runs toward the door, unlike the Manson chick waitress who has simply dropped to the ground, knowing full well that nobody will dispatch cops to a shootout in a reapjoint a block outside the Safe Zone.

"Stop!" Cass shouts at the Gacys, "Nobody leaves!"

Three more Mansons at the booth with the slain one rise and pounce like wild animals, leaping onto the table and finally making it buckle under the weight of six people. We all tumble to the floor, Mansons, Ian, Cass and I and the combat has gotten close. The Sons don't know what to do besides try and find where Joey's taken cover. They get up and start to look behind the booths. I've lost track of Joey, and can't really focus on finding the kid in the middle of this brawl. The Mansons are attacking with knives and teeth, joined by the ex-Ripkid leader who has pulled his swordcane and is getting ready to stab me in the stomach as soon as the Manson on me rolls off. The Gacys stop running and join the melee, leaping on top of the Manson covering Ian and I and lashing out with every part of their body that they can.

I have to wonder if this will finally be the end, torn apart by these animals. So quickly these people turn into the beasts they are. It reminds me of Orpheus. The love, the song that could tame the devils, brings on the end at the hands of those who crave the love. Those who want to be understood by their heroes, those who are most violent, most powerful feel dismissed and they set upon me and they tear me to shreds. The children of Dionyssus, disciples of the leopard, their teeth and claws could be the end. They could be, if it weren't for Joey's friends.

I hadn't thought I could count on these kids. I had suspected I could only intimidate them, but these kids have some brains too. These kids knew that the sadist with the swordcane who was getting ready to gut me had gone too far leaving Joey to die, and now they see that these kids are going too far. They saw all the bloodshed, knew what I, what Mr.400 had done, and still they know these kids, the jealous ones, the hateful ones who won't get the message, who can't grab peace from the song of love have gone too far and now they must be stopped. The Ripkids pull at the Gacys and the Manson on top of Cass and Ian and I. They pull them off and they hand us the guns lost in the tussle. But I don't take mine. This kid with the swordcane wants me dead, this hateful stupid kid thinks that he can do what Godless Jack and so many others failed to do.

So I let him, I let the little land shark come at me with the cane. He thinks he's going to cut me, and he's grown faster and more savage, so it's likely he might. It's even more likely he might because I'm distracted by a gunshot. I worry for Joey and look over at him. Joey's fine, but the Son of Sam that he's flanked and shot in the spine isn't. The kid goes numb and hits the floor like the Manson he had just killed. Another Son looks at what's happened, observes the shape of his friend, crumpled like tissue paper. Cass has become a regular Lone Ranger, though, quite capable of shooting the angry kid before he can blow Joey away. If only the kid had known what Cass had, that anger can make you weak, that anger can make you slow. There's one son left to look on all of his dead brethren and that kid drops his gun.

But I shouldn't have stopped to look. It lets the kid surprise me with a trip, something I don't expect him to do with the swordcane. I hit the floor and he leaps on me like the animal he is, like all the other animals are. I expect to die right then, take off guard without a weapon by somebody who sees no better way to prove he's worth something than to kill me. How pathetic. But he makes a mistake, the mistake Cass caught the Son of Sam on and the mistake Mr. Right might have caught Cass on were he not such a weakling and a coward. The Ripkid decides to be a sadist. Instead of just stabbing in the stomach and killing me, he punches me in the face. If it were a good punch, he'd have been able to stun me a second and let me suffer more, but it isn't. It barely makes a noise. When he moves to punch me again, I raise my good arm and I grab his hand. I twist hard and he screams. Then I reach for his arm, and with a bit of leverage, I knock him off me. He falls and that's all I need. I'm standing once more and he's on the ground.

One of the Gacys gets free of the Ripkid that's pinning him, more or less in the same way I just did. He's a big kid, might have played some football for awhile. He charges, getting ready to bring me to the ground again for the sadistic fuckhead I just pulled off me to get back to beating me. It seems the asshole's regained some status among the local Reapkids. The Gacy kid doesn't expect Ian to smack at the base of neck with the sawed off shotgun. Were these kids more observant, they'd have expected the poor stupid clown to get shot, but they don't expect that and they don't expect him to fall to the ground like the big, heavy sack of stupid he is. This does give the leader some edge, though providing a moment of chaos and hesitation that he can use to stand up again.

I give him a good old-fashioned jab to the stomach, and then I headbutt him. Were I not more certain now that I can bring this kid down in spite of his support and in spite of his savagery, I wouldn't have tried it, but I feel confident. Confidence is key. His balance isn't good enough for him to take the headbutt. It brings him down instantly. This kid seemed for a little bit, like he wasn't a weakling or a quitter, but it's clear that he is. He reaches one more time for the swordcane, but I don't let him get it. Anything even remotely like hope is gone from him when I take the gaudy, cheap, histrionic weapon for myself. He squirms, the animal in his eyes gone. I wonder if I should let this bully and this sadist live, if seeing him on the ground humiliated would be enough to get these animals to understand that the stupid things they love might be worth rethinking and resisting, that violence for the sake of violence is nothing. I don't give the kid mercy, and the act of violence against him is not to show them that I am tough or that I will kill them, but to show them what I am killing. Even though I see no Dark Ones near him, I know who their tools are and I know how to fight them. I raise the swordcane high, to let them see what I'm doing and the kid is too stunned too busy wetting his pants to move. I drive the swordcane into his heart, deep. In a truly Victorian fashion, I have staked this vampire. No longer are they to feed off blood.

When the battle of Murderland is done, I look around, at terrified ignorant Gacys, at the Ripkids who helped me win, at the Mansons who would never know better no matter what I told them, then at Ian and Joey, the lives I saved out of compassion instead of just disgust, at Cass, who is love, which is the only real reason to fight. The Gacys and the Mansons remain on the ground in shock, but not as much shock as I feel when the one surviving Son of Sam moves to leave with me. The Gacys and the Mansons find that violence is only so powerful because it has to be, and as many before me have thought; I find that those who cannot love, think, feel or be reasoned with, deserve nothing better than a canister of Sarin gas.

The God I once thought would let me be a martyr has given me much. He has given me friends, a lover and an army. The Dark Ones build their city behind the scenes, but I can tear it down with the hope in front of my face. After all I've been through, and all I've done, I see that I can only do the thing any man could and would in these circumstances: I can take the war outside of my head. I can walk the streets of America as it is, not America as it is doomed to be. I can only hope this is enough, because Murderland is everywhere and there are only so many bullets.

Reapchic.com, October 31st, 2006

Tonight, once more we celebrate All Hallows Eve, the night when the dead return to earth; seeking offerings and reminding the living of the precious gift they've been given. The emails have come to me, asking me to do the same thing. You've all written for me to bring you some kind of light and sanity in a changing world, and to remind you why we have chosen life and shunned death, why we embrace death's visage and venerate those who bring it. I regret to say that I have given all of the answers I could to these questions. I have been with you for five long years now, bringing this site from a little personal blog to one of the biggest forums and newsgroups about Reap on the net. I'm happy to have been able to give you this perspective and for all these years to tell you what I believed and what you should believe too. Like the epitaph, like the ghastly mask, I have reminded you of death in life and how we cannot deny it. I'm glad to have had the privilege.

But now, things are changing. Yes, things are always changing, but it seems like they've changed too much. Psychopomps used to be able to kill with impunity to show us that we lived in a dangerous world and to bring us a new dose of truly taboo excitement when there were no taboos left to entertain us. The fact that America changed enough to allow this was one of the biggest cultural shifts in history, one that will leave a mark on many a generation to come. Now, we are faced with a change just as large, and with as long lasting a consequence. Now, we are faced with Mr.400, a phenomenon I thought I had a handle on. A phenomenon most of us thought we had dealt with. Mr.400 was surely the newest evolution in Reap, or a bigger, riskier, extension of the things we believed. Now, I wish things were that simple. I wish I could say Mr.400 was just heralding a new age of Reap, but I can't. I can't tell you what Mr.400 is capable of, because I have not yet seen it, nor has anybody.

Godless Jack was more or less the founder of Reap. Even in death, he remains the founder of Reap. It was Jack that made us call into question, the ethics of killing to survive, that made us see that violence was a part of ourselves that could not be severed and that needed to be fed. Jack could not subsist without killing, and it is every man's right to subsist. How could we have argued with that? We all imagined what it would be like if the government told us we could not fulfill our urges, if policemen carted us away for masturbating, listening to loud music or eating too much, we wondered how we could deny a man the things that made him a man. We all watched *a*

Clockwork Orange and we took notes. We all examined our faiths and saw that death is transformation. We all made a series of excuses for Jack and we all decided that if he did not have the right to live, then we did not and that America had to be free.

So, we became something different thanks to Jack and America became something totally unexpected, it became freer. Our politicians saw that we were terrified of having some integral freedom taken away, and thought of how they would look for doing it. They thought about votes and human rights and they thought about the ends of their careers. They got scared like we did. They got scared of thinking that we were missing some integral freedom. So, in their eyes, Jack became a political threat, a Malcolm X or a Gandhi, a man who said it was okay for us to go nuts, okay for us to be ourselves, regardless of what that self was. America's advertising would fail if Jack did not go free.

Now Jack is dead, and many of us wonder if we are no longer free. I have received many e-mails asking what Reap is to become in the absence of its founder and what I planned on writing about the death of Godless Jack, the death of American freedom. You are still free. Free to kill in the Safe Zone, free to sniff all the modeling glue you want, have sex with whoever you like and gorge your brain on real, live murder. Don't worry about that, nobody can take that away from you, not even Mr.400. Mr.400 looks now to be a threat to a Reap-loving, free-loving, violent, exciting, living America, with his claims of our hypocrisy, of our absurd and his statement that our culture of violence is dead. Without Jack, you thought Mr.400 had already won and you had lost these freedoms you treasure so much. Don't worry about your freedoms, worry about your lives.

Worry because the more we kill, the easier it gets, not just to kill but to ignore the things that have driven us to kill. Outside of the Reap community, there is a war with China that will cost more lives that any psychopomp who ever lived or ever could. Outside the Reap community is an America that's just as confused as we are. Those Islamic terrorists are gone because they no longer entertain us, and it's become unpopular to bother with them. Somali warlords are gone because the cameras are gone. Before the cameras turned on, Mr.400 killed a lot of people and nobody knew or gave a shit, just because he decided to be invisible. This is why you should worry, because you can only see what you choose to, and you have chosen to see the wrong things, things that are done for you to see them. Worry about that. This Halloween, try worrying about all the screaming souls that must surely have no place to rest now. This Halloween, worry about the dead, and worry about us, the living becoming dead inside or dead altogether. Embrace and fear it. Understand it. Respect it.

I have led you astray, Reapkids and the time has come for me to stop. I'm going to go out and do the right thing now. I say goodbye to Reap and goodbye to the cult of death. I hope you have the judgment to do the same. I suspect most of you won't, but it doesn't matter. I might as well try. The time has come for everyone to try. Mr.400 is hope, and I for one, have chosen to embrace hope, and help some souls rest in peace on this Halloween night. To these lost souls, may you find your way home, may your screams and pleas be heard.

This is Ian Sterling, signing off forever.

THE END

Garrett Cook is an author and editor of Horror, Bizarro,  Dark Fantasy and Neopulp fiction. His books include Archelon Ranch, Jimmy Plush, Teddy Bear Detective and the upcoming Time Pimp. His fiction has been reprinted in The Decade's Best Bizarro Fiction and has appeared in anthologies alongside such authors as Michael Moorcock and Joe Lansdale. He is the editor of Imperial Youth Review and is available for freelance editing services.

EDVARD MUNCH

MURDERLAND | Garrett Cook

ALSO FROM Morbidbooks:

WELCOME TO HARBORSIDE DISTRICT HOSPITAL ... where three of a kind have come to live, work and kill. Born whole from the rectum of a dying patient, Morbid silently stalks the hospital's hallways, heinously dispatching the most helpless of patients and in the most painfully repulsive of manners. In the meantime, in order to pay for his

family and home that includes his ghost step-father Sammy and his pet aborted fetus Chip, Westphal has to ingest mounds of dangerous narcotics to get through his night shifts. Barely hanging on to his Care Tech gig by his fingernails, the last thing Westphal needs is to be accused of Morbid's evil deeds. You, on the other hand, simply want to find some solace. Terminally ill from a virulent infection, and dependent on Life Support, all You beg for a peaceful and dignified demise. Shirk has other plans for You. The ancient drug-snuffling demon makes You relive all of your deadly and venial sins as he tortures You. Night after night. Until eternal Damnation begins for YOU MORBID WESTPHAL, yet again.... NOW WITH EVEN MORE EVIL FLAVOR!

It looks like Carolyn and Mark are in deep, deep shit... Mark and Carolyn live in an alternate 1989 where Ronald Reagan is on his fourth presidential term. The USA has a rigid, long-standing caste system and abortions were never made legal. Being homeless is a crime that is punishable by imprisonment in an internment camp the inmates call Tent City. Most of Mark's ER patients are inmates at this camp and are victims of a new disease these illegals call the Transient Flu. This deadly and rapidly spreading disease mutates with each new host, collecting information, changing code. The disease evolves lightning quick, spreading like pond ripples and infecting everyone. No one is safe. Mark and Carolyn dig too deep and uncover

the brutal truth: Transient Flu was purposely made and is one hundred percent fatal. Carolyn's employer, Hudson-Smythe Pharmaceuticals, discovers the chain of evidence. It traces the pharmacide back to Hudson-Smythe and the crime of the century. Cost is no object and deadly force is authorized. Yes. Carolyn and Mark are in deep, deep shit.

Immanuel the Christ has some nerve. Jonah has already lost everyone he loves to Pilate the vampire and his Harbor drug violence. Jonah now trudges through his days staying as high on Plata as possible. He just wants to be left alone while he waits for his turn to die. The Christ has

other plans for him. She sends Her messenger, Pedro, to assign Jonah the very dangerous task of ordering the Herod to dismantle the Harbor's Plata trade. Jonah has a choice: fight or flight. He decides to run. But you can't run from God forever. As Jonah learns the hard way when the 'Edmund Fitzgerald' founders and goes down in rough seas, with the reluctant prophet on board. Job is Satan's Chosen One and he doesn't take kindly to orders from some upstart prophet. Rather than acquiescing, Job thinks caving Jonah's head in with a tire iron is the best bet. Jonah finds himself out of the frying pan, but firmly fixed in the fire. Then the Lord Herself starts dispatching Job's children. One at a time, until the Herod of The Harbor finally obeys.

Short stories of darkness and dismay, snorting souls, Satan and the New Christ make a bet; Pontious Pilate is re-born a vampire, evil ghosts and wicked demons. Dark shit from The Most Depraved Writer in Print. Rage creates a dismal post-industrial future, a look at man

defiled and in decline. Evil has arrived. Dominion has been taken by those who walk as the damned, demons, halflings, products of debauched rampages and sins against nature. Sex, drugs, and broken souls are the only things of value. Life is more like a disease, and the only salvation is the right amount of Plata to numb the conscience and, if one is lucky, to bring on a cleverly disguised demise. Through the sheer shock of his presentation, Rage forces readers to consider the

alternatives, to look at the garbage in the streets, to see what is swept into the gutters at night right before all decent people awake to see another cleaned up version of the day. He uses tradition to break tradition, to push the imagination in ways that are uncomfortable at the least and border on the offensive at worst. Yet, in doing so, he illustrates what real Love is.

Lines tell tales that without the right exposure live completely disguised within crevices that no amount of washing can remove. We yearn to have them clean - enough. Spend hundreds of dollars on this or  that to wash ... them ... clean. But some stains never come out, no matter how much we scrub, steam, or sterilize. And what becomes of the hands that are soaked in generations of sins committed by their owners, perpetual motion of offenses against their fellow man time and time again? Isn't there something that we've all done that we just can't seem to cleanse ourselves from? And what if you were Pilate? Steven Rage's "Pilate: A Brutal Bible Tale" explores the depths of sin, the way it stains our lives, and graphically illustrates the things we fear most. He forces us to look at true sin, true villainy, and truly offensive images of alternative realities. Sometimes it takes a shock to wake up!

"I'm feeling down and dirty, feeling kind of mean, so I give those fans my middle finger. Those poor bastards go nuts. My team looks at me in awe. My coach frowns and the opposing one begins to furiously scratch out new plays. The Warface is feeling her oats tonight and they all know they're in for a deep snag. I see our opponents and I almost feel sorry for the poor bastards. Their fans can't help them. Their coach can't help them. I'm going to run them off their own track in front of their own fans and there is not one thing they can do about it. I see my counterpart positioning herself on the outside line. I've got my eye on her and I've got her number. She is going nowhere. I'm going to body check her narrow ass off the track and into the third row. I hear the second whistle sound. The jammers are  starting to move behind us as I veer toward her. I lower my right shoulder. She sees me at the last second. I smile as her eyes open wide. I get speed, lean in deep and hit her. My jammer, Brute, slides up my left side. I see the opposing jammer shimmy through the wall and I give chase. Silly rabbit, no one gets past the Warface. Not tonight they don't."

www.ingramcontent.com/pod-product-compliance
Lightning Source LLC
Chambersburg PA
CBHW031600240626
47153CB00002B/582